NaiRobbery
Cocktail

Empress Ciku
Kimani-Mwaniki

MVUA PRESS

NaiRobbery Cocktail

By Empress Ciku Kimani-Mwaniki

Published by Mvua Press
5th Floor Rainbow Tower
32 Muthithi Road, Westlands
Nairobi, Kenya
Tel:+254 740 524 629

ISBN: 978-9914-9467-1-0

Cover Illustration: Lucy Ade
Font: Garamond

Foreword

Nairobi is, well, Nairobi. KaNairo, in slang.

Then there is the KaNairo that Ciku has written about. *The* Nairobi.

We have climbed mountains with Ciku (The Empress) and her husband Mwaniki. Danced in Nairobi nights, walked the Nairobi streets and events, and revised each other's manuscripts. Her fans believe she is 100 per cent noisy, yet she often lapses into long moments where she observes things. Now she is fifty, serving us her fifth Cocktail. As we sip from the pages of this fifth novel, it is clear that her keen observations are what enchant readers with her unique blend of imagination, wit, and profound insight.

In an absolutely stunning manner, she delves into the murky criminal underworld of Nairobi. The top gangster, Boss, is running the city, celebrated as a good guy. Yet, the new police boss is intent on dethroning him and installing his own puppet gangster as kingpin. All this unfolds through the eyes of the beautiful Naliaka, baptised with the "innocence turns to street smarts" that Nairobi serves anyone who stays more than an hour in it.

If John Kiriamiti's *My Life in Crime* has long been regarded as the top Kenyan crime novel, *NaiRobbery Cocktail* is the Godfather that delves deeper into the psyche, personal relationships and the intriguing pyramid of organised crime—from the lowliest foot soldier to the top honcho and all the grey-coloured policemen, pimps, clergy, and general society in between.

As usual with her Cocktail series, Ciku serves it with lots of romance. And sex. And betrayals. She delves into the depths of the human soul: exploring love, loss, and the enduring power of hope. Her writing is deceptively simple for everyone to enjoy, yet with such craftsmanship that literary critics mention her among the great contemporary African writers.

Indeed, if one wants to know Nairobi in all its layers, colours and peoples, this is the book.

I had to ask Ciku, "How do you know the Nairobi underworld this deeply?" I will never walk around Nairobi again without imagining everybody on the streets is not just an innocent civilian, but a member of the Boss syndicate playing their role as the criminal Nairobi ecosystem grinds on.

So, let us raise a glass to this remarkable author, whose words have brought joy, solace, and inspiration to countless readers. As she summits the literary landscape, may the pen continue to flow, and may the stories continue to illuminate our lives. Hongera, ki-Bro.

Simiyu Barasa
Author/Filmmaker

Dedication

To Mikie, and all those little souls who acquired wings too young. We remember you.

Acknowledgements

My bedmate should probably have a half of the royalties from this book going directly to his account, because the amount of time he takes to go through my manuscripts should count as a fulltime job. Thank you, Mwaniki Wa Njache.

Thank you, dear, dear readers, for your continued patronage, making it worth it to keep doing this again and again. I have to give special thanks to Carole Shiku who relentlessly hassles me to finish writing.

Simiyu Barasa, Kawira Muturi and Tony Gichuhi aka The Rogue Elder—my beta readers of this manuscript—thank you for your input, and for sacrificing your precious time to read and give your very helpful feedback.

Mvua Press under eKitabu, thank you for taking a lot of weight off my shoulders. Your team of professionals has made my life so much easier.

I must NOT thank the government of Kenya, for it is taxing me a lot. I hope I can thank it with the next book.

Chapter One

To be robbed in Nairobi is like a rite of passage.

Indeed, Nairobi city dwellers wear their robbery-victim belts with creepy pride and anyone claiming to never have been robbed is low-key frowned upon, like they do not deserve to address pulsating humans. For ten years, Boss and his band of thieves were responsible for these initiations into the cult-like Robbery Victims Association.

When in a pensive mood, Boss would wonder if that bad thing had not happened to him when he was a ten-year-old boy, and again when he was just exiting his teenage years, would he have ended up what he was, or would he have been an international footballer like he had always dreamed?

He is Boss, but before the transition, he was Kanja.

Flat beer. That was what his childhood memories tasted like. The few times Kanja remembered being excited was when he was kicking a ball with his friends, back when he had dreams of playing professional football after watching EPL reruns at the shopping centre's state of the art theatre. Sitting beside his friends on those terribly uncomfortable wooden benches, straining their necks to watch the old, dusty television secured with grill bars, hoping it would not rain because the only thing the rain did not touch inside the theatre was the well-covered television. Nothing 'state of the art' about it unless one was talking about the sun rays that the holes on the roof let in, but it was their only theatre, and they did not know better.

Kanja's casual labourer parents looked perpetually upset with life and only laughed in the company of outsiders, laughter that came out as muffled sounds, like they were embarrassed. As a grownup, Kanja would wonder if the lack of laughter was caused by misery, or absence of jokes.

Every weekday, the three left home at six in the morning. He would go to school as his parents went to work in tea farms. He would be the first to return home at four. His parents would saunter in an hour later, minutes apart, dog tired and expect warm water to soak their tired feet. By the time they arrived, Kanja would have washed his school uniform, collected dry twigs to start a fire, filled a *sufuria* with water and placed it on the *jiko,* already preparing dinner. If he worked faster, he would have a few spare minutes to kick a ball around with his friends.

As his mother made dinner, he would wipe his body with a wet cloth. He only had a full body wash on Saturdays at the Tigoni Dam with his friends.

It was one of those days as he was collecting dry twigs in a tea plantation when he was brutally grabbed from behind. He was too surprised to scream. By the time he thought of screaming, his mouth had been covered by one big rough smelly palm. For life, Kanja would remember the smell of the hand, a mix of different types of dirt and stale cigarettes. Somehow, he noticed the orange sun that was beginning to disappear into the horizon.

When the assailant turned him around, Kanja came face to face with a pair of red, crazed eyes. "If you scream, I will sneak into your house tonight and kill your mother." His attacker's bad breath registered before the threat. Kanja whimpered like a stressed puppy, nodding in quick succession.

Kanja had collected dry tea twigs every single day since he started school at the age of five. He had never had reason to be afraid of anything in the plantations. Often, he bumped into stray dogs that were more scared of him than he was of them. And now everything was happening so fast, all he could think about was when he would finish collecting the twigs.

The attacker was known to Kanja. He lived on his own, a few hundred metres from where Kanja lived with his parents. The man kept to himself, and often, Kanja and his friends would throw stones at his house, then run away. For a moment, Kanja thought he was being punished for the stone-throwing misdemeanours.

He was again roughly turned around, and his already torn shorts pulled down with a single move. He, Kanja, wondered why the man bothered to remove the shorts—they had enough holes anyway. "Lie down… no, not on your back, on your tummy!" He did as ordered.

Because he had his face pressed against the earth, he did not see his attacker coming down on him, but he felt him. He stayed quiet, and started counting, one… two… three… one hundred… one hundred and…

He did not know how long it all lasted. At some point he had accepted his pain. After what seemed like eternity, it stopped. The attacker's weight lifted off. Kanja heard the zipper, then he was alone.

He remained on the ground for what felt like another eternity. Eventually, he made himself get up, looked around for his torn shorts and wore them. He registered blood trickling down his legs, wiped it off with soil, picked the twigs he had gathered, and clenched his buttocks as he walked home.

At home, he collapsed on the earthen floor of the house where his mother found him.

"What is wrong with you? Why is there no fire? Haven't you prepared the *sukuma wiki*, you lazy boy? Wait until your father comes home and finds no warm water… you will have a good beating," his mother threatened. Kanja remained unresponsive.

"Anyway," his mother said with a shrug, "if you have decided to be like those naughty boys who never help at home, that is fine. Just know I am not including you for dinner." She then went around doing what Kanja usually did.

"What's wrong with him?" his father demanded as he entered the house.

"Your son has decided not to help around the house. He is not even talking to me."

He stood over his son and looked down at his immobile body. With a slight frown he gently nudged Kanja with a foot. "Are you unwell?" he asked. Kanja did not respond.

"He will be fine," his mother said quickly. Hospital visits were luxuries they could not afford.

The father gave his son one last look, shrugged, then used cold water to wash his feet.

Their one room abode had one bed at the far corner, his parents' bed. Kanja slept on a thin mattress that was stored under the bed at

daytime. Often, he heard muffled groans coming from his parents'
corner at night, sounds he knew he should not have been hearing.

For hours, Kanja's parents would step over his stationary body
when they wanted to get to the other side. Apart from the radio,
there were no other sounds in the house. His parents would exchange
bewildered looks now and then, shrug and step over him.

Until it was time to eat.

"Kanja get up, unless you want to sleep hungry?" his mother
asked, her voice softer with concern.

"If you do not want to eat, it is your problem. Your hunger will
wake you up in the middle of the night. Just make sure you do not
wake us up."

She served two plates of *ugali* and *sukuma wiki* for herself and her
husband. They started eating in silence, stealing glances at Kanja, as
their worry increased with every second. They shifted more on their
seats. They cleared their throats more. He was still motionless. If the
lighting in the house had been better, they would have seen the tears
running down Kanja's face.

"I have no memory of you not eating, even when you are sick.
What is wrong?" his father asked, putting down his near empty plate.

Silence, no movement.

"Are you dead?" his father suddenly asked, too loudly. He knelt
next to Kanja and bent over his face. That was when he saw the
tears. "Why are you crying?" he asked in sudden panic, shaking his
son violently. Kanja mumbled incoherently.

"He is running a fever!"

"My son is dying!" The mother screamed, throwing down her
plate. The father did not scream, but he groaned as he picked Kanja
up, ran outside, followed by a screaming wife. They stormed into a

5

neighbour's house, two compounds from theirs, one who had an old car that more often than not had no fuel, or needed jumpstarting the one everyone ran to when there was a medical emergency.

His father laid Kanja on the electricity-lit porch and banged on the door, ignoring the barking dogs that could have attacked them, but they did not, like they too sensed something was wrong.

"Uuuuuwi! He is bleeding!" His wife screamed as she turned over Kanja. "He is bleeding from his buttocks! What have they done to my child?"

* * *

The neighbour's car had fuel, and it did not need jumpstarting.

The doctor confirmed what everybody suspected. The parents joined their son in mute pain. Neither cried. Their silence lasted a day, Kanja's lasted years. At the hospital, Kanja only ate when he was force-fed. He only moved when he was moved. He stared unblinkingly at the ceiling. His dreamy and cheeky eyes had been replaced by a glassy look, like someone had placed a reflective mirror on the eyes to keep in the secrets of the soul.

They brought psychiatrists, he refused to acknowledge them, even when they sat right in front of him. "He is not ready—he will talk when he is ready," they all declared in resignation.

The physical wounds took two weeks to heal. He was declared physically well enough to be discharged. The same neighbour who had driven him to the hospital drove him back home, in silence. They were encouraged to take him to a psychiatrist. They did not know who a psychiatrist was. They did not ask because someone with a title like *psychiatrist* sounded like they would need to get paid. They were lucky that the hospital had waived their bill.

Kanja, in his silence and glassy stare, registered everything that was said. He heard the doctor's pessimism about his mental wounds. The smell of the man's hands and breath still lingered on him, and as long as he could smell him, he *decided* he would not heal.

His was not the first defilement of a minor in the village. Like all the others, Kanja's case was only whispered about. Even before Kanja cut himself off from the society, he had already been ostracised, like all the other victims—conspiracy of silence. His friends stopped playing with him——not that he wanted to play, anyway. Every breath he took was because he wanted to preserve himself long enough to outlive the rapist. Every meal he took, he took not because he was hungry, but because he needed to be strong enough for his plans… and a plan he had.

Kanja started working out, pushed himself to near exhaustion, which was the only way to have a nightmare-free sleep. Instead of playing football with his friends, he ran through the same tea plantation he was defiled in, up and down the hills; refused to flinch when the tea branches cut his legs. He found a spot in a nearby forest and put up a punching bag he made out of stolen sand, one he punched until he could not do it anymore.

He returned to school the following school term. Spaces cleared when he entered. Faces turned down or away when he passed. Even his teachers did not ask him questions. They did not check his homework, nor did they punish him even when the entire class was being punished. Kanja had turned into an invisible human.

His grades improved, but his new sceptic self wondered if he had really improved, or the teachers were too afraid to fail him.

* * *

Kanja's silence was a consciously calculated move. The first weeks after the defilement, trauma had knocked words and voices out of his system, but soon he realised people mixed up his refusal to talk with inability to hear. That was how, two years on, he overheard his mother discuss with another villager about a little girl. She was two classes behind him, and was defiled in the same tea plantation.

His buttocks clenched.

It was a warm August evening, and the darkness had already overpowered the light at six thirty. For two years, Kanja had acquired a new habit of taking a walk just before total darkness engulfed the village. Rain or shine, he had been faithful in the walks. The walks would take half an hour. It was six forty-five when he left the compound. With his athletic stealth, and determination summoned specially for the day, he walked to his defiler's gate.

Like he had done countless times for two years, he hid in the bush, camouflaged by his dark clothes and the darkness. It was a bush he had tried and tested many times and he only walked back home when a predictable Kimakia staggered into his compound. Kanja found it strange that Kimakia locked the gate when he left the compound, but either his alcohol brain forgot to lock it when he returned, or he had confidence that nobody would bother him while he was in.

Kanja followed Kimakia inside and just before he unlocked the door, Kanja lunged at him, pushing him forward. Kimakia groaned, then blacked out. Carefully, the twelve-year-old settled down and offloaded his rugged school bag. From it, he fished out a piece of cloth and used it to tie Kimakia's mouth, removed a rope and bound his molester's hands and legs. Next was a knife. He looked up at the skies, and just like the sunset had peered at him when he had been defiled, the near full moon was peeping through cloudy skies. He implored it to be on his side, unlike its sibling—the sun.

He ran his finger over the knife's edge and thought about the many days he had spent honing it against a stone outside the house. The two-inch wide knife belonged to his mother's limited collection of cutlery. Days over days of sharpening had reduced it to a fraction of its original size.

A crispy wind blew, ruffling the trees. Kanja imagined a few leaves losing the battle and dancing their way to the ground. Then it went quiet, just for a few seconds. A couple of village mongrels barked. Kanja took a deep breath and held it for a few long seconds.

He squatted.

It was near a full moon, but the cloud cover kept interfering with visibility. He stared even when he saw nothing. He was afraid, not of Kimakia, but of the prospect of potential failure. He considered abandoning what was starting to look like a stupid plan. He took another deep breath and held it.

He allowed himself to be nervous and let in a little bit of fear. For two years, he had studied Kimakia's habits. He knew he arrived home between seven and seven-thirty, drunk. He would stop by the gate to pee, and loudly spit phlegm into the bush. A couple of times, piss and phlegm had almost landed on Kanja, taking extra effort not to gag.

Kanja did not have a watch, but by somebody's watch somewhere it was seven-twenty-two when he unzipped Kimakia's trousers. The cold made him stir awake. He tried to move unsuccessfully. He tried to scream. Only muffles came out. The muffles and the struggle to free himself increased when Kanja drove a dagger through Kimakia's thigh. It was not in his original plan but as his victim lay right in front of him, his rage knew no boundaries.

Kanja had near cat-like night vision and the clouds had cleared way for the moon that had listened to his pleas. The dogs were closer, their barks vicious, but they kept their distance. Kimakia was groaning, too loudly, and he was struggling harder.

The dogs were inching closer, growling menacingly. Kanja picked a stone from the ground and threw it towards them and hit one by pure luck, it whimpered. It went quiet for a while to allow Kanja to concentrate. He cracked his knuckles and took a deep breath. Then he went to work. Just like it was done to him two years ago, he pulled down Kimakia's torn pants.

"What are you doing? Help!" That was what Kimakia said. The words came out as muffles.

Kanja punched Kimakia's jaw, then the other jaw. With his hand, he scooped soil from the ground, removed the piece of cloth covering the mouth and stuffed the soil in Kimakia's mouth. Kimakia choked. The dogs started barking again.

Kanja grabbed Kimakia's exposed penis. It was wet with pee. With precision that would have impressed a chicken butcher, he cut off what he thought was half of it. The relief he felt with that single brutal act was so huge, he groaned loudly. Then, I smiled for the first time in two years. He stood up, held his prize up, through the darkness and chuckled.

Kimakia did not scream. He could not.

Nobody knew better than Kimakia why this was being done to him. Only he knew the little boys and girls he had molested. Only he knew how he threatened them if they spoke his name. But Kimakia, as powerful as he felt, had always feared that one of his victims would either tell on him, or hurt him. He just never imagined getting his penis cut would be part of the punishment.

Kimakia passed out.

The dogs were getting closer. He threw another stone towards them, they retreated, just a little. Kimakia's one goat was bleating somewhere in the compound, nonstop. He dragged Kimakia back to the road where he would be spotted by the next passer-by. He wiped his hands on his shorts. With his rugged backpack on his back, he walked away, whistling all the way, the barking of the dogs fading with every step. He hoped they would, at least, eat the cut piece of the penis.

His first stop was the pit latrine where he threw his weapon. He washed his hands with soap in the *karai* just outside the door.

He opened the door to the house and looked at his parents. They were both holding cups, definitely with black, sugarless tea. They both paused to look at him. He smiled at them and said, "I am hungry."

His mother's aluminium cup fell to the floor. The liquid poured from the fallen cup, making several tributaries to *nowhere* on the floor. Nobody looked at it. His father slowly placed his own cup on the same floor over one of the tributaries, then lifted both his hands to the skies. His mother broke into tears. It was the first time they were hearing their son's voice in two years.

They were ten minutes into their silent, but happy supper when the piercing screams cut through the evening. For the second time that evening, dishes were dropped to the floor. The father grabbed a *panga* and the mother a piece of wood. When they rushed outside armed, they thought they were answering a distress call for thieves. In their panic, neither of the parents noticed Kanja's near stoic pose.

When his parents disappeared into the night, they did not shut the door behind them, Kanja did not bother to shut it, either. At that moment and time, he felt invincible.

The parents found a chaotic scene. Somebody had produced a torch and kept shining it on where Kimakia's full penis was meant to be. The men would groan emphatically from the sight and instinctively cover their groin area.

Kanja's father held his wife's hand and pulled her away from the crowd. They silently walked home, hands intertwined.

They found Kanja as they had left him—eating. They paused at the door. He looked at his father defiantly, and his father nodded and smiled. His mother started crying. The father studied his son, registering both pride and fear. The wife took a broom and started sweeping the food on the floor in silence.

* * *

Kimakia wouldn't die for some time. He would live his remaining short life with half his penis bandaged. Kimakia hanged himself with an old rope he used to tie his lone goat. The goat had taken advantage of the freedom and ran off. No one ever wondered where it had gone.

No one claimed Kimakia's body.

He was buried by the government in a shallow grave at the public cemetery. The dogs dug out and fed on his body.

Chapter Two

The air, even out in the open, had the acrid smell of the type of sweat that if it came into contact with eyes, it would feel like someone poured salty water in them. It was the only way for the air to smell because the midday heat was overheating the tarmac road, squeezing water out of every living thing by opening wide pores, humbling the trees enough for them to retract their shadows to invisibility and silencing the birds. In Utopia where poverty had no place, walking in that type of sun would have been considered suicidal. But Naliaka did not live in Utopia.

With a sad pair of eyes, she watched the *matatu* from which she had just alighted disappear into the horizon and only when she could no longer see it, did she turn to the direction of her way home. Earlier on, Naliaka had used her last money to buy drinking water, which left her no choice but to walk the remaining ten kilometres home.

On one hand, she held her blue school jersey and on the other, a terribly worn-out rucksack. She trapped the rucksack in between her knees, freeing her hands to tie the jersey on her bald head so as to protect it from direct sun, inhaled, closed her eyes, exhaled and took the first step.

A few minutes into her walk, Naliaka's body system started to overheat. She stopped to catch her breath, sip on water and adjust the jersey on her head. The road ahead was void of people, like shadows were not the only things that retreated from January's midday sun.

Sweat trickled down her spine, butt-crack and down her skinny thighs. She looked around to ensure she was really alone on the road, then rubbed her skirt against her thighs to soak the sweat.

A couple of kilometres on, Naliaka was too tired, too hot, too sweaty, out of water and teary. On most days, she hated her life. Today was one of those days, though for a good reason. She should not have been roasting in the heat, but she had been sent home from boarding school, because of an outstanding fee balance.

She kept walking, letting the salt of her tears and sweat become one.

* * *

Naliaka was midway up a hill, only hearing the sound of her panting and her thudding heart when the sound of wheels against the tarmac shook her out of the trance. Without turning, she stepped aside to let the car pass, then continued walking, eyes downcast, thus she did not notice the vehicle had stopped a few metres ahead. When she did, she stopped with a start, quickly looked around for an escape route, but before she could make a move, the electronic passenger window wound down with a whisper, revealing what Naliaka immediately considered a fascinating human.

The driver had a big afro blonde wig. Between the makeup and the wig, Naliaka decided the former was weirder. The driver smiled and exposed what looked like a double set of teeth. She noticed the large forehead that could have been larger, were it not for the headgear. The lips could have been smaller were it not for the red lipstick that seemed to pump life into them and her face was so red—probably because of the heat—but Naliaka chose to think of it as half-roasted meat.

Naliaka's tummy growled, reminding her that she was hungry.

Instead of running away, which she should have done, Naliaka stood hypnotised, peering at what the makeup suggested was a woman.

"Hi!"

It was a deep voice, but definitely feminine. Naliaka shook her head, more in consternation about why the woman was talking to her.

"Are you alright?"

The more the woman spoke, the less threatening she looked. Naliaka felt her shoulders drop in relaxation.

"I only stopped because you look like you need a lift."

Naliaka finally shifted on her feet, patted her head over her jersey and looked both ways before focusing on the woman again. She did need the lift. In fact, as she studied the strange woman, she wondered how she would make it home alive if she declined the offer.

"Come on, we don't have all day," the woman urged as she leaned over to open the passenger door.

Naliaka looked at the exterior of the vehicle with suspicion. It was like nothing she had ever seen. In her sixteen years, she had never been inside a vehicle that was not a *matatu*. She was looking at

15

a cream interior that appeared to repel dust. Naliaka looked at her dusty feet, then back at the smiling woman.

It took the woman another minute to convince Naliaka to get in. Even then, it was one foot in, same foot out, amused encouragement, then both feet in, hugging her backpack, sitting stiffly and eyes looking straight ahead.

"Shut the door, please." The woman said with a chuckle.

Just to have something to do, Naliaka uncovered her head and clutched at the jersey.

The woman drove slowly, once in a while taking her eyes off the road to study the girl beside her. She shivered with a familiar feeling that did not happen often, but when it did, it was ecstatic.

"I am Queen. What's your name?"

Naliaka clutched tighter at her sweater. "Naliaka," she whispered.

"Would you like some water?" Queen asked, and without waiting for an answer reached behind Naliaka's seat for a half-full bottle. Naliaka gulped it and swallowed loudly, nearly finishing it without pausing.

"So, where are you going?"

"Home."

"Are you not supposed to be in school?"

"Yes."

"Is it midterm already?"

"No."

"You don't talk much, do you?" Queen said with resignation.

Nyathuna Shopping Centre, lost somewhere in Kikuyu sub-county, was a sleepy red-dusty town sandwiched between a vibrant but red-dusty shopping centre of Ngecha and a chaotic market town of Wangige. Residents were mainly large-scale greens and tomato farmers who supplied Wangige market, or workers of these farms. The workers and the employers were often hard to differentiate, because they all wore overalls and rubber boots, often covered in mud.

"I want to get off here," Naliaka softly but urgently said when they reached the outskirts of the shopping centre. She did not want to be dropped at the heart of the shopping centre where young idle men, or those done with work, went to hang about to watch life go by.

"You live close by?" Naliaka nodded as she fumbled for the door handle. "Here, take this card. It has my name and telephone number on it. If you ever need anything, anything at all, call me."

Naliaka took the card, but did not look at it. She was more worried about being seen by someone who could tell her, other than that she was seen alighting a vehicle.

"You are a very, very beautiful girl," Queen whispered just before Naliaka shut the door behind her. Queen did not see the smile on Naliaka's face, she did not see Naliaka running two fingers on her right cheek, nor did she see the sudden sparkle in her eyes. It was the first time anybody had ever complimented her on her beauty, and it felt good.

* * *

Under the still scorching sun, a cold wind that lasted a few seconds hit Naliaka's face. She stopped. That was when she looked ahead. A group of people stood outside the gate of the plot where they rented a room, their heads close together like they were blocking the wind from carrying away their secrets. Then one of them spotted her, whispered something to the others who all turned to look at Naliaka, wide-eyed before scampering off.

Naliaka picked her pace again, nearly running the last fifty metres into the compound. Their one room house was among several similar rooms, wooden structures that offered little privacy or security, but good enough to shield occupants from rain and direct sun. In the compound, there were people in clustered groups.

Naliaka dropped her bag and sweater before letting out a scream. Her knees gave way, and she ended up on the ground. Her stomach churned, not with hunger like before, but with doom. She screamed again. And again. She kicked at nothing. When she was not kicking, she rolled on the ground until her whole body was covered in red dust. Some women approached her, going on their knees to try and contain her.

"Naliaka, how did you know?" one of the women asked.

Naliaka screamed her mother's name and passed out.

When she came back to her senses, she was inside the familiar *nothing* of their room, surrounded by worried faces. The evening passed in a daze. She remained mute, mostly unmoving. She did not eat or drink. Somebody told her that her mother had succumbed to a rabid dog bite and by the time she was rushed to hospital in critical condition, she was beyond treatment. Naliaka slept a dreamless night, which made her feel guilty when she woke up and remembered that she was technically an orphan.

A pauper's burial took place three days later at the government cemetery. There were no flowers, or tears, not even from Naliaka whose tear ducts had long dried by then. The local area Member of Parliament donated a casket after an appeal. There were less than twenty people in attendance, mostly jobless young men with nothing better to do.

In the pauper's cemetery, the dead buried themselves.

For two weeks after the burial, Naliaka locked herself in the room, only venturing outside to use the pit latrine. She only took a sponge bath when she started smelling her own sweat after days. Neighbours brought her food in silence—they were too busy wrestling with their own poverty to burden with somebody else's problems.

Reality came calling when the landlord knocked on the door. Naliaka was given a week to come up with rent or to vacate the room. She went from door to door asking for help, but none came through. She did not blame her neighbours—they were all collectively poor. As it were, they were already getting tired of donating food to her and the donations were getting less and less every day.

Not knowing what else to do, she took the rucksack she had not touched since she arrived from school. She removed her school books and tossed them carelessly on the floor, then started packing her few clothes inside the pack. That was when she saw the business card that Queen had given her.

She reached for her mother's *kabambe* phone, one that had been on for two weeks but nobody had called it.

* * *

Queen's house was a seven-bedroom mansion located in the north of Nairobi on Limuru Road, right between Ruaka and Ndenderu. The three-storey structure, built on a vast piece of land, was not visible from the road and there were no immediate neighbours. The perimeter stone wall was ten feet high—against the stipulated seven feet. Thorny trees planted on the inside flowed over the wall. The

19

manicured lawns were mowed and watered twice a week with flowers tended like favoured children. The big lawn umbrellas, planted on different spots around the garden, provided the occupants an opportunity for privacy.

Queen occupied the whole top floor. Decorated and painted with different shades of purple, it was a house within a house with every imaginable amenity, including an underused hot bath tub.

The other six bedrooms, located on both the middle and ground floors, were spacious but only when not compared to Queen's. They each had two, five by six feet beds separated by colourful curtains in the middle. The bedrooms were all shades of grey and red. The occupants were all women of different ages and sizes.

The house was officially a massage parlour. Unofficially, it was an elite whore house.

The brothel was only by appointment and membership was by subscription. All new clients were vetted and had to be vouched for by an existing client. Queen ran an illegal business. Everyone, including the authorities, knew what she did, but she kept them all financially happy and silent. It helped that her clients were wealthy, powerful men.

Queen's well-travelled clients often brought her expensive drinks from their travels. She let the girls drink everything else but the champagne, which she drank every once in a while. Naliaka's call found Queen at the balcony lying on a recliner seat, nursing a glass of champagne, gazing at the skies through her dark sunglasses.

She responded to the vibrating phone with a quick glance, frowning a little because of the unrecognised number.

"Hello?" she answered in her most official voice. Someone on the other side whimpered. It was a familiar sound. Girls who came to her were usually at a bad place. Making a call to Queen was the last resort, an acceptance of defeat. The final humiliation.

"Who is this?"

"Naliaka," came the whisper. Queen was good with names and faces—she smiled.

"Are you okay?" she asked, a familiar surge of adrenaline rushing through her. She carefully placed her champagne glass on the glass stool, stood up and leaned on the balcony rail.

"No."

"Where are you?"

"At the shopping centre."

"Wait for me at the same spot I dropped you." Queen did not bother to change from her *dera*, she just slipped into sandals. She grabbed her car keys, and shouted for one of the girls.

"Julia, follow me!"

Julia, dressed in a cropped top and a short skirt, both too small for her size, did not bother to look for her shoes.

Sometimes the girls would call, but by the time Queen arrived, they would have developed cold feet and disappeared. Their phones would sometimes be switched off. Some would call back with apologies, others would disappear forever. The less time they had to think things through, the better chance Queen had to get them.

Queen missed the miserable looking figure seated on the grass hugging her knees and rocking back and forth, the tattered bag lying carelessly tossed on the ground next to her. Naliaka only stood up when the car passed, making a weak effort to run after it but then gave up and started walking instead. Queen took a U-turn and spotted the haggard figure.

'How dirty can someone be?' she asked rhetorically, stopping the car.

Still, when she came out of the car, she hugged Naliaka before opening the back door to usher her in.

"Hi." Julia's voice made Naliaka jump.

Naliaka stared at Julia's outfit. Julia would, several times after, narrate how Naliaka recoiled into herself like a snail into its shell. Tenderly, Julia took Naliaka's hand. As hot as the weather was, the hand was cold, lifeless. It was rough and bony. It had dirty fingernails. Julia squeezed it a little with reassurance and held on to it.

Queen turned off the radio, only the humming of Queen's V8 engine was audible. Naliaka, her hand still in Julia's, looked outside the window. A river of tears silently ran down her cheeks beside her nose, over and inside the mouth before finally dropping into her old clothes that were turning wet with each tear drop. She didn't see Queen adjust her rear view mirror to look at her.

Chapter Three

Naliaka, with stooped shoulders and inability to look anywhere but the ground in front of her, alighted from Queen's car and allowed Julia to lead her inside the house. She did not once look up, not even when they went up the stairs into a room that had different shades of purple.

In silence, Julia helped her out of her clothes, ran a shower and washed her like she would wash a baby. Naliaka had never experienced a shower or scented soap before then, but it would be days before she appreciated all that.

She was given a room of her own. It was smaller than any other, but bigger than the one that had housed Naliaka for all her life. It had a television set and a wall-to-wall wardrobe. When Julia left a music channel on, Naliaka did not even notice it.

For days, Queen dropped in and out of the room multiple times during the day. Sometimes, she would sit next to Naliaka on the bed and hold her hand, rubbing it reassuringly. At first, it made Naliaka tense, afraid that she was expected to make conversation. Every night before sleep, Queen hugged Naliaka and at that moment Naliaka would break down and cry herself to sleep.

Meals were delivered to her room and Naliaka would eat under Queen's watchful gaze. Once a day for an hour, Naliaka went outside to get some sun. Once a day, she got a massage from one of the girls. The first day, it was Julia who gave her the massage. She did it while Naliaka was fully clothed. "This would feel so much better if you had less clothes." Julia suggested to a hesitant Naliaka. "Wear shorts and a tee-shirt."

"I don't have any of that," Naliaka answered, thinking of her tattered clothes still inside a tattered bag. She had never worn shorts in her life.

"Queen always has spare clothes."

She liked to look through the window, into the vast manicured compound. Or the front yard from the opposite window. She watched scantily dressed women, laughing and smoking. They looked happy, carefree.

She may have been naive in the ways of the world, but she knew there was something sinister about the home. The men, all in suits, would walk in a hurry and walk out slowly, dragging their feet, like they did not want to leave. Sometimes, Queen walked them to the car and waved them off until they disappeared out of the high gate.

* * *

Naliaka was watching the women through the window as they soaked up the sun when Queen walked in. Naliaka jumped like she was caught in mischief. On one hand, Queen held up a pair of jeans and another blue item. On her other hand was a pair of red doll shoes and some lacy bits that turned out to be a panty and a bra. Naliaka looked at Queen with silent questions.

"Naliaka, how are you this morning?" Queen asked as she shut the door with her foot. Naliaka shivered but smiled shyly walking to the bed. She sat down, palms under her thighs. Queen dropped the stuff on the bed, then folded her arms across her chest, standing over Naliaka.

"You look much better and prettier. The week of rest has done you good."

Naliaka risked a glance and smiled.

"It is however, about time you got out of the hideous nightdresses."

For a week, Naliaka had been changing from one long nightdress into another, all provided by Queen. She had not been wearing underwear because she had not carried any, except the old one she had on the day she left Nyathúna.

Queen pointed at the clothes, her eyes stuck on Naliaka.

"I am sure I got the sizes right."

"Thank you," Naliaka whispered, giving the items a side glance.

"Take your shower and change into those. You and I are going shopping."

For hours, Queen and Naliaka moved from shop to shop at the Two Rivers Mall. Naliaka gasped at the price tags as she watched Queen pick the clothes, all short and tight, then make her try them all. She found them too short, or too tight, or too bright, but Queen would look at her hunched figure and nod, "perfect". They bought shoes, more underwear and a makeup set. "The girls will have fun showing you how to use makeup.

They finished at a barber shop where Naliaka learned shaving hair did not just involve running a pair of scissors over the head.

"Why do I need all these?" Naliaka finally asked, more in embarrassment than curiosity. They were having lunch at an open food court, beside them bags over bags of shopping.

Queen took her time to answer as she tried to lock Naliaka's eyes.

"Because, Naliaka, I need you to start working."

She stopped chewing and shifted on her seat.

"Where?"

Queen gave her another long look as she continued chewing.

"For me, of course."

"Doing what?" She whispered involuntarily and roughly scratched her freshly bald head.

Queen cleared her throat and used a paper towel to wipe her mouth.

"Do you know what happens in my house?"

Naliaka half-shrugged, looking away. Queen sniggered before answering.

"My goodness! Where did you grow up?" It was a rhetorical question, but Naliaka had answered, "Nyathúna."

"Sex does not happen in Nyathúna?" Queen asked, resuming her eating.

Naliaka looked at Queen with her big eyes, face going red.

"You would have to learn how to give proper massages, of course." She cleared her throat and sat up straighter. "Those girls you see in the house entertain men, and they get paid for their effort."

Naliaka pressed her back on the seat. She looked around to see if anyone else had heard Queen.

"You want me to be a prostitute," she finally said, squaring up to Queen.

"A-ha! So you do know about these things." She picked a piece of fry, ignoring the fork.

Naliaka shook her head, eyes shining with tears.

"I can't. My mom…"

"Naliaka, your mom is dead, remember? She left you with nothing. With no one. I am offering to help you."

"I… I…"

The tears running down her face were hot. She wiped them with the back of her hand, along with the snort. Queen handed her a paper towel which Naliaka used to wipe her hand.

"I will not force you to do anything you are not willing to do, but I would hope you have an alternative plan."

Naliaka cringed at Queen's tone.

"I mean, you just lost your mother, you already told me you have nobody in this world. So, tell me, how are you going to fend for yourself?"

Silence.

"I am giving you a way out. You are a beautiful girl. Pretty soon, men are going to want to do things to you, whether you stay with me or not. Men will lie that they will help you, marry you, even educate you but all they want to do is get inside your pants. You will try to resist because you are a nice, innocent girl but when hunger strikes, you will give in. The men who come here do not misbehave, but out there is an open jungle."

"How about school?"

"Do you have school fees?" Queen scoffed.

Naliaka cried more. Queen continued chewing on her food, while staring down Naliaka.

With a soft tone, Queen spoke to Naliaka, laying down the possibility of how, whatever else she chose, poverty would be her sidekick. At some point, Naliaka stopped crying, but her eyes were red and puffy. Her nose was running, and she was going through the paper towels very fast.

"More often than not, there is always a price on sex. You can choose to be ahead of the game, or you will join millions of women who feel short-changed because they were faithful to their men, but all they got for their troubles was unfaithfulness, and disrespect, and being stuck at home with spoilt brats for children as the man pursued other women, and a life."

Queen had used that speech many times. It often worked like a charm because many of the girls who came to her were from abusive relationships or broken families. Others were like Naliaka—clueless and lost.

Naliaka could feel herself losing all willingness to think. Prior to meeting Queen, she had never thought about sex or what it could or could not bring her. Her mother had warned her against premarital sex, especially against being friends with girls who looked like they were already having sex. Prostitutes, loose girls who will never find husbands, she had called them, seemingly forgetting that she too did not have a husband.

"If you really want to go back to school, I cannot stop you, but you would have to work for the money. We can work out something." Queen pointed at Naliaka's half-eaten food. "Come on, finish your food. We need to get going."

They ate in silence. They drove back home in silence, with Naliaka shivering occasionally.

* * *

For two days, Naliaka stayed in her room in near solitary.

Queen no longer turned up and the massages stopped. Only once did she see Queen through the window as she drove out. Over and over, Naliaka replayed her conversation with Queen, and as much as she hated to admit it, Queen was the only one with a viable solution, as unpalatable as she found it.

The day she saw Queen drive out, Naliaka decided to see if indeed she was allowed to walk out. She slipped into the same pair of jeans, same shoes she had worn when they went shopping, a new tee-shirt and carried a sweater in her hand. She tiptoed to the ground floor, ignored the girls who fell silent as she passed them as she walked towards the gate, heart racing faster with each step.

"I want to go out," she told the security man, who shrugged and opened the gate in silence. Naliaka hesitated. She had expected some resistance. Her walk beyond the gate was slower. The sun was hot, like it had been that first day she had met Queen. She covered her bald head with the sweater, the same way she had covered it on the day she had met Queen.

The main road was coming closer and closer and her steps were getting slower from indecision. When she got to the road, she looked both ways, then, for no particular reason, went right. She had no idea how far or how long she walked for, but she stopped suddenly and retraced her steps. With a pinch of shame, she realised she did not want to be out there. She wanted a comfortable bed and three tasty meals a day. She wanted to belong, anywhere.

The odds were stacked against her, and so was the sun. The stakes were also against her—she was a minor with no family. She had no friends, but she had Queen.

With the same indifference, the security guard let her back in.

Back in her safety, she sat on the bed, feet sunk in the softness of the lush carpet. She took in the furniture and the purple room and sighed. With a new sense of determination, she stood up, undressed and took a shower.

Through the window, Naliaka saw some of the girls sitting on the grass, all of them holding a bottle of soda, a couple of them smoking. They were laughing loudly. She wanted to be able to laugh like that. They saw her walk out of the door and waved at her. They cheered as she approached. She smiled shyly.

All the girls gave her high five. One of them asked how she was feeling and another one offered her soda.

"I know where to get another," she said.

She was drawn to Julia, the one who had accompanied Queen to pick her up. Everyone else seemed to be competing for Julia's attention, leaning towards her. Julia was older and most voluptuous. She wore a pair of shorts and a tight top that pronounced several layers on her midriff. When she laughed, her whole body shook like thick jelly.

Julia looked like somebody's beautiful mother, not a prostitute.

"So how are you feeling now?" Julia asked.

"Much better."

"Good. Because you need to start working, otherwise your ass will be thrown out."

The other girls laughed uncomfortably, but they nodded their heads in agreement. Naliaka looked at the grass.

Julia, like that first day, took Naliaka's hand.

"I am sure you already know what we do here?"

Naliaka nodded.

"I am telling you this because as good as Queen has been to you, she is not a charitable organisation. In fact, you should know how lucky you have been—with your own room, and meals delivered by Queen."

"Queen does not serve anyone," one of the other girls cut in.

"Exactly."

Naliaka sighed. She used her free hand to scratch her head, eyes cast down.

"There is something about you. It's in your eyes. Like you haven't seen the worst of life. It must be the reason that Queen has a soft spot for you. You seem like a nice girl, not like these mad women I live with."

They all laughed. Naliaka looked up at them and smiled.

"Sorry about your mom by the way, but accept that life is not fair. You need to decide if you want to do as Queen wants you to or not, otherwise..."

The other girls were nodding in agreement. One of them was blowing gum loudly. Another one was clearing her throat equally loudly.

After a moment of silence, Naliaka looked up at Julia and asked, "How is it?"

"The sex?" Naliaka nodded.

"It is just sex. It is the same sex you have with a boyfriend behind the bush. The only difference is we get paid for our troubles."

Naliaka cocked her head, neck seemingly shrinking into her body.

"But I have never had sex!"

First, there was silence, then a splatter of drinks to and from all directions. Someone choked on their cigarette smoke. Another short silence followed, like the calm before the storm. The laughter that followed sounded like a bad piece of music from a choir of drunks. When they finished laughing, they were all sprawled on the ground, holding their ribs. Naliaka's face was red with embarrassment, but she giggled.

"This is way too funny!" Julia was the first to recover.

"How old are you?"

"Nearly seventeen."

"Wah! *Jameni* at your age, I had five years' experience in sex, and a child to boot."

"You have children? Where are they?"

Julia's face dropped.

"With their idiot father."

Naliaka shook her head in confusion.

Julia waved her hand dismissively. "He is rich, ugly and abusive. I hate him."

"Julia wanted, still wants, to kill him," someone offered.

Naliaka was happy the conversation was no longer about her, but she shifted in discomfort. She knew about abusive marriages. She had neighbours who had vicious fights that ended with bad injuries.

"Why haven't you killed him, by the way?" someone asked so casually, Naliaka held her breath for a moment.

"He may have been, still is a bastard, but he is the father of my children and to give the devil his due, he is actually good to them." She paused, looking thoughtfully into the distance.

"Tell her how you ended up here," someone else said.

"Moment of madness," Julia said and went silent.

Naliaka thought that was it, and was about to ask something, but Julia spoke again.

"I followed him here because I was convinced he was having an affair. I hid in the maize plantation on the other side of the wall, waiting for him to leave the house so I could shoot him—I had stolen his gun. As I waited, I saw several men drive in, and out. It was easy to work out what happened here. After he left, I walked in and offered my services…"

"What?"

Julia shrugged. "So I went back home, took my teenage children to my sister, packed my clothes and moved here."

"Does he, you know, still come?"

Julia nodded.

"He's okay seeing you here?"

Julia shook her head. "This place is only by appointment so I am able to know when he is coming."

"He doesn't know?"

"I have been right under his nose for years. The stupid fool…"

Everyone laughed.

Naliaka studied the other girls. None of them looked shocked, but she was shaking inside with the information and sudden curiosity. She wanted to know everybody's story, everyone's journey to Queen's castle. Julia was talking again.

"His idiot brother is my client," Julia declared. Naliaka choked, splattering the soda.

"H… how?"

"His brother is a malicious nasty piece of work, likely worse than my husband if you can believe that. But he hates his brother more than I do. I suspect he sleeps with me to spite his brother.

Naliaka shook her head.

Then Julia sighed, sat up straight and shook her body a little.

"Everyone here joined Queen at a low point. This place," she looked at the house, "this place is our refuge."

The other girls nodded.

"I do not remember how we started talking about me. You, young lady, need to make a decision. But… there is an issue here… your virginity. I do not know any prostitute who lost her virginity to a client. Is Queen aware?"

Naliaka shook her head.

"Let her know."

Julia paused and rubbed her nose, all along staring at Naliaka in disbelief.

"*Heh*, I do not envy you. I believe that virginity was a calculated punishment for women," she sighed and rubbed Naliaka's back. "Good thing you only lose it once."

* * *

Naliaka drew the curtain in her room and squinted at the blinding morning. She scratched her arm and continued to scan the compound, specifically where Queen's car was usually parked.

It had been three days with no sighting of Queen.

She walked back to the bed and sat on it, slowly and gently, like she was afraid of offending it. She ran her hand over the soft beddings and smiled. She looked up at the ceiling and took in a deep breath, letting the lavender scent travel down her throat and penetrate her lungs. Queen's house smelled of either lavender, marijuana, or spicy food.

She took a shower and slipped into a pair of tights and a sleeveless top. As usual, she tiptoed down the stairs, an unnecessary act because the hallway and the stairs were carpeted and she was barefooted. There were no human sounds, but piped music played loudly.

She spotted Malaika sitting under a tree, dangling an unlit cigarette between her lips while peeling an orange with her long yellow nails. When the orange was fully peeled, Malaika broke off a section and popped it into her mouth while holding the cigarette between her index and ring fingers. Naliaka watched with fascination for a while, taking in the near sensual sight of the petite girl sitting with crossed legs.

Whenever she peeled a piece, she would trap the cigarette between her index and middle finger and pop it in her mouth. Naliaka watched her for a while, taking in the near sensual sight of Malaika sitting with crossed legs.

Malaika looked up at Naliaka in what looked like nonchalance and nodded, pointing to the ground with her mouth before popping another piece of orange.

"Where is everybody?" Naliaka asked unnecessarily.

She spoke with the cigarette trapped between her teeth.

"Wednesdays are always busy days. I am in-between clients."

Naliaka swallowed loudly. "I have not seen Queen for days."

"She is out of town."

Malaika offered a piece of orange to Naliaka. They chewed in silence as she stared at nothing in particular. Naliaka watched her, spellbound by the unlit cigarette.

"Does everyone here smoke?"

Malaika nodded. "Except Julia and Queen."

Naliaka nodded thoughtfully, still staring at the cigarette.

"How are you doing?" Malaika asked after she was done with her orange, squinting her eyes at Naliaka.

Naliaka smiled and shrugged. "Okay, I guess."

"Mh… so you will join us in the *fun*?" she cocked her head at Naliaka.

Naliaka shrugged. "I do not think I have a choice."

Malaika nodded. "You really do not want to be out there on your own. It is unkind." Malaika lazily looked at Naliaka. Malaika's big eyes were beautiful, but they lacked emotion. They had a glassy look that made Naliaka slightly uncomfortable.

Malaika was more on the skinny than slim side. She was as dark skinned as Naliaka was light skinned, teeth so perfect, like someone worked on them with precision. On her head was a blonde wig that should have been a mismatch against the dark skin but only enhanced her colouring.

Her voice was hoarse, like someone who was recovering from a throat infection. Naliaka watched her strike a match, finally lighting the cigarette, blowing smoke that blew in Naliaka's direction.

"I was hoping I could talk to Queen today," Naliaka said after a long silence.

"She is always going on and off. You enjoy your freedom for now because once they start scheduling you, there will be little rest."

Naliaka cleared her throat. "How many men do you… you know?"

"Have sex with…?"

Naliaka nodded.

Malaika blew a ring of smoke, looking into the skies. "Depends. Sometimes one, sometimes four, or more… you stop counting after some time."

"So, how did you end up here?"

"*Ai*, this has been my life since I was ten."

"Ten!" Naliaka screamed. "How?"

"My mother, a proud Majengo Estate resident, was a prostitute. My father could be the estate drunk or the president. When I turned ten, she started offering me for sex to her clients."

"What?"

Malaika shrugged. She lit another cigarette. "I grew up with sex everywhere. Some man humping on top of dear mother is most likely my earliest memory." Malaika paused and rubbed her nose vigorously. "There were many kids in my situation in the neighbourhood, and I probably lost my virginity at five to a boy the same age."

Naliaka shifted her bottoms, lost for words.

"We used to hump each other left, right and centre, and by the time my mom sold my body when I was ten, I was an expert." She laughed and coughed. A loud, bitter laughter and a cough that told of a congested chest. "I had done it with older boys and even though my mom offered me to her clients as a virgin, I was anything but.

"Being here is certainly better than being in Majengo, and the money is better, and the clients cleaner. The drugs are free, have a medical cover and constant food. That the clients are afraid of Queen is an added advantage because it means they cannot beat us up, as I got beat up a lot in my previous life."

"How about school?"

"I made it to class eight. I hated school, so no loss."

Malaika suddenly stood up. "Telling my story is always so draining. Come on, I have a few minutes before my next client. I am the official makeup artist around here, and I want to work on your beautiful face. Those bushy eyebrows need trimming."

* * *

Naliaka's mind was floating like the steam from the shower she was having when Julia loudly drew the shower curtains. Naliaka screamed and covered her nether areas with her hands, pressing her body against the wall.

"What are you hiding?" Julia asked with a snort. Naliaka did not move. She was staring at Julia with enlarged pupils. "My dear, pretty soon nakedness will cease to be an issue for you. Come on, finish up. Queen just called and will be here in half an hour." Julia drew back the shower curtain and walked away.

When Queen drove in, Naliaka emulated the smiles of the other girls who all stood outside waiting, but she felt queasy with nerves. She had selected a short blue dress that hugged her body at the right places, but her discomfort showed in how she hunched her shoulders and crossed her arms.

Queen hugged and asked after each girl. Naliaka, standing at the far end, was the last to get a hug.

"Look at you!" Queen exclaimed, holding a blushing Naliaka at an arm's length. "You are smiling." She finished with another hug that lasted longer than the other girls.

As the other girls helped each other pull the suitcases, Queen tagged at Naliaka's dress.

"I guess we are ready for our talk."

Naliaka nodded as she twiddled her fingers.

* * *

Naliaka and Queen were sitting on Queen's bed when she blurted out, "I am a virgin."

Queen laughed. At first, it was a short and sharp laugh. She looked at Naliaka like she expected to be told that the statement was a joke. Then she laughed again, long enough for Naliaka to get concerned.

"I thought I was the only adult virgin remaining," she finally said as she wiped tears of mirth with the hem of her dress.

Naliaka gasped. "You are a virgin?"

Queen nodded with a chuckle. It was Naliaka's turn to laugh.

"How?"

"Really, you are asking me that? Look at me. I am built like a brick and I have an ugly man's face—I do not inspire sexual desire." Naliaka shook her head in confusion. She had never heard anyone speak so negatively about themselves. "Anyway, I am going to have to auction you to the highest bidder, but before that, we have many do's and don'ts to go through."

Suddenly, Queen was all business. She spoke, Naliaka listened.

"I know I cannot keep you all here forever, but I want to know that, if and when you leave, you will have financial backing to help you out there. Save your money—you don't need it anyway since I provide everything."

Naliaka, with that single statement, was starting to understand why the girls adored Queen.

"On the week you are on your period, you take the week off. That is on top of your one day every week. You are required to do a complete medical test every three months."

She spoke about what the clients expected, and what she could not allow to be done to her.

Saturdays would be her days off.

"You are allowed to leave the compound. If you intend to spend the night I need to know and your phone must never go off."

* * *

Three days later, Naliaka got to meet the highest bidder. Kaggai.

Queen dressed Naliaka in red lingerie, did her makeup, and then made her drink a glass of wine, "It will help you relax," Queen said as she patted Naliaka's scalp gently. "Weed would be better, but because you have never used it, there is no way to know how you would react."

Kaggai, looking like an unpleasant, sweaty giant, walked into the room panting like he had been working out. He smiled at her, a smile that got Naliaka wondering if it was meant to relax her or scare her. It was a hot day, but Naliaka shivered and rubbed her arm.

* * *

Wearing a sleazy smile, Kaggai said he would be gentle.

Naliaka watched him undress what she immediately concluded was a hideous body even though she had no other male body to compare with. When his trousers fell off, she cringed with both shock and fear. He lifted his tummy to expose his manhood. She gasped and shut her eyes. He pushed her down gently, moved her legs wide apart, tied and adjusted and re-adjusted some ropes to each of her limbs, then to the four corners of the bed, and he nodded with satisfaction.

He applied something very cold on, and in her vagina.

The overweight man lay on top of her skinny body. The first thing she felt was his wobbly tummy slapping on her body. She recoiled internally, because he made it physically impossible. His full weight restricted air in and out of her lungs.

She whimpered and bit her lower lip to suppress a scream.

It was an excruciatingly painful process.

He humped, not gently. Endless pain.

She lay under him, eyes tightly shut, still, praying for the end of the episode or her life.

She whimpered more, tears blinding her. He groaned. Then he continued to groan more for what seemed like a lifetime.

NaiRobbery Cocktail

Chapter Four

They made a strange pair.

The tall woman in her late twenties had a long face set upon high cheekbones. Her melanin-dripping skin was flawless, and when she smiled, even the wind seemed to pause, as if to pay tribute to the smile—only she hardly ever smiled.

Her eyes were a striking shade of brown that stood out against her dark chocolate skin. Against the midday sun, the eyes sparkled like micro stars and the rest of the time, her many misgivings about life took away the sparkle. Her hair was long and naturally straight, the only gene from her mother that trickled down to her, thankfully. She spoke softly, like one who was keeping secrets from the wind. When she laughed, it was a soft, half-hearted laugh.

She moved gracefully, like a happy cat. When it was dusty, her feet remained dust-free. When it was muddy, the only trace of mud was found at the bottom of her soles. Her name was Kerubo, official occupation—shop manager in a car parts shop on Kirinyaga Road.

Then there was the man. He was the official mad man of Kirinyaga Road, a title he relished. He stood at six feet two inches and the dirty-looking sacks he wore did not hide his broad muscled body. Beneath his *mad man's* attire and the muscular body was a clean, white vest and clean white underwear. Somewhere in the confusion of clothes and sacks was a gun.

When he was not walking up and down Kirinyaga Road, he would be at a disused bus shelter on the same road, pretending to doze on and off, sometimes just staring at passers-by. Once in a while, he would get into impromptu workouts and entertain passers-by with push-ups and air-punches.

For people who took in little details, they remembered one day the disused bus shed being empty as it had always been since it was put up by the county government, then one morning, as people went to work, and as children went to school, a *mad man* had taken it over. He was ignored or avoided by people in their rat races.

Like the proverbial mad man, he loved collecting rubbish on the streets. What was now known as Chizi's shed was packed with plastic bags and other indistinct paraphernalia. Underneath his collection, however, were clean blankets he used to protect himself from nights of stinging cold.

Except Kerubo, everyone else, including other *mad men* and criminals, left him alone. Lovers fumbled in his presence, like he was invisible. The dreaded county government *askaris* left him alone as they chased everyone else. School children avoided him when they were not throwing off-target stone missiles at him.

He was known as Chizi Samuel. Samuel was the name he mumbled over and over, to no one in particular. Samuel was the answer to any question from anyone with enough guts to talk to him. Only he and

Kerubo knew he was more sane than half the people who passed by his shed. Often, because the shed was close to the popular Grogan mechanics' gathering, bored mechanics would shout greetings at him, greetings he often ignored or answered with Samuel.

Every two weeks, Chizi Samuel would disappear for a week. The regulars would hardly miss his presence, too engrossed in whatever had brought them to the city.

Chizi Samuel liked lingering around idle groups of people and his years on the streets had taught him to discern body language. He would shut his eyes and nod his head now and then, feigning sleep, although that would be when he was most alert. Sometimes he let his eyes roam, looking out for anything out of the usual chaotic norm.

Every morning and lunchtime, Kerubo delivered home-cooked meals to Chizi Samuel, and sat with him until he was done eating. That was when information was exchanged. Sometimes, because many years of meeting six days a week for three weeks a month had turned them into more than colleagues, they shared jokes and managed to ignore curious glances.

* * *

Kerubo was not sure what irritated her more between the dust and the heat. The baseball cap she covered her braided hair with felt wet around the rim. What was worse, she had to keep her dust coat on for two reasons; one, to keep her gun out of sight and two, because the county *askaris* would give her a hard time if she did not wear one.

It was a slow business hour, and she took the time to go through the dailies. She was reading a story in a newspaper, when she clicked her tongue.

"What?" Selina was her shop assistant and friend.

"It's the crime rate in the city."

With a pen she untucked from behind her ear, Kerubo tapped on the story, over and over.

Selina shook her head. "Why do you keep reading these stories when they make you so angry?"

"Ignoring them will not change reality," she scolded.

Selina shrugged.

"Ignorance is bliss, and I sleep better at night—unlike you."

And Selina should know. They went out occasionally and would sleep in each other's houses depending on where the night found them when they had gone out. Kerubo's turning and tossing would have Selina opt for the sofa.

"They could target us."

"Reading the story will not make them not," said Selina.

"But what if we all did something about it?"

"Like what?"

"Like telling on the thugs. Surely these thugs are somebody's husband, neighbour, brother?"

"Do you have a sibling?"

Kerubo shook her head. "You know I don't."

"A husband?"

Another head shake and an eye-roll.

"What's your point?"

"You have no idea how difficult it is to tell on a loved one."

Selina sneered as she walked away. From their many drunken conversations, Selina had let it slip that she suspected her elder brother was an armed robber.

"He says he is a car salesman, but there is something about him that is just off."

Kerubo thoughtfully looked at Selina as she disappeared at the back of the shop and sighed. She folded the offending newspaper, put it away beside the cash machine, removed the food dish from under the table and went to Chizi Samuel.

NaiRobbery Cocktail

Chapter Five

Father Joshua loved sex, and sex with prostitutes was his chosen way because they were easy to discard. He long stopped feeling guilty, so much so that he even stopped speaking to God about it—something must kill a priest.

Father Joshua started as an altar boy. He was a catechist by the time he sat for his secondary school exams. Becoming a priest was the next natural thing. That he had the gift of the gab was never a matter of doubt. When he preached, he was in his element. His sermons mesmerised congregants.

Perhaps, he sometimes thought, if their house girl had not been doing things to him when he was a little boy, making him discover the little and big pleasures of the flesh, he might have been a model priest. Father Joshua genuinely believed in God, certainly in the power of forgiveness, ironically the reason he kept sinning. He also knew he was not the worst sinner, and he should know from taking his congregants' confessions. At least he had never forced himself on a woman. He didn't touch little boys or girls. That there was always a worse sinner vindicated him on a daily basis.

One of Father Joshua's favourite Bible stories was when Jesus told his detractors that he came for the sinners, not for the already redeemed. Unlike Jesus, though, Father Joshua had no interest in helping redeem anyone in any drinking dens, least of all himself.

Thus, every Friday or Saturday after the six o'clock mass, he would remove his priestly regalia, wear jeans trousers, a T-shirt, a dapper jacket and shoes that always matched his belt, then leave for the city.

Nairobi by day is as chaotic as Nairobi by night with throngs of people in a rush to get somewhere. Father Joshua loved the buzz, a nice change from his peaceful existence in the countryside.

It was eight o'clock when he took his corner at his favourite pub, right at the heart of the city centre on Moi Avenue. All around him were groups of people. Everybody was trying to talk over the music.

Holding a beer, he scanned the crowd, zeroing in on a couple of women, each sitting alone. The pub was not especially popular with prostitutes, but like any pub anywhere, there was always a random one trying their luck with the advantage of little or no competition. He focused on one. In front of her on the table was a bottle of the pub branded water. She was tense, though trying hard not to appear so. Like him, she was scanning the crowd, trying hard not to be obvious.

Kiki liked Nairobi by night. It matched her dark heart.

Her caramel skin was perpetually on the verge of blushing. Her eye makeup matched her outfit of the day. Somewhere along her "career", she had discovered fake eyelashes which, combined with the kohl, brought out the best of her doe eyes. Her wig was big and afro.

The pub was semi-lit, but Kiki's eyes locked with Father Joshua's from across the room. She sat up a little straighter, squinted her eyes to try and work out his features; tall, dark, possibly handsome. She could see his arm muscles pressing on his tee-shirt. A man's physical appearance should never have mattered, but over time, she had discovered that she had a type. He looked like her type.

She flashed him a two second long smile. If he was interested, he would join her.

For a good while, the two sized each other. On and off. A smile here. A shift of the body there. Then he stood up, she straightened up, but instead of approaching her, he walked towards the toilets. With a shrug, she resumed scanning the room for another potential customer.

When he returned, he walked straight to her table.

"Is this taken?" He was pointing at the chair next to her.

"Yes, by you." She knew all the lines.

"My name is Paul." Paul was his chosen sin name, but if the name Saul did not sound ridiculous, it would have been his choice because the story of Saul of the Bible gave him hope that one day he may be a changed man in all ways.

"Kiki."

She was Kiki, but only at night. She offered her hand. His was soft, unfamiliar with hard labour. She turned his palm over to study the nails. Short and clean. She smiled. She liked this one. Kiki encountered so many unkempt men, clean ones were always a welcome treat.

"So… Do you come here often?" he asked when he settled.

"Nope," she lied. "Do you?"

He shook his head. He was also lying.

"Would you like to go somewhere less noisy?"

She smiled. It was coded language. She nodded. "Sure. I get to pick the place, though."

He shrugged. "Sure."

Kiki led the way, giving him the opportunity to study her from behind. Small, shapely butt carried by endless legs. She wore a tiny black flared skirt, and a tiny red top that left her midriff bare, exposing a flat tummy. She wore a pair of knee-high two-inch heels. In her hand was a clutch bag.

* * *

Father Joshua had met prostitutes so bright, they should have been the ones running the economy. Women so beautiful, they should have been beauty queens or models on the catwalk. Others, he was unable to describe because they were a combination of many fascinating factors and Kiki was in the last group. He approached such with caution because he worried about undercover cops. "Priest Caught with Koinange Street Women" was an imagined headline that gave him frequent nightmares. Even worse, a video leaking on social media.

When they entered the room, and even before he kicked off his shoes, she stretched out her hand and asked for the money.

"I like to get paid first," she said with a shrug when he glared at her.

"How much?"

"Three thousand shillings per hour."

"That's a lot!" He protested. It was.

"I do not negotiate." She started pushing him towards the door.

He put up his hands. "Relax…"

"Also, do not imagine you can trick me. The reception and security already know you are here with me. If I don't tell them to let you out, they will not."

Father Joshua sniggered. "You take your security seriously, don't you?"

"With a good reason. Women like me have been robbed, or killed."

He nodded.

Kiki started undressing, starting with the boots.

"You are beautiful..." He whispered, mesmerised.

She shrugged. Next she removed her wig and placed it on the bedside table. "Beautiful," he whispered, looking at her bald head.

She removed her top and danced down her skirt. She stood in front of him, wearing a white bra and a white thong.

"So, how do you want to do this?" she asked with a husky voice. "Do you want *wham bam bye* or do you want to pretend to be romantic?"

He chuckled, genuinely amused. "How do you want it?"

"You are paying. Just remember, we are already ten minutes into this." She glanced at the clock on the wall.

Father Joshua looked at the clock and felt panic rise. One hour suddenly felt like a few minutes.

"Sit here," he tapped the bed. "I want to remove what you still have on. Also, would you undress me, please?"

"You are paying, so you make demands," she reminded him, slightly amused. She was not used to gentlemanly customers.

"I want to pretend I am being romantic. Can you do the same?"

"I pretend for a living," she said with a smile.

* * *

Father Joshua lay his exhausted body next to Kiki's. He should have slept right after, but he did not. Instead, he was watching her sleeping, running a hand over her arm once in a while. He was also keeping tabs on the clock on the wall when he made a sudden decision.

"Kiki?" he nudged her.

"Mh?"

"How much do you charge for the whole night?"

She sat up, yawned and rubbed her eyes. The request was not unusual—in fact, she always anticipated it.

"I want you to stay all night," Father Joshua said, lightly pinching Kiki's small breasts.

"I charged you three thousand shillings for one hour. Let's see… how many hours do we have?" She looked at the clock. "Six hours to go. You want to stay the night, you get a discount. Ten thousand shillings." She looked at him defiantly.

It took Father Joshua five seconds to make the decision. "Okay." He reached for his wallet and counted the notes, handing them over to Kiki.

"Now, I own you," he declared as he ran a hand over her thigh. "First, though, I need to make a phone call. I cannot make it to work tomorrow."

"Who works on Sundays? Are you a priest?" The question was meant to be a joke. She could have asked if he was a cop.

He laughed. "Guilty as charged."

Kiki burst out laughing. "No way!" She made a sign of the cross. "Forgive me, Father, for I have sinned."

"Are you Catholic?"

"All the five times I went to church, it was a Catholic church." She almost added the last time she was in church was at her mother's burial, but she let it slip.

"It's your lucky day, you can confess to me."

"Now I have seen it all."

He retrieved his phone, searched the phonebook and called a number.

"Father Matthew, this is Father Joshua."

He heard Kiki giggling. He ignored her.

"Look, you might have to take the six o'clock mass for me. I am out of town and having car trouble… yes. In Nyeri… perhaps I can take all the afternoon ones? Oh, thank you very much. God bless you." He disconnected the call and winked at Kiki.

"God knows you are a liar, and you will go to hell."

NaiRobbery Cocktail

Chapter Six

Five years ago, Jonte met Boss in a spectacular way.

Jonte's eyes appeared like they had not blinked in years, but that was because chewing khat had that effect on the eyes. Just before entering the club, he spit out the green substance and wiped his mouth off any residue, but his tongue was still green and it felt tangy. He stopped by the counter and bought a soda, looked around the slowly-emptying club and that was when he spotted him.

Boss occupied a leather couch on his own, head thrown back, like a man sleeping. Jonte sat a few metres from him. With every minute, he inched closer to the sleeping man. Jonte loved this hour of clubbing because the waiters were too tired to be alert, the bouncers too busy kicking out drunks crowding the door, and the patrons usually too drunk making them easy prey. Three in the morning was his golden hour.

But how was he to know that Boss had bodyguards sitting a few metres from him, watching his every move?

Before his slimy fingers found his intended victim's pocket, a big pair of strong hands grabbed his neck from behind. He yelped. To date, Jonte has no recollection of how one moment he was inside the club trying to rob someone and in a blink of an eye he was rolling down the stairs. By the time he got to the bottom, someone was waiting for him with a big foot and equally big boots were stomping on him.

"Stop!" An authoritative voice interrupted. "Put him in the car."

And like he weighed the same as a feather, he was picked up and thrown inside a car boot.

He had no idea how long the car was in motion. Jonte was too worried about his body breaking into pieces as the driver seemed to enjoy accelerating over bumps. Finally, the boot was opened and he was roughly lifted off and carried inside a house, one that was so tangibly cold that he started thinking of ghosts. A house with such eerie silence that he thought of a multitude of ghosts.

He was ordered to remove his shirt and later he would come to know that the boss ordered those he was unhappy with to stay topless. He was made to kneel and not look at the Boss.

"So, you tried to rob me."

"Sorry…"

"Shut up! Do not talk unless I ask a question."

Jonte was about to say another sorry, but caught himself in time.

"So, you tried to rob me," Boss repeated. "You are lucky I am in a good mood, otherwise you would be in some graveyard as food for stray dogs. What is your name?"

He said his name.

"Anything else you do apart from stealing?"

"No."

The questions came quickly and went on for a long time. Some were asked multiple times and the sun was up by the time they were done. His knees were aching. He was shaking from fatigue and there was no doubt that Jonte would be working for Boss.

"And if you try to cheat me, I shall kill you."

If Boss was older, he would have been like a father to Jonte.

* * *

If one believed in fate, they would claim a partnership between Oti and Jonte was meant to be.

Oti and Jonte were different in many ways. Although they grew up in different parts of the city and only met in adulthood, they were both eight years old when they first stole. Jonte, driven by hunger, first stole food from a neighbour's house. Soon, hunger stopped being his trigger to steal when the thrill took over.

Oti, driven by both hunger and spite for his family, stole his mother's purse, then watched her beat the hell out of his nine siblings because of a crime he had committed. In his opinion, they all deserved it, because whenever he went out to play with his friends, they would eat the food that his mother saved for him, then laugh at him when he cried from hunger and anger.

While Jonte grew up in Kayole as the first born in a family of nine, Oti grew up on the opposite side of the city in Kibera as a middle child in a family of nine. In their respective families, the two grew up competing for everything with their siblings, especially food and space. Jonte did not particularly hate any of his siblings, they were just mere irritants, though he and his sister, Selina, had a special bond. Oti categorically hated all his siblings equally.

From his corner of the overcrowded cell, Jonte nonchalantly watched the police drag in a bloodied Oti, and wondered why they kept bringing dead men to the cell instead of taking them to the mortuary.

With the same detachment, he watched the other inmates roughly kick the newcomer as far away from them as possible, the half-dead body ending up next to Jonte's feet. Jonte pulled his knees up and rubbed his nose. He hated the smell of freshly clotted blood more than he hated the constant stench of excrement in the cell.

The half-dead man's eyes were swallowed by the swollenness surrounding them, and drool dripped out of the swollen lips, like a tap that had not been properly tightened. The clothes were in tatters with a sleeve missing. The only thing intact was the waistband of his trousers. He had one torn sock and no shoes.

For the two weeks that Jonte had been in the cell, three thieves had been dumped in the cell in a similar state. Two of them had been dragged out when rigour mortis had set in. As he looked at the new arrival, he wondered how it felt to die.

Jonte may have been sharing a cell, but he was a privileged inmate. Sometimes he paced up and down the cell in agitation, but mostly, he seemed at peace. Every meal time, a policeman would unlatch the cell locks loudly and shout his name. On his return, he would sometimes be wearing fresh clothes, sometimes with a fresh haircut, but always had cigarettes and enough food to feed the entire cell.

Jonte was much smaller in stature than everyone else in the cell and possessed a look softer than the majority of the inmates. He should not have scared anyone, but when he spoke, everybody paid attention. When scuffles broke out, Jonte stopped them without even having to stand up.

The morning after Oti was dumped in the cell, Jonte returned with not only food and cigarettes, but also a first aid kit. As the others gobbled food down, Jonte, like the seasoned doctor he was not, worked on Oti swabbing every wound he could locate, which was just about the whole body. He checked for broken bones—here didn't seem to be any. He fed Oti water, tried to feed him some fries, but his mouth could not hold anything. The other inmates watched in fascination.

"Do you know him?" one inmate asked.

Jonte shrugged without looking up.

"No, but I am bored."

He put disinfectant on cotton wool, cleaned around Oti's eyes, ignoring the flinching and the moaning. He was telling the truth about being bored. Sitting in the cell, counting seconds, trying to ignore the constant foul smell and only succeeding in doing the opposite was boring enough. He hated watching other inmates doing nothing except watch each other, burp loudly, fart as loudly—farts that smelled as bad as the cabbage they were served—and once in a while. Bicker or fight. He was fed up with wondering how much longer Boss would punish him by keeping him in this hell-hole. Had he not paid enough for his misdemeanour?

* * *

It took Oti three days to become mildly aware of someone poking him once in a while, trying to feed him water. On day four, he was able to turn when asked to. On day five, he used the toilet unassisted and the swelling went down enough for him to see.

For days, Oti observed his surroundings in silence.

He finally found his voice after a week. The other inmates were gathered at a corner, noisily playing a card game donated by Jonte. Some were smoking, filling up the small cell with smog that choked. The smell of cigarettes was, however, better than the smell of urine and faeces and unwashed bodies.

Oti and Jonte were sitting side by side, knees pulled up and backs against the wall watching the men. Oti shifted and leaned closer to Jonte.

"So how come you get preferential treatment?" he whispered.

"What treatment?" Jonte did not turn to look at Oti, and Oti did not see the slight smile that formed on Jonte's mouth.

"You know what I am talking about."

After a short silence, Jonte turned to Oti, studied his face, felt a little pride in his work on Oti's face, and then shrugged. "I have people who care. Do you have anyone?"

Oti sneered and snorted a short, bitter laughter that hurt his ribs. He thought about his family and his lack of friends. The only person who may have missed him was the broker in the ghetto. He shook his head.

"So maybe everybody here is like you, except me," Jonte said, observing him closely.

"But," Oti said, not giving up, "Why do they always bring you extra food?"

"Because they can afford it."

"Why have your connections not got you out of this hell hole?" Oti sounded bitter.

Jonte shrugged. He knew why he was still in the cell.

"I will be leaving soon. Is there anybody on the outside you would like to know that you are here?"

Oti scoffed and shook his head. "No."

Jonte turned away and smiled wider.

* * *

Officially, Jonte was a car salesman with a basic salary taxed by the government. Once in a while, he made appearances at the car yards that his boss owned and unsuccessfully attempted to sell. In reality, he was an armed car thief. What his victims did not know was that the guns held against them were never loaded.

"If you are good at what you do, you never need to ever shoot anyone," Boss would tell his band of thieves during initiation.

Robbing was risky. Sometimes, victims were armed and their guns had bullets. Jonte had bumped into a couple of those. It was the very reason that he did not have a partner at the moment. Wafula, his partner of four years, had been shot by an intended victim. Jonte had only escaped because the victim was a bad shot who had got lucky with the first shot. Boss's argument was always, 'stealing is a risky affair anyway, with or without a loaded gun. You are always knocking on hell's doors.'

'No robbery should happen unless Boss knows about it'. That was the number one rule that Jonte had broken, why he had been stuck in a police cell for close to a month. He blamed his now ex-girlfriend for his predicament. She had wanted him to furnish her house and Jonte had needed extra cash because she wanted all her furniture bought in a showroom. He had reckoned that doing just a single side job would not hurt. The job was a success, so was the disposal of the car. He had furnished his ex-girlfriend's house, but two weeks later, Jonte confirmed what he already knew, that nothing ever escaped the Boss.

* * *

A few weeks earlier.

When Boss knocked at the door, Jonte was watching a karate movie, wearing a vest and a pair of shorts, an empty plate next to him. He clicked his mouth in irritation and paused the movie, swearing to punch whoever it was at the door. It was the Boss and he was smiling, which was often not a good sign. Jonte felt the food he had just eaten threatening to eject.

"I could just kill you now," Boss said, pushing Jonte aside to let himself in.

His two burly bodyguards followed, one of them roughly pushing Jonte to the ground before shutting the door behind him.

Jonte shivered from the cold floor and fear and implored his bladder to behave, wondering how long Boss had known where he lived, right in the middle of Umoja Estate chaos, wondering if he was just about to die. Unlike the gun Jonte carried, Boss and his bodyguards carried loaded ones.

Boss, with arms crossed, stood over him, his men nearby with clenched fists.

"Sit up." Jonte did.

"Remove your vest." Jonte did.

Boss slapped him, a slap hard enough to dislocate a lesser jaw. He did not touch his cheek, but remained immobile.

"I have a very strong urge to just kill you, but spilling blood is often so unnecessary." Boss started walking the room to and fro, slowly. He spoke quietly; Jonte had to strain his ears.

"I hate betrayal, Jonte." He stopped just next to him.

"Sorry."

"Shut up!" Boss raised his voice. "I knew within hours what you had done. The only reason I waited this long is because I wanted to see if you would do it again. For not doing it again, you get to live."

He started pacing again. Jonte stifled a sigh.

"I cannot let you go scot-free, though. I am going to have you arrested." Jonte gasped, attempted to talk and quickly changed his mind.

Jonte nodded.

"I am trying to make an honest thief out of you."

Jonte could have laughed, but he knew better.

"As you know, we lost Wafula. Find me someone to replace him among the delinquents you will be sharing the cell with.

* * *

Back to the cell.

"What do you do?" Jonte asked Oti. They sat at the same corner, shoulders touching.

"What do you think? I am the boss of Kenya."

Jonte laughed.

"You know what I mean… What sort of stealing do you do?"

"Why don't you tell me how many types there are, then I can pick one."

"Touché," Jonte said with amusement. "Do you grab bags on the streets, do you threaten people with weapons in dark alleys, do you break into houses, do you steal vehicles?"

Oti laughed but instead of answering, he asked, "Which one are you?"

"I asked first."

Oti was quiet for a while, then inhaled deeply before answering. "Do you remember many years ago when someone stole your phone, twice, within minutes?"

Jonte turned to Oti so fast, he felt his neck snap. He cocked his head, this way and that way. Oti was still full of unhealed wounds, but his bloodshot eyes were familiar. Jonte laughed long and hard for everyone in the cell to stop what they were doing to look.

"Wow," Jonte finally said to Oti. "I saved you from a lynching back then, and still here you are!" Jonte shook his head in amusement, remembering that rainy day three years ago, just a couple of years after meeting Boss. He remembered it clearly because it was the only time anyone had ever stolen anything from him

Alongside other Nairobians, he was queueing for a matatu, letting himself get soaked by the rain because he did not care for sharing umbrellas like most people—close contacts were perfect breeding grounds for pickpockets. When it rained, people stopped worrying about anything other than the rain, but Jonte worried, yet Oti still picked his phone. By the time Oti stole Jonte's phone, he had already stolen three others within minutes; Jonte had his phone in the back pocket and with the feather touch that Oti had mastered so well, he slid it out. Just before he walked away, Jonte grabbed Oti's arm so tight, Oti yelped.

"Give it back!" Jonte muttered through clenched teeth. Oti gave him the phone. "Thank you," Jonte said as he put the phone inside his front trouser pocket. "You are good, but there is room for improvement," Jonte whispered, releasing Oti.

Oti was so confused, he could not find the strength to walk away. He thought that it was a trap, that as soon as he started walking away, his failed victim would scream mwizi, thief! So he folded his hands across his chest and locked eyes with the man who held his fate at that particular moment. "Don't you want to leave?" Jonte asked casually, removing a pack of chewing gums from the pocket and slipping a piece in his mouth. He offered Oti one. Oti took it, eyes still locked onto Jonte's. "Come on, scatter and get busy elsewhere."

So Oti scattered. Only when he was about twenty metres away did Jonte realise his phone was missing. Then he saw Oti waving at him, holding the phone. Jonte laughed, impressed. He waved back.

Oti often felt some guilt about robbing the man who had literally spared his life. He nearly returned the phone but decided that only fools pushed their luck that far. Instead of selling it to the broker, he started using it for himself, to remind him of that man who could have gotten him killed through a mob justice, but did not.

Oti should have stuck to pickpocketing where risks of getting caught were low. But fate was providing him with another opportunity. One evening, he was taking a random walk after relieving passengers off their wallets and phones in a packed matatu. It was dusk, on a lonely path that served as a shortcut to the ghetto. In front of him was a sluggish looking man carrying a backpack. Those backpacks, Oti had learned from the ghetto broker, more often than not contained laptops. Very good money in that, the broker had encouraged.

But Oti underestimated his victim on the basis of his lazy walk. As soon as he reached for the bag, the man seemed to transform into some super kind of man. He moved fast and grabbed Oti's hand, Oti heard his own scream. Within seconds, Oti was on the ground and he was being stumped on by an angry, overweight man. And the man was screaming mwizi!

The police saved him from a lynching.

Oti had no memory of having ever fallen sick, had never even met a doctor, but he knew he needed urgent medical attention. The police, after saving him, threw him at the back of a police pick-up where he landed with a thud. They drove him not to the hospital, but to the police station, where they dropped him down from the vehicle and dragged him to a cell.

"So, are you going to stop stealing?"

Oti gave a sarcastic laugh. "And do what? It's the only thing I know how to do."

"So this did not scare you?"

"What are you, a priest?"

"Answer me," Jonte insisted, looking Oti straight in the eye.

Something in Jonte's eyes discouraged Oti from negotiating. "It did scare me, but like I said, the only other option is to die of hunger."

Two hours later and Oti had no memory of ever talking about himself for so long, or ever at all.

* * *

When the policeman on duty opened the cell doors shouting out Jonte's name, everyone, including Jonte himself, assumed it was his breakfast call. He, however, returned after a few minutes with extra clothes.

"Wake up."

He threw the clothes at Oti.

"*Vaa hizo, tunaenda.*" Get dressed, we are leaving.

Oti sat up with a start. Everyone else in the cell paused to watch the two, open-mouthed.

"Where are we going?" Oti finally asked after rubbing his eyes repeatedly and subconsciously slapping his thigh.

"You have two minutes to get dressed, or I am leaving without you."

As Oti got up, letting his dirty clothes fall to the floor as he wore his ill-fitting new clothes, his eyes did not leave Jonte's. So focused was he that he did not hear other cell mates lament about no longer getting princely meals and free cigarettes. Within minutes, a policeman noisily opened the cell door again and let the two out. It was not a conscious act, but Oti was tagging on Jonte's shirt all the way, out of the cell and out of the station building into freedom. He did not look at the policemen at the reception, the ones Jonte was jokingly telling he hoped never to see them again.

Only when they stepped out did Oti let out a deep sigh, even risking looking back at the building that had been his home for weeks.

"You can let go of me now," Jonte shook himself free from Oti's grip.

"How… how did you manage to get me out?" Jonte was walking fast towards the gate. Oti, still sore from the beating and prolonged lack of mobility, was struggling to keep up.

"There was nobody to press charges against you. No witnesses either."

"Oh!"

So many questions he wanted to ask, if only his chest was not heaving. With a measure of amusement, he thought how he would have to get his feet back if he was to resume his life of crime.

Oti, who was no longer tagging at Jonte's shirt but walking closely behind, bumped into him when Jonte suddenly stopped outside the station's gates. Oti tried to stretch, but every joint in his body ached. He took deep breaths, letting the air of freedom flood his lungs. Nairobi had a distant smell of sewage, but to somebody who had spent weeks next to a defecation bucket, unwashed bodies and the stench of stale cigarettes in a small airless police cell, the air outside was like a gift of pure oxygen.

He watched a lanky marabou stork struggle on a weak branch. He kept blinking at the brightness. After being indoors for so long, the light was overwhelming his eyes—a small price to pay to see open spaces.

"Let's get out of here," Jonte said as he led the way towards the city.

"Where are we going?"

"To see Boss."

"Who is Boss?"

Oti considered running away, then he remembered his stiff joints. Not that he had somewhere to go, because Kibera landlords did not recognise tenant rights. He had not paid rent for over a month and his few belongings had most likely been sold to off-set the rent.

He was also curious, o so he followed.

"There he is," Jonte pointed at an illegally parked 4x4 ahead. Its lights flashed twice before the back door was opened by an invisible hand.

"That is our lift," Jonte said heading for the car.

"That big car?" Oti, who had been like a shadow since they left the cell, hesitated for a few seconds to look at the car. For the countless number of times, he wondered what he was getting himself into.

Jonte entered the vehicle first, Oti followed hesitantly.

"Shut the door."

There were two occupants, the driver and his passenger. Oti was not sure who ordered him to shut the door, but he did very quickly. For a long while, they drove in silence. Oti bent forward and tried to peep at the passengers at the front, Jonte pinched his thigh.

"You both stink!" someone declared before spraying the air with air freshener.

Jonte shifted on the seat and cleared his throat.

"Welcome back, Jonte!" The speaker did not turn.

"Thank you, Boss!"

"Welcome, Oti!"

Oti coughed in surprise. He looked at Jonte who ignored him. Oti had never seen Jonte afraid—not of the tough-looking cell-mates, nor of the harsh cops, but at that moment and time, he looked petrified. He felt himself tense.

"Thank you," he whispered.

"Boss… Jonte added quickly.

"Thank you, Boss," repeated Oti.

Oti, being Kibera born and bred, knew the neighbouring estate of Ngumo like the back of his hand. At first, he thought they were taking him home, but they turned towards Ngumo, and into one of the mansions. Boss came out of the vehicle first, leaving the door open. By the time Jonte and Oti were out, Boss had already disappeared into the house.

Oti, for lack of anything better to do, studied the driver. He was huge and unsmiling. He wore a dark suit that looked too tight on him. Then Oti gasped and took a step back when the driver's coat flapped, revealing a gun.

"*Unaangalia nini?*" What are you looking at? The burly man demanded.

"*Pole msee… hata siangalii.*" Sorry, I wasn't looking. Oti answered quickly and stepped farther back. He had never seen a gun up-close, despite all his years as a criminal, and it unnerved him.

When Jonte started walking towards the house, Oti quickly followed, throwing the driver a nervous look at the same time trying to control his suddenly erratic heart rate.

The smell of food hit their nostrils before they stepped inside the house. Oti felt his tummy grumble, gun momentarily forgotten.

"You need to shower first! Bin those clothes. Shave, as well—I don't want lice infestation."

Oti had to look for the voice talking to them. It was coming from one corner of the room, a dining area. Boss was already seated and going through a newspaper. He had already seen that Boss was tall, but seeing his face and considering what he was, Oti felt some confusion. He was looking at probably one of the most handsome men he had ever seen, the type of men he imagined had big jobs in big offices. His hair, a few inches long, had some wavy hairstyle. He was clean shaven and looked like he had never broken a sweat in his life. And was that an ear stud?

Jonte jolted Oti out of his stupor by pulling him by the hand to a bedroom. In silence, they shaved each other's hair and showered in turns. Jonte selected clothes for both of them from the wardrobe.

Boss was still at the dining area, clearing the last of his food, when the two returned. He pointed at the dishes on the table. "That's your food. I will be back in twenty minutes."

Oti studied Boss's back as he disappeared, taking in extra details. Boss was not nearly as big as the driver, but between the two Oti would be more wary of Boss. It was the eyes—something Oti had seen in the two seconds their eyes had met, something that had triggered a chill in him.

Seven flat minutes later, they cleared everything. Oti burped. Jonte hit his back hard. "Behave," he whispered.

Boss returned carrying three beers and offered each of them one. Oti downed his within a minute, letting out a loud burp in appreciation. He missed the venomous look from Boss as he was too busy basking in the pleasure. Jonte cringed. He was too far to hit Oti.

"Why do you think you are here?" Boss suddenly asked.

He was sitting at the head of the table, the two other men sitting on either side.

The question caught Oti off-guard. He looked around, as if the question had been directed at somebody else. Boss repeated the question.

Oti rubbed his freshly shaved chin as he thought.

"Jonte invited me."

"Do you know why?"

Oti shrugged.

"You are a thief." It was a statement Oti cringed at. "We are thieves, too, so you are in good company, but unlike you, we are a little more polished."

Oti coughed, keeping his head down.

"We steal cars." Boss took a swig of his drink. Oti cocked his head. "But we try not to harm people."

Oti nodded, but there was visible confusion on his face.

"Can you drive?"

Oti shook his head.

"No worries. Jonte is a good driver."

It was another hour of tough talk and tougher questions from Boss.

In the end, Oti knew he was not being given a choice. He could already recite the rules without pausing. Not that the guns they carried were loaded, anyway; do not hit anyone unless it is absolutely necessary and if you do, do not hit to kill; do not target vehicles with women and children; do not do side-jobs; do not talk about your job to anyone; all money comes to Boss, unless you have a death wish.'

Oti had a problem with the last rule, and he spoke to Jonte about it later when Boss left. They were still sitting at the dining table, several empty cans of beer lying on the table.

"Do you really give all the money to Boss?"

Jonte nodded. "Except the phones. He does not like disposing of stolen phones, so we keep those."

"But how would he know how much you robbed?"

Jonte laughed. He had wondered the same thing at first.

"He has ears, everywhere. And that includes the police. He gives consideration for the cash figures reported, because some victims exaggerate what they lost."

"But why would I take all the risk and give him everything?"

Jonte shrugged as he walked to the backyard to smoke weed. Oti followed.

"You can do it, and see what happens."

"Will I get killed?"

"By any other name."

He took a drag of the stick before handing it back to Oti. "I have been with him for over five years, and he takes care of me like I am his kin. But he does not like betrayal—that was the reason I ended up in the cell. I got off easy, unlike others."

There was a long silence between them, too stoned and drunk to realise the silence had lasted for long.

"You still have twenty-four hours to decide if you want to work for him or not."

"What happens if I do not want to work for him?"

"He will let you go, if you are lucky.

In the end, they were unable to walk back to the house. They blacked out on the grass, only to be woken up by security dogs licking their faces.

Chapter Seven

Naliaka was in the middle of unpleasant smells. That should have been bad enough, but there was the ducking, the pushing and the shoving with strangers. If it was not a motorbike rider looking determined to knock her down, it was a *matatu* driver aiming for her head with the side mirror. The minute she thought she had the *matatu* and the motorbike in check, there would be a blind-acting *mkokoteni* pusher to avoid.

At some point during her walk to what looked like the godforsaken part of the city, everyone started running in different directions. Only when she barely made it inside a shop before the shutters were brought down did she realise she had just escaped a battle between illegal hawkers and city *askaris*.

Crowds made her edgy. She would rather have been sleeping on her couch, watching movies, but she liked to keep promises, and she had promised *him* that she would go.

At the entrance of the building, Naliaka looked around, wondering how the very polished man who had asked her to go to his house would choose to live at the edge of downtown Nairobi, Kirinyaga Road.

In spite of it, she smiled because she liked him. The two times she had met him had been weird and as she negotiated her way through the unfamiliar street, she wondered if the third time would be as weird.

They had met in a club, one of her prowl joints. He wore a blue pair of jeans and a black short-sleeved shirt. His fancy haircut was just right and his bright eyes shone through his chocolate dark skin. He was staring at his phone, pressing keys here and there. It was not the first time she was seeing him, but it was the first time she was paying attention to him.

There was nothing about him to suggest that he would be interested in her services. Six years of being a prostitute had taught her that men interested in prostitutes did not have a particular look, but there was always something unexplainable—he did not have that *something*. She was studying him because it was a slow evening and he was interesting to look at. She was also wondering if she had ever seen him with any company because at that point, he was sitting alone.

He suddenly looked up from the phone and straight at her; the suddenness of his movement made her choke on her soda. A coughing fit followed. The waiter passing by stopped to rub her back. When she could breathe properly again, she looked up, and the man was standing in front of her wearing an amused smile.

"I am glad someone found my near-death experience funny," she said accusingly, wiping away tears with a tissue the waiter had given her. She blinked a couple of times to check if her fake eyelashes were still in place, then used the same tissue to blow her nose.

"It was funny, plus it was nowhere near death," he answered, placing his hands on the table and leaning on it. A hint of his cologne penetrated her nostrils.

Then he sat down and stared at her. Kiki, as much as she held his gaze, found it unsettling. On a good day, even on a bad day, she was never flustered by men. She prided herself in having met all sorts in her line of work.

"Would you like to go home with me?" he asked, still unblinking.

"Hell ... no. But you could come to my hotel with me."

"Why a hotel?"

"Because I play it safe. There are psychos in this town."

He smiled. "I suppose I look like one?" he chuckled and sat back on the chair.

"They do not have a look."

"Alright, Kiki."

She choked again, spluttering on the table. "How do you know my name?"

"I have my ways."

She peered at him, working her memory.

"If you are wondering if you and I ever got it on, the answer is no."

She felt herself blush.

"You are a regular, so am I. You are interesting to watch."

"Have you been stalking me?" she demanded, looking around for a friendly waiter.

He chuckled again. She hated that she liked how he chuckled.

"How much?" he asked instead.

"I charge per hour."

"How much?" he didn't flinch.

She named double her usual, for two reasons. One, she was not sure she wanted to go with him as he was making her uneasy and two, he looked like he had money.

"Okay."

He was already standing up.

"You are mine for the night."

"I don't think I want to go with you."

He sat back down slowly, his gaze, once again, digging into her in the same way that left her feeling exposed.

"I did not know prostitutes are choosy."

She shook her head slowly. She was feeling hot and knew her face was red. She started fanning herself, then shrugged.

He sighed, folded his hands and studied her again. When he stood up, she thought he was leaving, but he fished out his wallet, sat down and opened it.

"That's your money. Count it."

She didn't take it. She crossed her hands and ignored the sweat that was now running down her face. She shook her head.

It was a battle of who would blink or look away first. She lost and grabbed her soda, nearly dropping it, then drained it all, her throat making gurgling sounds that upped his amusement.

"You are a very beautiful woman," he said between chuckles.

She sneered at him or tried to. Most men liked to use boring and used lines, like "have I seen you before?", or "I have been waiting for you all my life". She knew all the cheesy lines, and they helped to break ice, plus she suspected that men used the lines because they were trying to convince themselves that they were hooking up with a *nice* girl. This one did not look interested in niceties and he wanted her to know he knew she was a prostitute.

"Why me?" Kiki asked, looking around for other prostitutes. She could spot at least two, sitting on their own. "There are others here who would be willing to leave with you."

He shrugged and swept a hand in front of his face.

"Because it is you I want."

He bent closer to her, she pulled back.

"Your phone, please."

Like one in a trance, she fished out her phone from her bra, he smiled at that. She unlocked it and gave it to him. He keyed in his number, called himself and returned her phone to her. A few seconds of him keying something on his phone, and a money deposit message reflected on her phone.

"Your money is in the phone. Now you have a paper trail, in case the DCI needs it."

He laughed. She did not.

"Come on, call your cab guy and take me wherever you want."

He stood up and offered her his hand. Slowly, she accepted it, for a moment feeling like she was being led to a slaughterhouse.

Only when she shut the hotel room door behind her did she allow herself to relax. She was on familiar grounds.

As he stood hands akimbo, looking at the room critically, she entered the bathroom and minutes later emerged wearing red lingerie and renewed makeup. He was lying flat on the bed with his head popped up with the pillows, fully dressed, looking at his phone. He even had his shoes on. He looked up and smiled. Feeling too exposed, she crossed her arms.

"Are you not getting undressed?" she demanded.

He shook his head.

"I am not here for sex."

She had had men who just wanted to talk, but on those times, the men had looked broken. This one, however, looked like a man who had the world at his feet. She looked back at the bathroom where her clothes were neatly folded, feeling a sudden urge to get dressed.

"Keep that on. I want to look at you."

"Just, look at me?"

"Nothing else."

He pointed at the space beside him. She only hesitated for a moment.

"So, tell me why you sell your body?"

She sighed, irritated by the interrogation.

"It's something to do."

"With your beauty, you could just about tie down any man you wanted."

She allowed one side of her mouth to half-smile. It was not a new conversation, and it always amused her that men assumed that only so-called ugly girls should be prostitutes. The reality was, *ugly* prostitutes would not survive, because men wanted to pay for pretty things. "Why do people assume women become prostitutes because they are too ugly to get a man? There are so many factors, like, sometimes we just do not want to be owned."

"How old are you? Twenty years old? What would you know about not wanting to be owned?"

"I am twenty-three, and I do know," she said stubbornly.

"Is it the sex?" he whispered, patting her bald head gently.

"What about the sex?"

"Is it that one man cannot satisfy you?"

She would have wanted to tell him that it was not the sex. From her experience, sex was taxing and overrated. It was a blank feeling that came with financial benefits. The only time she found it good was when she was doing it with Father Joshua.

She pulled herself up and swung out of the bed, walked to the window, peeped through the curtains, all along debating with herself on if she was willing to indulge a wanna-be psychiatrist.

"Am I going to answer questions the whole night?"

He chuckled again, swinging off the bed and joining her at the window. He hugged her, gently. She was shorter than him, and when he nudged her head to rest on his shoulder, she relaxed.

"What do you want from me?" she whispered. His cologne made her miss the priest.

"I told you, I just want to talk," he whispered back.

"About me?"

"Put it this way, I am curious as to why a girl like you would choose such a demeaning job."

He pulled her at arm's length and studied her. She held his gaze, thinking his eyes looked gentler than they had all evening. She felt herself relax more. When he asked her to return to bed, she went willingly. He stripped to his underwear and they both slid under the white duvet in-between white bed sheets before assuming their earlier pose.

In the end, she had ended up talking. The first five minutes were difficult—she hated her life in general, talking about it was not something she had done before, not in such detail. Not even to the priest, a man she had started considering as a friend. She paused intermittently, she hesitated mid-sentence, but he was such a good listener.

Two hours later, when Kiki's mouth was dry from overuse and his ears ached from listening, they fell asleep in each other's arms. In the

81

morning, she turned down his offer to have breakfast with him. She was not willing to go out in daylight dressed the way she was, and she didn't want him to see the *buibui* she always carried in her bag. After he left, she freshened up, wore the *buibui* and took a taxi home.

With the money he paid her, she did not need to work for a few days. She would have stayed home even on day four, but he called.

"Meet me at the same hotel. Let me know when you arrive."

She opened the door for him five minutes after she arrived. He gave her a curt smile and a pat on the back, then sat on the bed.

"Do you want me to change into lingerie?"

He shook his head, and they sat on the bed, talked, laughed, and fell asleep in each other's arms. At midnight, almost as if he had set the alarm, he tapped on her shoulder gently. At first, she thought that he wanted to have sex. For a woman who always managed to arouse men with a mere look, his attitude confused her.

"What?" she had asked groggily.

"You have been talking about yourself, but I have not told you anything about myself." She sat up against the headboard to give her full attention.

"I cannot have sex." His confession was typically abrupt.

"What do you mean? Cannot or will not?"

"Cannot. Something happened to me when I was a boy."

"Oh."

Even to herself, her response sounded stupid, but it was all that came out as she shifted on the bed.

"That is the long and short of it. I have never had sex in my life."

"Ever?" He shook his head.

"Well, trust me, you have not been missing much, there is nothing phenomenal about it."

They both laughed uneasily, squeezing each other's palms.

"You don't enjoy sex?" he asked, almost hopefully. Misery loves company, he thought.

Kiki shrugged. "Put it this way; I do not know what the fuss is all about. People kill, maim for sex—I don't get it. At all."

"My name is Boss."

"Is that a legitimate name?" she asked between giggles.

"People who work for me call me Boss… maybe one day I will tell you my real name."

"So, Boss, why have you been stalking me and telling me all this? Is this something you do with random prostitutes?"

"Believe it or not, you are the first prostitute, the first woman I ever shared a bed with."

It was true. Almost half of his female employees were ex-prostitutes, but he had no contact with them after getting them to work with him. "But to answer your question, I like you, and I want you to stop selling yourself?"

She laughed loudly.

"I am not joking. I can offer you something better."

"What, sexless marriage?" Even as the words came out, she knew it was a bad and tactless choice of words.

"Do not make a joke of my situation, please."

"Sorry." And she meant it. "I am just confused about what you want with me… it is strange. Usually, I deal with men who cannot have enough sex, not the other way round."

He grunted dismissively.

"Haven't you ever thought of doing something different?"

She shrugged. "Like what? I am a form two school dropout. My mother is dead, I do not know my father, or any relatives. It was either this or slaving for meagre pay as a housemaid. I suppose I could get married to a rich man, but I doubt the men I meet would want to marry me."

He nodded.

"What do you have in mind?"

"A chance to work for me."

"Doing what?"

He cleared his throat and shifted on the bed. She asked the question again, this time round with a little more force.

"I am a robber."

She jumped out of the bed, went to the door, seemed to change her mind about leaving, went to the window, peeped through the curtains and finally looked back at him. He was still in the same position, his expression like someone deep in a poker game.

"You want me to be a robber?" It was slightly higher than a whispered question.

"Do not judge me, it's not like you are a priest!"

"I am not judging you. I am just concerned that you want me to become a robber!" She glared at him. "Besides, I do not hurt people, they come to me willingly."

"And who said I hurt people?"

"What robber does not?"

"I do *not* hurt people. They are usually too scared to resist."

"Robber..." she sniggered, moving back to the bed, sitting on it and facing him. "What kind of robber are you?"

"Vehicle."

She laughed.

"As in, carjacking?'

"Whatever you call it."

"That's it?"

"That's it. I no longer do it myself, I have people doing it for me."

"How do you know they do not hurt people?"

"I have ears everywhere."

"Even with the cops?"

He shrugged. "I said I have ears everywhere."

"So, you want me to steal cars? I cannot do that; I am sorry I have to decline the offer."

Because she was right in front of him, it was easy for him to hold her hands. It was a gentle but stable hold. "You do not have to agree, but if you say no, I am good at disappearing, you may even wonder if you did ever meet me. Obviously you cannot talk about it to anyone, ever."

"Okay."

"If you say yes, you will be my favoured protégé."

Two months later, she called him because after much thought, she decided she was done with prostitution and needed a new *challenge*— however, deep down she knew she missed him. She could not stop thinking about him. She had never missed anyone in her life, except her dead mother. And that was why she was in the middle of Nairobi chaos, seeking Boss."

* * *

Her patience in negotiating the chaos finally paid off. She stood in front of the building, taking in the frenzied surroundings, still unable to reconcile the polished Boss and this neighbourhood.

It was only when a mad man pushed her with his sack full of whatever mad men carried that she shook herself. For a brief moment, her eyes and that of the mad man locked, but she looked away quickly and as quickly stepped into the entrance.

Chizi Samuel watched her disappear inside.

The ground floor consisted of tiny shops displaying all sorts of wares; hardware shops, car spares shops, mirror shops, clothes shops. She took the stairs to the first floor. It was calmer. Shut office doors, someone pulling the seat, a cough, a laughter, a couple of people taking cigarette breaks in the corridors.

She hesitated at the foot of the stairs leading to the second floor, reached into her jeans' pocket and fished out her phone, dialling number.

"Kiki?"

"Hi. I think I am lost."

"Where are you right now?"

"I am standing on the stairs on the second floor. There doesn't seem to be anything up there?"

She was peeping at the grilled door that looked more disused than used.

"Take the stairs and open the grilled door. It's unlocked."

When Naliaka landed on the top floor, she paused to take it all in. The corridors were clean and tiled. The walls had a soft green coat of paint. Potted plants graced the corridors. "This is beautiful," she muttered to herself just before a door opened.

"Kiki!" His smile under the natural light disarmed her for a second. "Come in."

"It's daytime. My name is Naliaka," she said as she gave him a long look. He was wearing a fitting white tee-shirt, grey slacks and white socks. She felt her body stir up in excitement.

"Come in, Naliaka," he said with a grin, holding her gaze.

When he shut the door, when she gently kicked off her sneakers, Naliaka was ushered into a different world. The walls were a soft orange colour. The softest cream carpet caressed her bare feet, reminding her of her room in Queen's house. The carpet led her to a massive sitting room with black leather recliner seats. A large flat screen television took up a big chunk of one wall; below it was a glass shelf full of seashells and other paraphernalia. She did wonder for a moment whether he collected them during travels or he bought them from a shop.

A large painting of an African family was on the opposite wall. The room was simple, cosy and minimalistic. At one corner was the dining area with a table and six chairs.

Boss was having problems of his own, reconciling the woman in front of him with the one he met at night; the one whose memory of a soft, warm body still gave him sleepless nights. Had they met on the streets instead of his house, the only reason he would have looked at her was because she was beautiful, not because she looked familiar. Now, he was observing her as she took in the surroundings, soaking in her fascination with his house and her beauty. The wig was gone; in its place was a shiny bald head. She wore huge bead earrings, and a loop nose ring.

In place of her short skirts, she wore a pair of fitting blue jeans and a black top that revealed a hint of her midriff. Her sunglasses were on her forehead—he had never seen a forehead so huge and lovely. No trace of make-up, except for clear lip gloss.

"You look so very different," he finally broke the silence.

"I am a different person in the light. That is why I changed my name as well." She turned to look at him, giving him a once-over.

"You look different, too. And your house is very beautiful."

She turned her attention back to the room.

"Thank you."

"Who would have thought… and in such an area?"

He laughed. "In my line of work, you have to know how to hide and disappear."

The statement reminded her of the reason she was there.

"Come on, wash your hands. The sink is right that way. Let's sit down because that food is not going to eat itself. Wine?"

"I do not drink alcohol. I have enough vices."

"Ever?"

"Sometimes I take a glass or two," she explained as she noisily slumped on the leather sofa instead of the dining area, folding her legs under her.

"I am waiting for two other people, they should be here any time."

As if on cue, three systematic taps on the door interrupted them. Naliaka did not know it then, but if Boss's door was knocked any other way, it would be time for the bodyguards to cock the guns as Boss hid.

He opened the door, letting in Jonte and Oti. Naliaka studied them from the sofa and frowned. One of them looked nearly as polished as Boss, but his companion was heavily scarred with a look of someone who had it rough in life.

"Right. Boys, this is Kiki. And Kiki, this right here is my right-hand man, Jonte. This is Oti, his right-hand man. You may just be seeing a lot of each other."

"Hi!" she said, slightly amused at how the two were gawking at her, mouths slightly opened, eyes wide, looking slightly stunned. They nodded at her, unblinkingly.

"Come on boys, we were just about to eat. Wash your hands and we can get on with it."

Naliaka was a slow eater. Food was not something that occupied her mind, she ate because her body was aware that it needed to eat something. She had no favourite food, and as a result, she ate anything, if only a little of it. As Jonte and Oti gobbled as if it was their last meal, she more or less played with the little she served herself, staring at them in disbelief. Boss, on his part, studied her as he ate his food with much more decorum.

NaiRobbery Cocktail

Chapter Eight

In his thirty years of life, and without counting his childhood friends, Boss had only made three friends. Two of them, Mato and Monde, were dead and the one remaining, his high school teacher, did not know the type of man that Boss had become. As he thought about Naliaka, whom he was still struggling not to think of as Kiki, he missed having a friend.

He would confide in that friend over a drink that he believed he was in love. He would tell that friend that the first time he set eyes on Kiki, he had wanted to have her for himself. When he could, for a moment, forget that he was doomed to *never* experience the full pleasures of a woman except vicariously in blue movies and saucy novels, he imagined himself making love to Naliaka. His senses would, however, return but not before he wondered if it was possible to date without sex.

Of late, he loved it when he woke up with a smile right after dreaming about her. He loved it that when he day-dreamed about her, he would smile enough to rattle his bodyguards who did not know him like that. He loved it because several times, his penis had attempted to rise when he thought of her.

That first time he saw her, he was sitting alone, as usual, his bodyguards a few decent metres away from him. She wore a black spaghetti top that had a pair of nipples pressing against it. Her light brown skin had looked even lighter against the blond wig. The lips were too red for her complexion, the eyebrows too dark, and her eyelashes too long and obviously fake. Her eyeliner, too, was too dark. He studied her as she walked to the toilet. She was tall and slender, long and slim, with shapely legs under a short-flared skirt.

That first day, he was disappointed by the male species letting a woman like that do what she obviously did for a living.

It was six in the evening when he saw her, but he watched her until the natural light disappeared, then he continued watching her through the dimmed lights of the club. He observed her, felt his heart sink whenever she had sat up straight after identifying potential *prey*.

He watched her position herself strategically, crossing one leg over the other and running her long fingers on her bony knee, ever so lightly. He followed the movement of her fingers and noticed the red fingernails. Her body language was well-orchestrated to give a come-on to the identified *prey*. She reminded him of those beautiful male birds he often watched on the National Geographic channel, those birds that made fools of themselves, dancing ridiculously in front of usually difficult-to-impress female birds.

Boss gulped down his beer, some of it made its way down his chin, onto his tee-shirt. He wiped off the one on the chin with the back of the hand, all along his eyes glued on her. He tasted bile and the veins on his temple bulged with pressure and rage as he watched her walk out with that man, and the subsequent ones on subsequent days.

After that first day, watching her became a sport, but unlike other sports, this would leave him melancholic. It left him plotting murders of the men she walked out with.

Boss was at peace with his impotence. Several times over, especially during those rare times when his penis was twenty per cent alive, he considered trying to have sex, but if he was not afraid of anything including death and life in incarceration, the two possibilities that were very likely in his line of work, he was afraid of the men working under him losing respect and fear of him if his condition became public knowledge, like that time back in secondary school.

Boys in his dormitory, and in the bathroom, especially in the mornings, would chatter with excitement about their penises rising. He remembered watching in fascination as they walked the corridors, chests thrust forward, naked, hands in the air triumphantly, hard as wood and dangling in front of them, triumphant grins on their faces. He always hid his own shrivelled one under a towel.

He would listen to them talk about masturbation. When he was alone, he tried to masturbate. He would squeeze his penis, hit it, pull it, but the moment he released it, it would fall on his thighs, like a piece of wet fabric. He stopped having unnecessary relationships with his penis, only looked at it by accident, only touching it while peeing or taking a shower.

He learned to take the teasing, because it was difficult to explain why he always covered himself. They called him a woman. They called him gay. He learned to walk away with feigned dignity, but it made him want to hurt people.

Amidst all that, Kanja made a friend in one of his teachers. Mr Choka was his favourite subject teacher, physics. They never went directly into it, but Kanja always felt like the teacher understood him. Once in a while, because misery loves company, he suspected Mr Choka knew what was wrong with him, that perhaps he suffered the same. After all, he was the only unmarried teacher, and he was not exactly young.

Those moments Mr Choka would summon Kanja to the staffroom for random chats, those visiting days when Kanja had nobody to visit him, Mr Choka would pass him bread and soda, which helped to make Kanja's boarding school experience worthwhile.

* * *

Twelve years ago when the secondary school national exam results were announced, Kanja was working in a farm, wiping his brow every few minutes because the sun was very hot. He only learned about it in the evening at supper time, through the radio.

His parents had one of the rare episodes of excitement. Like someone who could see the future, Kanja stopped himself from joining in the excitement. High chances were that he did very well, but there was always that imposter syndrome lurking at the back of his mind.

"When will you go for the results?" his father asked, catching Kanja in his daydream mode.

He shrugged.

"I don't know. But there is no rush. Universities will not be admitting until later in the year."

Kanja finished his supper, downed it with cold water from a tin cup and excused himself to go to sleep. He had rented a separate room only a few metres away from his parents since he started earning.

Over time, his mundane life in the village started gnawing on him. He did hard, manual labour for eight hours, six days a week. His already muscular arms felt like the only thing that was improving. And he had more money. Between his sun-charred skin and his mental state, he could not decide which one made him want to leave the village more.

The decision was made as he and other workers were having lunch, shielding themselves from the hot sun under a tree. One of them recounted his meeting with a former colleague.

"He is now working in Industrial Area."

"Where is Industrial Area?" Kanja had asked.

"In Nairobi," his colleague answered with a shrug.

He had never been there. None of them had ever been there. The only times Kanja had been to the city was during his journeys to and from boarding school.

"Is he making money?" another one asked.

"He looks better than we do, so I guess he is."

The four young men instinctively studied their rough hands.

"I think I will try Industrial Area too. There is nothing for us here except poverty and getting married to a village girl."

It was a bitter statement. The others nodded.

"Talking about getting married, Kanja, we have been wondering, how come we have never seen you with a girl?"

Kanja's heart skipped as he stood up.

"None of your business," he said as he feigned a yawn and a stretch.

"But if you must know, I do not want to make a village girl pregnant and have to get married to someone I do not like, like Mose here," he pointed at one of the young men who found himself married to a girl he had only had sex with once, against a tree, under the cover of darkness, village dogs circling from a distance with excitement. A couple of months later, the mother of the girl had dragged her to Mose's shack, carrying a plastic paper bag on the other hand, one she proceeded to dump at Mose's feet before declaring, "That's your wife."

*   *   *

Two weeks later, Kanja bought himself a new pair of trousers, a tee shirt, a jacket and a pair of canvas shoes. As he walked to the village bus stop with all his monetary wealth hidden in different parts of his clothes, he felt conspicuous. Near shy. Being so smartly dressed made him feel out of place.

It was on a Monday, in March, a day that could not seem to decide if it was going to be hot or cold. He looked up at the partially cloudy skies, squinting at the sun that was peeping through one of the cloudy gaps. He shrugged and pressed on.

He felt a little guilty for lying to his parents. As far as they were concerned, he was off to get his exam results. His father had even pressed a few notes in his palm for lunch. In his defence, he planned to go to the school, just not yet. His immediate priority was to make enough money and set up his parents for a business. He would install some dignity in them. But first, he needed to find a job in Industrial Area. His predecessor had promised to host him for a while, and he was going to meet him at Jeevanjee Gardens in the city.

Once in the city, he walked aimlessly for a while, marvelling at the tall buildings, the traffic, the harassed-looking people shoving this way and that way. Eventually, he found Jeevanjee Gardens, sat on a bench and bought a soda and cake from a hawker, then started watching the world go by.

Months later, he would think how stupid he had been for not being suspicious of the stranger who sat next to him, who ignored other empty benches. That he also sat too close to Kanja instead of the other end of the bench. But he was a trusting villager.

"It's very cold today," the stranger remarked. They both looked up at the skies. Kanja nodded. "I think it will rain."

They spoke about the weather for a minute before the man offered him a piece of chewing gum. The last thing Kanja remembered of that encounter was when he put the gum in his mouth and thought it tasted very bitter.

As the man, along with another one who appeared when Kanja lost most of his senses, started helping him to his feet, they looked like two people helping a drunk, or sick friend.

When he came to his senses, he was in a dark alley, and it was cold. He did not have his jacket, or shoes. He did not have to check for his money to know it was gone. He started weeping, at first silently, then he howled.

Big and unfamiliar city. Cold. Angry. Scared. He forced himself to stand up, his head felt woozy, and throat was dry with thirst. The buzz of the city's nightlife found him wandering aimlessly. There were happy people, drunk people and people in a hurry. Darkness did not seem to slow them down.

He finally lost his strength next to a disabled man who was hawking, using his wheelchair as the sweets and cigarettes shop.

"*Wewe, ni nini mbaya?*" What's wrong? The disabled man asked in alarm, poking him with a stick. "Are you sick?"

Kanja, in foetal position, nodded and whispered for water. The man gave him water, Kanja downed it fast.

It took ten minutes to recover enough to recount his experience.

"They drugged you," the man declared. "This city is becoming too much! Have you eaten?"

Kanja shook his head. The man gave him a soda and a cake. "The sugar will help you recover."

It was the tastiest meal Kanja had ever tasted.

"Do you live far?"

"No," he lied, unwilling to burden him more.

"Thank you. When I get the money, I will come and pay you."

"You will find me here… if I do not die first," he said with a big laugh. Kanja smiled for the first time in hours.

He walked away, aimlessly, for hours. It was past midnight when he finally identified an alley, he thought was safe, because it was dark. He sat down, against the wall, brought his knees up and tried to ignore the cold, though his body was going into violent shivers every few seconds.

When he saw the silhouettes of five male figures walking towards him, every nerve and sense in him told him to run, very fast. He did not. The cold and dejection he was experiencing had taken away all his energy and resolve. He sat frozen and held his breath. Plus, could it get worse? By the time they surrounded him, he knew that it could get much worse. Like a dead mass, his body remained still as they quietly turned his empty pockets inside out. He felt their quiet fury when they found nothing. He offered no resistance when they all took turns in sodomising him. Cold tears cutting through his hot face as he relieved the same experience many years ago.

When his aggressors walked away as quietly as they had walked towards him, his eyes followed their evil figures disappearing. He stared at the horizon they had disappeared into, only blinking when his eyes became too dry. The tears had long ceased flowing.

Morning found him in the same alley, same foetal position. He no longer shivered. The city was once again abuzz, but he might have as well been an invisible man, or a piece of discarded paper, or the alley shit that people stepped over. He felt like a character in the biblical Good Samaritan story.

Just past midday, he woke up from a nap he was not even aware he had taken, but someone was softly nudging at his ribs. Still in pain, hunger and anger, Kanja opened his eyes and came face to face with a pair of bloodshot eyes. The stench on him, on a different occasion, would have choked Kanja. His hair was several inches too long, too shaggy and too dirty. The rest of him was as dirty as his hair. He was carrying a dirty sack, plastic bottles peeping through the holes in the sack.

"*Wewe unaitwa nani?*" What's your name? the red-eyed man asked. His voice sounded like he had a bad cold.

For an answer, Kanja blinked and shifted his body for the first time in hours. The man put down his sack and sat on his legs, peering into Kanja. His eyes studied Kanja's vertical body, understanding flooding into the red eyes.

"*Boss, walikutia.*" They raped you. It was a statement, not a question.

"*Pole jo!* Have you eaten?"

Kanja was a little confused with the stranger's concern, and found it weird that the kindness he was experiencing was coming from a person he would have run away from under different circumstances.

He shook his head. The stranger walked away, leaving the sack beside Kanja. He returned carrying a bag of hot chips and bottled water. He sat down next to Kanja, lifted Kanja's limp body and used his own body to support him. With dirty hands, he fed Kanja. City dwellers passed and stared at them curiously.

The dirty and stinky man left Kanja again, and when he returned, he had two younger boys in tow. "I am going to *Inda,*" he addressed the younger ones. "Do not leave him alone, *mnaskia?*" The boys, high on glue, sat quietly on either of Kanja. Once in a while, they incoherently spoke to each other. They even offered Kanja their water and glue. He declined the latter. At dusk, the older boy returned with an empty sack, and they all supported Kanja to a *safe* place.

* * *

Mato was everybody's big brother, but only because he was not old enough to be a father. It was hard to determine his age, not that he knew it either.

"I was alive when Kenyatta died," he liked to say.

A group of street children lived on Kirinyaga Road, with Mato as their leader. Sometimes they would be fewer when some of them disappeared to somewhere, other times they were more when they had visitors from other street families. Kanja, for the longest time, did not consider himself a part of the family. He was only with them because he was not well enough to either go to Industrial Area, or back home. But that was before this life had become the norm.

Their home was a shed made of tattered, plastic bags that protected them a little from night chills and rain. Kanja spent nearly three weeks lying on a bed made of dirty clothes. At day time, as most of the family scattered, Mato would choose two boys as Kanja's caretakers. They were in charge of feeding, protecting and medicating him.

Although Mato collected plastic and sold it for recycling in *Inda*, short for Industrial Area, Kanja soon learned that they did not all do honest jobs. There were thieves among them. They plucked side mirrors from parked cars or in traffic. They snatched mobile phones. The heist would quickly be sold to ready buyers along Kirinyaga Road. The younger ones begged for money and food. The girls sold their bodies, a realisation that shocked Kanja—that there were men, clean ones, willing to have sex with street girls.

"When you need to have sex, all your other senses take leave," Mato chuckled as he answered Kanja.

Sometimes, they all went to the Globe Roundabout and bathed in the dirty river. The baths left them as smelly as before, if not worse.

"It's not about being clean, it's about cooling off," Mato explained.

In his second month on the streets, Kanja had blended in with his street family, courtesy of his dirty, rough look and worn-out clothes. To complete the look, he carried with him a bottle of glue, but it was more for show because he hated the smell. The day he plucked his first side mirror from a packed vehicle, he was nervous, though there were five boys standing guard and encouraging him.

* * *

Evenings on the streets became fun for Kanja. They would huddle around a tyre-powered bonfire and laugh about their day's escapades

101

like running from an irate public, or a rant against the broker who underpaid them. Sometimes, they cooked a meal in an old *sufuria* that was hardly ever washed. Strangely for Kanja, he ate more meat than he had ever done in his life. Butcheries were often more than happy to give the rotting meat to the street boys, and they rummaged in restaurants' bins. None of them ever got food poisoning.

After meals, sex clusters would be formed around the shack. Some masturbated, often in front of each other, as if it was the most normal thing to do. Others would be heard groaning behind the shack. Some had sex with the girls, some boys had sex with each other.

Kanja would remain by the fire and stare at it angrily, like it was the cause of his woes. When the lump of jealousy constantly blocking his throat during those moments got too much, he would sit a distance away and watch their figures in the dark, move against each other rhythmically and choke with envy as they performed mass masturbations and orgies.

Sometimes, the girls offered him sex. He hated that they offered it to him out of pity, he could hear it in their voices. He would walk away, unwilling to display his sadness to them. Like the boys in his secondary school, some high-on-anything street boys and girls would accuse him of being gay, prompting some of the boys who preferred to have sex with each other to offer him the same.

One cold July, he got his respect. And the nickname Boss. Kanja had an old and smelly blanket around him as he mostly listened to sexual sounds, blank look on his face, stubbornly refusing to walk away from the warm fire. One of the bigger boys, known for preferring other boys, roughly pushed him to the ground.

Kanja was strong, way stronger than any of his street siblings, but he had been caught off-guard. The boy was on him, grappling with Kanja's blanket that landed on the fire, then his trouser. In that one moment, Kanja re-lived both his rapes.

What he did next was discussed among his street family for a long time. He blamed the incident on the metallic taste that flooded his mouth. One minute he was on the ground, the next he was the one on top, strangling the big boy and the other boys were struggling to get him off.

He had no memory of reaching for the boy's throat and squeezing it with both hands; none of throwing off everyone else who tried to get him off. He did not even hear them scream when the rubber fire caught his attacker's foot. Those were things he was told later when he was calmer.

"Kanja! Boss!" It was Mato's voice.

"Boss, *wacha hizo*. Don't kill him. He is stupid!"

Mato's voice was calm and firm.

Slowly, Kanja got off the immobile boy, took slow steps back as he stared at his own fists, like he was seeing them for the first time.

"Is… is he dead?"

He hardly recognised his shaky voice.

"Somebody pour water on his face now!" someone shouted.

It took five minutes to revive the attacker.

"Listen here, all of you," Mato finally said when there was order. Everyone but Kanja and Mato was huddled together in one corner, shaky from what they had just witnessed. The boy Kanja nearly killed was lying on the ground in foetal position, quivering. "You all need to leave him alone. When he wants to have sex, he will let you know.

You have seen what he can do to you. He is boss, and you better remember that before you attempt your foolishness."

They left him alone. They stopped looking at him straight in the face. When they did, Kanja saw fear, or perhaps it was respect. Whatever it was, Kanja loved it, and he loved that they all started addressing him as "Boss".

Chapter Nine

Naliaka, occupying a high stool at a vantage point at the counter, shifted her bottoms and turned her head this way and that way. There was a whiff of adrenaline in the air. A discreet sniff of her armpits confirmed she was the guilty party. She fished out a little bottle of perfume from her bag and dashed a little of it on her neck and armpits.

On the outside, it was just another day on the prowl, but on the inside, the turbulence of her heart and the nerves in her stomach told a different story. It was on a Friday, one of the busiest drinking evenings in Nairobi.

She surveyed the crowd through her thick fake eyelashes, and could pick up Boss and the two house-size men who discreetly trailed his every step with their watchful eyes. One was sipping on soda and the other one on water. A few tables away were Jonte and Oti, both on water. That they were not facing her did not deceive her; she knew they could see her every move.

On any other day, she would have already identified her target and they would be well on the way to the hotel. Not tonight, because she was starting her new hustle.

Someone interrupted her nervous thoughts by approaching her from behind and covering her eyes playfully.

"Who is that?" she demanded as she tried to unlock the fingers. A few seconds later and a chuckle, he let her go.

"Do I know you?" she asked, cocking her head.

"Do you mind if I sit down?" he asked instead, pointing at the empty stool next to her with his chin.

She shrugged, like she usually did when in the mood to play. "It's free seating."

"Waiting for someone?"

"Yes, you."

He smiled and stepped closer.

"Your place or my place?"

"Depends. Where is your place, and are you sober enough to drive to wherever you live?"

"Ruaka, and yes, I am sober enough to drive and do other things."

She didn't hear what he said next because she was busy texting multiple texts about the possible location and to affirm there was a car. She looked up to see Jonte and Oti walk out. They would be waiting outside to begin the trail.

"If you are taking me that far out of town, you would have to either pay for the taxi back, or have me the whole night. I get paid in advance."

"How about the whole night?"

She named her price. He agreed.

Twenty minutes later, Naliaka sat nervously next to the man whose name she did not know. She felt the urge to look behind and see if Jonte and Oti were behind, but she needed to act as natural as possible. She did, however, keep looking at her phone and at some point, her companion asked her whether she was on social media.

"I don't do social media." It was true. She had absolute zero interest in social media. She had tried Facebook once, but it just made her feel miserable about her life because it appeared that everybody out there was having a great time.

"For someone who does not do social media, you are quite busy on that phone."

"I do have clients who would like to have me for the night, you don't mind if I tell them I am booked, do you?"

He shrugged, but through the darkness Naliaka did not see the shrug.

They were just past the Village Market when Jonte and Oti struck by cutting them off, forcing them to veer off the road. Naliaka screamed and covered her head. There was a pain on her chest as the seatbelt locked and tightened across her. Within seconds, Jonte and Oti were inside the car, Naliaka was roughly pulled out of the front seat to the backseat, with Oti sitting next to her while Jonte took over the passenger seat. It was so quick and scary.

Jonte and Oti had their guns pointed at the driver. "Drive, and don't try anything stupid," Jonte growled, slightly knocking the man's head with the gun. The man nodded and complied. Their first stop was about a hundred metres into Gacharage, towards Gachie, a lonely road at any time.

"Drive towards the quarry," Jonte ordered.

In less than a minute, they relieved the man of his two phones, wallet, rings and a watch. They took Naliaka's phone and purse. "If either of you has hidden anything and we find out, I will shoot you…"

"I swear that's everything… I can give you my ATM card pin number," the man was volunteering information in a shaky voice.

"Good man. You keep it up, you will come out alive. What's the number?"

"Four, five, six, seven…"

"Did you get that *múriũ*?" Jonte asked Oti.

Jonte took over driving, with Naliaka sitting at the front and the man behind with Oti. He drove the car towards Gachie, ordered Naliaka and the nameless man to get out just after the shopping centre as they drove off into the night, leaving a genuinely shaken Naliaka and the victim by the roadside.

Naliaka paced up and down in tears. The victim sat on the ground, hugging his knees and rocking himself. He was howling. Seeing and hearing a grown man so frightened was what made Naliaka realise it was going to be way harder than she thought.

* * *

"We should go to the police," the victim finally whispered, launching himself up and wiping his tears with his shirt. He pinched his nose and blew it loudly, discarding the phlegm on the ground.

"I am a prostitute. I do not deal with the police."

"But I have to report the theft."

"It's your car, not mine," she said stubbornly, crossing her arms.

"Don't you want to report the theft of your phone?"

She shrugged.

"You want me to leave you on the road alone, at night, after what just happened?"

He finally looked up at her. "Are you crazy?"

"I can handle myself better than you think. Besides, I doubt lightning would strike twice. I will hide in the bush until morning."

He went to say something then seemed to change his mind, shrugged and walked away. Naliaka felt for a snap knife carefully strapped on her wrist, unstrapped it, held it on the ready as she watched the man stagger away until darkness swallowed him.

She shivered, suddenly aware she was alone, in the middle of the night. What if her rescuers did not turn up? Maybe she should have accepted Boss's offer of a loaded gun? She jumped when the phone started vibrating in her bra. *There will be a five minute window after the boys abandon you. That should be enough time to get rid of the victim,* Boss had instructed earlier. She had not even realised the five minutes were over.

"Are you alright?" he sounded anxious.

"No! I am scared," she said.

"There is a vehicle with hazard lights on… can you see it? It is coming from the same direction you came from."

"I see it."

"Flag it down."

In the safety of the car, Naliaka started shivering uncontrollably. As they drove past the crime scene she had helped create, she turned away, unable to watch the abandoned vehicle and the police surrounding it.

"Turn around," she ordered the driver.

"What?"

"I want to go to see my friend. She lives in Ndenderu."

"But Boss asked me to take you to him."

"Boss does not own me."

"He owns me, and I do what he says." He pressed harder on the accelerator.

Naliaka pulled out her phone and called Boss.

"I want to go and see my friend in Ndenderu. Could you please ask your faithful goon to take me there?"

"What friend in Ndenderu?" He sounded alarmed.

"I really need to go to Ndenderu right now."

Boss hesitated, catching himself just before asking if the friend was a man, or a woman. He sighed.

"Alright then, but come to my house tomorrow by midday."

At five minutes past midnight, Naliaka called Queen on her new number.

"It's Naliaka."

"Naliaka!" Queen's constant excitement whenever Naliaka called always made her consider returning to the whorehouse.

"What are you doing with a new number? Are you now a thug?"

It was a joke, but Naliaka cringed.

"No… it's… I just wanted another number," she answered defensively.

"Why are you calling me so late? Is everything alright?"

"Are you at home?"

"Why?"

"Can I come over?"

"What a silly question. Of course you can. I am not at home, but I shall be there at some point tomorrow."

When Naliaka still lived in the house, it was common knowledge that Queen was gentler with her. When Naliaka left, she did not expect Queen's fussing over her to continue, but it did. It wasn't strange for Queen to make random calls, just to check up on her. To invite her for lunch. Once, she took her to Mombasa and introduced her to everybody as her daughter.

"You are the daughter I shall never have."

Naliaka went along with it. On the one hand, she hated Queen because at her most vulnerable, Queen had taken advantage of her. On the other hand, she loved Queen in her own dark way, ironically because of the same reason, that she had picked her up at her most vulnerable.

* * *

Ngari the gateman was in his forties but often looked well into his sixties. He was the only father figure most of the girls in Queen's house had, and Naliaka had loved to sit with him at the gate for lengthy chats. She often felt sorry for him because of the things he had to witness, especially because he had two daughters; when he talked about them, Naliaka could tell that he worried that they may end up like the women he guarded. Those were the moments he looked sixty.

Ngari peeped into the car and exclaimed excitedly when he saw Naliaka before ushering her in.

The house was quiet, but the front door was open. Queen had most probably called the live-in housekeeper to leave it open. There was always food, packed in containers, stored into the fridge or the freezer.

She warmed some chicken and rice in the microwave and put on the kettle to make coffee. She ate quietly, thinking about her evening. The shivers nearly made it impossible to eat.

Her thoughts kept going to the victim, the same one who had so playfully hit on her. Where was he now? Did the police help him? Had he blocked his bank accounts before Jonte got to them? Would he ever be able to drive at night again? Had they just cured him off picking up prostitutes?

She did not even realise she had eaten all the food until she reached for an empty plate. She downed the coffee, poured a glass of wine and then went upstairs to her room. She was the only girl with a permanent room in the house, even though she no longer lived there.

She took a long shower, and although showers always made her feel sleepy, she turned and tossed in bed for hours. She turned on the lights, turned them off, switched on the small television in the room and turned it off. She went back downstairs and poured herself another glass of wine, then went to the window to stare into the darkness, crying on and off. Finally, at dawn, she fell into a disturbed sleep.

* * *

Somebody was noisily drawing the curtains. The light burned through her shut eyes. She groaned and pulled the duvet over her head, sinking deeper in the bed.

"Wake up, sleepy head" It was Queen.

"What time is it?"

She was vigorously rubbing her eyes, begging them to behave.

"Eleven. What's your problem anyway? You got drunk last night?"

She was looking at the empty glass on the bedside table.

Naliaka giggled and shook her head. "I only had two glasses of wine, but I was exhausted." She sat up and stretched her body.

"When did you come back?"

"A few minutes ago, only to be shocked to learn the girls do not even know you are here."

"They were all asleep when I came in."

"Of course they were. Unlike you, they are not nocturnal animals." They both laughed and hugged.

"How are you, Naliaka, really? Last night you sounded very tense."

Naliaka pressed herself against the headboard and stretched again. For a few seconds, she considered confessing to Queen what she had been up to. But only for a few seconds.

"I am fine, really. It was just one of those nights."

Queen cocked her head, eyes full of doubt.

"You know you can tell me anything… Remember I swore to you I would be there for you, no matter what."

"I know, and I appreciate it. But I promise you, I am fine."

Queen shrugged.

"How is business out there?"

It was Naliaka's turn to shrug.

"I cannot complain."

"You know you are always welcome to come back to the house."

"I know, but it's fun being out there. The city can be a very interesting place."

"Have you made any friends?"

Naliaka shook her head. "Nope. Not close ones anyway, which is how I prefer it."

"It bothers me that you do not have friends. What young person doesn't have friends?"

"You told me you never had friends even when you were young!"

Queen laughed.

"But I was ugly. You are beautiful, and beautiful people need friends."

Naliaka laughed. "I am alright. The girls here are the only friends I need."

Queen smiled as she smothered Naliaka's head.

"I woke you up because I am leaving in a little while, but the girls will be glad to see you. If you are sure there is nothing you want to talk to me about…"

"I am fine. I just missed you all."

* * *

Naliaka was in the garden with the girls, laughing and catching up, when they were interrupted by a ringing phone.

"I think that is your phone ringing," Julia told her, pointing at the phone with her mouth.

The phone was on the grass. For a second, Naliaka looked at the unfamiliar phone in confusion before grabbing in and walking away.

"Hey!"

"Naliaka!" Boss was mad. "Where the hell are you?"

"Erm… at my friend's."

She had forgotten she was supposed to go and see Boss.

"Why are you not here?"

Naliaka laughed. Not with amusement, but in disbelief.

"Don't shout at me!"

"When I tell you to be here, I mean it."

Naliaka laughed again, this time louder. She stole a glance at the girls, they were looking at her curiously.

"I forgot, and that's the truth, okay? Stop shouting!"

"Who do you think you are talking to?"

"I. Don't. Care. I don't care how everyone else talks to you, but you need to stop talking to me like I am a child. Now, if part of this deal is to order me around, I don't want it."

"Naliaka…"

She didn't hear the rest. She disconnected the call. She was seething. The last time anyone had such expectations on her, expectation to report even when she was going to the toilet, was when her mother was alive. That was a long time ago. Even when she was under Queen, she still had a big chunk of her independence, as long as she met her target. When she left Queen's house, she lived as she liked. Worked when she wanted. Slept when she wanted. Ate when and what she felt like. She wasn't about to start taking orders from anyone, least of all an armed robber.

Her phone was ringing again as she walked back to the girls. She looked at it and threw it away in anger.

"Whoooah! What's your problem?" Malaika demanded in between exhaling cigarette smoke.

"That's a very expensive phone you are throwing away."

"You can have it!" Naliaka answered angrily.

She sat on the same spot she was sitting on before the call and glared at anyone who dared to look at her.

Then the other girls started laughing. Eventually, she joined in the laughter.

"You are in love, aren't you? Only a boyfriend can get you so angry."

"No! It's just some stupid man who thinks he can tell me what to do," her anger was back.

"Careful. If your face gets hotter than it is, you will set yourself on fire!"

They were still laughing.

"This is very good news. Prostitutes can get boyfriends... you hear that, girls? Do not give up. There is hope. Our Naliaka is dating," Julia said in-between laughter.

"I am not dating!"

"You are. Come on, Suzie, get that phone for her. When she calms down she will need it to call her boyfriend and apologise."

They all burst into laughter. Naliaka did as well, reluctantly. She was still angry, but she realised her anger was fuelling the teasing. She accepted the phone from Suzie. It had already registered five missed calls within two minutes.

* * *

Boss was seething as well. But unlike Naliaka, he was angrier at himself than he was at Naliaka, for losing his cool and making himself feel stupid.

Since Naliaka told him she was going to see a friend, he had been on edge. The driver who had dropped her had reported to him how happy the gateman had been to see her.

"It has to be a man!" He muttered. He had felt the hint of the metallic taste and quickly went to the toilet to spit inside the toilet bowl.

He drank all night, thinking about Naliaka and how sensitive she was to him. Perhaps, he thought, bringing her on board was a bad business idea. He had slept at six in the morning and set his alarm clock for eleven. Then, he walked to the central business district and bought a large pepperoni pizza to share with Naliaka.

Come midday, he had already showered and slipped into a white tee shirt, black shorts and white socks. Every five minutes, he checked his phone and heard imaginary knocks at the door. By the time he called her, his anger and anxiety had peaked. Then he had been angry at her for not being apologetic, for having the audacity to tell him off. For sounding like she was fine without him. That was new, at least in his new life. He could not remember a time when anyone dared shout at him, drop calls on him and to rub salt to an injury, refuse to pick subsequent calls.

Then he laughed because he finally understood why over and over, the romance books he read and romance movies he watched, love seemed to make people act stupid. He was partly happy, that he was capable of falling in love, that his earlier suspicions of being in love with Naliaka were now confirmed, but he was partly disappointed with himself that he could lose his cool like that because of love.

At two-thirty in the afternoon, he called the driver who had dropped Naliaka.

* * *

At three, Naliaka was itching to leave Queen's house. They had laughed, eaten and now they were all taking naps or with clients. Thoughts of Boss were distracting her. She needed to speak to him to make it clear that her terms and conditions included independence, outside work.

She felt sad, as she always did whenever she had to leave the comfort and the unconditional love Queen's house provided, but the thought of being in the same compound with Kaggai cured her.

"Kaggai is obsessed with you," Queen had once told her. "Usually, he goes for the youngest one, but he keeps coming back to you. Perhaps it is because he broke your virginity?"

Naliaka always tensed with the memory of her first time with Kaggai. It didn't matter that he had never asked her to have anal sex again. He had instead seemed to try and make up for that first time by being gentle, but he disgusted her.

And she could not forget what he did to her.

She waved her goodbye at the gate and started walking towards the road, grateful that she still had some of her clothes in Queen's house. The night before, she had worn her usual short outfits and heels topped with a blonde weave. Right now, she was wearing a pair of sneakers, a pair of jeans, a sleeveless top and a jacket to shield her arms from the sun.

Ahead of her, close to the road was a car. It was facing the road. She thought nothing of it because such vehicles were always going in and out of Queen's house.

Then someone came out of the back seat. She jumped and squeaked, for a second wanting to run back to the house. Then she straightened up, put one hand on the hip and glared.

"How did you find me?" she demanded.

Boss was leaning on the car, studying Naliaka from head to toe with an expression she could not work out.

"I see you changed your clothes."

She grunted, shifting her feet.

"So?"

She shrugged.

"Nothing. I was just making conversation."

"How did you find me?" she repeated, still standing on the same spot.

"Have you forgotten one of my guys dropped you here?"

"What do you want? To shout at me again?"

Boss opened the car door and pointed at it.

"Get in."

"What if I don't want to?"

"Stop acting up. What do you think I will do to you, kill you?"

"It's a possibility I am aware of," she retorted.

"Please..." he mocked with a tongue click. "If I wanted you dead, you would be gone by now. Get in!"

She stood her ground, but only for a few seconds because a car drove into the driveway and stopped next to her. The driver wound down the window and Naliaka nearly gagged at the sight of the gappy smile she had come to detest so much. She took a step back.

"Naliaka! So good to see you. Where have you been? Are you back? Why are you standing here like this? Is this man disturbing you?" Kaggai was already out of the car, walking towards her with open arms.

Naliaka took another step back before dashing into Boss's car.

Boss, almost reluctantly, because he was studying Kaggai, entered after her and shut the door.

"Take us home," he instructed the driver as he turned to look at the man Naliaka had run away from looking at their disappearing car, looking hurt.

It was a drive that bordered on being amusing. Naliaka was shaken and angry. Her constant fear whenever she went to the whorehouse was bumping into Kaggai. The timing of his turning up had been so wrong, considering that she had meant to punish Boss for his arrogance. She stubbornly looked ahead most of the time. Her hands were crossed and she deliberately kept the sneer on her face, aware that Boss kept looking at her and shaking his head. By the time they stopped outside his house, her muscles ached from the tension.

119

He led the way up the stairs, she followed silently. He opened the door and let her in first. She walked in and slumped herself on the sofa, turning on the television immediately.

"Drink?" he asked after he locked the door.

She glared at him then went back to looking at the television.

"Suit yourself."

He was back within a minute, with a beer can. He opened it loudly, placed it on a stool before sitting next to Naliaka.

"What are you watching?" he asked.

She had been staring at the television for minutes, but had no idea what was on. "Something…" she muttered.

"I bet you have no idea what is on," he said, taking the remote from her hand and switching off the television.

"What?"

"We talk… enough of this imaginary lovers' fight."

Naliaka chuckled.

"You wish. I am just upset that you think you own me."

"I don't, but I think it is rude to tell someone you will turn up and then forget to even call them to excuse yourself."

She sat on her legs before answering.

"I overslept."

"Heavy night?" he asked.

"You ask that after what you know I did last night?"

She looked at him and rolled her eyes.

"That's not what I mean. Whose house was that?"

"Does it matter?"

"Perhaps not. But I am curious. Whose house is it? I saw a couple of men driving in." He had actually seen more than a couple of men driving in. By the time the fourth car drove in and two out, he had put two and two together. He still wanted to hear it from her.

"It belongs to my friend."

"Tell me about 'your... friend'"

"Why?"

"Because you are my friend and I want to know about your friends."

"I don't know about your friends," she said weakly.

"Two of them are dead. The other one lives very far away."

Out of spite, just to get back at him for being so arrogant, she wanted to keep the information to herself, but that stolen glance at him and that his two friends were dead softened her.

"I will tell you, but you must first promise not to behave like you are my mother. I had a life before you, I will still have a life away from you. I realise you are used to giving orders, but I am not one of your boys. I will do what you need me to do, but if I want to go to Mombasa, I shall not ask for your permission."

They glared at each other, then he nodded and put up his hands in mock surrender. "Deal."

* * *

"My goodness!" Boss muttered when Naliaka finally finished telling the story of her life, then he crushed the fourth beer can. "And I thought I had a shitty life!"

She giggled.

"We are a crowd!"

"Two peas in a pod!" he added, taking her hand and squeezing it gently.

"I am so sorry."

"Mushy doesn't suit you."

"You are right," he said and smiled, then dropped her hand. "How about I make a fresh cup of coffee for you?"

When he came back with another steaming cup and placed it on the stool, Naliaka was in the toilet. She returned to find him stretched on the sofa.

"Well, that's selfish."

There were other seats in the house, but he lay on her comfortable spot.

He spread his legs and tapped on the spot in front of him.

"Let's cuddle."

She looked at him and took a sharp breath; found herself wondering what making love to him would feel like.

"Are you paying for this?" she quipped as she slowly took the spot.

"Don't be a wisecrack. You don't mind, do you?"

She shook her head as she let her back rest on his chest, taking time to relax between his legs. When she was well settled, he wrapped his hands around her.

"You know," he said, almost to himself. "I watch a lot of romance movies. I know all the moves. I have always wondered how it feels like to do a lot of stuff."

He was running his hand, gently, on her bald head.

"You really have never?"

"I really have never. You are the first woman I ever held."

At that very moment, she decided it was her mission to have sex with him.

"For someone who has never had any practice, you are doing very well."

Naliaka, a woman who long ago lost count of the number of men she had slept with, was not that familiar with sex preambles. Most of her partners, understandably so, were more interested in penetration—wham bang thank you ma'am. Her thoughts took her to the priest, the one man who went out of his way to be gentle to her, to worship her body. It did not matter if he did it for her, or for himself, but it left her feeling good about herself, not dirty.

"At this rate , my second cup of coffee, too, will go cold."

"My beer may do the opposite."

"Tell me about the man who stopped to talk to you at Queen's gate."

He felt her body tense. But she did tell him. By the time she was done, his anger and hate towards Kaggai was neck to neck with hers.

"That is some heavy, sick shit," he declared, fighting the metallic taste.

"Why... how did you finally get out of the house to be on your own?"

Naliaka remembered the day too well. The hate towards Kaggai had been building up for years. It reached its peak one week when he went to the whorehouse every day and spent two hours with her. She suspected that he had increased his dose of Viagra. She could not satisfy him, and the worst part, he thought she liked it because part of her job description was to convince the client that she liked having sex with them.

"I can't sleep with him anymore," Naliaka had walked into Queen's bedroom one evening after a session with Kaggai. She had found Queen half-dressed. Naliaka had not bothered to look away, and Queen had not bothered to cover up.

"Kaggai? Did he hurt you again?" Queen had asked in alarm.

Naliaka shook her head as she moved to sit on the bed.

"No. But I cannot stand him. He is disgusting. He makes me want to throw up."

"Naliaka, but you know you cannot choose whom to sleep with."

"Julia does," she countered.

"That's different, and you know it," Queen answered as she finally covered her big body with a *kikoi*.

"Different, how?"

"Her husband does not know she is here."

"I want to leave," she declared and glared at Queen.

Queen laughed sarcastically.

"... And go where?"

Naliaka shrugged.

"Anywhere very far away from that buffoon."

Queen sat next to Naliaka, taking time to speak. When she did, she started with another sigh.

"Listen, I understand where you are coming from, but what you are asking is hard. Kaggai is our biggest client, he gets what he wants. Is it more money you want?"

Naliaka shook her head, tears finally flowing.

"It can't be that bad."

"It is. I want to leave," she repeated more boldly.

"You are serious!" Queen said as she moved to look through the window.

"Where will you go?" she repeated her earlier question, but without the sarcasm.

"I will find myself a house."

"And do what for a living?"

Naliaka shrugged.

"I will figure it out."

Queen shook her head. "You don't know anything about life out there."

"I cannot be here forever either."

"Why not?"

"Because I cannot sell my body forever. I do not want to be Julia's age and still be doing this."

"What else will you be doing?" Queen's voice was growing exasperated.

"I said I will work something out," she snapped.

"I refuse to sleep with Kaggai, ever again. I don't want to see him either. He disgusts me when he smiles at me, like he thinks he has a good smile. I keep wanting to knock off his remaining teeth and cut the extra fat on his body. I want to put more scars on his ugly face, his whole body. He makes me cringe. I... I keep wanting to hurt him. The other day I carried a kitchen knife to the bedroom..."

"Naliaka!" Queen gasped, moving to kneel in front of Naliaka. "I didn't realise it was this bad."

"If I ever see him again, I feel like I will not be able to stop myself from hurting him... please, let me go."

Then, Queen did something that would leave Naliaka forever confused. She cupped Naliaka's face and kissed her. A kiss that felt wrong but good, good because Naliaka could not remember ever being kissed like that by anyone. It was gentle. Even sensual. She let the kiss go on, only stopping because she lost her breath.

"I am sorry about what you have been going through. I feel terrible," Queen said as she stood up, like the kiss never happened.

"Will you let me go?"

Queen nodded. "Of course. I will pay your house rent for two months. I owe you that. If at the end of the two months you still want to be on your own, then you will have to take over the rent yourself."

"Thank you."

Naliaka had seen Queen angry, not emotional. She felt like she was witnessing something she was not supposed to, so she looked away as Queen spoke.

"Promise me that you will keep in touch. Promise me that you will come back often to see me, to see us."

"I promise."

Naliaka moved into her one bedroom flat furnished and paid for by Queen. For a week, she stayed in bed, watching television, sleeping and overeating. The second week, she decided to go out to town. She had no intention of getting herself a client, but she had. She had gone to his house, and he had had sex with her but refused to pay, then kicked her out of his house at dawn. Naliaka had waited outside the gate for daylight before getting into a *matatu*, attracting all sorts of unpleasant looks from the early risers. She had still been wearing her short dress and heels, and her makeup was smudged.

The following day, Naliaka went to several hotels within the city to ask them if she could rent a room for a few nights a week. Five of them, knowing what she meant, had turned her down. The sixth one agreed.

"You really would like him dead?" Boss asked when Naliaka was done.

"Very dead," she answered innocently. "Let's just say he is lucky that I am no killer." She even giggled. Boss, who had a sudden urge to brush his teeth, did not respond.

126

"Hungry?" he suddenly asked, pushing her away so he could get up.

"Starving," she said with a yawn.

"I hope you do not mind cold pepperoni pizza…"

"Sorry about that." She was, by now, feeling sorry for standing him up.

"Cold pizza and a hot cup of coffee would be great."

"Don't you want to check missed calls, or how much I paid you?" Boss asked as he saw her items still on the table.

Hours later, after eating and watching a romantic movie, Naliaka suggested a combined shower. She saw him tense.

"I swear, it is just a shower. I promise not to take advantage of you," she joked to reassure him.

He smiled, attempting to hide how vulnerable he suddenly felt. If he allowed her to do what she was suggesting, she would be in the position of power. Then he shrugged. She already knew what his issues were, they had slept in the same bed, naked. He shook his body and tried to relax before allowing her to undress him. Appreciating her gentle hands on him, her kisses on random parts of his body. He risked a look at his penis and cringed at how unresponsive it was, but he allowed her to lead him to the shower. Allowed her to scrub his body, every part of his body. He enjoyed doing the same to her, even for a moment forgetting his sexual troubles.

"You want a tee-shirt to sleep in?" he asked tensely, unable to look at her straight in the face.

"Absolutely not. We are sleeping naked."

"We are?"

Naliaka peered at his tense face, at his limp penis, then nodded. She uncovered the bed and lay down, facing up. "Of course we are. We have done it before. Now, lie on top of me," she whispered.

He looked at her inviting body then shook his head.

"It won't happen."

"Who said I want anything to happen?" she countered.

He did. Hesitantly. Afraid of hurting her with his weight. She was a slim girl, he was a muscular man.

"It's okay," she whispered in encouragement. "If and when you get too heavy, I will tell you."

He smiled and sunk on her. Body part to body part. He felt the warmth of her womanhood on her manhood.

"See, I do not bite," she said, gently biting his ear.

He laughed, genuinely amused.

"You are a terrible tease, you know that?"

Chapter Ten

It was Naliaka's fifth month, two or three hits a week, and she no longer worried or lost sleep over the victims. All the jobs, except two when the victims had tried to fight back, had been smooth and bloodless. The resisting victims had been left unconscious on the ground with gushing wounds on their heads, courtesy of Oti's gun muzzle.

The first time Oti had hit the victim so hard that Naliaka was sure she had heard the skull crack. She screamed, the bile in her gut threatening to spill out.

"Do you have to be so brutal?"

"If you see a man willing to fight someone who is holding a gun, it means they also have one, and are looking for an opportunity to shoot you. You have to incapacitate them before they kill you," Jonte explained as he watched a gum-chewing Oti wipe the bloody muzzle on his jeans.

* * *

Father Joshua had not seen Kiki for months, and it was getting on his nerves. Her number no longer went through but every weekend, he would religiously try to call. With a sense of loss, he started accepting the possibility that she may have died, because how else could someone disappear like that?

Every Friday, sometimes on an odd day, Father Joshua turned up at the pub where they first met. A few hours later, he would make the lonely drive home, disappointed.

On this Friday, he spotted her immediately he stepped into the pub. He missed his step and nearly bumped into someone. His instinct was to run and hug her, drag her to the lodging, then he would ask her where the hell she had been. Instead, he collected his dignity, smiled what he hoped was a casual smile as he took long and bold steps towards her. Naliaka's face lit up when she spotted him.

It was a hug that went on for long enough for Jonte and Oti, sitting a few metres from her, to notice and sit up straight.

"Where have you been?" Father Joshua demanded, his earlier resolve to be calm forgotten.

"Your number never goes through!"

He was still holding her hand, his other hand smoothening her face, unwilling to let her go, secretly reassuring himself that he was not dreaming.

Naliaka laughed, amused by his emotional display.

"I changed my number."

"And you didn't think to inform me?" He was still upset.

"I do not answer to you, Father."

"I am your client!" he protested, looking genuinely hurt.

She chuckled.

"That is no way to treat clients."

She laughed as she took back her seat. "Have a seat, please."

"I would rather we went to the hotel.'

"Come on, sit down and relax a little."

Naliaka felt her phone vibrate with incoming messages. She ignored it because she knew it was Jonte asking what was happening. She could bet on her last shilling that Boss already knew there was something different tonight.

"You have never wanted to sit and relax."

"Dear, dear Father, Christmas for you has come early and you can have me tonight for free. Perhaps you will find it in your heart to ask God for my forgiveness."

"What is it with you?"

He was peering at her, one side of his brow arched, like he was expecting to see in her eyes whatever it is he thought was wrong with her.

"Prostitutes also give back to society. Sit. Have your beer, I will even pay for it."

Naliaka was more excited to see Father Joshua than she was willing to show. Seeing him made her realise that for months, she had been at the butt end of a gun; a real life prop in robberies. Seeing him gave her a sudden urge to take a break for the dangerous humdrum life she had been living.

She needed sex. The whole nine yards. Spending a night, every fortnight, in Boss's arms was nice and Boss had even learned how to use his fingers and tongue on her. It was amazing, for both of them. Whenever she writhed in pleasure, his manhood would get excited, and it turned her on. Whenever he paused to breathe and look at the marvel that was her womanhood, things happened to him, and it was exciting to witness.

But she needed more. And she needed a life outside Boss's circle of criminals, though knowing Boss and his dangerous mix of ego and insecurities, there was no way he would be okay with what she was about to do.

Naliaka looked at Father Joshua, but did not see him; heard him but did not listen to him and nodded once in a while in agreement of what she had not heard. She smiled when he laughed, rubbed his thigh in assurance.

"You seem a little distracted. Are you okay?" he suddenly asked, looking concerned.

"I am fine, I promise. I need to use the toilet, though."

She stood up, but he was hanging on to her arm.

"You are coming back?"

She laughed.

"I am only going to the toilet. Do you want me to leave my handbag as insurance?" The question was in jest, but he grabbed the bag from her. She was thankful for having her phone in her hands. As she walked towards the toilets, she saw Oti and Jonte follow her.

The toilets were busy. She had to wait to get a cubicle and as she peed, she dialled Boss's number. He picked on the first ring.

"What's going on?" he demanded tensely.

"I need the night off."

"Are you unwell?"

She told him she was fine.

"Is it about that man Jonte told me about? Who is he?"

"An old friend."

"Friend." It sounded more like an echo of her words.

"Yes, friend. I want to spend time with him." She was whispering into the phone because there were people waiting to use the toilet after her.

Boss swallowed hard. When he spoke, his voice was a croak. "This is not right. What do we do with Oti and Jonte?"

"Just give them a day off. You can give them my pay from the next job as compensation. And Boss, this man must not be robbed."

"Why not?"

"Please," she felt close to tears.

"Don't make this a habit."

"I will make sure I give you enough notice next time."

"Next time?"

"So you will call them off?"

"Yes, Naliaka, I will," she could hear him sigh heavily.

"Are you going to take him to the hotel?"

"I am not sure. Remember I no longer have an arrangement with them." Besides, she was not sure if Father Joshua would be okay with her going to his house but if he was not, they would find another hotel.

"Come and see me tomorrow." His tone had softened.

"What time?"

"You will have lunch with me so be here, latest by two." He sighed loudly.

"Also, calling me while you are peeing is a bit rude." She chuckled before disconnecting the call.

Her two shadows were hovering around the corridor outside the toilet. She winked at them, they shook their heads simultaneously

133

in obvious confusion. One day, she decided she would really have a conversation with her teammates.

She found Father Joshua, looking comical as he stood facing the direction of the toilet, still clutching at her bag.

In the end, when Naliaka told Father Joshua she no longer had access to the hotel, he begged her to go home with him and that he wanted to wake up next to her, to serve her breakfast in bed.

"You mean go with you to the church?"

"Stop asking unnecessary questions."

* * *

When Boss felt composed enough to not sound shaken on the phone, he dialled Jonte's number.

"Follow them and stay with them until she leaves."

Jonte and Oti would discuss Boss's relationship with Naliaka. They would wonder if they were *doing* it or not. They would agree they were doing it. They would wonder how he could let her go home with another man. They would decide the only plausible explanation was that the man had something that Boss badly needed, that Naliaka needed to have access to whatever that thing was.

An hour later, Jonte called Boss, interrupting his melancholy and the metallic taste. He looked at the phone screen in near disgust, wishing Jonte would have just let him continue wallowing in self-pity.

"*Sema…*" He answered with a dry mouth.

"They went into a church compound."

"Who?" He was that confused.

"Kiki and the man."

"You think he works in the church?"

"I think so."

"Tomorrow, you will be going to church, if he goes."

"What?"

"Tomorrow is a Sunday, you shouldn't have trouble accessing the compound. I want to know what he does for the church."

"I don't go to church."

"Good for you, Jonte. Tomorrow, however, you will be among peers, because the biggest thieves hide in church." He heard Jonte chuckle.

When he disconnected the line, Boss started giggling until his giggles turned into full blown laughter.

"A church man?" he asked himself loudly, getting up to fetch another beer from the fridge.

"What is the world turning into?" He was no longer angry, his mouth did not feel dry anymore. The taste of metal also disappeared.

"I believe my mouth and evil thoughts just experienced divine intervention!"

* * *

As Boss slept off his hangover in Kirinyaga Road, Naliaka, wearing Father Joshua's tee-shirt and nothing else, was picking nuts one by one from a bowl and sipping on her coffee as she watched a comedy show on television, trying not to burst out in laughter every twenty seconds. Her urge to laugh had nothing to do with the comedy.

She could hear the church choir. She could hear children running outside. She laughed at the scandal that would be if anyone discovered their handsome priest had spent half the night eating from the forbidden tree.

"I will be gone for no more than two hours," he had said to her earlier, looking more serious than she had ever seen him. She stifled a giggle.

"Father Matthew lives next door. Keep away from the windows as well. If anyone knocks, do not open."

"Perhaps Father Matthew has a woman in there as well?" Naliaka quipped, enjoying his attempt to be serious.

"That's not the point."

"You two are wild!" she laughed loudly.

"Shhhh…"

"Why so serious?" she mocked as she sat against the headboard, naked and deliberately exposing her breasts, watching him secure his priestly collar.

"It's not funny," he protested as he grabbed the rest of his attire and nearly bumped into the door.

"I will be right here when you return," she called after him.

Two hours later, the music stopped. Muffled voices from congregants leaving the church followed. Car engines started. She walked to the window, drew a little bit of it and peeped outside. She could make out Father Joshua standing at the top staircase of the church, shaking hands.

She was bored. There was only so much television one could watch. She was tired of reheating her coffee. She was out of nuts, and she did not feel like munching on the biscuits, the only other light food available. Then she heard his voice. He was talking to someone. She jumped from the seat and disappeared into the bedroom, shutting the door behind her softly.

"Thank you, Michael. You can place everything in the pantry. Don't worry about unpacking—I will do that later."

"What was Michael helping you with?" she asked coyly when he opened the bedroom door and found her lying on the bed, naked.

"Offertory," he answered as he stared at her.

"You are the reason I will surely go to hell," he whispered as he lay beside her.

* * *

Boss slowly came out of sleep. First, his mind was aware that he needed to get up. Then he registered a headache and a clogged head. Neither of those was a surprise. He had drank late into the night. The cold was what finally persuaded him to get up. He sat up on the bed and groaned, putting his head between his hands.

His phone rang. He grunted as he picked it from the bedside table. His shaky hands almost dropped it.

"Sema…"

"We went to church!" It was Jonte, sounding excited.

"I hope you did not confess your sins. What was the sermon about?"

"That dude who lied to his blind father about being the first born… like, how stupid was the father?" Jonte laughed.

He loved it when Boss was in a joking mood. It did not happen often but when it did, he took full advantage.

Boss laughed, despite his entire body's discomfort.

"Why do you imagine he was stupid?"

"I do not have children, but you would think differentiating your children's voices is basic."

Boss laughed.

"So, did you see the man?"

"You will never guess what he is?"

"The cleaner?" Boss asked.

He didn't think whoever the man was, was a cleaner, but Jonte sounded like he needed humouring.

Jonte took the bait and laughed.

"Wrong. He is the priest."

"Huh? Like a preacher?"

"Worse, a Catholic priest."

Boss chuckled, more in confusion than amusement.

"Aren't they supposed to be celibate?"

"Clearly not this one."

"Kiki?"

"She is still in the house as far as I know. Oti stayed outside the church just to keep an eye on the house."

"Right… you can go home now."

His headache disappeared miraculously after the conversation. He was not a religious man in any way, shape or form, but the least he expected of religious men was for them to fear the Supreme Being.

* * *

Later, still wrapped around each other's sweaty bodies, Naliaka shifted.

"So, you keep the offertory food?"

He sniggered as he stripped off his collar.

"It is always too much so I share with the less fortunate."

"What a nice job you have. What the hell do you do with your salary?"

"Pay for nice stuff… you are nice stuff." They laughed.

"And buy nice clothes, I guess. Go on holiday," Naliaka rolled her eyes.

"But seriously, I give out most of my money. Usually, I pay school fees for several students, and I help educate my family."

"That sounds like your ticket to heaven."

"But there is you!" He was tracing his fingers along her jaw.

"You make me think about things… things I never thought about before."

"What things?" she asked, unable to hide a sudden panic.

"Like, how would it be to leave priesthood? How would it feel to get married?"

She pushed him away. "Stop thinking such nonsense. You leave your calling for me, I shall certainly disappoint you. My life is dark."

She went to the window and peeped outside, thinking of Boss.

"So is mine."

"Well yeah. Still, do not do anything stupid because of me."

"We shall see," he whispered.

"Anyway, I need to go. How are you sneaking me out of this priestly house?"

That little discussion, and that Father Joshua looked very serious had put her on flight mode.

"Already? Can't you stay another night?"

Naliaka chuckled and shook her head.

"When can I see you next?"

She thought about the potential fight she was likely to have with Boss for abandoning duty. She thought about her cuddly nights with Boss, and whether she would prefer to have sex with Father Joshua or have *alternative* sex with Boss. She wanted both, at different times. She needed to work it out.

"A month from now."

"That's too long. Can I not see you next weekend?"

She shook her head emphatically.

"No. Sorry. I am booked."

He looked crushed.

An hour later, Father Joshua sneaked Naliaka out of the house. He first checked if Father Matthew was in—he was not. He reversed the car close to the entrance, made sure there were no prying eyes around before opening the back door of the car, one he had backed very close to the main door, covered her with clothes until he was sure they were safe, about five kilometres away.

* * *

Boss had a cook who came in three days a week. Sunday was not one of those days. Instead of the fast food he relied on when the cook was away, he decided to cook.

There was not much to choose from, but he spotted some leftover *sukuma wiki*, and there was meat in the freezer, and he could make *ugali*.

He liked it when people were afraid of him, but he loved watching the fire in Naliaka's eyes whenever she defied him. That she dared to cancel on a job was shocking. Nobody had ever done that and survived. As he turned the onions with a wooden cooking stick, he knew he had no intention of harming Naliaka. If anything, it made him more protective, needier of her presence, attention and body.

He needed to know more about the priest. Why he had been the one to make Naliaka lose focus. Why, if he could believe Jonte, she had been so excited to see him. Was she likely to be seeing the priest again, and again?

By the time the food was ready, his head was spinning. He removed his apron and went to take a shower, touching his manhood, willing it to back him in his fight for Naliaka. He gasped when he touched and felt hardness.

* * *

Three taps on the door.

"Hey. What's with the head thing?" he asked when he let in Naliaka.

Naliaka's head was covered with a red head-wrap.

Naliaka laughed.

"It's a cold day, my head was freezing."

It was true, the day had started hot and promising but by the time it was midday, it was like a different season altogether. She was also wearing a long, light cotton coat and a pair of black boots over her jeans. She removed the boots, revealing a pair of thick socks. She removed the coat, revealing a tight-fitting black top.

"When did you change?"

What he wanted to ask was, did she also have a change of clothes in the priest's house?

She shrugged as she slumped on the sofa.

"What do you mean?"

He shrugged, sitting next to her and facing her, displaying more courage than he felt. "You didn't go home last night."

She shrugged again, turning away.

"I went home in the morning."

"Right," he stood up and rubbed his hands. "Come on then, wash your hands. We need to eat before the food goes cold."

"Great. I have not eaten a proper meal all day."

She was lying. Father Joshua, before getting ready for church, had prepared an elaborate breakfast for both of them. She had only managed half of it and she was still feeling stuffed, especially because she had fed on nuts out of boredom.

They ate in silence for a few minutes. Naliaka was as usual playing with her food. "This is good. Who made it?"

Boss laughed. "I did, except the *sukuma wiki*. I just reheated that."

"Very nice. I suck at cooking."

"You suck at eating too."

"Funny," she hit him playfully across the table. "If there is any left, I may just carry some with me."

Boss did not answer, and when Naliaka looked up from her food, he was staring at her and he wasn't eating. She licked her fingers before speaking.

"You are giving me very strange looks."

She pushed her half full plate away and glared at him, trying to feel and look defiant. She knew she should have been more afraid of him but could not bring herself to be.

"Are you jealous that I slept with someone else last night?" she suddenly blurted out.

"Why should I be?" he retorted, immediately regretting his tone.

"It's your business if you want to sleep with all the men in Nairobi, but I do not want my work to suffer."

"I said I am sorry!"

"So, who is he?" He was testing her honesty.

"Why are you so interested?"

"Because you work for me and I need to know the people who are likely to confuse you during work. Because for months you have worked for me and have never absconded. Surely you cannot blame my curiosity."

She shrugged.

142

"His name is Father Joshua…"

Boss found himself laughing loudly, and to his surprise, it was a genuine laugh. He still thought it unbelievable that the man was a priest.

"What's funny?" But she was giggling as well.

"Father. Is that his first name?"

"He is a priest." Then they both laughed.

"Are you not afraid of being struck by thunder?"

"I am not responsible for his sins, I have enough of my own to worry about," she said dismissively, pulling back her plate, slicing a bit of *ugali* with her fingers and using the piece to wipe soup on the plate. She put it in her mouth.

"You know, he is actually a really nice guy. I feel sorry that he has to do this. I don't know why he cannot just walk out of priesthood and sin legally."

"Legal sin? That's a new one."

"He is very passionate about being a priest, but his body lets him down."

"Tell me how you met."

"More or less the same way I met all the men I have slept with."

"But you like him more than you like all the others?"

The room was suddenly getting hot. She fanned her face with her hand, watching him, trying to work his mood. It was possible that Boss was just curious about Father Joshua, but she knew it was also possible that he was bothered about there being another man in her life.

"I do. He was respectful from the word go. You do not get a lot of that in my line of work."

He sighed. "So you will see him again?"

"Yes, I will."

She did not miss the look on his face.

"And Boss, please, you will leave him alone."

"I don't know what you mean," he said without looking at her.

"I am not stupid. If anything happens to him, I will blame you."

He put up his hands in surrender.

"Okay. Between me and his God, we should be able to keep him alive for about a hundred years."

"It's not funny!" But she was laughing. She had worried about Boss's reaction to Father Joshua. She had worried about exposing him to Boss, for showing him preference so blatantly.

He was staring at her again.

"What?"

"Do you enjoy sex with him?"

The question ruffled her, but she shrugged casually, like someone used to such questions.

"I don't, actually," she lied. "But he is nice and clean and he treats me well. He is also the only man who ever spoke to me like I am human, like he actually believes I have a brain."

"I think you have a brain," Boss said defensively.

"You are different. I do not sleep with you... not like that!"

"Would you sleep with me tonight?" The question was a near whisper.

She raised her brow.

"Why?"

He shrugged and looked away.

"Because I miss you... it's been two weeks. I thought you would come here last night."

"I am sorry."

"So, will you stay?"

She held his gaze for a while.

"How could I say no to that?"

She smiled, reaching for his hand and brushing it with her soft hands.

"What do you want to happen tonight?"

She was still sore from last night's and that morning's sex. Not that she had much hope in Boss's ability to get her sorer but even oral sex she was going to say no to.

He shrugged.

"I just want to hold you…"

* * *

"You know, besides my parents, you are the second person I have ever told about the man I killed—come to think of it, I did not really tell my parents, but they worked it out." They were sharing a sofa and a blanket as they watched a music channel.

She laughed, "I am honoured… I think."

"What do you think of it?"

"You mean what do I think of you doing what you had to do? I would have done the same."

She shifted on the seat.

"I just get angry that he turned me into the person I am."

"Who was the first?"

"A teacher in high school. Perhaps, one day I will tell you the risks he took for me." He still vividly remembered that one Saturday afternoon during one of his staffroom chats with Mr Choka. It had been a particularly dark day for him for no particular reason. He started crying and then was unable to stop the confessions pouring out of his mouth. Mr Choka had listened with a straight face, like a man who already knew the truth before it was said. Kanja, with every word, had felt relief with every word he spoke, had not even stopped to consider the consequences. After that day, Mr Choka became more protective of Kanja.

"Do you see your parents?" Naliaka snapped him out of his secondary school memories.

He shook his head. "I do not see them. Long ago I opened a bank account for them, sneaked there at night and slipped the bank card under the door with a note. I deposit cash every month and monitor the account so I know they are still alive—at least one of them is."

"Does it bother you that you do not see or talk to them?"

Boss took his time to answer. He had asked himself, enough times, the same questions. Over time, he had convinced himself that it did not bother him, that it would be better to let his parents be.

But he knew the truth, that he was both ashamed and afraid of seeing them. They would probably give him one look and know exactly what he had been up to for the ten years he had stayed away. Most important, he did not want to expose them to his enemies, and he was aware that they often monitored his movements.

"I think it bothers me, but I would rather not dwell on that."

Naliaka thought about her dead mother, and how much she would have loved to see her, how much different her life would have been if her mother had not died.

"I think you should go see them."

"Perhaps, just not yet."

Chapter Eleven

"You are late," Chizi Samuel grumbled. He did not look up. He studied his feet, the same feet he was tapping on the ground.

"How do you know? You do not even have a watch," Kerubo countered as she slammed herself carelessly beside him.

He looked up briefly at the sun, squinting at it. "I no longer need a watch."

"Whatever!" She placed the lunchbox on the bench between her and Samuel before crossing her long legs and arms.

"*Kula.*" Eat.

"I miss *chapati*. Did you make *chapati*?" Chizi Samuel asked with a yawn, finally sitting up and turning to Kerubo.

"And I am coming down with a cold and I need a warm bed."

"Gosh, you are a grumpy one!" Kerubo said with an eye roll as she handed him wet wipes to clean his hands.

The script was familiar. They went through it every two or three weeks. She tried to understand him because, as Chizi often told her, *living on the streets can turn anyone into a right bitch.*

"I really feel unwell this time round," he insisted as he rubbed his nose noisily, wiping it with the wet wipe he had just used to wipe his hands. He missed Kerubo's sneer.

"So were the other thousand times—the problem with crying wolf is, I may not believe you when you are really sick. If you are serious, however, I could get antihistamine."

"What, you are a doctor now?" he snapped as he picked the lunchbox.

"That kind of snapping has to come from a sick person. Is there something else you want, except *chapati?*"

Their eyes met, locked for seconds before he winked.

"You know what I want."

She rolled her eyes at him.

"Mscheeew!"

"If it is sex you want, you should just say you want sex, unless you are looking for pity sex, and that kind of sex is boring."

"I want sex. And *chapati.*"

"See! That wasn't so hard," she smiled, wishing she could rub his thigh but knowing there may be prying eyes that may find it strange that a woman like her would be tenderly rubbing the thigh of a dirty *mad* man.

"If you behave, you may just get both, assuming I am not going to see the Kamau's this weekend."

She sat back against the shed, discreetly watching him eat the pork ribs. She loved how he chewed. Slowly, deliberately. Thoroughly.

Sometimes she tried to emulate his chewing style, but she lacked the patience to chew her food slowly, fifty times, before swallowing.

"There is some change with our guy," Chizi said without looking away from his food.

Kerubo sat up straight, fast. "What changed?"

"A woman…"

"A woman?" Kerubo asked after a prolonged silence.

He turned and looked at her curiously.

"Yes, a woman… oh dear, you still have hang-ups for that guy?" he asked, covering his mouth with his dirty attire so he could giggle.

"Incredible… considering you did not even get to shag him."

"Why would I have hang-ups?"

"Because he didn't want you?"

"I don't want to talk about that. What have you seen?"

"I want to talk about *that*. What is it about the guy that gets your goat so bad?"

Kerubo sat up, folding her hands stubbornly. She was good at keeping calm, but she had been working with Chizi Samuel for so long that he knew her only too well, and that annoyed her. "He just kills me with curiosity. What is he? What does he eat? Who are his friends? Is he straight, bisexual, asexual or gay?"

Chizi chuckled in between chewing.

"I think he is straight, otherwise what else would he be doing with that woman in his house? I have seen them leaving together, in his car, and they certainly are more than friends."

"Who is she?"

"That's what we need to find out. Every great man falls because of a woman he loves."

"You don't know if he loves her."

He looked at her and lifted one brow.

"He looks pretty smitten."

"Mh…"

Samuel was thinking about how tasty the food was, how much he wanted to eat a hot, fresh *chapati* straight from the pan. He thought about what he wanted to do to Kerubo. Kerubo, on her part, thought about the woman, what she was likely to look like, what it is the woman had that Boss had not seen in her.

She thought about the time Boss rejected her advances.

It was months into her Kirinyaga Road assignment when her curiosity to know more about Boss threatened to explode. She begged to be allowed to get close to Boss, so she wore makeup and a wig as a disguise, just in case he had spotted her on Kirinyaga Road before.

Boss was in one of the tens of pubs along Moi Avenue. He, as usual, sat alone. Kerubo, wearing a pair of skin-tight jeans and a tight sleeveless top, watched him from a distance. She was watching the bodyguards, too, careful not to let them see her watching him too much.

She watched him as he sipped on his beer, slowly. She watched him as he spent so much time on the phone, scrolling, answering and making calls. For someone with no known friends, he spent a lot of time on the phone. Then, she walked to his table after she watched him dismiss a hooker.

"Hi!" she put on her best smile, looking down at him.

She faltered because, at close range, he was an unnervingly good-looking man. He did not lift his head fully when he answered her, more like letting his eyes go up and down her body.

"Hi, may I help you?"

"I was wondering if I could sit with you."

"Why?" he asked, finally looking up.

"Because I need to sit somewhere and all the other seats are taken... oh," she added quickly. "I am not trying to be picked up. I am genuinely looking for sitting space."

He laughed and nodded towards the seat.

"Feel free."

She sat down quickly, smiling appreciatively.

"Thank you. I have been standing for so long and it is hard to enjoy a beer while standing."

Boss grunted and went back to scrolling the phone. Usually, it took a few minutes for the men she was trying to trap to hit on her. Not this one.

She looked around and beckoned the waiter, ordering for a beer. That seemed to pique his interest. He looked at her and smiled.

"You don't look like the sort to drink a beer," he remarked, finger still on the phone.

She smirked. "Is there a look?"

He nodded.

"Yes, and you do not have it. You look sort of... delicate?"

"Well, I am not!"

"And what is a beautiful woman like you, one who is not a prostitute, doing here? Alone, in the middle of a hungry men-jungle?"

"I wanted to come for a drink... so I did."

"Why alone? Don't you have friends?"

She shook herself, trying not to look sorry.

"Nope. I don't like baggage."

He laughed.

"That makes the two of us."

"You don't have friends?"

He shrugged.

For a moment, she had thought he was about to confess to something, and that would have shocked, if not alarmed her. But he did not. He shrugged again.

"So, how many of those can you down?" he asked, pointing at her beer.

"Why, you want to compete?"

"Maybe."

"Don't. I can drink you under the table and still walk in a straight line."

They both laughed.

"Somehow I believe that. You have only sipped twice and your beer is halfway."

She shrugged. "We all have vices."

She saw the look on his face. "Don't worry, I am not an alcoholic. I can go for months without a drink… okay, not months, more like days." They laughed again.

"I like you. It's not often you meet women willing to show you their nasty side." She laughed.

"That's because those women are out looking for potential husbands."

"… As opposed to?"

"Looking for someone to have sex with."

Their eyes locked. She saw him pull back a little. "I thought you said you were not a prostitute."

"Because I am not. I don't charge."

He laughed. "I don't know what's worse." He let their eyes lock for a moment. "You look like the sort of girl I would have fun with, but I am a faithful husband."

She laughed to stop herself from accusing him of lying.

"Too bad... perhaps one day you will want to go out of town... I do out of town trips too, and I can even cater for my transport."

She winked at him. He laughed again.

"Are you what they call an independent woman?"

"You could say that."

For hours after that, they sat and drank and laughed some more. He was still constantly on his phone, sometimes he left the table to speak on the phone.

They had been the last in the pub. He offered her a lift, she had hoped he would drive to his house, but instead he had instructed his driver to take her home, she directed them to Chizi's apartment.

He did not ask for her number. Did not ask if he could see her again.

Kerubo had worked as a honey trap since her university days, helping in bringing down drug dealers and rapists in the university. She had done many things as a honey trap, like taking drugs and even having sex. She had lost the number of times she had done those and many other unpalatable things, but she had never, ever, not been able to trap. Until Boss. Years later, she still held a grudge against him.

Chizi Samuel interrupted her trip down memory lane.

"The girl... I... well, I *kinda* know her."

"How?"

"I met her once in a club."

"She is a prostitute."

It was a statement.

Chizi and Kerubo were regular sex partners, but there were no rules. No expectations. They had sex with each other when they were both available and if not, they did it with other people.

Because of the nature of his work and fear of commitment, Chizi preferred prostitutes as he did not have to explain to them why he disappeared for three weeks somewhere. Kerubo was being truthful when she told Boss about picking up random men. Like Chizi Samuel, her dislike for commitment and trust issues did not allow her to date, not forgetting her job required her to sleep with random men because the end justified the means, and information had to be extracted by any means necessary.

Chizi Samuel nodded.

"She is."

"Have you been with her?"

He nodded thoughtfully as he tried to retrieve a piece of meat stuck in his teeth. "When I first saw her going into Boss's building, I thought she looked familiar but she looked very different at night. By the way, she kind of reminds me of you."

"If you are trying to make me feel better, I am not jealous!" she snapped.

"No, really, she does. There is a certain allure about her that is so you. The night I was with her, I thought of you all the time."

"That's disgusting," she declared with a frown.

"Well, shoot me!"

"So Boss is dating a prostitute?"

"It still bothers you that you did not trap him, doesn't it?" he finally asked.

She turned to him slowly and studied him. There was irony in the situation. According to Chizi, Kerubo and the girl Boss was seeing had similarities. Whether they were imagined or not was beside the point, but Kerubo remembered how she had found Boss similar to Chizi, but not the street Chizi; the one who could scrub up. Perhaps it was the height, they were both tall. Perhaps it was the skin colour, they were both chocolate brown. Perhaps it was the muscles, or perhaps it was the look in their eyes. The kind of look that people who had seen death and caused death ended up having, like the eyes reflected the dead souls.

"It doesn't bother me," she spat.

* * *

Seven years ago.

Mato was unwell.

For months, Boss watched life draining out of Mato, like a battery light going out of charge, slowly and surely. Every morning as he fed him a breakfast of tea and *mandazi*, Mato seemed to be a kilogramme lighter than the day before. Then he got too weak to make his plastic collection rounds, that was when Boss took over. Whenever he was around, he fed Mato, sat with him, and rubbed his back when he coughed and spit out bloody phlegm.

"You know, I have never really told you my story," Mato spoke with laboured breath. "I was born on these streets. Everyone I knew back then is dead, including my mother who died when I was ten or so—I can't be sure. Like you, like so many of the boys here, I was sexually molested by those big boys, repeatedly, for years," Mato paused and winced. Boss clenched his butt.

155

"Until the day I got my dagger and stabbed one of them to death. They left me alone after that but I made it my mission to protect other street children from them. I have been killing them, one by one.

Boss nodded, shocking himself with his own calm. He knew Mato always carried a dagger under his clothes. He thought about how he, Mato, would disappear at night, then return with a bloody knife, only wiping it when inside the shack. "He is *bloodthirsty*, and a devil *worshipper*. Once in a while he needs to kill someone…" one of the boys had once whispered to Boss as they watched Mato clean his dagger with soil.

"There is no reason to rape anyone," Mato continued after catching his breath.

"There is a lot of free sex on these streets, as you know." Boss nodded.

"I have killed several of them, but they grow in numbers all the time, like we do. You may have to kill the rest for me."

Boss caught his breath.

"Do not pretend that you do not know I am dying."

"You just have a bad cough," Boss answered weakly.

Mato laughed and coughed.

"It's not just a cough. Look at me… I am wasting away!"

He spread out his hands to display skin and bones. Boss looked at him, but he did not need to look at him to know.

"You are not dying," Boss muttered under his breath, more for his own benefit.

"You are stupid. I have the big one—I got tested by those people who go around testing us."

"What is the big one?"

"You are being stupid, again. I have HIV/AIDS. I have antiretroviral drugs but I am tired of living. I want to die," Boss broke down.

"Stop crying, you are not a baby!" Mato snapped, surprising Boss with the strength of his voice. He wiped his tears and took a deep breath.

"Take care of them, and kill those rapist bastards, or I will haunt you," he laughed and nearly choked on his phlegm. "They are beasts."

He paused to take a deep breath and when he spoke, it was in a voice so low, Boss struggled to hear.

"It shouldn't be hard for you to kill again."

"What do you mean?" he asked, but he was looking away from Mato.

"I know that look in your eye. When you have taken a life, something happens to your eyes. I see that look every time I look at you."

They were quiet for a while, both lost in their own thoughts about death.

"I didn't mean to, but he deserved to die," Boss eventually whispered.

"I am sure he did. I am hardly one to judge you." Mato coughed and winced again. "My only regret about dying is having to go before those rapists. Funny, that we kill people, then we all eventually die. Death is such a humbling event."

Boss swallowed hard.

"I want you to have my dagger." He removed it from under him and handed it to Boss.

"Use it well."

He made Mato comfortable, then left the shack because he did not want Mato to see him cry.

*   *   *

Mato succumbed, but unlike his life, his death was eventful.

A grim mood among the street siblings during the last days replaced the orgies and the squabbling. Instead, they sat around the usual tyre-powered fire, stared at it, muscles tense, like a group of people afraid of breathing. One hot December night, as Mato sat up supported by Boss, he literally sunk into himself. One moment he was half-upright and the next, his torso appeared to sink inside of him.

Boss eased him to the ground and shook him gently as he called his name. The younger boys and girls started crying, Boss ordered the bigger boys to make a stretcher out of wood planks. It was way past midnight, but a large group of street children started the long walk from Kirinyaga Road, through the Central Business District on Kenyatta Avenue, through Uhuru Park, past Community in Upper Hill to Kenyatta National Hospital.

When the hospital security tried to stop them, the sheer numbers and determination of the street children got them through. They pushed their way into the hospital grounds, to the casualty department, led by Boss. Boss's intention was to demand that their friend be attended to immediately, but the minute he looked at all the sick people waiting to see the doctors, he imagined if God had a waiting room, it would look like that. There seemed to be a competition on who would die before the other. The nurses and the doctors were constantly on the move, looking harassed but determined.

Two hours in, and Boss made a difficult decision to leave Mato's lifeless, drooling body at the casualty reception. He looked at him one last time, lying on a bare, cold floor, a floor as cold as his body had become, and muttered an apology. He signalled the others to follow him outside.

"He is dead," he announced when they all gathered around him outside the casualty department. A few of them started crying again.

Boss walked towards the gate first and fast, but only because he did not want anyone to see him crying. The others reluctantly followed him, most of them wailing Mato's name.

That night, Boss sniffed glue, but it was the first and last time he did.

That same night marked the beginning of his reign as The Boss.

* * *

Boss's street life changed constantly, but some things remained constant. The years did not rush, neither did they drag. Days turned into nights, nights turned into days. Some of them had grim weather, others were full of sunshine; sometimes, the stars could be seen above the city lights. He liked to watch the stars, but he never was up to watch the sunrise, and he had developed a strange relationship with sunsets—they made him uncomfortable.

Some of his street siblings died from lynching, others, like Mato, from diseases and drugs, others disappeared, but with each death, there were new additions.

With each addition, Boss's reputation preceded him; new members were warned beforehand. It helped that he was the strongest, and because he was the only one who did not do drugs, he was the healthiest.

* * *

Mato's death was a blow, and Boss became clingy to Monde, the disabled hawker who had fed him after he was drugged and robbed. Monde's makeshift shop was where Boss went to cry after he lost Mato, it was where he went to if he needed adult conversations, it was where he went to watch the city go by.

Besides being a friend, Monde was many things to Boss, including a teacher on how to be street-smart. He was a genius at reading people. "That one is a pickpocket. See how shifty he is, and how he looks at handbags."

"Do you see that man wearing a suit and asking different people for directions? Don't be deceived, he is drugging people." Boss peered closely at that one, trying to work out if he was the one who had drugged him.

"That one is a city council official... terrible fellows."

"You see that one over there, leaning on that wall? That's an undercover cop." Boss studied the cop longer than he studied the *dragger*.

"Do you smoke *ganja*?" Monde asked the question so casually, that Boss asked him to repeat it.

"Of course not," Boss had answered, picking a sweet from Monde's table and throwing it in his mouth.

"Have you seen what drugs do to the street kids?"

Monde laughed.

"You can still do drugs and not turn into an idiot."

"That's a lie. Why are you asking me that, anyway?"

Monde leaned closer to Boss, who was sitting beside his wheelchair on the floor, and whispered.

"I have some here… high grade, from the land of Haile Selassie, Jah, Rastafari."

"You do drugs? In your condition?"

"What condition?" Monde snapped defensively. "My legs may not be functional, but everything else is!"

"Whatever. So you do drugs?"

"No way. I do not want to turn into an idiot." They laughed. Monde leaned again.

"I sell."

"What? To whom?"

"Hah!" he sneered, sitting back up.

"Clearly you do not know that half the people walking the streets are on some sort of drug or another."

He pointed at passing crowds. Boss followed his hand as it pointed, looking closely at people's faces.

"If you think it is possible to make proper cash by selling sweets and cheap, illegally packed untreated water, then you are proving that you do not need drugs to be an idiot. *Hii Nairobi lazima ujanjaruke.*" In Nairobi you have to be a step ahead.

"I wondered how you could afford expensive clothes by selling sweets."

"You could help me sell."

"Sell what?"

"Shoes… idiot! You look like a clever guy on the outside but I am beginning to think the inside is full of stupidity… Listen to me."

Boss found himself leaning towards Monde.

"You could make some good money. I know my customers, but I cannot take the drugs to them, obviously."

He looked at his legs.

"I had a guy who used to do that for me but two days ago, he was lynched."

"For selling drugs?"

"Of course not. Drug dealers get shot, not lynched. The stupid fool used to double up as a thief. His forty days were over."

"Oh."

"But life goes on. People need their fix. I got another guy, but he is stealing from me. I need someone I can trust."

"… And you thought of me… how sweet."

Boss chewed on his lip thoughtfully, his eyes fixed on a man he was sure was an undercover agent.

"What if I am arrested?"

"If you stick to the rules, you will be fine."

"What if the cop over there…" he pointed with his mouth. "What if he arrests me?"

"The only reason he would arrest you is if I refused to give him his cut."

"He knows you sell drugs?"

"Dude, it's the only way I stay in business, and alive. Take it from me, if you are going to choose to do illegal stuff, you need the law on your side."

Boss laughed.

"How does that even make sense to you?"

"We have crooked cops, and they are the ones you need to keep happy."

"How much is in it for me?"

"Enough to get you off the streets. Enough to buy you soap and wash that stinky body of yours."

"I don't stink!"

"You do, too. Very badly." They chuckled as Boss smelled his own armpit and sneered.

"If you say yes to this, you may have to leave the streets, perhaps stay with me for some time until you can sort yourself out."

"Give me two days to think about it. I have a whole family depending on me."

Chapter Twelve

Oti had always worried about his next meal, or if the money he had would last until the next job came through. He was born by worried parents who bred worried children. Unlearning all that was hard. Part of his unlearning involved going to the supermarket and buying stuff he had no use for but that he bought, anyway, because he could afford it.

One evening while watching a movie and drinking beer, the shopping bags sprawled on the floor between him and the television kept obstructing him. At ten o'clock, he hauled all the bags to his parents' house. That was the first time he did that, it was not the last time. During those times, he would put the bags outside their door, knock on it and quickly hide at the corner and wait. His mother always opened the door.

She would look at the branded supermarket bags first, then look both ways before picking them and shutting the door behind her. Sometimes she would do it quietly, other times she would thank the invisible philanthropist.

The third time he made a delivery, his mother peered into the dark, the opposite direction of where he was, something that had made him chuckle.

"Oti! Oti! I know it is you. Thank you for this, but remember the days of a thief are forty. Forty only. You just remember that."

It was possible she meant that she would catch him at his delivery at some point, but he doubted.

That shopping for his parents had nothing to do with his duty as a son. He shopped because he had too much money. Money he could not bank, because he had no bank account. He, like all of his siblings, was born at home, his mother assisted by other slum mothers. None of the births were reported, and as far as the government of Kenya was concerned, he, Leviticus Otieno, did not exist.

A few months into working for Boss, Oti moved to a bigger, better house. He could afford to move out of the slum, but Kibera, in the midst of the chaos and the dirt, provided anonymity and security he did not believe could be found anywhere else. That was before Jonte told him that Boss knew where he lived.

"How? Did you show him?"

"If you are asking that, you still have a long way to go before understanding how Boss works."

Kibera was a maze only understood by those who lived within it. Were it a straight line, his new house would be not more than five hundred metres from his parents' house. It did not however, stand on faecal matter, or next to the railway line, and he did not have to listen to his neighbours having sex, or snoring, or gossiping. It was a one-bedroom mud-house, but one could only tell that from the outside. Inside, the smooth whitewashed walls kept the secrets of the building material hidden. One corner of the sitting room was designated for the kitchen. The toilet and bathroom were within the house, but it was a long-drop toilet—he often wondered how they had dug it, and what would happen when it spilled over.

He had two sofa seats, an average size flat screen television standing on a wooden stand, a coffee table covered with both full and empty cans of beer, and his three remote controls. When he bought a carpet, it had taken him weeks to remember to leave his shoes at the door.

A five by six feet bed was his most prized possession. He had grown up competing for space with his siblings. On the bed, he could stretch in whichever direction. Often, he woke up with a start in the middle of the night, having dreamed that one of his siblings was asking him to make space for them.

The mini fridge had no food in it, but it had beer. He did not own utensils except for two plastic tumblers he used to drink water. He ate in food kiosks near Kibera.

Oti's days were spent within the confines of the slums, his house. His nights were either used to terrorise Nairobi car owners, or spent with prostitutes in lodgings.

At first, through the excitement, Oti kept count of the robberies, but after so many, he decided to only keep count of his money that was kept in a wooden box, under lock and key, under his bed, and at various spots up on the ceiling. He spent it carelessly, gave it to his parents, upgraded his prostitutes, and still couldn't get through it.

* * *

It was a slow day at the shop. With all the other workers at the back of the shop having lunch, Kerubo sat behind the cash counter, chewing her nails thoughtfully, once in a while scratching her head,

167

and in between thinking how she needed to visit the salon to sort the scalp itch.

When the man walked in, she felt him, rather than saw him. Since she started working at the shop, she had always wondered how she would react if there was a robbery, if she would use the gun. The man did not make her hair stand on end though, so she did not reach for the gun. It was just a light feeling of discomfort.

If your hair does not stand on end, chances are you are fine. Adrenaline from a criminal always triggers those hairs. That was Samuel's repeated advice.

Slowly, she brought her head up and looked at him, gauging him. She knew he was a criminal, but she also knew he was not there to rob her. Perhaps on recce. She smiled.

"Hello," she said, standing up with feet astride, something she had learned from Cecilia whom she often partnered with when honey-trapping needed more than one person. Kerubo was very good at flying kicks and was certain if need be, she could easily do one across the counter.

He had a beautiful smile. Most criminals did.

"Hi, I am looking for my sister."

"Your sister?" Kerubo asked, lifting her brow.

"I believe she works here."

He was looking around the shop at the products. "Her name is Selina."

"Oh."

The *oh* was said as she took a step back, thinking about all the conversations she had had with Selina during their tête-à-tête. How she suspected her brother was a thief, but there was no proof. Kerubo peered at him, studying him. He may have had an evil aura around him, but somewhere in his face was the face of Selina, like a darker version of her. "You do resemble her."

"You must be her boss," he smiled.

"I am. I will fetch her for you."

She was back within a minute, a confused Selina in tow.

"Jonte, what's wrong?"

"Hello to you too, dear sister."

"Sorry. I just did not expect you. Is everything okay?" Kerubo, standing beside Selina with crossed arms, looked from one sibling to another, taking in their tension and distrust, wondering what her life would have been like if she had a sibling.

Jonte laughed.

"Nothing. I was in the neighbourhood and I realised I have never come to see you. That's all."

"Oh," Selina sounded relieved.

"Will you excuse me?" Kerubo asked, picking Chizi Samuel's lunchbox.

"I will let you two catch up." She could feel both their gazes on her as she crossed the road to the bus stand, to Samuel.

"You are early, and flustered," Chizi remarked, looking at her through half-closed eyes.

"Yeah. Selina has a visitor," she said, placing the lunchbox on his lap.

"Good for her," Chizi answered, spitting on the pavement.

"Why do you keep spitting on the ground? It's uncouth!"

"Sorry," he said, sounding anything but sorry.

"Once in a while I need to spit out the taste of the streets."

"It's her brother. I am sure I have told you that she suspects he is some sort of thug, which is just a nice way of saying he is one."

He nodded.

"Okay. There are a lot of criminals walking the street, some we even know by name, yet we don't care about them unless they interfere with you-know-who, or if they actually carry out their criminal activities here. Is there a reason why we should care about this one?"

She shrugged.

"I don't know. Maybe there is nothing to worry about but for all the years Selina has worked at the shop, he has never visited."

"There is always a first."

"I would be okay if Selina did not look so shaken when I told her he was looking for her."

"Mh… families, ey?"

Kerubo shook her head.

"He said he was in the neighbourhood and… you know. What if he is here for recce? What if he is looking for you-know-who?"

Samuel shifted on the bench.

"That's a possibility. What do you think?"

"Perhaps follow him as he leaves the shop?"

"Okay."

"Come on, eat quickly. He may not be there for long. They don't look like they have a lot to talk about… oh, wait. There he is," she pointed with her mouth, using her hands to take away the half-opened lunchbox.

"I will bring the food later. Come on, quick before he disappears."

Kerubo returned to the shop and found Selina sitting on a bag of cement, staring into space.

"You okay?" she asked cautiously.

Selina turned lazily to her friend and sighed. "Yeah. I am, thanks."

"So why do you look like someone died?"

Selina shrugged.

"I… I don't know. Jonte, my brother… he… he just gave me a lot of money."

"Shouldn't that be a good thing?"

Another shrug. "Under normal circumstances, yeah."

Kerubo counted five seconds before asking the next question.

"Why are these not normal circumstances?"

Selina allowed her eyes to linger on Kerubo for a few seconds.

"Dad needs this money. Jonte wants me to give it to him."

Another pause.

"Why can't he do that himself?"

Selina focussed on Kerubo again, like she wanted to see if she could be trusted.

"I have told you before that we suspect Jonte is not very straight?"

Kerubo nodded.

"Sometime back, Dad told him to get an honest job. Jonte was offended, and insisted he is a car salesman. He called Jonte's money blood money, and said his Christian faith did not allow him to accept any more of it from Jonte."

"Wow."

Selina sighed before covering her face with her palm. "Dad is unwell…"

"You never told me that!" Kerubo said accusingly.

Selina shrugged. "He needs an urgent heart operation. I do not know who among my siblings told Jonte, but one of them did."

"O… okay. What do you want to do?"

Selina shut her eyes like one in pain, then shook her head in frustration. "I don't know. I just don't know. I need this money. But what if we are right and it is blood money?"

Kerubo shrugged, unable to see the dilemma. "The blood is not on your hands."

"It would be, because I know it is blood money. What would you do?"

Kerubo looked at Selina for a while then looked away, unable to take in the frustration, the uncertainty in her friend's eyes. She knew what Selina wanted to do, she also knew that Selina wanted Kerubo to give the go-ahead, perhaps to shift the blame of blood money to someone else.

Kerubo remembered how unmoved she was when Mrs Kamau told her that her mother was ailing. How she never felt compelled to attend her father's burial. "If I loved my father and was desperate for him to live, I would take the money without a second thought."

Selina gave a long sigh of relief.

"But how will I explain the source of the money? As recently as yesterday, nobody had any." She touched her jeans, allowing Kerubo to see the bulge.

"Tell him I lent it to you."

Selina broke down.

"Thank you."

Chizi Samuel trailed Jonte, but the trail lasted ten minutes because Jonte hopped into a *matatu* destined for somewhere in Eastlands.

* * *

That evening.

Chizi Samuel waited for Kirinyaga Road to retreat into the shell of silence and darkness.

At day time, people moved about like triggered safari ants. Drivers honked impatiently at the constant gridlocks, motorbikes were ridden on pavements, sending the rightful users jumping into shops for safety. The mechanics were a cheerful and loud lot, but they were a menace to anyone not interested in having their vehicle repaired when they insisted on diagnosing perfectly working vehicles stuck in traffic. The tropical sun seemed to burn hotter in downtown Nairobi, making everyone jittery and edgy.

At night, the tentacles of madness recoiled. Unlike the richer parts of the city, there were more dead street lights than working ones. The lit houses were occupied by Asian families who stubbornly refused to vacate the convenience of city houses, houses their forefathers had occupied during the scramble for Nairobi. A street family, the same one that had brought up Boss, the same one he still controlled, lived on the same spot at the end of the street.

When Kirinyaga Road went to sleep, it was the cue for Chizi Samuel to transform himself. Tonight, he was starting his one-week break from the streets. Cleaning his face was always the hardest part of his job. He would use sheets on sheets of disposable face wipes, and only stopped when his skin started feeling raw. Then he would shed off his sacks and wear jeans and a tee-shirt.

The stink was harder to get off. The smell of crime and days of not having a shower penetrated deep into his skin. It was a smell that the sponge bath with bottled water never got rid of. The stink no longer bothered him, but it bothered other people he came into contact with. The disgusted looks he got from people in public

173

transport was the reason he stopped riding *matatus* or taxis home, why Kerubo now drove his car to the city and handed him the keys at lunch time.

* * *

As Samuel climbed up the stairs to his third-floor apartment, the speed and force of his heartbeat threatened to destabilise his footing. He was not unfit, but the excitement was always so much that by the time he opened his door with shaky hands and shut it behind him, he would have to lean on it for a while to calm down.

He flicked on the light switch and continued standing by the door, taking in the room, not only to re-familiarise himself, but to check if there was anything out of place. Satisfied that nobody had broken in, in his absence, he kicked off his shoes and went straight to the bathroom to run a bath. He would have two of those. The first one would stain the bathtub with grime and grease and stink. He would drain that, clean the tub with an antiseptic before running a second bath, one he would lace with a cocktail of his favourite aromas. Two scented candles would be at the foot end of the bath. By the time he was satisfied there was no smell of the street, his skin would be creased like an old piece of cloth. He would then oil every accessible part of it.

Only then did he walk into other rooms, starting with the kitchen to fetch a cold can of beer from the fridge. As he downed the beer, he went to the home office to file reports, something he liked to get over with as soon as possible. He would then check emails from his clearing and forwarding business.

In between, he longingly looked at the one side of the wall filled with books. They were some of the things he missed most when he was on the streets. Books and a woman's naked body next to him.

Tonight, as he did with every first night he was home, he ordered for a takeaway. Like he always did on his first night back, he got drunk, and watched television. Not even his priced books would be touched, those would have to wait an extra day to get his attention.

* * *

As Chizi Samuel settled in, Kerubo sat in her house in Ngara and like she often did, she thought about her life. How she had come to be what she was, mostly damaged, a diagnosis she readily gave herself.

Unwillingly, because it left her feeling melancholic, she thought about her childhood. She grew up under violent and alcoholic parents but luckily, they were just violent with each other. She was simply ignored. Their fights were both physically and verbally vicious, and she found herself caught in the crossfire several times before she learned to escape in time. Sometimes, they would go for days without speaking a word to her. Other times, they looked at her like they had never seen her before. She believed in miracles, because it was a miracle that she grew up.

She had hated them, but as she grew older, she felt nothing for them.

Often, they forgot to feed her. Sometimes, they arrived from work or alcohol dens carrying *mútura,* then use their dirty fingers with even dirtier nails to pinch off a small piece for her.

Benevolent neighbours fed her, but her main source of food was the rubbish bins at the market where she spent most of her days doing everything from rummaging to sleeping behind shops to staring at well-fed humans, yet, she had no memory of falling sick. She also had no memory of when or how she started scavenging, but she remembered pretty much taking care of herself from the moment she woke up. Many were the days she would not see her parents because by the time they returned home, she would already be on the floor, asleep, careful not to be in their way as several times she had been stepped on.

Mrs Kamau found Kerubo rummaging through the market bins, and Kerubo's life changed. She was six years old.

"What are you doing?" Mrs Kamau, with a *kíondo* on her back, paused to ask.

Kerubo stood up, ready to bolt. It would not have been the first time. Strangers often told her off, demanded to know where her parents were. Sometimes they chased her from the dumpsite. She would hide and wait for them to disappear, then resume.

Mrs Kamau was different. She had kind eyes, and she offered Kerubo a banana from the *kíondo*.

"Have you eaten anything today?" Kerubo shook her head.

"You poor thing. Where are your parents?" Kerubo shook her head again, as she looked into the distance. With a limited social life, her speech was still struggling to develop.

"Come with me." Kerubo looked at Mrs Kamau's stretched hand with suspicion.

"I will buy tea and *mandazi* for you as you tell me about yourself." At that moment, her stomach rumbled with hunger and excitement.

Inside the market hotel, Mrs Kamau watched Kerubo put chunks of *mandazi* in her mouth, chunks that should have choked the little girl. She watched her, in silence, as she drank the hot tea fast, like one who had a timeline for finishing the food.

Five mandazis and two cups of tea later, Kerubo burped.

"What's your name?" Mrs Kamau finally asked.

"Kerubo."

"How old are you?"

Kerubo averted her gaze.

"Where are your parents?"

All Mrs Kamau got was that distant look before the little girl turned away to look through the glass window, shoulders stooped to a near slump.

"Can you show me where you live?" Kerubo nodded again.

They found a group of laughing women in the compound. Some were doing their laundry, others just watching the washers. All that stopped when Kerubo and Mrs Kamau walked into the compound. She pointed at the house where she lived. It was locked.

Mrs Kamau turned to the women. By the time they finished narrating Kerubo's harrowing life story, Mrs Kamau was fighting tears.

Within a month, with the help of the area chief because the parents could not be bothered, Mrs Kamau had enrolled Kerubo in school. Every morning on the way to school, Kerubo would stop by her benefactor's for breakfast and packed lunch. After school, she would pass by to wash herself and eat supper.

Kerubo topped the primary school national exams in her district. For a week, she became a mini-celebrity that everyone from the common man to the leaders wanted to be associated with. That week, her parents managed to keep off alcohol, or at least look half-sober. They still looked at her like a stranger would. They received food and clothes donations, stuff that her parents sold to raise money for alcohol once the excitement died.

And she was sponsored through high school by a well-wisher, saving Mrs Kamau the trouble.

She qualified for university.

"Will we get gifts like last time?" her drunken mother asked when she delivered the news of her exam results.

Kerubo walked out, a lump in her throat, tears so blinding her that she almost bumped onto the door frame. That was the day she started feeling *nothing* towards her parents.

She moved out. To sustain herself, she did casual jobs that included washing clothes and working on farms.

Her parents may have lived a few hundred metres from her, but the day she walked out was the last time she would see her mother alive, and her father barely alive.

* * *

Chizi Samuel was an ex-soldier familiar with sleeping rough. Sleeping in the bush alongside snakes and possible human and wild predators had been daunting when he was still an active soldier, but he preferred that to spending nights on the cold pavements of the concrete jungle.

He was a man used to sleeping on the ready, with all his senses on alert, and that was why, when Kerubo's call woke him up the following day at nine in the morning, he was still holding a still upright half-full can of beer.

"You sound nicely groggy. Did I wake you up?" Chizi Samuel grumbled.

"I guess you deserve to *ass* around. Anyway, I am calling to tell you that I am taking Mrs Kamau to see her mother in Nyeri."

Samuel forced himself to sit up, careful not to make sudden movements because his head was banging.

"That sucks," he said and yawned. "I had such beautiful plans for us."

"I was *kinda* looking forward to taking care of those cobwebs you are dragging about." They both laughed.

"I will probably see you on Monday evening."

He was disappointed, but not heartbroken. He liked spending time with Kerubo for more than the good sex they had together. Kerubo was his female version, and he loved her. They thought alike, both wanted a better world, both accepted the world was messed up, but were both still willing to do their part.

He placed the beer can on the nearest stool and stretched his body, starting with the neck. Satisfied he had not developed brittle bones in his sleep, he went to the kitchen for the previous night's leftover food and a beer as he planned his day.

First, I need to roast goat ribs and eat, he thought. He also needed to visit his barber, get a massage, buy new underwear, and stop by the supermarket to stock up for the week.

* * *

By six in the evening, Chizi Samuel had ticked everything on his to-do list, except having a woman. At eight o'clock, he left his apartment.

When he picked the same pub he had first met Kiki, there was only a glimmer of hope that he would find her there. The pub was busy, humming with conversations and bursts of laughter. He selected a table at a vantage point that allowed him to observe, ordered for a beer and allowed his eyes to sweep across the room.

When he saw her, he spluttered his drink, which found its way to some people on the next table. He apologised without looking at them, his eyes digging hard towards Kiki, blinking several times to ensure he was not hallucinating. His instinct was to walk to her immediately, but he held himself back.

He watched her. She was still on the prowl, he could tell that from her body language. That confused him a little. Was the biggest thug in Nairobi okay with his woman peddling herself? Was it possible that the two were just friends? Over the weeks, he had watched them many times, and there was nothing but sexual gestures between them.

Having observed her for over twenty minutes, he noticed that she kept looking towards one point, not for long, but for someone trained to look for details, he noticed. So he followed her eye-line and nearly spluttered his drink again.

"I will be damned!" he declared, looking from Kiki to Jonte, back to Kiki several times.

"What the heck is going on?"

He dug out his phone. He needed to talk to Kerubo. Then he paused, because Kiki was talking to a man. She was laughing, flirtatious even. Samuel cursed under his breath, then relaxed when he saw Kiki shaking her head, dismissing the man. So maybe she was no longer selling herself. But then there was that exchange of quick looks with Jonte.

When Samuel dialled Kerubo's number, he let his eyes linger on Jonte who was drinking bottled water, while his companion was on soda. They both sat facing Kiki's direction. Was it possible that they were her bodyguards? He knew Boss used bodyguards for himself, perhaps he was doing it for his girlfriend?

"Hey, missed me?" Kerubo answered.

"Goodness, are you in hell? It's noisy, wherever you are."

"And how is Nyeri?"

"Nice and quiet. I can count the stars, and it's a full moon."

Chizi Samuel smiled, soaking in her jolly tone.

"But you did not call to ask me how Nyeri is. What's up?"

Chizi Samuel smiled.

"I am out and about, and you will never guess who is in the same pub with me?"

"Boss and his prostitute girlfriend?"

"Ouch. Do you have to call her prostitute?"

"She is one, isn't she? Plus we do not know her name."

"I once knew her name. Anyway, she is here, Boss is not. Someone else is though."

"You are killing me with suspense."

He smiled again, imagining her rolling her eyes with impatience.

"Jonte."

"Which Jonte?"

"How many do you know?"

"Selina's brother?"

"Bingo!"

"They are together?"

He shook his head. "No and yes…"

"What does that even mean?"

"I am trying to work it out. They are sitting separately, but they are exchanging knowing looks. Jonte is with another man. Rough looking *kinda* guy. I am wondering if they could be her bodyguards."

"But you do not sound convinced. You think Jonte knows Boss?"

"I don't think, I know he does."

Kerubo took time to answer. He could imagine her head working.

"What do you want to do?"

"Get to the bottom of this."

"Please do not try and pick her. If she is his girlfriend, you do not want an altercation with him."

"I cannot try and pick Jonte. I prefer women because they are softer and they have boobs."

She giggled. "You know what I mean."

"Do not worry about me. I am a big boy. She has already rejected two men in the last ten minutes. I may be the lucky number three."

He disconnected the call, stood up, touched his waistline to feel for his gun, and then remembered he had left it in the car.

She saw him approaching, and smiled. He tried on his best smile. Kerubo often told him to smile often because he had a good smile. It seemed to work. He was also a little disappointed because she did not seem to remember him.

"Hey…do you mind if I…stand next to you, seeing that there are no free seats?"

"Absolutely not. I was getting fed up talking to myself," she said charmingly. He noticed her looking towards Jonte.

"Surely, that cannot be. A *hot* woman like you cannot be allowed to be on her own." He was leaning sideways towards the counter, facing her. She turned her whole body towards him, giving him the full view of her short skirt, one that just needed to ride higher an inch and it would reveal the secrets of her underwear. She placed one of her manicured hands on her lap, rubbing it softly. He watched shamelessly.

"I have had some offers for company, they were all boring." She said this as she leaned closer to him, giving him a partial view of her bust. It was a small bust, he already knew that from their previous encounter, but he loved it.

"It's your lucky day. I am as charming as they come," he said, touching her chin with his index finger, feeling the excitement of danger.

Then she sat back suddenly, peering at him. "Have we met before?" Naliaka's head was working furiously, trying to remember if it was before or after Boss, that she had met him.

"Good memory," he said, impressed.

"Yes, we have met before. It was interesting."

She cocked her head. "How interesting?"

"Oh, I don't know how to put it, but certain parts of me still miss you," she laughed, touching his freshly shaved scalp.

"I just may give you a repeat."

"Admit it—you miss my prowess."

"Such faith in yourself!" she said with a giggle.

He looked at her empty glass and nodded towards it. "Would you like your soda refilled?"

She looked at him, then at her empty glass, back and forth several times before finally settling her eyes on him. "What do you want?"

"Well...this may surprise you, but I just want to chat."

She almost believed him. He looked so serious, but there was that hint of a smile that appeared after a few seconds.

"Puh! And I want to be a bishop. Men like you don't want to chat with me."

"That is really sad, but believe it or not, I would like to chat, besides other things," he said and winked before rubbing his nose vigorously, leaving Naliaka to wonder if the rubbing was a part of the joke or his nose was actually itchy.

She chuckled. "What would you like to chat about?" she asked, deciding to indulge him.

He shrugged.

"Have you never just wanted to chat, about nothing in particular?" Samuel was half serious.

In his line of undercover work, he did not get to talk to many people. Kerubo was at the top of his list, and he appreciated that he could talk more than work with her. He spoke to Onyango, his boss, but not often enough. He spoke to his fellow undercover agents, but only about work.

He was an only child of rich but now dead parents, and they never were the chatting type. He was a soldier who retired prematurely, and it often saddened him that he had not made any real friends while in the army. When he picked up women, he did so with crossed fingers that he could have above average conversations with them.

"I have, but right now I am working. If you just want to talk, you still have to pay me." She took the empty glass and started sniffing at it, eyes trained on him.

"So if I pay you, you will listen?"

"That's what I said. But I charge in advance."

He laughed.

"I believe that is what they call cut-throat business." She nodded.

"Where do you live?"

He caught himself in time, about to ask why she was not taking him to a hotel like last time. He remembered her insisting that she did not go to strangers' houses.

"Here and there, but tonight, Kitengela. It's a long ride." He did own a house in Kitengela, where he took women who were not Kerubo.

"Are you sober enough to drive?"

He laughed loudly.

"I believe I am."

His phone vibrated in his pocket. As he checked the message from Kerubo warning him to be careful, he saw Naliaka tapping on her phone furiously. At the other corner of his eye, he saw Jonte on the phone. Again, he knew there was a possibility of him being paranoid, plus there was still the strong possibility that Jonte was a bodyguard and she was telling him she was leaving.

I will be fine. He tapped his reply to Kerubo.

"Girlfriend?" Kiki was asking.

He looked at her in confusion.

"I mean, is your girlfriend disturbing you?" she asked, pointing at his phone with her mouth.

He laughed.

"You could say that, but tonight, I would like to call you my girlfriend."

* * *

Naliaka and Chizi Samuel walked out hand-in-hand, like old lovers. A couple of times, they looked at each other. He grinned at her, she giggled. He pinched her bottoms, she yelped playfully.

As he opened the car door for her, a sudden feeling of doom descended on him. At the same time, he had a feeling of being watched. He looked around him, but there were many people going about their business—he could not see Jonte. His phone beeped with a message. He did not bother with it.

"Are you okay?" she asked from inside the car. He had been standing outside her side of the door for almost a minute.

"I am fine. I was trying to decide if I should take a piss in the club toilets, or if I can hold it all the way home."

She laughed.

"Do like every other man does and piss behind the car."

"The horror. I have a urine-shy dick," he said as he sat behind the wheel. Samuel hated taking a pee in the open during his time off, because he spent most of his time peeing on the streets.

He eased his Mercedes Benz out of the parking lot and drove off. In his rear view mirror, he saw a vehicle behind him, then another one, and he laughed at himself. It was a Saturday night, it was only natural that there would be many vehicles on the road. His gun was never in the glove compartment, he preferred to put it in the door pocket beside him. He touched it and felt reassured, just before tucking it in his sock.

"You are busy on the phone," he remarked.

She laughed. "I am just chatting to a friend. I am done though."

He put his hand on her soft thigh. She squeezed his hand.

"You are such a beautiful woman, you know that?"

She still looked as beautiful as he had first seen her.

"Aren't you going to ask me why I do what I do?"

He chuckled.

"Why would I do that? I did not ask you last time, I will not ask you today. I want to have sex with you, not redeem you."

She laughed loudly, feeling genuinely amused.

"You are funny."

"I hear that a lot."

She laughed again.

"So you get many men asking you that?" His hand was riding up her thigh.

186

"Like you have no idea. It's actually a very annoying question because, if they were genuinely bothered by what I do, why do they come to me?"

He shrugged.

"It is their way of trying to convince themselves that they are not bad people; that they are trying to make you see the error of your ways."

"By shagging and paying me for it? Please…"

There was still a vehicle behind him.

"Remind me your name."

"Kiki."

"Nice. Mine is Samuel."

That was when it happened, and he had time to compose himself because he saw it coming. They were approaching the junction that branched off to Imara Daima when the vehicle behind him suddenly accelerated and cut him off. If he had not screeched to a stop, they would have bumped his side of the car and activated the airbags. Kiki screamed. He cursed and felt for his gun. Times like these were the reason he wore sports socks, the only ones that could hold his gun safely. His other sock had his spare phone and some money.

Just in time too because within seconds, Jonte and his sidekick were with them.

He could have easily taken them, shot them both within seconds, but he did not. He was curious.

Oti had a gun on his temple and warned him against any resistance, and Samuel put up his hands in submission. Jonte roughly pulled Kiki out of the passenger seat, pushed her in the back seat, replaced Kiki on the passenger seat, and then Oti joined Kiki. It must have all taken about ten seconds.

"Drive!" Jonte ordered.

With calmness that slightly bothered Naliaka, Chizi Samuel reversed the car, drove round the car blocking him and pulled away. "Drive faster!" He did. "Stop!" He pulled by the side of the road just before the intersection going into the JKIA. "Quick, give me your phones and wallets. Both of you!" They did. "What's your bank pin number?" He gave them. "Now, get out!" They did, and they both stood, shivering in the night cold, and watched his tail lights being quickly swallowed by distant darkness.

Then Samuel started laughing.

Naliaka started crying.

"Why are you laughing?" she demanded, feeling slightly irritated. He was changing the usual script. He was supposed to be hysterical, like all the others.

"What the *eff*? I just got jacked!"

"And that's funny? You just lost an expensive car. They took your phone and your money. They will probably sweep your bank. They took everything I had. What's funny about that?"

"I don't know about you, but the car will stall in about two minutes, and the minute they put the wrong pin on that phone, it will be useless. They better be able to run very fast too, because they are already being pursued."

Naliaka gasped. "How… how?"

He laughed again.

"Because, when you can afford such a car, you can afford to stop thieves in their tracks, literally. I activated a security code through a button inside the car. Lastly, I gave them the wrong pin—everything they have taken from me is useless to them."

She was thinking how upset Jonte and Oti would be. Then she started smiling, then stopped because the phone hidden in her bra was vibrating.

"What's that?" he demanded.

"A phone... I have two phones and I hide one... well, in my boobs."

Then he burst out in laughter for the second time.

"I like you." He meant it. "Well, pick it."

She did. She started crying on the phone, explaining how she had been carjacked with a friend and abandoned on a dangerous section of Mombasa Road.

"It is alright. Do not come for me. I will call an Uber," she concluded before disconnecting.

As she spoke on the phone, Samuel was taking a piss and watching her at the same time. Through the darkness, through the lights of one or two vehicles that passed by, he noted her body language. His heightened senses knew she was acting, but he did not worry too much. He was happy enough that the puzzle of Boss, Kiki and Jonte had finally fallen into place.

* * *

Seconds turned into minutes, the two figures stood by the road. Every taxi they summoned cancelled as soon as they realised they were being summoned to the middle of nowhere.

"You cannot really blame them. If I were them, I would cancel too," Samuel joked in encouragement.

The weather was not kind either. The area surrounding the airport was known to behave like desert weather at night, crispy, cold and windy. In her skimpy clothes, she was shivering, he could hear her teeth clutter. He pulled her towards him, encamping her inside his jacket. She shivered again then sighed.

"Thank you," she whispered, letting her head rest on his chest and breathing in his cologne.

"You are welcome. This way, if the lions find us, they may hesitate to attack because we will look like confusing prey—big with four arms and four legs and four eyes." He meant it to be another joke, but he felt her tense and lifted her head to look around her.

"There are lions?"

"We are at the periphery of Nairobi National Park."

Neither could tell who initiated the kiss. It was long, and sensual, and comforting, and it provided both with the warmth both their bodies craved for. Then they started to giggle.

"We must look a sight," he remarked, pulling away from her. "Do you think there will be social media posts about us with videos from people driving by?"

She giggled. "They probably think we are ghosts."

"I can even imagine the stories; that we must have been lovers, we had an accident on this very spot and our ghosts have refused to rest."

They laughed.

"Anyway, we better find a way to get out of here. Give me your phone."

He could have used his own phone, but he was hesitant about letting her know he also had a secret phone.

"Who are you going to call?"

"I have a friend who lives around here. If he is home, he will rescue us. You are still welcome to come to my house."

As Chizi Samuel made the call, Naliaka considered the pros and cons of going with him. She wanted to, at least her body wanted to. Even her mind wanted to because he was so funny and calm, and she wanted to know a little more about a man who could manage to be so calm in such a storm. But also, she was hesitant, because she was feeling vulnerable around him, afraid that she may let something slip.

In the end, she opted to go home. Chizi Samuel's friend, who was really a workmate, had picked them up, and they dropped her home first.

* * *

Kerubo was laughing on the phone.

"You are kidding me, right?"

Chizi Samuel, on the other end of the phone, was also laughing. When he was dropped home, he showered and had a can of beer, one he had hoped would bring down his adrenaline levels, but they had remained up there. Morning found him watching television, opening his sixth can of beer.

"I wish I was kidding."

"I told you to be careful, but you didn't listen."

"I didn't get myself shot, did I? In fact, you should be congratulating me because I now know how Boss operates. I even doubt Onyango knows this."

"What are you going to do now—with the information, I mean?"

Chizi Samuel shrugged to himself. He had thought about it a lot, he still did not know. He could volunteer the information to Onyango, he would definitely know what to do with it, but then again, he had not been asked to find out how Boss worked. Maybe it was supposed to be a secret and confessing that he knew would just be similar to poking a hornet's nest. He told Kerubo as much.

"For now, this information is just between you and I."

"I understand."

They worked in an industry that did not allow anyone to trust anyone else completely for self-preservation.

"But what are you going to do next?"

"I am going to find her."

"Why would you want to do that?"

"Just… we have some unfinished business."

Kerubo clicked her tongue.

"The fall of every great man has been caused by thinking with the wrong head."

"But think about it, being close to her can only be a good thing."

"… or your death sentence."

"I will take my chances…"

* * *

At about the same time Kerubo was on the phone with Samuel, Naliaka woke up with a start. The first thing she did was check her phone. There were ten missed calls, nine of them from a persistent Boss and one from Queen. She checked the messages, there was one from Queen, reminding her that there would be a party later at the house to celebrate her birthday. She confirmed attendance on text and then called Boss.

"Hey, are you okay?" He sounded worried.

"I am okay. Sorry, I didn't hear the phone ring."

"What happened last night?"

"It was crazy!" she started. And the more she thought about it, the crazier the experience sounded.

"It happens once in a while. Usually, that kind of calm happens with people who have been jacked before, people who understand it is not a matter of life and death if they remain calm."

"Oh?"

"People in disciplined forces also tend to be calm, but likely to counter, so I doubt he is one. I will however go with the wealthy— they don't get hysterical about losing material things, as long as they can stay safe. They have everything insured. His vehicle stalled in minutes, by the way."

"Please tell them to get rid of the phone as well. It is extra-tracked."

He nodded, not sounding surprised.

"They already have. They know the type of phone not to keep around." He sighed.

"I am glad you are alright. What time do I send the driver to pick you up?"

It was now a ritual. The day after a night job, she would go to his house to collect her phone and handbag. They would eat, laugh and he would give her oral sex, something he was getting very good at. A couple of times, she had performed oral sex on him and although it had not turned up the way both expected, she smiled when his penis went up and down, like it was having repeated false starts, and she had loved it when he had sighed with pleasure.

Naliaka was spaced out when she was picked up and remained spaced out in his house. Boss kept repeating himself, interrupting her thoughts of Chizi Samuel. Eventually, she told him about the party at Queen's.

"Are you alright though?" he asked with concern.

He was a man who operated at optimum by knowing what people around him were thinking. A slight change in behaviour alarmed him.

"I think I am just a little tired."

"Not sick?"

She shook her head.

"Possible. It was very cold yesterday and we were exposed for a while."

He relaxed.

"Yeah. That could be it. I could ask you to let me take care of you, but I also know when you need to see Queen," he said with a smile.

"It's her birthday."

"We need to get her a present. What does she like?"

"Queen loves her gold jewellery."

"Then we need to buy some for her. And a cake."

"She will have cake, though. You can never have enough cake."

She laughed, looking at him quizzically.

"You sound like someone who enjoys birthday parties."

He laughed. "If there were parties to attend, I would enjoy it, but I have never had an opportunity."

She smiled in appreciation and when he bent down to kiss her, she let him. She let him suck out all her negative thoughts, her frustrations about things she could not understand, like how she could be enjoying what Boss was doing to her right now and at the same time think about Samuel.

Boss kissed her, gently pushing her down on the sofa, parting her legs with his own, continued to dry-hump her, not letting his mouth leave hers, his hands seeking her pleasure points on different parts of her body, until she whimpered.

194

Chapter Thirteen

It was an afternoon of scorching sun, burning bright and the skies azure blue from horizon to horizon, like a single-colour wall-to-wall carpet. The wind blew lazily, begging to take shelter from the orange ball of fire. Walkers on the grind walked in strained paces, shoulders hanging in submission to the heat, their heads covered with whatever item was available to them, including handbags and newspapers.

The vehicles on the road moved slowly, as if they, like the people walking under the same sun, were feeling the heat. Among the vehicles caught in the snail-speed traffic was a big black car, windows tinted as black as the vehicle's colour itself, making it look like a big moving black blob.

There were four occupants in the car, two of them shifty-eyed men who could have been twins from different mothers. They sat at the front, one driving. Their backseat passengers were Naliaka and Boss, the air-conditioning shielding them all from the non-discriminatory tropical sun. Naliaka, behind the safety of the big black blob, found herself thinking about the day she met Queen. It had been so hot.

"Queen does not allow men into the compound on her birthday," Naliaka told Boss earlier. "But I am sure she will not mind if you come in, just for a bit. It will get her off my back."

"What do you mean?"

She shrugged shyly. "She knows there is someone special in my life. She's been itching to meet you."

"I am special?"

She nodded coyly.

Boss wore a white polo shirt, blue jeans and a pair of sports shoes. Naliaka, who now had enough clothes in Boss's closet, wore a bright yellow spaghetti top, skinny blue jeans and bright yellow sandals.

They stopped by Two Rivers Mall. Boss personally selected two gold chains, one with a queen's crown amulet, the other a love heart. They then stopped at a cake shop and settled on a carrot cake.

"She's going to love you for this," Naliaka said, hanging on Boss's arm as they walked back to the car. "Thank you."

"You love her," Boss said with a shrug. "And that makes her important to me."

She turned to hug him, wrapping her arms around his neck, her head on his. He wrapped her waistline with his hands, squeezing her in assurance before kissing her forehead. He pushed her away gently after a little while, fishing out the chain with the love amulet, and securing it around her neck.

"For you," he whispered and kissed her neck.

"Thank you," she said, touching her chain.

"Apart from the stuff I used to get from Queen, nobody has ever given me a present."

196

"What a shame."

Hand-in-hand, smiles on their faces, they walked back to the car.

From the mall to Queen's house, it was a silent journey, the bodyguards lost in their usual silence to concentrate on driving and looking out for trouble, the passengers lost in their own thoughts about the confusing present and the uncertain future.

Ngari, the fatherly security man, was on duty. As happy as he was to see Naliaka, not even his soft spot for her could convince him to open the gate for a car with male occupants. "Queen told me not to allow any... any man here today. I am sorry Naliaka."

It took a call to Queen to get him to open the gate. Queen was already waiting at the door when they drove in.

"She reminds me of a Nigerian Oga's wife," Boss remarked as they looked at Queen through the car window.

"How would you know about those?"

"I have watched many Nigerian movies."

Naliaka laughed. It had always been a consensus among the girls in Queen's house that she, Queen, would make a good wealthy Nigerian wife in a movie. Her heavy makeup. Her bigger-than-life personality. Her booming voice. Her stern look and once in a while, like today, her dressing. She was dressed in a flowery purple *kitenge* outfit with a matching headgear.

"Isn't that heavy on her?" Boss whispered amid giggles.

Naliaka shoosh'd him before opening the car door, opening her arms for Queen's hug.

"Happy birthday my Queen!" Naliaka did a mock curtsey before hugging Queen.

"My baby girl! How are you?" She was sizing Naliaka from arm's length. "And how is it possible that you get more beautiful every time I see you? You must be happy."

Naliaka giggled, turning to look at Boss who was now standing behind her, hands in his pockets and hiding behind sunglasses.

"Queen, meet my friend, Boss."

He stepped forward, extending his hand for a shake and using the other hand to draw up his sunglasses.

"Great to finally meet you. I have heard so much about you."

"Have you now? I wonder why I haven't been told about you," Queen said, shaking his hand and looking at Naliaka accusingly with a raised brow. Naliaka shrugged and grinned. "Also, you and I have something in common—we have awesome names. We must be relatives."

They laughed.

"Sorry I brought him on your special day, but I really wanted you to meet him."

"Trust you to be the one breaking the rules." She peered into Boss's car. "There are two giants in the car. Are they not coming out?"

Boss swept his hand in the air. "They are fine. They stay there, unless they have to get out."

"Oh…" Queen let her gaze linger on Boss for a while before looking at Naliaka. "Well then, you must come in and meet the other girls."

"Are you sure? I only wanted to meet you, not gate-crash at an all-girls party."

Queen adjusted her headgear and grunted before turning to walk towards the house. "It's my party, I can change the rules. Besides, the girls will be happy to see you. They are used to seeing buffoons! I declare you the party treat."

And with that, they followed Queen into the house and out to the backyard.

It was a full-blown party. Loud music. White tent. Multi-coloured balloons. A food table and a bigger one for drinks. Girls dancing. Those not dancing sitting in a circle, trying to talk above the music and each other, laughing loudly. Cigarette smoke from multiple cigarettes forming itself into a genie-like formation before disintegrating into the air. All the girls were wearing tiny clothes.

The girls spotted Naliaka. A cheer went up in her name. She waved at them. Then they saw Boss and temporarily froze. Naliaka giggled. Boss pulled down his glasses and approached hesitantly. Queen was already on a seat, watching the effect Boss was having on the girls.

"Come on, they won't eat you," Naliaka whispered encouragingly to Boss.

"They sure look like they could. I even spotted a few fangs," he protested weakly in whispers.

"Girls… girls… you can snap out of your shock now," Queen boomed. "Where are your manners? We have a distinguished guest. Come on, welcome him."

"Can we eat him?" It was Malaika who asked in between smoking.

"No you cannot," Naliaka answered amid laughter, taking turns to hug all the twelve women. When she was done, she turned to Boss, who looked completely mesmerised. "Say hello to my friend. His name is John…" Naliaka finally said after hugging everybody. She heard Boss chuckle.

"Hi John!" They said in unison.

"Hi ladies. You are all looking very beautiful."

Boss shook all their hands, willing himself not to crumble. He had never been around so many women. What if they touched his gonads and laughed at their softness? They sure looked like they could. The women were fearless in their gestures and one or two of them poked his palm with their fingers, making him cringe. Another couple may have pinched his bottoms, making him clench them. He had had enough.

"It was nice to meet you all, but I shall leave you to your party," he announced, ignoring Naliaka's glare.

"So soon?" Queen protested. The other girls grumbled. "I hope it wasn't something we did," Queen chuckled in understanding. "Alright, then. I shall walk you to the car."

"John? Of all names you could have picked up, you chose John?" he asked Naliaka when they were out of earshot, Queen walking behind them.

"It's a nice name," Naliaka answered. "If you knew the girls, you would know introducing yourself as Boss would breed questions I am not willing to answer."

"It is really nice to meet you," Queen said when they reached the car. "I could invite you back, but as you can see, I keep predators disguised as human girls."

"I felt like my life was in danger." They laughed.

"Thank you, and keep taking care of this girl. She means a lot to me."

"That is something we have in common."

Boss was looking at Naliaka. Naliaka was looking at her yellow sandals and red toenails. The two people discussing and declaring their love for her were criminals from whatever angle one looked at them, but they were her family.

"But, before I forget, I have something for you." He dug into his pockets and removed a small box. "Happy birthday."

"Thank you!" Queen choked, turning to Naliaka.

"Where did you get this one from?" she asked, smiling through wet eyes.

"I like him very much."

"There is something else…" Naliaka went to the car and removed the cake, handing it to Queen.

"I am not sure I can handle this anymore! If you have another present for me, please keep it until next year."

Boss laughed.

"It's your lucky day, I do not have another one," he said, kissing Queen on the cheek before turning to Naliaka and kissing her full on the mouth.

"Talk to you later."

The two women, holding hands and wearing smiles on their faces, watched him until he disappeared out of the gate.

"Wow," Queen turned to Naliaka. "I… I am speechless. Who is he?"

"My friend."

"That man is head over heels in love with you. I am also thinking he is not a pastor," she nudged Naliaka knowingly.

"What does he do? Is he a politician?"

Naliaka turned to look at Queen and nodded. "Today is your day, let's focus."

Queen grunted. "At some point I am going to have to hear all about him. He seems… what can I say, he looks like the kind of guy who would understand this life." She pointed at her house.

Naliaka laughed.

"I am happy for you, Naliaka… you deserve to be happy."

Two hours into the party, two hours of answering questions with untruthful answers about Boss, her phone beeped with a message. She read it and smiled, calling the girls to attention.

"Girls, does anyone want to go out to town?"

Over half of them did. The rest looked on hesitantly.

"Your lucky day. John just sent me some money to treat you all."

"What, like going out to the city? All of us? And not pay for it?" It was Malaika, pausing a cigarette halfway to the mouth.

"Yes. Like go out to mingle."

"Count me in. I can't dance, but I am very good at keeping watch of the bags, and punching anyone misbehaving towards any of you," Julia volunteered.

* * *

Chizi Samuel spent the day sorting the inconveniences of the night before. His car had been found, with the phone inside, but not his bank cards and identity card. It would however take a few days to have the police release everything.

At five, sitting behind his computer in the house and trying to make sense of the reports about his clearing and forwarding business, the grumbling of his stomach and sudden surge of acid reminded him that he had neglected his stomach for hours. He warmed some leftover meat and *ugali*.

At seven o'clock, he showered and headed to the city, to the same pub as the day before.

Like the night before, he had little hope of bumping into Kiki, even less than the night before. But she was there, sitting with several loud and boisterous women. She sat, back straight, one palm supporting her chin, looking at the women with mild amusement. She looked out of place, yet she seemed to fit right in.

He watched them, taking in all the different ages, sizes, skin tones, his curiosity rising. Who were they? Was it a *chama* meeting? Did they also work for Boss? Samuel's eyes roamed the rest of the pub. He was looking for Jonte and his sidekick, or a couple of others like them.

He called Kerubo.

"Oh lord… are you out again?" she greeted, referring to the noise.

"I am lonely without you…"

"You are just horny. Where are you?"

"Back to the same pub."

"You never learn, do you?"

"She's here," he said instead.

Kerubo paused. "Are you with her?"

"Not yet. I don't think she is out robbing vehicles tonight. She seems to be having a girls' night out."

"She can afford it. She's a thief!"

"You are jealous!"

"Piss off!"

He chuckled. "The boys are not here though. But I am going to talk to her."

"Please don't get yourself killed. Not for her."

"I will be careful, I promise." He paused, "When are you coming back?"

"Tomorrow. I will come and spend the night at your house."

Chizi Samuel held his breath and sat up straight. Did he just hear a pleading tone from Kerubo?

"Do you want to see me?" he asked cautiously.

"Do you want to see me?" she asked instead.

"You know I do, but…"

"But you will be going home with her. I get it. Don't worry about it, just do whatever you need to do."

"Kerubo, are you alright?"

Another sigh.

"I am fine. Just ignore me, I am probably ovulating," she laughed.

"Honestly, it's alright. Just be careful and let me know if you find anything."

He muttered to himself and shrugged, turning back his attention to Kiki's table. Kerubo's weird behaviour put aside, he made a beeline for the table, approaching from behind.

He tapped her shoulder. When Naliaka turned, she did so with a smile. The smile froze on seeing Chizi Samuel, then it slowly turned into what could have been fright. The rest of the table went quiet.

"We must stop meeting like this."

"Chizi Samuel…" she whispered.

"Kiki. How are you?"

"This is too much!" It was Malaika, declaring in feigned exasperation and lighting a cigarette she had been holding. Samuel gave her a quick smile, knowing the club bouncers would be arriving to ask her to put out the cigarette.

"She gets all the good looking guys and what do we get? Baboons!"

"Malaika, shut up!" Janet whispered roughly, but Chizi Samuel laughed.

"Can I talk to you?" he asked, turning to Kiki who had managed to compose herself.

"Now?"

"Now."

"I am with my friends."

"They look like they can survive without you," he answered stubbornly.

Reluctantly, she allowed him to lead her towards the exit. Unlike the previous night, there was no flirting, just a pregnant silence.

"You got another car?" she asked when he opened the car for her.

"It's a rental."

"Nice."

"Get in."

"I can't leave my friends."

He probed her in.

"You are not. I just want to talk. In the car."

For a minute, they sat in silence.

"How are you? After last night, I mean?"

She shrugged, crossing her hands on her chest. "I am okay. You?"

"Good. And alive. That's what matters, right? One has to appreciate a robber who doesn't hurt them. If I could, I would get in touch with those guys and thank them."

Naliaka swallowed hard.

"Anyway, I have something for you."

"What?"

He bent across to the glove compartment and removed a box, handing it to her.

"A phone?" she asked in shock. "For me?" He nodded. Subconsciously, she touched her chain. "Why?"

"Why? Because I feel responsible that your phone was stolen."

"It wasn't your fault," she said guiltily, knowing her phone was safely inside her purse.

"Still."

"How did you know you would find me?"

"I didn't, but I live in hope. Plus, we have unfinished business."

She went silent.

"Tonight?"

She shook her head. "I don't know."

"We had a deal yesterday. What has changed?" He was peering at her through the dark, wishing he could see her expression. Nothing told a story more honestly than facial expressions.

She looked back towards the club. "My friends… I made them come out."

"They all seem like grownups." She didn't answer.

"Alright. Here is the deal. You stay as long as you want but when it's time to leave, you leave with me."

"Are you giving me a choice?"

He shook his head. "Let's put it this way; I will do anything to go home with you, anything short of kidnapping you."

* * *

Morning after.

Boss was upbeat, enough not to hit the punching bag in his home gym, not like it was responsible for every bad card that life had dealt him, but like sparring with a friend. He still punched it with fury because it was the only way to hit a punching bag, countless times, until his muscles threatened to lock, until the sweat running down his body started sprinkling the floor around him. He stopped suddenly, hugging the punching bag, allowing it to see-saw with him until it calmed down.

He had been in the gym for an hour, something he did on a daily basis, at least whenever he did not have a painful hangover.

Working out was his perfect antidote for stress, his escape from the grim realities that haunted his life, and his way to keep his body looking the way it did. Today's gym session was different because throughout, through the sweat and humping, he smiled.

He dared to think he loved Naliaka, like a man could love a woman, to imagine settling down with her, perhaps leaving his evil ways behind and making a couple of babies with her. It's not like he needed the money he made from crime because, unlike most of his peers, he invested heavily, and there were two car yards that actually did genuine car sales. If he never got involved in crime again, he would not have to change his lifestyle.

But he was the Don, and as much as people thought Dons held the ultimate crime power, he knew different. He could not just walk away, not without endangering his life and the lives of people close to him.

The little, literally, matter of his manhood, was his biggest impediment. As he stripped off to get into the bathroom, he let his hand grope his balls, squeezing them softly. When he was grinding on top of Naliaka, usually fully clothed, when he was giving her oral pleasure, when he listened to her moaning with pleasure, his penis danced with the tune.

His scatterbrain led him to think about his parents. Usually, it was easy to suppress thoughts of them, but today he let himself.

It had been more than ten years since he last saw them, when he was a naive nineteen-year-old with big dreams of making a decent living. He laughed a little about that thought, how he had thought working as a casual worker in Industrial Area could have made him wealthy. He thought about Mato, the man who made him.

He thought about Monde, another instrument of his destiny. Monde had died in a road accident. He still remembered how, as usual, he had gone to Monde's spot to collect weed for delivery. Hours later, he decided to go to Monde's house, thinking perhaps he was sick, although he had wondered why Monde's phone was off. The house was locked. The next door neighbour had casually told him that Monde had been hit by a lorry while crossing the road in his wheelchair and died on the spot. Like Mato's, he did not attend Monde's burial because he did not know anyone connected to him.

Monde's death had opened a whole new world for Boss, a world of crime bosses and assassinations, corrupt lawmakers and enforcers. He had been working for him for a long time and had come to know all the people who made the illegal trade smooth, including the supplier, the cops and the customers. Boss was the natural successor. He wondered how his life would have turned up if he had not met the two.

He allowed himself to admit that he was tired of being a crime boss, and there were things happening on the streets that could signify the end of his reign.

* * *

Naliaka, wearing nothing but a gown, stood at the balcony looking beyond the white Kitengela dust into the vast land stretching for miles.

"Kilimanjaro," Samuel announced as he joined her, holding two glasses of freshly squeezed juice. He stood beside her, wearing a pair of boxer shorts.

"What?"

He used his mouth to point to the horizon. "That right there, is Mount Kilimanjaro. Watching it on clear sky days is my favourite pastime."

She turned to look back at it, sipping the juice. "I have never seen a mountain higher than Ngong Hills."

"I love mountains."

She laughed uneasily. "I would die if I tried. I am so unfit."

"That's a strange thing because you have the body of someone who works out."

"Mother nature," she laughed.

They went quiet, both looking at the mountain peak glittering like a star against the sun.

It was the morning after a night full of passion. The only reason they had stopped having sex was because they had run out of condoms and Chizi Samuel was still debating on whether or not to go to the shops for more. But then again, what they were having at the moment, talking and looking at the peeping peak of Kilimanjaro was great.

Earlier on, he prepared a heavy breakfast, one she had hardly touched but had consumed most of the freshly squeezed juice. She was still asking for more.

"What's your favourite food?"

"Oh… nothing really."

"You cannot, not have a favourite dish."

"I don't. I am either hungry or I am not. When I am hungry I eat what is available, otherwise I pretty much ignore food."

"What do you want me to make for lunch?" he asked in near frustration.

* * *

Chizi Samuel put together a vegetable stir fry to accompany the dry-fried lamb marinated with garlic, ginger and bay leaf, then made plain white rice. By then, the mountain peak had been swallowed by the clouds, but they still sat facing it.

"This is really tasty," Naliaka remarked.

She was using her fingers to pick the meat, licking them slowly with every bite.

Samuel laughed. "This is one of the most basic meals on my menu."

"You are a show off," she quipped.

"But I am not lying."

"Thank you."

"Do you always have beer with your lunch?"

He nodded. "Whenever I can, yes. I am away a lot, and I am not able to drink when I am away. When I can, I make up for it by drinking too much."

She turned to look at him. "Why are you away a lot?"

"Mh… is this where we start talking about ourselves?"

She shrugged, a knot in her stomach. She still had not decided how much truth she would mix with the lies. She was still confused as to why she felt compelled to tell her life story to a total stranger, except that she really felt like it.

He piqued her curiosity. He was such a good-looking man, a man who was obviously doing very well for himself financially, a man, who unlike Boss, could hold his own in bed, a man who, unlike Father Joshua, did not have to resort to prostitutes. What was his story? How had he escaped the claws of *decent* women out there?

She sighed. "Might as well. At some point I would have to leave, and it's way into the afternoon."

"Why can't you stay?"

"Because I refused to charge you last night. I am not willing to give two nights for free?"

"You mean last night was on the house?"

She giggled. "You could say that, although I think the new phone more than compensates."

"Stay. I will pay for tonight." He was trying to lock his eyes to hers, his hand holding hers.

"We can hook up another time."

"Next time would have to be when I return. I am leaving town in two days." It was not entirely true. He still had another five days out here, but the five days were packed with plans. He still had not spent time with Kerubo, and he was missing her. He had not gone to give his verbal report to Onyango, and that took a whole day. He still needed to spend a day or two with the manager who ran his company.

"So, what is it you do?"

Another sip of his beer to wash down the food. "Why don't we start with the easy stuff, yours?"

She laughed, genuinely amused. "Dude, I am a hooker. How can mine be the easy stuff?"

He turned to look at her seriously. "I am telling you, yours is the easy stuff. How did you end up doing this?" She squeezed her glass with both hands, looking away, this time not at the peak but away from it.

"I thought you said you are not interested in why I do what I do."

"What I am not interested in is trying to redeem you, but it would be interesting to know how you ended up here."

She sighed again, took his beer from his hand and sipped it, cringing from the taste but going ahead to do it for the second time. "This stuff is nasty."

"Acquired taste."

She sipped again and cringed again. "Yeah… it's a very tasteless story, my story…"

"Let me be the judge of that."

So she did.

"So, why are you out here on your own?" he asked after she was done talking. She did not tell him about Boss, but that did not surprise him.

"Years in that house with no choice of who I had sex with, I was craving for freedom. But I go back often because that's all the family I have. The owner is the mother I do not have. She really is an awesome woman."

"That's debatable, but life has a way of dealing us difficult cards."

"Like it did with me. Now, society thinks I am scum. What society would have wanted for me was to marry, at seventeen. The man would have most likely abused me, physically, sexually and emotionally because I was naive and powerless. Then society would have stepped in, not to help me, but to feel sorry for me." She paused to chuckle. "You know, when Queen took me in, she told me something about society preferring sexually repressed and oppressed women. That men will use you for sex one way or another, but we as women have a choice to turn it to our advantage, so screw the society. Those words ring true every day."

"Interesting perception. But does that mean that you do not believe in happy endings?"

She shrugged. "I am sure there are many, many happy endings that do not make it to the headlines, but I also know there are many tragic endings that could be avoided if only women were empowered enough to walk away from doomed relationships. If men treated women like human beings, not like goats." She thought about Julia and her abusive husband. "If only society did not frown upon women who seem to be enjoying sex. Why, for instance, are we the prostitutes yet you, as my customer, get away with it?"

He shrugged. "What can I say, it's a man's world. But if it makes you feel better, I am a prostitute, but I am the paying side of the prostitute."

She laughed out loud.

"Purely out of curiosity, do you ever imagine settling down?" he asked.

"Like settling down in marriage? With children and stuff?"

"Correct."

"Who would settle down with an ex-prostitute?"

"I know I would."

She flashed him a smile. "You do not have to be nice like that. I think the only people who would settle down with someone like me are criminals."

For a short second, Samuel's heart paused. That was the closest she had come to making reference to Boss.

"Not strictly true, but that's a discussion for another day. So, are you actively looking for a criminal to settle down with?"

She laughed and looked at the peak.

"I wouldn't say actively looking, but in my line of work, I have met several nice ones. Perhaps, if and when I am ready to settle down…"

She took a deep breath, turned to him with a tired smile.

"Enough about me, let's see whose life sucks more."

"I am in the army." That was the half-lie he had chosen.

She turned to him, wide-eyed, remembering what Boss had said about calm people. But why had he not attacked his assailants? "Fighting terrorists?"

"And then some. Also, I own a clearing and forwarding company."

"Oh. When do you get to run it?"

"I don't. Being stuck in an office would be the worst punishment for me."

She laughed. "But why start a company you hate running?"

"My parents did. Then they decided to die." When Naliaka looked at him to say sorry, he had this distant look.

"What happened to them?" she asked instead.

"My father had an awesome business brain, but unfortunately, that was the only good thing about him."

"Oh?"

"I know we shouldn't speak ill of the dead, but I say he screwed that. I am an only child, at least I thought I was, for the longest time. I didn't turn out the way my father would have wanted because I did not inherit his brain, I struggled academically. I got whipped so much for being nearly at the bottom of the class." He laughed, but it was not a happy laughter.

"Sorry."

He swished the air dismissively, but his hard line face remained.

"I grew up in violence, and with a father who was constantly ashamed of me. He called me a woman enough times." He laughed, "Like being a woman was the worst thing that could happen to anyone. The strongest people I know are women. Anyway, he told me I should have just been born one—because I was weak. I was the kid who got beat up by other kids, and whenever I came home with a black eye, he would give me another one."

"Gosh… your mom?"

"She got as good, or bad in this case, as I did."

Naliaka took a deep breath before asking the next question.

"But you do not look like a guy who could be bullied."

He shrugged.

"When I joined secondary school, I was constantly bullied and humiliated. I was on my own, unlike before when mom and I suffered together. It finally hit me that I was the only one who could take care of myself. When I went home for the holidays, I joined the gym and started learning karate. By the end of the year, I had become the bully. Life was quite smooth after that and I learned lessons I still carry with me today—be sure you can beat anyone." He smiled at this.

"I sat for my final exams and failed, at least according to my father. According to me, I had done pretty well because they were the best results I ever posted. Not being admitted to university was the ultimate humiliation for my father. He attempted to hit me, I blocked his hand and squeezed it as a warning. I needed him to know I was tired of his violence."

"Wow."

"He retreated, but he told me to move out of his house. That if I thought I was man enough to fight him, I was man enough to look after myself."

"Where did you go?"

"For months, mom secretly paid my rent, fed me and even bought me alcohol… and I drank a lot. Then I joined the army because mom could not pay for my college with the little allowance she got from dad. It was the best decision I ever made.'

"How… how did your parents die?"

He faced the peak before continuing.

"Dad killed mom, but I really do not want to go into details. But their deaths left me wealthy, although I have no desire to work in the same office as my dad."

Chizi Samuel's parents had died of HIV/AIDS, and years later he still got mad about it. His mother discovered her status first and went on medication. She asked dad to get tested but instead he beat her up and accused her of cheating on him. He was in the army when all that was happening, but later he learned that his father threw away her antiretroviral drugs and forbade her from ever leaving the house. The watchman was warned of dire consequences if he ever let her out. So she wasted alone in the house, with her long-time house help taking care of her. Then his status went full blown, but he refused to take medication. He died within months.

He was still haunted by what he had seen when he first arrived; two women in the living room, but he only recognised the house-help. He asked her where his mother was. When the house-help pointed at the skin and bones woman next to her, Chizi Samuel broke down. The last time he had seen his mother, she was a heavy-set woman who needed to lose weight. The woman being pointed out for him was not, could not, be his mother.

He collapsed on her feet, placed his head on her bony lap, nearly cringed when her bony hand touched his head.

Chizi Samuel cried for days, but not for the loss of his father. It was for the near-loss of his mother. Plans to bury his father were put on hold because he refused to be involved until his mother was stabilised. Then he insisted on cremation because he did not want a grave as a reminder.

The day before the burial, a court order arrived to stop the cremation. Three women were claiming to be his father's wives, and they all had one child each, and they wanted part of his father's property.

"They can have his bloody body and equally bloody money!" he had declared, throwing the court order on the ground, stumping on it and walking out.

Two days later, he was calm enough to listen to his mother. "You cannot have them take all the money. It is your money by right. You suffered under that man, the least he can do is leave his money to you."

"I do not want his money!" he protested.

"I want you to have his money. We are not debating on this. This is what you are going to do. You will request a DNA test for each of the three children. If they are his children, I certainly want them to share his wealth. You will keep half of his property and they can share the other half."

"What if they contest? This could be a long process and I haven't got energy for a court battle."

"They will not contest. The will is clear on what is mine. If they want to fight, you give them a fight. Show your father's ghost what you are capable of."

His father's death had brought out a new kind of woman out of his mother.

The DNA had turned positive for two of the children, a boy and a girl. He made his offer to them, and the women took it.

His mother died within the year.

He shook himself out of those memories and smiled at Kiki.

"So you see, Kiki, you and I are some sort of kindred spirits. This life has served us shit, but we take the shit and make manure out of it."

Naliaka laughed.

"I think it's lemons."

"Nah... I like shit better."

She laughed again.

"Oh, and my name is actually Naliaka, Kiki is for my night shenanigans."

* * *

Kerubo did not sleep well. Earlier, she had a hairdresser fix braids on her hair, and they were too tight. At night, she let a shower run down her head. The cool water gave her some relief, but not enough to allow her to put her head on the softest pillow.

After hours of turning and tossing, she sat up and started reading. The reading only worked for a few minutes, then her thoughts decided to face several demons that were haunting her, starting with Mrs Kamau and why they were in Nyeri, which was the reason she had lost her cool with Samuel, allowing him to see a side of her she never let anyone see, the pathetically emotional one. She considered telling him what was happening, if only to justify her behaviour, but she needed to do it face to face; she needed to be in his arms as she told him.

Mrs Kamau had been unwell for months. Diabetes, or so they told her.

"Nothing to worry about, I just need to watch what I eat."

Kerubo went online to research, and drew up a diet plan for Mrs Kamau, on top of accompanying her to the doctor.

"This should sort your sugar levels pretty fast, but you have to follow it strictly. And take your medication."

That Friday when she drove to Mrs Kamau's in Gachie and opened the gate for herself, she found Mrs Kamau sitting outside, catching the last rays of the sun.

"Oh my goodness! I know my diet was going to make you shed weight, but I never realised how fast it would work!" She said, half worried, especially because Mrs Kamau's eyes looked hollow.

Mrs Kamau laughed lazily, tapping on the seat next to her for Kerubo to sit. She did, cautiously, keeping her eyes on Mrs Kamau.

"Are you unwell? I mean, is there something more than diabetes?"

"You could say that... how are you?"

"I am fine. Where are you ailing?"

"Ah, my daughter, you cannot start shooting questions at me even before you wash your hands, before you prepare tea, before you prepare dinner for us. I have so missed eating your *chapatis*. Do that, then we can talk?"

Kerubo looked at her defiantly, with every intention to protest, but something in Mrs Kamau's eyes stopped her. Perhaps, it would be for her own good to hold on to the questions until later.

"Where is baba?"

Calling them mama and baba had come naturally.

"He went to the shops. He should be back any moment."

Kerubo, through the window as she kneaded the *chapati* dough, watched Mr Kamau help his wife up from the seat. She watched them walk slowly to the house, Mrs Kamau a former shadow of herself, a far cry from the energetic woman who had rescued her over twenty years earlier. It was not just the passage of time that had taken its toll on her, it was something bad, something big and she, Kerubo, started preparing herself mentally for the worst.

In place of the bright-eyed, plump woman she had known most of her life, Mrs Kamau's eyes were sunken, swallowed by her own skull. Her skin was darker and flaky. The same forces that were swallowing her eyes from within were also feeding on her fleshy body.

Kerubo served everyone in silence. Only the low volume television saved them from complete quietness. They ate in silence, washed down their dinner in silence. By the time she finished washing the dishes, she was ready to punch a wall.

"Alright, what's happening?" she asked, standing hands akimbo in front of Mr Kamau.

He cleared his throat, looked at his wife briefly before asking Kerubo to take a seat beside him.

"There is no nice way of saying this, but mama is dying."

Kerubo did not react, not physically. She had already imagined the worst case scenario. In her silence, Kerubo did a quick journey of her life with the Kamau's, concluding that without them, she would probably have died as a child.

"Liver cirrhosis," Baba continued. "Acute. She should be in the hospital but she wants to be here. This means…"

"Yeah, I know what that means," she said. "Why didn't you tell me earlier?"

"What would you have done, except worry?" Mama asked weakly. "I went in too late, and I have accepted it."

Kerubo tasted her tears, tears that were flowing down her nose to her throat on a salty path, instead of escaping through the eyes.

That night, Kerubo hardly slept, and hardly stopped crying.

Now, as she thought about the imminent death of mama, she thought about her last conversation with Samuel, one in which she came off as jealous, and she was cringing with the thought of how confused she left Samuel . His call was ill-timed, and she had projected.

Then she thought about the prostitute.

Kerubo was happy to believe that Boss was asexual, or just faithful to a wife somewhere in the village. Her failure to lure him had rubbed her off in a bad way, and it felt worse to lose him to the prostitute.

Then there was Samuel. Her best friend, the only person who knew everything she was willing to share about herself. They were a team, not just on the streets, but emotionally. They were each other's support system. What bothered her was not that he was sleeping with Kiki, but she could tell he was getting emotionally attached. She knew him well enough.

* * *

In a desperate attempt to awaken her senses, Kerubo had a cold shower, then prepared strong black coffee to slowly sip on the drive back to Nairobi.

"Is something wrong?" Mama asked as she accepted a yoghurt from Kerubo. "You have been very quiet, and you have been crying."

Kerubo smiled, but within, she was angry that she couldn't hide her tears.

"I am fine. I just did not sleep very well. My hair was braided too tightly."

Mama looked at Kerubo's hair and nodded. "It does look tight. But it is beautiful too. Are you too tired to drive? I can drive, you know."

Kerubo shook her head. "The coffee will help."

"I worry about you," she whispered.

"Why would you worry about me? I am fine!" Mama grunted.

"I worry about you because you are determined not to feel."

Kerubo shook her head.

"I don't understand."

"You are working very hard not to break down about my condition."

Kerubo winced.

"You are ashamed of showing weakness. I know you broke down when you went to the bedroom. I listened outside the bedroom. Your eyes are red right now. You hid and cried. Kerubo, it is okay to be weak. I remember how you behaved when your parents died."

Kerubo felt the tears fall and momentarily blind her. She pulled over by the roadside and allowed herself to cry in Mama's arms.

"I bet that felt better," Mama said encouragingly after Kerubo calmed down. "You have trained yourself too well about not feeling things, to hold down emotions. I feel like I have failed you, that I have failed to reassure you that there are good people in the world, that your parents may have hurt you, but not everyone will."

Kerubo blew her nose loudly. She thought about Samuel. About Boss. No, she was human. She was hurt and she was jealous.

"You have this shield around you, and it is stopping you from feeling things, like love."

"I love you," she cut in quickly in defence.

"I know, and I love you too. But you love me because you are sure I would never hurt you. Your life is about nothing else but the shop job."

That mama believed Kerubo was just a shop manager made her feel guilty once in a while, but not enough to tell her what she really was.

"You do not have friends… you have never had friends. You do not have a boyfriend… you are not getting younger my dear. You need to have children before your eggs become too old!"

If the mood was not so grim, if mama had not started the conversation with her looming death, Kerubo would have laughed. She would have told mama she did not want to get married or to have children; that she did not care how old her eggs became, she had no intention of using them.

"I have a boyfriend!" she blurted out, then immediately regretted it.

"Oh, you do? How come I do not know him?"

"I was going to introduce you to him, but then you got unwell and I thought I should give you time to recover."

"I am not going to recover. I need to meet him before I die. What's his name?"

"Samuel," she said through clenched teeth, then turned on the ignition.

NaiRobbery Cocktail

Chapter Fourteen

The unfamiliar shrill of a ringing phone from the bedroom interrupted Boss and Naliaka's lazy breakfast.

He excused himself and Naliaka heard him mumbling in a conversation. When he returned, he was in a pair of jeans, a tee shirt under a light jacket. His exit was abrupt, only telling Naliaka he would be back shortly. She followed his exit thoughtfully. Only when he shut the door behind him did it hit her that it was the first time she was on her own, in his house.

She got fidgety as she fought the temptation to snoop around. As much as she did not know nearly enough about Boss, she knew enough to know there was a high probability that pinhole cameras were peeping at her from every wall. From her favourite sofa, she let her eyes scan the walls, looking for clues. The other possibility was there was nothing to find. What she was sure about was he would not be stupid enough to leave anything incriminating lying around.

So she watched spy movies and slept on the sofa. And ate two biscuits and drank a glass of milk. And thought about stuff. She even thought about going for a walk, quickly ditching the idea when she remembered she did not have a set of his house keys. There was no balcony and for a little while, she felt claustrophobic.

He returned after four, having been gone for most of the morning and afternoon. Boss shut the door behind him, leaned on it with a heavy sigh before giving her a smile that neither reached his teeth nor his eyes.

"Are you alright?" she asked, sitting up. "You look like you are in pain."

He did. He was cringing and when he started walking towards her, he did so while dragging his feet. For a scary moment, she thought he was injured. She stood up but he waved her off and she sat back down.

"I am just tired."

He reached for her hand and squeezed it, then forced a smile.

"Have you eaten?"

She nodded. "I left some for you, if you are hungry."

He shook his head. "I could do with a beer, though. But first, I need to freshen up. The sun out there could roast an egg."

He walked halfway towards the bedroom then paused, looking back at her.

"Please don't go home today."

She nodded as she held his gaze.

When he returned twenty minutes later, Naliaka was still on the sofa, but the stool in front of it had an unopened can of beer and a glass of wine. With a measure of amusement, he paused to look at the wine then at Naliaka.

"You look like you need company," she said with a shrug, sipping the wine.

He laughed, popping the beer loudly, taking a huge gulp before sitting next to her. "This," he said, taking another gulp, "this is how you take a gulp of alcohol."

"I am learning."

"What are you watching?"

"A movie."

"Is it interesting?"

She shrugged. "So-so. Same old storyline I guess."

"So you don't mind if we turn it off?"

She studied him for a while before taking the remote control and pressed the power button.

He took another gulp of the beer, placed it back on the stool before sitting back. "There is so much going on in my head right now and I cannot think of anyone more suited to listen."

She took a sharp breath. "That's almost scary, considering I do not know you that much."

He laughed, not a happy laugh. "That's actually part of my point. Nobody knows me well enough. If I dropped dead right now, there would be a mighty confusion." He paused and took another sip. "I trust you."

"Thank you," she whispered.

"*Me* trusting you is not necessarily a good thing because I cannot stand it when someone breaks my trust, and there is always a chance the person you trust most will betray you."

"What?"

He put up his hand to quieten her. "Let me do this before I change my mind," she nodded. "I have been betrayed numerous times. It goes with the territory. It also goes with the territory that snitches suffer. Everybody who has betrayed me has either ended up dead, or close to death."

He turned to look at her with dilated eyes. She did not look back at him, but he saw her swallow hard.

"I… that I love you makes it all scarier. If you betrayed me…"

"Erm…"

His hand went up again.

"It's alright. Don't say anything."

She nodded and took a bigger sip of the wine and swallowed loudly.

He spoke firmly. "I love you, and I would like to swear to you here and now that I would never, ever do anything to hurt you. That I would happily chop off the head of anyone who hurt you, but I am afraid what would happen if…"

"If I betrayed you," she said quickly.

He didn't stop her this time.

"I cannot imagine what would make me."

He shrugged. "A moment of weakness. Torture, especially. I am good at torture, my enemies are as good. But no woman has ever been tortured because of me. Then you came into my life."

"I am glad I did."

He shook his head sadly.

"Perhaps you shouldn't be. When I recruited you, I did it because it is what I do, besides the fact that I thought you were, still are, the most beautiful woman I have ever seen."

She blushed and hunched her shoulders shyly.

"I have other girls working for me. I have never invited any of them here. I don't even talk to them unless it is necessary. The only people who come to this house are Jonte, his dead partner, Wafula,

Oti, my bodyguards, and another man you may or may not meet at some point." He did not think she was ready to learn he had a body double.

"And you. You being this close to me puts your life in danger."

"It cannot be that bad."

"It is, and then worse. I hold a position that is desired by many. I have protection from rogue law enforcement, something every criminal wants. We have had gang wars. Wars I have emerged as the victor, but not without bodies. The dead ones knew what they were signing up for, like every soldier does. You did not sign up for it. I don't know what I would do if you were caught in a crossfire."

She took a deep breath. "Why are you telling me this? Why now?"

He shrugged. "Because I want to give you the choice of walking away from me before it is too late. Because, as much as I would miss you, I want you to walk away from it, for your own sake."

"Don't be silly.'

He grabbed her arms, a little too roughly, and turned her towards him.

"Naliaka, this is not a game. It is deep shit. Do not be deceived by how I treat you. I am a nasty man. I am ruthless. I have tortured people, the kind of torture you see in espionage movies—plucking off nails, one by one, without anaesthesia."

Naliaka cringed. He was hurting her and she was too scared to tell him.

"And that's the nice stuff. I made countless women widows, mothers son-less."

He rubbed his nose noisily, eyes shut, for a moment looking tormented. "This," he circled his face with his index finger. "This persona is reserved just for you. I am not a nice man."

He released her. She rubbed her arms.

She swallowed hard.

"My rivals are as nasty, if not worse. If they decided to get me through you, you would end up with guys who look scarier than Oti, and they do not treat women well."

She felt herself shiver.

"Like, rape?"

He nodded. "It has happened. Not to any of my girls, but it has happened."

She shivered again.

"I am also telling you this because something has been building up for a while and for your own sake, you need to stop coming here. You need to stop being seen with me. I am hoping they don't already know about you, but chances are, they do."

Naliaka was shaking, and she was crying.

"Your friend, Queen…"

"What about her?"

"Can you stay with her, just for a little while, until I know what is going on?"

"Can I not stay in my house?"

He shook his head. "You could, but only when I am sure you are safe. I like where Queen's house is, it is easy to secure."

"What the hell are you talking about, secure it?"

"I am going to provide you with security."

"What? What will you tell Queen?"

He shook his head. "She doesn't have to know."

"It's really bad, isn't it?"

He nodded.

"When do I leave?"

"Tomorrow when the city wakes up, someone will take you to Queen's."

"I am so confused."

"Better confused than dead. I am so sorry I got you mixed up in all this."

She let him hug her, she let her tears flow, and she let her body shake with fright.

"Remember I said I trust you?"

She nodded.

"I need to ask for a couple of huge favours. But you are free to say no if it makes you uncomfortable."

She nodded. "I need you to go and see my parents."

She was still struggling with a dry mouth, so she just shook her head.

"Naliaka, I may not come out of this alive."

"What do you want me to do?"

Naliaka asked after minutes upon minutes of quiet, as she struggled to control her shaky body and dry mouth. In the end, she was calmer than she thought she should have been.

"For the next few weeks, at least until all this is sorted, there will be no jobs but everybody will be compensated. No need to worry about your income."

Naliaka nodded.

"But, if the worst happens…" he let the sentence hang as he searched her face. She wouldn't look at him.

"If the worst happens, someone will let you know. And you would need to tell my parents."

"You are not going to die."

"We all die, eventually," he said dismissively.

She nodded, eyes downcast.

"Give me a minute, I will be back."

He returned carrying a huge briefcase. She looked at it suspiciously, butterflies flipping over and over in her stomach. He pulled the coffee table and placed the briefcase on it. He entered a combination but before he opened it, he turned to look at her.

"Are you ready?"

She shook her head, then nodded.

"Ready or not?"

She gasped and covered her mouth with both her palms. She could feel her eyes growing wider, for a moment afraid they would pop. She pinched herself quickly, just to make sure she was not dreaming, quickly returning her palm to help the other palm cover her mouth.

"Emergency escape plan," he said, studying crispy notes upon notes of dollars, packed neatly in the briefcase. And tens of pieces of gold jewellery.

"I want you to keep it for me."

Naliaka whimpered and shook her head. He didn't acknowledge her discomfort.

"I am not sure how much is here, but it is a lot."

"I can't!" she protested. "I cannot take that."

"You will."

His voice, she noticed, had gone flat, business like, like someone else was speaking his words.

"If you do not take it, and they get me, they will take it. You will take it, because you cannot let the people who may kill me take it. Do you understand what I am telling you?"

Even his eyes had changed with his voice. She didn't like what they looked like, or how flat and emotionless he sounded.

She nodded.

He picked a brown envelope from the same briefcase.

"These are my documents and bank cards. Pin numbers are in the envelopes. If I die," she whimpered again. "...if I die, you will make sure my parents are taken care of."

He shut the briefcase with a snap. She jumped. He continued.

"My teacher, I told you about him."

She nodded.

"I would like him taken care of as well."

Five years earlier when Boss had finally gathered the guts to visit Mr Choka, carrying money in the same briefcase, he told a confused Mr Choka to do whatever he wanted with it.

A month on, Mr Choka had called Boss to tell him he was a proud owner of a piece of land that he was already building on.

"If I die," he continued. Naliaka winced again. "I would like you to visit him. His contacts are inside this envelope."

At this point, Naliaka was out of whimpers and resigned herself to looking at Boss, in shock, in disbelief.

"Another important group of people—this one may shock you."

"As if I am not shocked enough," she managed to grumble.

"Street children," he said.

Naliaka's eyes grew wider. Then he told her about Mato, and the street family.

"They are my eyes on the streets. This may be asking for too much, but once in a while, it would be good to check up on them."

"How?" she asked incredulously.

"You see my bodyguards?"

She nodded.

"And their bodyguards? And their bodyguards' bodyguards? The whole pyramid to the bottom knows you."

She shook her head, dying to ask the specifics of his statement but too afraid to know how much about her life was known to random street boys.

"They are the reason I sleep peacefully, why I know everything going on."

"What do they get in return?"

He took a deep breath.

"It is difficult to totally rehabilitate someone used to living on the streets—the streets are rough, but there is a certain freedom that comes with it. I have managed to get most of them off the glue, but they will still carry those bottles around for appearance. A street kid without glue would stick out. But there is a condition for being under me—you must attend school. So, I have a school in Mathare, teachers and all, government-recognised. They all must attend for three hours, every weekday. None of them does exceptionally well, but we have several who have made it to secondary school. They can read and write and all the basics.

At eighteen, they get their identity cards and driver's licence, for obvious reasons, but a few of them have chosen the *righteous* way and broken away. They still turn up once in a while to see the young ones. I still keep tabs on them for obvious reasons."

Naliaka inhaled and shook her head, but she remained quiet.

"Some work at my car yards, but most choose the heavy duty work you help in.

"Have any of them tried to betray you?" he asked.

"Not just tried. They have."

"...And?"

"You do not want to know the gory details."

Naliaka shook her head again. "This is too much!"

"I am not asking you to take over my dirty job, I am asking you, if you can, to see to it the school stays open."

"This is too much!" Naliaka declared again, taking the wine and downing half of it. "I want to get drunk."

He shrugged. "You do what you want, but we started this, we are finishing it. I want you, when you make the choice, to make an informed one."

She put down the glass. He continued. "If they kill me, my lawyer will get in touch with you. He will know how to find you."

"Are we done with this? I don't think I can take it any longer. It's too heavy."

"Do you want to sleep on this decision?"

She shook her head emphatically. "No. I am in."

She was not sure whether it was the alcohol making her bold, or along the way, she had decided she was already in it, that she may as well dive in with all her clothes, but as she accepted his proposal, she felt a hundred per cent sure that it was the right thing to do. "Please, could you try and avoid getting yourself killed?"

"I will give it my best shot."

He picked the envelopes and handed them to her.

"My real name is Kanja, although you will not find it on those documents. That is the name you would use with the people I asked you to see."

She nodded, accepting the envelope.

* * *

235

NaiRobbery Cocktail

Boss's relief and fear were at par.

It was two in the morning, hours after he had one of the most difficult conversations of his life. He had been staring at his bedroom ceiling in the dark.

He could have patted himself on the back for baring all to Naliaka, but he could not ignore the reason behind his confession.

Also, he preached water, and drank wine. Often, every time one of his boys did something stupid, it was because of a woman. A criminal worth his salt should never trust a woman; that had always been his mantra.

He hated it when someone had leverage on him, yet he had willingly armed Naliaka. She could destroy him at the speed of a blink. He sighed and pulled her closer to him, for she was lying next to him, naked, out like a light because she had taken too much alcohol.

The past two weeks had been tense. He could have continued pretending that everything was okay, until earlier in the day. The tension up there was intense, his enemies were zeroing in on him, and it was getting dangerous for Naliaka. He had every reason to believe they did not know about her, but he did not want to take chances.

* * *

The call that had got Boss nearly running out of the house, the one that had come through his emergency phone that never delivered good news, had seen him brisk-walk to Uhuru Park with his bodyguards and *their* bodyguards, in tow.

The call was from a contact to his invisible bosses.

"Uhuru Park in half an hour. We need a boat ride."

236

It was nothing new, taking a boat ride in Uhuru Park. It was the one place they were sure walls could not listen.

Judas, like he was known among Boss's circles, was there before him. Boss did not need to see his face to recognise him. He knew his lanky figure and his twitchy stance. He knew he would be the guy with a baseball hat pulled down and sunglasses to boot. He would be the guy wearing a long coat, whatever the weather.

What Judas did not know was that Boss knew him, where he lived, who he was married to, where his two children went to school and his two mistresses. It had taken Boss's network almost a year to crack his identity. They would follow him into town, but he always picked busy buildings to disappear into, and the trail would be lost.

The day they finally got him was cold, and either Judas had been in a hurry, or he had let his confidence get to his head. Instead of walking to a building, he entered a vehicle parked on the streets. Excitement among Boss and his people had followed. Two riders who usually paused as *boda boda* riders followed him out of town. Within twenty four hours, Boss had a fat dossier on Judas. Within a week, he had a dossier on ten associates of his.

Now, in utter silence, the two got into a boat, cycling it in the same silence to the centre of the artificial lake at Uhuru Park. They stopped rowing and continued with the silence for a few moments.

"There may be trouble," Judas broke the silence as he pulled his hat farther down his forehead.

"There is always trouble. Be specific."

"The new station boss. He is not satisfied with his cut and he wants more involvement."

"He is stupid. Does he know what happened to the last one who tried that nonsense?"

No answer, but Boss, from the corner of his eye, saw a shrug.

"So what happens?" Boss asked.

"There is no decision yet, but if he carries out his threat to start a rival group…"

That got Boss turning to face Judas.

"He wouldn't dare!"

But even as he said that, he knew the man had already started daring. It explained the unusual activity on Kirinyaga Road. He had seen it coming and it had felt like waiting for a volcano that may or may not erupt. His watchers reported newbies on the streets, people who should not have been there, and they were watching his building. On top of that, there have been a couple of carjackings that were not committed by his team.

"He can do whatever he wants… or so he thinks," Boss muttered.

"Be careful."

Boss nodded. "I am always careful."

"There will be war on the streets. May the best man win."

Boss shifted on the boat's plastic seat, "So, is this my fight?"

"You know the answer to that. If there is a fight, you fight it. On your own."

He sighed. "I need to be sure, to know I can do it my way."

"Don't do anything yet, until you hear from us."

Boss shrugged, unwilling to make any commitment, but unwilling to argue as well.

"As usual, I am happy to do battle, but I have a condition this time round."

"You have no bloody right to make demands."

"I do, actually. I am risking my life as a lot of you have warm dinners in your warm beds in your posh estates with your beautiful wives. I am not the only one who benefits from this arrangement, yet if shit hits the fan, I lose it all. Now, like I said, I have a condition."

"What do you want?"

"I want out."

"What the…"

"I am tired. Really tired."

"You cannot just walk away."

"I know, but I am not just walking away. I am asking you to let me walk away."

"And if we don't?"

Boss shrugged. "Then we all lose."

"What the hell do you mean by that?"

"You should know you haven't been as careful as you think you have been in keeping your identity and that of everyone else. All of you. I, for instance, know all your names."

"You don't!"

Boss laughed. "How about Corporal James…"

"Shut up!"

It was a growl. A growl full of shock, anger and disbelief.

"You dared me."

"Are you blackmailing us?"

"Absolutely not. I am just telling you I have insurance, a ticket to walk away, alive, when I win."

"You son of a…"

"Oh, please. Did you expect me to just sit and take orders?"

"I could just kill you right here and throw your body in this very shallow lake."

"I do not doubt that, but right now, we are being watched by... what, perhaps ten people? And they are recording evidence. Perhaps, perhaps I am recording this conversation."

"I searched you!"

"Don't be daft. You are a cop and you should know better. I know you are recording me as well."

"You fu..."

"Save it. Anyway, it is in my interest not to use the evidence, but if you force me, I will. Trust me."

He sighed. "I will pass your message."

When they got off the boat, each took opposite directions. The rogue cop kept looking over his shoulders, but even with his trained eye, he could not pick out who was following him, yet he knew he was being followed.

If he had looked lower than his level of height, he would have seen the high number of street boys hovering around. He saw the men with cameras, but he could not tell the difference between the regular Uhuru Park photographers and Boss's photographers.

Now, as Boss looked at Naliaka next to him, he wondered if he would die before ever having experienced an orgasm.

* * *

Many years ago, a violent twist of fate brought Onyango and Samuel together, creating a mismatch of friendship that would last a lifetime.

It was at an estate bar where undesirables and the part-time elite were brought together by their love for rhumba music.

The pub, an open hall with plastic tables and chairs and a thatched roof to boot, was buzzing with alcohol and cigarette smoke and noise, mostly laughter and drunken declarations of love for rhumba and big-bottomed women. Most tables were empty, but only because the patrons were dancing. The few still seated were watching the dancing ones, nodding their heads or slowly moving their bodies to the slow beat.

Samuel and Onyango sat two tables apart. Samuel was on his own. Onyango was in the company of a woman. It was hard to ignore the two as they were constantly canoodling. 'They are married, but not to each other," Samuel muttered to himself and rolled his eyes.

They sat at the far end of the pub, facing the dance floor. Hours on, from his vantage point, Samuel saw four men enter the bar, stop at the entrance and scan the crowd. He sat up straight, because he knew they were not there for the music. Instinctively, he reached for the gun and cursed, because it was in the car.

On alert, he continued watching them. At first, he thought they were robbers, but soon realised they were looking for someone, and that *someone* was in trouble. Samuel gave the canoodling couple a quick glance. He turned back to the four men to find one of them pointing in his direction. They walked towards him.

"Now what have I done?" Samuel wondered to himself, holding his bottle of beer, ready to land it on the forehead of the first person who dared to hit him. A few metres away, he relaxed a little, because they were not there for him.

Like a group of choreographed dancers, they stopped at Onyango's table and started punching him from all corners. The woman screamed. Onyango managed to throw a weak punch that hit none. His bent position and that they were behind him and by his side put him at a disadvantage.

When Samuel joined the ruckus, he meant to separate the one-sided fight, but one of the men punched him on his shoulders, so he punched him in the face, sending him hurling blind to a table nearby before hitting the floor. He turned to the others.

The woman finally found her legs. She screamed before jumping over a seat, running towards the entrance. She was a big woman and in the midst of the chaos, Samuel quipped to himself how it should have been scientifically impossible for someone her size to jump over a seat and run so fast.

When he grabbed a second man from behind, dislodging him off Onyango, Samuel was on turbo charge. He punched him squarely on the face, like the first one. The first rule of battle engagement, especially when faced with an enemy who could win not by strength or prowess but by sheer numbers, was to hit the core. If they could not see him, they would not attack him. So he blinded the second one and kicked his groin, throwing him towards the first victim who was still groaning and rubbing his eyes. The two, piled on top of each other, groaned together, broken beer and glass bottles everywhere.

The two remaining attackers were still punching Onyango who had put his head under the table, a clever tactic that protected his head and groin. Samuel grabbed one of them, but unlike the first two, he was not so lucky with his punch. It missed the man's face. The man returned the punch that landed on Samuel's stomach. Samuel caught the third punch halfway, twisting the man's hand. He screamed.

Someone else screamed. And another. Then another one. Within seconds, it was a scramble for the door. The two downed men were crawling towards it. The one whose hand Samuel had twisted was begging to be released. Onyango, with less adversaries, was out of his *hole*. Samuel did not see how it happened, but when he turned towards him, Onyango was holding a gun against the fourth attacker's forehead, his other hand grabbing him by the shirt.

"Don't shoot me!" The attacker cried in terror.

"He's got a gun!" someone else shouted, and the scramble to the door intensified.

For a second, Samuel observed an impossible number of people trying to fit through the door. He released his victim who quickly rushed to join the brouhaha for the exit.

"You don't want to waste a bullet on a guy you could just slap," Samuel said calmly.

Onyango, bleeding on the lip, turned to look at Samuel, like he was just seeing him for the first time.

"Was it you who just helped me?"

He nodded. "Let him go. He ain't worth your silver."

Onyango looked at his whimpering prisoner then relaxed.

"You are right," he said. "But I need to know who the hell he is, why did they just try to kill me?" he shook the man violently. "Who the hell are you?"

"Sorry."

"I asked who you are."

The man whimpered more. Samuel cleared his throat and took a careful step towards Onyango and his captive.

"Let him go. I know why you were attacked."

"What? You know them?"

Samuel shrugged. "I don't need to. Let him go, the poor guy has already wet his trousers and if you are not careful some will land on your expensive shoes."

Onyango looked down at the man, made a disgusted face and a rude remark, released him and kicked him for a push. The man fell several times before disappearing out of the door.

"The hell… who are they?" Onyango asked, tucking back his gun.

"The woman you were trying to eat alive belongs to the person who paid them."

"What?"

Samuel shook his head, trying not to laugh at Onyango's naivety. It was not wise to laugh at the man with a gun.

"It was obvious to me, and I don't even know either of you. The urgency of your canoodling was that of teenagers trying to beat parental curfew. You were obviously both in a hurry to get back to your significant others."

Onyango allowed himself to be impressed, just for a second.

"Who the hell are you?"

"Guy who just saved your ass."

Onyango grunted. "Please, I could handle those slapdash kids with my little finger."

Samuel laughed. "They were *gonna* kill you. You are bleeding by the way."

"What?"

Samuel touched his own lip. Onyango mimicked him. He looked at his fingers and cussed.

"Also, we had better leave the premises right away. By my calculation, we have just about thirty seconds before the police come in with their bigger guns, or the crowds with blunt objects."

That sobered Onyango quickly. The two men walked out of the now empty pub that still had the music playing, the DJ having run out with everybody else. The immediate outside was empty too, but they could see silhouettes of people lurking from a safe distance.

"We could make a run for it."

Samuel shook his head. "No. It's too dangerous. If we walk toward them, and I can assure you by now the story out there is we are robbers, they will get us with stones and sheer numbers. Your Glock-17 has how many bullets left out of the seventeen?"

"What the... how do you know what gun I have?"

"You held it for all to see."

"But..."

"We don't have time for this. We need to get out. You can only shoot seventeen people if you are a good shot. The other two hundred will slaughter and drink our blood. We need an alternative escape route."

"Who the hell are you?" Onyango demanded, but even as he asked, as his private investigator instinct knew this man was not just another reveller, he followed him back to the pub, struggling to keep up because he was not as agile.

"I can answer you as you buy me a drink later. For now, we need to get out."

Samuel led the way into the kitchen situated at the back. The kitchen had been abandoned as well, various dishes in various stages of cooking. He led the way out to the back door.

"Every kitchen has a back door for fire exit and taking out trash," Samuel said unnecessarily.

"No back gate, unfortunately," he announced, scanning the stone wall.

"Can you jump over the wall?"

"Do I have a choice?"

"Yeah. You can remain here and wait to be murdered."

"In that case, I can climb a wall. I don't know how, but I suspect you do."

"Correct."

Samuel did not have to search far. Close to the wall was an empty drum. He put it upright, helped Onyango on it, waited for him to scale the wall before doing it himself in seconds.

"How do we get down?" Onyango wondered.

Samuel jumped down.

"This way."

Onyango did, landing with a thud. He groaned in pain. When he started walking following Samuel who was already walking away, he did so with a limp.

"I don't know why you are helping me, but remember I have a gun just in case you want to harm me, and it's cocked."

"I am not helping you. I am helping myself. Those people out there do not know we are strangers, but I was seen fighting for your side. I don't want to die because of some horny dude who can't keep his hands off people's wives…"

"Watch your mouth. I still have the gun!"

"You need to be fitter than you are by the way. You are panting badly. Come on! We can get behind that building and first lose the crowd."

When they did, Onyango's chest was on fire.

"You are right… I need to get fit. Can we find a place to sit, just for a few minutes?"

"We can get into that pub." He pointed at a pub, a similar one to the one they just escaped from.

"Are you crazy? What if someone recognises us?"

"Only five people could, four of them are receiving first aid for their injuries, and the woman will probably never be seen around again."

They took a corner table near an exit where they could watch the main entrance. They ordered drinks and imbibed in silence for ten minutes.

"I am Onyango. So who the hell are you, and I don't mean just the name?"

* * *

Now.

"From a distance, you look like a clever guy. Then I heard your car was stolen and I decided you only look clever from a distance." Those were Onyango's first words to Samuel when the latter walked into the former's office the following day. Samuel had decided to text Onyango about the carjacking, but he did not tell Kerubo that he had done so.

"Nice to see you, too," Samuel said, inviting himself opposite his boss, and going ahead to drink his tea.

"Nice tea. Pour yourself another one."

There was a flask, another cup and sugar in a tray on the desk.

Onyango growled, but there was no anger in his growl.

"I see they haven't started teaching you manners on the streets…"

"They are. We no longer walk naked!"

They laughed. The banter between the two men was as old as their friendship.

"So tell me, how does someone with your credentials get outsmarted by thugs?"

Samuel slurped and shrugged. "I wanted to experience carjacking. But seriously, how was I supposed to know the woman I had picked was one of Boss's?"

Onyango chuckled. "I told you, you need to get married, then you will not have to go picking up strange women in bars."

"Going by the he-goat tendencies you possess, we can conclude getting married does not cure that sort of thing."

They laughed.

"Talking of Boss, what's happening downtown?"

Samuel assumed a serious face by taking a deep breath. He was about to edit some truth to a friend, a boss, and that was nearly as bad as lying. Overridden by a desire to protect Naliaka, he had decided he would not tell all.

"There may be something, or not."

Onyango shifted on his seat expectantly. "Go on."

He shrugged. "I know every regular on that street. I know those who are there every day, those who come once a week, those who come once a year." He took another sip of the tea. Onyango did the same. It was tasty ginger tea, but neither of the two men were currently paying attention to the taste. "I noticed the strangers because they are obviously cops. Do you know anything about that?"

Onyango looked away. "Perhaps. But let's hear what you have."

"They are never together. They hover around, near you-know-who's building, and they suck at staying invisible. There is a new shoe-shiner on the streets, and he sucks at shoe-shining."

Onyango placed his cup on the table noisily, cleared his throat and blew into his palms. "We are running out of time."

"What do you mean?" It was a question calmly asked, but his insides had just done a somersault.

Onyango shifted again on the seat. "My person is annoyingly economical with the truth, but from the snippets, I think the new police boss is unhappy about his cut."

"… and he wants to replace Boss with someone more agreeable to his greed," Samuel cut in.

Onyango nodded. "We cannot allow them to kill Boss. I am going to need to bring somebody else to help you, at least until we know where this is going."

"Someone I know?"

"Cecilia, one of my best agents, is about to become a vegetable seller somewhere close to Boss's house, perhaps near the shoe-shiner."

Onyango sighed deeply, stretched his arms and sat back on the seat.

"Pretending to get rid of criminals is as old as civilisation. America, arguably the most advanced democracy in the world, will not get rid of crime, not because they cannot, but because crime is important for the human ecosystem. China and her socialist dictatorship still have jails. Countries with Sharia laws, enough of them brutal, have criminals. Who are we to imagine that we can live in a world without criminals? Crime, as terrible as it is, balances life. There cannot be good without evil, and unfortunately, evil is good for world economies."

"You make a good case, but what is our reason for preserving Boss?"

"Think of the Italian mafia—criminals by any other name. Many are tolerated by the law enforcement, at least as long as they don't become cop killers. The mafia have grassroots advantage. As ridiculous as it sounds, they control the masses better than the authorities. You know why? I will tell you why. Because they have grassroots support through feeding the needy, giving them jobs, protection—which is more than we can say about the government. In their own skewed way, they keep order.

"Boss has managed to do what the police force has failed to do. He has reduced the number of shootings during carjacking, for starters. That the shootings have reduced allows the law enforcement to record less shootings, and they take credit. Boss, being in charge of almost every parking lot in the city, has reduced vandalism to parked vehicles."

Samuel nodded. He knew all that, but he let Onyango talk.

"Boss has made the city safer. Other criminals are hesitant about doing their criminal activities in the city and immediate surroundings. Some have tried, but they did not live to tell the story." Onyango paused again for tea break.

"Boss has admirers in the force. Add that to the fact that he keeps their pockets very well lubricated. He is not greedy, and finding a thief who is not greedy is an event that only happens once in a century. A lot of people want Boss to stay because he makes their work easier. Several people have tried to estimate the number of people Boss has directly employed— it could be as many as five hundred."

"That's a whole conglomerate."

Onyango nodded. "And he probably pays better than the said companies. He has the toughest, roughest criminals as his subjects, and he is good to them. Boss has the city by the balls."

"I am almost impressed."

"I am constantly definitely impressed."

* * *

Hours later, Samuel picked Kerubo up in Ngara. As he watched her walking towards him, he found himself comparing her to Naliaka. Nothing similar, except they were both gorgeous, with the weights of their childhoods on their skinny shoulders. Yet, he could not see one and not think of the other.

He knew Kerubo well enough to immediately pick out that she looked sad.

"Hey…" he flashed her a hopeful smile when she took the passenger seat, bending to kiss her. She let him.

"Hey you. Have you any energy left to do me tonight?"

He laughed, louder and longer than the jibe allowed. He laughed because he was happy she still had her humour.

"Damn, I have missed you. How are you?"

He was already easing onto the road. He needed to leave the city before the rush hour traffic.

"Dog tired. I haven't slept well for two days…"

He looked at her sharply before asking why.

"I can explain the lack of enough sleep. You see this stupid hairstyle? It is so tight and whenever I put my head on the pillow, I feel like I am being stabbed on the scalp with toothpicks."

"It's beautiful."

"I don't care. If the pain doesn't ease by tomorrow, it's coming off."

"*Pole sana.*"

She shrugged. "Right now, I badly need a drink."

So he pulled over, went to the boot and came back with two cans of beer.

NaiRobbery Cocktail

"Warm beer is terrible, but it is better than anything. Thank you," she said as she opened hers loudly, pouring the liquid into her. She burped.

He laughed. "Such a Philistine!"

She downed some more. "You know, besides some shit happening in my life right now, shit that demands I get drunk, I have figured out the only way to get some sleep tonight is to make sure I don't stop drinking until I blackout."

Samuel laughed.

"Drink away. I promise not to take advantage of you."

"Nice ride, by the way," she finally said, looking at the car with disapproval.

"Liar. Your face tells the truth better than your mouth."

Kerubo was more relaxed by the time they arrived in Kitengela. She made the *chapati*, he made the stew and the greens. They watched a movie as they ate, washed the dishes and discussed everything that did not include what was bothering her.

By late evening, stuffed with food and half-drunk, they sat on opposite sides of the sofa, legs intertwined and sharing a couch blanket, each with a can of beer.

"You are doing a shit job at hiding that something is seriously bothering you."

Kerubo studied Samuel from the opposite side of the sofa and swallowed hard.

"You are fighting tears. Come on, spit it out," Samuel prodded her.

"Mrs Kamau is dying."

Samuel did not react. Not externally. "Shit, that's heavy. I am sorry. What's wrong?"

252

"Cirrhosis."

"When did you find out?"

"She has been sick for years, but she also has diabetes. They only told me about diabetes."

As she spoke, her tears flowed, she choked with them and emotions. Samuel hugged her, and wiped the tears for her, until there were no more tears to cry.

"I am so tired of crying, Sam. I am tired…" she concluded, pushing him away.

"You mean you are tired of being emotional? You do know you are human, right?"

She side-eyed him and shrugged. "So are you. I have never seen you cry."

"It doesn't mean I don't."

"Still, I am tired. I need something else to think about. How was your meeting with Onyango?"

"You don't want to talk about that right now."

"If I didn't I wouldn't have asked you," she snapped.

He put up his hands in surrender and told her.

* * *

"I don't know what to be more shocked about. Why didn't you tell him about Kiki's deep involvement with Boss?"

"Naliaka. Her name is Naliaka."

"Whatever! Why didn't you?"

"What value would it have added? It's not like she told me anything worth reporting."

She grunted. "What's the plan?"

"Gosh, you almost sound like you are looking forward to trouble."

"What would you rather I do instead?"

He thought for a while. "I don't know. Just don't sound excited."

She chuckled. "Anyway, it will be good to see Cecilia again."

"She's hot, but too serious."

"Don't even think about it. She would rather have me than you."

"Arrgh! That explains it."

"Sorry, not everyone thinks you are sexy."

"Ha ha! Anyway, the plan is to stay alive, to constantly have your gun cocked and to keep your eyes open."

"I understand."

"You look really tired. We can discuss this at length tomorrow. In the meantime, would you like to have sex?"

She chuckled, then laughed. It was a laugh he was familiar with.

"I will pass tonight. Let me catch up on my sleep arrears. That should give you time to recover from your Kiki."

"Naliaka."

"Whatever. Oh, I told Mrs Kamau I have a boyfriend, and his name is Samuel. What a coincidence."

"The hell?"

"I am about to introduce you to her as my future husband. We are going to see her on Friday."

"Today is Wednesday!" he protested in panic. "Oh, good! We have enough time to go through the lies we shall tell her."

Chapter Fifteen

One moment, Naliaka was in the gentle arms of Samuel, watching a beautiful sunset over Mt Kilimanjaro. The next moment, she was standing on a beach watching a similar sunset, standing next to Boss, enjoying the feeling of the wet beach sand up through her toes. But the beautiful moment turned into a nightmare when a tsunami kind of storm started rising from the horizon, swallowing the sunset, rushing towards them. The storm frightened her, but she stood rooted on the same spot, hypnotised by its beauty. She woke up screaming Boss's name.

She sat up so fast that she knocked her head on the headboard. "Ouch!" she groaned, rubbing the head before opening her eyes. Disorientation took over for a moment. Then she remembered. It has been three days and two nights since she moved in with Queen.

The three days had been a reminder that time could either sprint, or crawl, depending on what one was up to, or not up to. For two days, she looked through the window with jealousy down at the laughing girls soaking up in the sun, yet feeling no desire to join.

The nights were worse with elusive sleep, and when it came, the abyss of nightmare after nightmare would take over. In one of the nightmares, she was a bank robber. She managed to break the vault but just as she was about to leave, a backpack similar to the one Boss had given her was strapped on her back reading, "Boss shot her".

In another nightmare, she had fallen in love with Kaggai and just as she was about to kiss him, Boss had walked in on them. "You betrayed me!" he screamed before shooting at her.

She was weak with fatigue, anxious with worry, and starting to wonder how long she could hold on to her sanity.

Slowly and unwillingly, but knowing she had to, she got out of bed, stretched her tense body, dragged her feet to the window and drew the curtains to look outside. It was a wet morning. The long rains, the ones that had been preceded by a scorching sun, had broken the skies the night before. She spotted one vehicle at the parking lot, Queen's. She turned to look at the clock on the wall. Eight in the morning.

There was a soft knock at the door. She adjusted her shorts, rubbed her eyes and sides of her mouth to rid them of any white stuff from the night and ran a hand over her bald head. "Come in."

Queen popped her head in. "You are up."

Naliaka smiled. "Been up for a minute." She sighed and rubbed her face again, walking to the bed and slumping herself on it. She bounced on the mattress a few times before throwing herself flat, hands spread out.

"Argh! What I would do to get some decent sleep."

Queen shut the door behind her softly and sat next to Naliaka, studying her with concern.

"Eye bags don't suit you. I hear cucumbers work wonders on them."

When Naliaka arrived, Queen had been on the way out, when two unfamiliar vehicles drove in. Naliaka emerged from the first one, and left two burly men inside. The two occupants of the second car, as burly, never left the vehicle. None of them acknowledged Queen. Later, the gateman on duty would tell Queen that a third car with four occupants had remained parked a distance from the gate.

Naliaka and Queen hugged without exchanging a word. The hug had gone on for long, and when they broke it, Naliaka waved off the men before walking, hand-in-hand with Queen, to the house. The other girls were still in their rooms and Queen and Naliaka quietly walked to Naliaka's usual room.

"Do you need anything?"

"Shower. Breakfast and sleep... is it... is it okay if the maid brings my breakfast?"

Queen went to say something but changed her mind and nodded instead.

She brought it herself.

She sat with Naliaka for a while, in silence. Queen watched a spaced out Naliaka, head turned towards the window, slowly chewing on her breakfast of two sausages and two slices of toasted bread, once in a while sipping on her tea. As soon as Naliaka was done, Queen kissed her forehead, picked up the breakfast tray and walked out. When she returned at night, the lights in Naliaka's room were off.

Day two, Naliaka feigned period pains, her reason to Julia when she came up to the room to ask why she was not joining everyone else downstairs. The rest of the day was spent in Queen's bedroom watching television.

Day three. She was not feeling any better mentally than day one, she did not have any answers to the questions she was asking herself. She was afraid of the questions Queen would ask, questions she would have to give honest answers to. She wondered if being honest to Queen amounted to betrayal to Boss, a thought that increased her stress levels.

"You want to tell me what the hell is going on? And don't tell me crap about period pain and other fabricated stories. Is there trouble in Boss's paradise?"

Naliaka sighed again and sat up, facing Queen and letting her eyes linger on her for a few seconds.

"Let me show you something," Queen's eyes followed Naliaka as she walked to the wardrobe and retrieved the backpack which she handed to Queen. "Open it, please."

Queen gave her a questioning look but took the backpack.

"Why can't you open it yourself?"

Naliaka shrugged. "Please…"

As Queen unzipped the bag, Naliaka's eyes were on her, taking in all the different emotions that played on Queen's face. There was uncertainty just before opening the bag, then shock that came with a gasp. Then surprise and finally confusion. It was the same confused face she turned to look at Naliaka with.

"What the hell is this? Whose money is it?" Queen demanded, letting the bag slip off slowly to the floor, some of the money and gold pieces pouring out of it. Like someone trying to wipe off traces of the bag, Queen rubbed her palms together in quick succession.

"Boss."

"You stole it?" It was a roughly whispered question. She stood up, put her hands on her waistline, glaring at Naliaka in disbelief.

"No! He asked me to keep it for him." Naliaka saw the anger leave Queen's face, but the confusion remained.

"Why?"

Naliaka sighed again. Even she was tired with the number of sighs she was giving. "There is something I need to tell you. I don't know if you will still want me to be here. I will understand if you do not."

"Get on with it already…" Queen said with exasperation.

"Boss is a robber," she said quickly.

Queen paused for a moment. Then, started to laugh.

* * *

"At this rate, I will end up being a seasoned drinker. I got really drunk the other day," Naliaka said, accepting a refill from the near empty bottle of wine that Queen had opened.

"Certain issues cannot be discussed with a sober mind."

Sitting and standing positions were changed several times within the hour. They laughed. They cried. And now, they were exhausted and Naliaka was feeling drunk but relieved.

"You know," Queen said, dubbing her eyes with her tee shirt. "When I still had illusions of having a man in my life, I always wanted a thief for a boyfriend," she chuckled. So did Naliaka.

"I was convinced a thief would be the only type of man to understand the type of person I am. *Ole wangu*, even the thieves did not want me!" Queen giggled. Naliaka smiled. "Now I know why. If Boss is the type of thief available, of course I was doomed from the start. That man is too good looking for his own good."

Naliaka cleared her throat.

Queen chuckled.

"When you have lived as long as I have, experienced as much as I have, watched women go through hell, you end up soaking in all their problems and then feeling guilty at the same time for using them to make yourself rich, then you learn how to look at the bright side of life."

Naliaka nodded.

"This… this Boss business is serious. It puts you in danger not only from his rivals, but the law as well. By extension, it puts me and my entire network in danger."

"I am sorry… I could leave…"

"Rubbish. You stay right where you are. What we do is find a solution."

"What do we do?"

Queen shrugged. "I am with Boss. Stay here, out of the way. I can, in the meantime, enjoy the security he is providing. Just do not steal the contents of that bag."

"I wouldn't know what to do with it, anyway." She looked at the bag, still lying haphazardly on the floor.

Queen chuckled. "We could hope Boss gets shot dead, then you end up with everything… ah… things you could do with that money."

"Queen! I don't want him to die."

Queen shrugged. "It could happen."

* * *

"So why are you here, pretending to have period pains?" Malaika, the one person who could be relied on to ask direct questions, shot the first. The four of them, Malaika, Julia and Susan, a new girl, were having their lunch in the dining room. The rains had relented, but the grounds were too wet for anyone to sit outside.

"I wasn't lying."

"You were," Julia asserted with an eye roll.

"You lived here for years and we would have known if cramps were your thing."

"It could have started when I left."

"Unless... unless you are having an abortion?"

Naliaka gasped, horrified. "I always use condoms."

"Accidents happen."

Naliaka shook her head. "I just wanted to be alone."

Telling part of the truth suddenly appealed to her better than letting anyone think she had an abortion.

"Boyfriend trouble?"

"I am okay now."

"How long are you going to be here?" Malaika was relentless.

Naliaka shrugged. "I don't know."

"Will you start working again?" Malaika pressed.

"Here? No."

"Lucky witch. And you still get to live here, for free, in your own room."

"You sound jealous, Malaika."

"Of course I am! The day I tell Queen that I no longer want to work here will be the day she asks me to pack all my belongings. Yet, here you are, swaggering in and out like you co-own the house."

"What would you do if you left?"

"Start some shit business, I guess. I have the capital, but I don't know how to do business. I hate to think of the day I will leave, because I am happy here. And I can't take care of myself out there. It has been so long."

Naliaka reached out for Malaika's hand, squeezing it reassuringly. "You can. I didn't know how to take care of myself either, and I survived."

"You are sober, and brainier."

"I think you are brainy… if only you were not stoned most of the time."

"Right there is the problem. I can't be sober. I don't want to be. Do you know I have been on one type of high or another since I was twelve? You think I can live without intoxicating myself? I don't even remember how it feels to be sober."

"Stop being such a defeatist."

"It's pragmatism. I will stay on until Queen kicks me out, and I suspect it is going to be soon. I am nearly too old for this. Even my regular clients have started preferring younger and newer women…" Malaika said, shooting an accusing glance at Susan who had been listening to the conversation quietly, nibbling on her breakfast.

Naliaka sighed in defeat, turning her gaze to Julia who was lost in thought.

"But Julia still gets clients and she is older than you."

"Julia is Julia. The men who pick her do so because they are looking for someone motherly. She has more longevity than all of us."

"Do you ever plan to stop?" Naliaka asked Julia.

Julia shrugged. "I could stop *yesterday*. The only thing keeping me here is because I am waiting for my husband to die. Why won't he die?" She was looking at each of the three other girls in turn, like she was expecting an answer.

* * *

Kerubo sat in a near stoic state, staring at the television. On the sofa, she tucked her long legs under her, chewing her nails, one at a time, an intense look on her face. She had just left the bed, still wearing Samuel's oversized tee-shirt, and nothing underneath. She should have been feeling better because the night before, she had finally slept properly.

Samuel emerged from the kitchen, chewing on a slice of toasted bread. He stopped to study her.

"I didn't know you were up."

Kerubo turned slowly to look at him, pausing on her nail chewing. "Hey."

"Anyone would think I was the one taking you to meet my parents. You are more nervous than I," he said, offering her his half chewed piece of toast. She accepted it, replacing the nail chewing with the toast.

"I think this is the stupidest idea I ever came up with. I just have a bad feeling about this…"

"I could agree, but it is too late to pull out. In fact, you should already be in the bathroom. It's ten and if we do not leave in an hour, we will be late."

"Why do you sound like you are looking forward to this?"

He chuckled. "I am. I have never, ever been introduced by a girl to her parents. I always wondered how that felt."

She smiled. "Only this is a lie…"

Samuel shrugged. "A noble lie. Besides, you and I shag. Isn't that what boyfriend and girlfriend do?"

"You don't think she will work it out that we are lying?"

He shrugged. "If they want us to demonstrate by having a quickie, we can…"

"Piss off!"

"Breakfast? I was just preparing something light."

She shook her head. "Just coffee."

* * *

At midday, Kerubo and Samuel pulled into the Kamau's' compound. It was quiet and still. Kerubo shivered as she opened the gate, expecting, hoping to find mama basking in the sun like she had found her the last time.

"It's so quiet," she whispered to herself as Samuel parked the car next to the Kamau's.

"Perhaps they are not in?" she said hopefully, but she knew baba hardly ever left without the car, even when he needed to go to the town only a kilometre away. He had developed problems with his knees and too much walking left him in pain for days.

"So…" Samuel interrupted her thoughts.

"We go in."

She had a spare key, but when she tried the lock, it opened. She put her head in first, looking around before calling out.

"Hello… is anyone home?"

Silence. Kerubo started shaking. She had been in many scary situations, but not even the one she had been on the verge of being raped next to Cecilia could measure up to the kind of fear that was engulfing her, bit by bit, starting with her feet, swallowing her body like quicksand. She took a deep breath and straightened up. Whatever it was, if it didn't have a gun, she could handle it.

"Have a seat as I check upstairs," she said full of hope.

She took two stairs at a go. She softly knocked on the Kamau's bedroom door. No answer. When she opened the door, she couldn't decide what repulsed her most. There was the smell. A diseased kind of smell that not only penetrated her nose, but her eyes as well. Her throat contracted. Then there was the darkness. It was well past midday, but the dark curtains were drawn, locking out the light. She squinted her eyes, focusing on the bed. Two figures huddled together, still as death. She squeaked. Or perhaps she screamed because the squeak could not have been heard by Samuel, yet he ran upstairs.

He found Kerubo grabbing on the door handle, knees buckled, trying to stop herself from hitting the floor. He stabilised her as he went through the same emotions Kerubo had a few seconds ago. The smell. The darkness. The stillness.

"Oh shit..." he said, his way of acknowledging the two still figures, then he turned to Kerubo, gently pushing her out of the door completely.

"Get the hell out of here!" He grabbed her hand, leading her downstairs. She followed, like a robot, unblinking. When he got her to sit on the sofa, he located the kitchen and got her a glass of water. She took it but held it without drinking. He ran back upstairs.

They were dead.

Kerubo had spoken on the phone to baba the previous night to confirm their visit, Samuel had been present during the phone call. She had not spoken to Mama because according to Baba, she was resting in bed. Now he wondered. Burglary? He dismissed that thought immediately. A murdering burglar would have left evidence in the form of messy rooms. Suicide? Murder and suicide? Death and suicide? It had to be one of the above because, as far as Samuel knew, Baba was not sick enough to die.

The first thing he did was to draw the curtains and open the windows. Then he turned to look at the bodies. How peaceful they both looked. He poked them—hard and cold, rigour mortis. He sighed and looked around. On the side of the table was a note written in red. There was a jug of water and a couple of empty bottles of pills. He picked the letter.

"Kerubo. I am sorry it had to be this way, but we discussed and agreed it would be better to leave together. You were aware of mama's debilitating illness, but we did not tell you about mine, colon cancer, stage four, diagnosed a month ago. I have watched mama suffer. I refuse to suffer like that, especially when I know the only person who would end up taking care of me is you. You need to live your life. You are a great woman, you deserve to be happy, and I wish you nothing but happiness. We are so happy that you finally found yourself a man to love, it means we shall die in peace; may he make you happy. Do not worry about informing our children, I already sent them an email but please, do not let anyone else know how we died.

All our love"

"What is that?"

Samuel jumped guiltily. He had not heard Kerubo walk up the stairs. She stood, legs and arms crossed, watching him. And she was looking… normal?

"What are you doing here? Are you okay?"

"I am fine," she said, walking to him with an outstretched arm. The handwritten suicide note was dangling between his fingers, she bent a little and grabbed it. She went to the window, leaned on it and started reading. Samuel studied her, all the fifty-five seconds she took to read the letter.

"That's it, then," she said, looking up at him. He realised she was avoiding direct glances at the bed.

"Kerubo?"

"What?" she snapped.

"Your parents just died…"

"Erm… this might sound strange, but this is *kinda* the second time it is happening."

"Kerubo…"

"What!" she screamed.

"Look, I don't know what you expect me to do. They are dead, I cannot resurrect them. I did not cry when my own parents died, I have no intention of doing it now. They chose to die, together, good for them!" she shrugged and walked out.

Samuel remained on the same spot, looking at the door she just walked out of, and only moved when he heard the microwave turned on.

"That woman is mad!" he muttered and turned to the dead bodies.

"I guess it is you and I… oh, nice to meet you, dead or alive…" he chuckled at the last statement, immediately reprimanding himself. He fished for his phone and called Onyango.

The police arrived, so did the ambulance. Samuel and Kerubo were questioned together, but he answered most of the questions.

* * *

Kerubo often wondered why people smoked. The smell of cigarettes should have been bad enough to dissuade anyone, the dangers of smoking were worse, and nobody looked cool. But, as she sat on Samuel's balcony holding a can of beer and staring into the horizon, she suddenly wanted a cigarette.

It was evening, hours since the discovery of Mr and Mrs Kamau's bodies. She had not shed a tear, but she had done what needed to be done, ensuring their bodies were preserved at the mortuary and answering the questions from the police. With Samuel by her side, she had secured and locked up the house, and then in silence, they went to Samuel's house in Kitengela.

Samuel was a silent presence, only speaking when spoken to, just what she needed. He was by her side holding a beer as well, soft music playing inside the house but seeping through to the balcony, when she started talking about something she was usually successful at making herself forget. Her biological parents.

"I never told you how I lost my biological parents." Her words were slurry, but they were clear enough. Samuel shifted on the seat, preparing himself for what was obviously a confession.

"No, you never did."

"I am not even sure what they died of, you know. They were alcoholics, so their bodies could have just given up. But I never was invested enough to find out."

"That bad?"

"Worse." She cleared her throat and took a sip of her drink. "Did I ever tell you how I met Onyango?" Samuel looked at her in confusion.

"Stay with me—the two tales are connected."

"No, you never told me how you met Onyango."

"See, I spent most of my time at the Kamau's, especially after their children left home. If I was not there, I was at my one-room house close by. I never, ever went to see my own parents although they lived a few hundred metres away."

Samuel nodded. He knew only bits and pieces of her severed relationship with her biological parents, and he had worked it out pretty early that she did not like to talk about them. When he had told her about his relationship with his own father, it was in the hope that she would open up, but she had not.

"The Kamau's never gave me any pressure to see them, they knew our history and besides, they did not trust my parents with me. But this one time, Mrs Kamau suggested that I should go and see my mother because she was ailing. I knew for her to tell me that, it was bad. So, I left and walked towards my former home, but when I got to the gate, I could not bring myself to go in. I walked past, and kept walking."

Kilometres away, the skies went dark. The first fat drop of rain hit her forehead. She wiped it off with her sleeve and looked up. The next drop entered her eye. She turned back and tried to outrun the rain, but it was faster. The police station, the building closest to her when the rain caught up, looked like a good place to take shelter. A young policeman, looking terribly bored, looked at her with disdain, one eyebrow up.

"Yes?" he asked as he flipped covers of a tattered occurrence book.

Feeling a little silly, Kerubo shook her soaked body, water dripping onto the floor around her.

"What do you want?" the policeman asked again, this time forcefully. "Do you want to report something?"

Kerubo stood on the same spot in the middle of the room, looking at the dripped floor and wondering how she had thought taking shelter in a police station was a good idea. She shook her head without looking at the policeman.

"Well, is there someone you want to see?"

She shook her head.

"A police station is not a place for idlers, so if you have nothing to do…" he pointed at the door and went back to flipping the pages.

"It's raining."

"Oh, who would have thought?" the policeman sneered. "Now, get out!"

"May I see your boss?"

That she asked shocked her as much as it seemed to shock the policeman.

The policeman laughed in disbelief. "Which boss? I have many."

"The big boss. I need to ask him something?"

"What do you want to ask?"

"I would rather talk to your boss, please."

"Listen here lady, this is a police station, not a social office. You do not get to see my boss unless I know what it is you want to ask him. If you cannot tell me, I repeat, you need to leave, right now."

Kerubo sighed and turned to look at the persistent rain. Suddenly the rain looked better than arguing with the policeman with a bad attitude. She turned to go, only to bump into a formidable figure at the door.

"Sorry, sir!" she mumbled as she stepped aside, taking note of his superiority of uniform and obviously, rank.

He furrowed his brow at her. "Young lady, are you alright?"

Kerubo nodded before stepping outside.

"What is her problem?" He asked the policeman at the reception.

"*Afande*, she is a nuisance. She said she wants to see the boss…" The young cop answered, starting to laugh but quickly realised his boss did not get the joke. "Sir!"

He went to say something to the cop manning the reception, but changed his mind and instead beckoned Kerubo to follow him.

In the end, Kerubo sat with the OCS in his office, shared a cup of tea and told him that she was on a long university break, and was looking for a job.

"Obviously I cannot employ you, seeing that I work for the government, but I know someone who just might." So he called his friend, Onyango, who hired Kerubo immediately. For months, she did the filing, made tea and did deliveries within the city. Onyango's office was where Kerubo went to work whenever she was on university break, including weekends and the days she did not have lectures. Over time, she was trained in martial arts, taken to shooting ranges and then given honey-trap assignments. She never left Onyango's employ even after graduation.

"Anyway, I never did go to see my mother, and she died two weeks later. I did go to the burial but stood at the back. Dad died soon after and I did not attend his burial. According to Mrs Kamau, they had TB."

After a long silence, Samuel asked, "Do you feel guilty?"

Without hesitation, she said, "I should, but I don't."

Samuel understood. Many times he had wondered why he never, ever, felt guilty for hating his own father in life and death, but it was the only honest way to feel.

NaiRobbery Cocktail

Chapter Sixteen

"You took precautions." It was a statement that Boss said without looking up from his phone.

Jonte paused at the door in confusion. It was not his first time to be summoned by Boss. He, Boss, often used him to deliver personal messages to contacts. Once in a while, he was invited for lunch, but those lunches always involved a lot of picking of Jonte's brain.

It was, however, the first time he had found the house crowded. It unnerved him, especially because the call that had summoned him had been short and terse. It had left him nervous now that he couldn't think of anything that he might have consciously done wrong.

He cleared his throat and stood straight, feigning courage he did not feel.

"I did," he answered, but he was busy calculating his chances of survival. He knew four of the men present. Two were Boss's regular bodyguards, one was Boss's body double, and there was Boss. The other three were strangers who reminded him of Hannibal Lector, like they regularly fed on raw human brains.

The only people seated were Boss and his double, strangely assuming the same pose of sitting against the sofa with spread out legs. They were dressed in similar clothes; white tee shirts, blue jeans and similar haircuts. They were like identical twins, only that boss was a shade darker than his double.

"Would you like to sit?" Boss asked, finally looking up.

"What?" Jonte heard the question, he was just having a hard time processing it.

Boss grunted. "Sit over there," he pointed at the dining table area with his mouth. Jonte slowly took a seat, his eyes never leaving Boss.

"Would you like something to drink?" Boss continued with what Jonte started considering as gentle torture.

He tried to talk but instead swallowed hard. The first tickle of sweat was emitted from his nose tip. He wiped it with the back of his hand.

"What would you like?"

"Water?"

Boss shrugged and nodded at one of his bodyguards. "Bring him water, and a beer for me, and a drink of whatever everyone else is having".

Jonte was trying not to look at anyone, but his eyes did so involuntarily. He was watching everyone in turn. How nobody looked threatening, not that any of them looked particularly friendly, but he had seen most of them at their worst, and this was not it. In fact, unless his eyes were deceiving him, he caught Boss looking at him with a bemused expression.

The bodyguard returned carrying a tray with everyone's drink.

"I am sure you are wondering why I called you."

"Yes, Boss."

"It's because I need you to take a break from your... erm, field operations."

"Boss?" In his pessimistic state, he understood Boss's statement to mean he was fired. Boss did not fire people though, he killed people.

"Relax, I am not about to kill you."

"Oh." He picked his water and drank half of it in one go.

"Do you think Oti can work with someone other than you?"

Jonte hesitated. He liked Oti very much, but he also knew Oti was a loose cannon with crazy ideas of how they could break away. Oti was tenacious, a born renegade. He was annoying, too, but Jonte found his character amusing. Not many people would.

"I... I am not sure."

"Jonte, be very careful with your answers. We are not in the business of protecting friendships. I will ask you again and I expect an honest answer."

Jonte returned Boss's stare and saw, in that look, a fiery warning. It was the look of the ruthless man he knew his boss was, not the friendly face that had welcomed him and offered him a drink only a minute earlier. He took a deep breath and nodded.

"Can Oti be trusted if paired with someone else?"

Jonte shook his head emphatically. "He is not used to taking orders. He has been a lone ranger since he was a kid, but he is generally a good person."

"Good for him," Boss said sarcastically, sitting back on the sofa. His body double next to him mirrored him. "I am sure Jesus will take note of his good nature on Judgement Day. So, what would you do with him?"

Jonte gasped. "Me?"

"Was I talking to anyone else here?"

"I… I would keep him close to me. I can control him."

"How?"

"I talk to him when he sounds like he is going off the rail."

"So you are willing to be a babysitter to a full-grown adult?"

Jonte looked down at his black socks, what he had thought were both black socks, but what he was looking at was one brown and one black. He pulled his legs under the seat, hoping nobody else had seen.

"You are going soft on me," Boss's tone sounded so disappointed. "We do not have time for emotional decisions." He thought of Naliaka and how emotional he got around her and allowed himself to feel like a fraud, just for a second. "Emotions cloud your judgement. They make you hesitate. They make you start rationalising stuff. So I ask again, 'What would you do with him?'"

"Kill him," Strangely, Jonte felt no guilt at saying that.

Boss smiled and nodded. He sat up. His body double did the same. Their copy and paste movements were starting to bother Jonte.

"That's one option. The other option is to have him get himself killed."

"Sorry?"

Boss cleared his throat. "Oti is not why we are here though."

"Oh?" He asked with relief.

"You see these people here?" Jonte looked at each of them in turn.

"These are the most important people you will ever have as your friends. Like soldiers, they will take a bullet for you, and they are the reason I am alive. Respect them. Consult them. Treat them well," he cleared his throat before continuing. "You know my bodyguards, of course?"

Jonte nodded. There was more sweat running down his back.

"You know Boss2?"

Boss2 was the body double. Jonte nodded.

"These other three are arguably the most important. They head the surveillance team."

Jonte swallowed hard. The three men looked scary, scarier than the ones he had met during interrogation of enemies.

"With time, you will get to know them."

"When... when does my eem... break start?"

"Tomorrow. You however still have today to take care of pending business, like telling Oti that he is getting another partner. Like moving out of your current house."

"Move out?"

"To Ngumo. It is easier to secure. Oh, and break it off with Mary."

"Mary?" He asked stupidly.

"Isn't Mary the name of your new girlfriend?"

Jonte fought an urge to laugh, instead shifting on his seat. He had been dating Mary for not more than two weeks, having broken up with his previous girlfriend. He side-eyed the surveillance team, impressed.

"She is."

"You change your women too often. No women in Ngumo."

Jonte was feeling like a child who had been caught stealing sugar.

* * *

It made sense that the rooftop was only accessible from Boss's house as he had the whole third floor to himself. Only five people had access to the rooftop; him and his four bodyguards who worked in shifts of two. It was accessible through a wardrobe door in his bedroom. Behind the clothes was a door that had been drilled through a wall, with a ladder going up to the roof. There was another ladder on the roof, a foldable one that could get close enough to the street floor for someone to jump down safely.

If it ever came to him escaping through the rooftop down the ladder, he would land next to the shack he spent many years calling home, and from there he could disappear to any of different directions, helped by tens of street children.

Nine o'clock found Boss on the rooftop, alone. It was not a place he liked going to, except when he was emotionally overwhelmed. It was too windy and he could smell the filth from Nairobi River. There was nothing much to see from up there except other old buildings and dirty streets. It was also not the most comfortable of places to relax, not even with a beer. There were no seats, only a couple of concrete slabs. On those cold slabs, he sat and thought and sipped his beer. He also walked round the rooftop, gazing down to the streets below.

He should have been feeling more relaxed after speaking to Jonte, after his top management agreed that with a little polishing, Jonte could indeed make a good replacement. He had, just before Jonte arrived, told them about his intention to retire without disbanding the organisation. There had been protests, he had expected that. He begged them to agree to monitor Jonte, to test his ability and resilience, at least for the next one week.

"If you are not impressed, I will gladly stay on."

His retirement depended on how well Jonte fared, because if push came to shove, he would never be able to live with himself if he walked away from the hundreds of people working under him, tens of street children who looked up to him. The promise he made to Mato on his deathbed meant more to him than his freedom, even more than his desire to run away with Naliaka. That promise included keeping the rapists off the streets.

As much as the afternoon had been a success, he was far from relaxed. He was putting faith in too many people at the same time, including Jonte and Naliaka, and that felt more strange than scary.

He sighed and walked to the edge of the rooftop and looked down at the shack. That shack was an integral part of his fiefdom. Through the bad lighting of the street, he saw a smouldering fire inside, most definitely an old tyre fire. He heard laughter and smiled. Nothing changed much. If he listened keenly, he could hear the clicking and clacking of aluminium spoons against aluminium plates. The family was having dinner. After dinner, they would tell stories, or have orgies. The memory of the orgies made him grunt with jealousy.

He let himself think about Naliaka. He smiled, a short happy smile that warmed even his morbid heart, a smile that ended as quickly as it came. He hated the likely possibility of never seeing her again. He hated the possibility of being betrayed by her.

They had not spoken since she left, not because he couldn't, but as much as his heart ached for her, he needed to give her time to process the heavy stuff. On the bright side, the security had assured him that she stayed indoors.

* * *

The rain was beating gently against the roof, and like the Pied Piper, baiting Naliaka and Queen to sleep. It had taken Queen's horror reaction at the time to get both of them to decide to watch a movie. "We cannot sleep at nine-fifteen. We are not babies," Queen had declared.

They changed into warm night clothes and sat against the headboard, feet under the duvet to wade off the chill. The chill made Naliaka worry about Boss's Boys. Queen dismissed her worries with a single statement, "They probably have already put up a structure inside the farm, or dug an underground tunnel." So they settled in.

Their cosy set-up was interrupted ten minutes into the movie. She did not hear the phone ring because it was on silent mode, but she saw the screen flashing. Unnecessarily, she peeped at the caller ID though she already knew who it was. She took a sharp breath anyway, when Boss's name displayed on her phone.

"What?" Queen asked, pausing her glass of wine halfway to the mouth. Naliaka nodded at the phone.

"Well, what are you waiting for? Pick it."

"What do you think he wants?"

"How would I know, child? Pick it."

Naliaka picked it, cleared her throat and tried to stay calm.

"Hello?"

"Naliaka, hey. How are you?"

"You are okay…" She said with relief, looking at Queen and smiling.

Boss laughed. "I know I am. You?"

"Okay, I guess."

"You are sure?"

She nodded.

"That's great."

"How… how is everything?"

"Same, same. Things are quiet, but it's definitely the calm before the storm."

"Can't you just... run away?"

Boss sniggered before answering.

"Run to where? There is no place far enough to run, unless it's six feet under." He regretted his choice of words when he heard her gulp. "Let's not talk about that, though. I just called to check on you. I miss you."

It was a five-minute conversation, one that could have been a romantic one if only both of them were not constantly thinking about tragic endings.

"You okay?" Queen whispered after the call was over.

"Can I sleep with you?" she asked instead of answering.

* * *

Before leaving the house in the morning, Queen gently shook Naliaka from sleep. "Listen, sleepy head, if I return in the evening and find out that you haven't gone for a walk, I will whip you with a belt."

Naliaka groaned and pulled the duvet to cover herself. She wished never to wake up because the night before had been nightmare-free, and she was still enjoying dreamless sleep.

An hour later, Julia stormed in to find Naliaka still asleep.

"Goodness... almost ten years in this house and this is the first time I am having access to this room!" Julia's voice was what woke Naliaka up. The former was going from one end of the room to the next, opening the walk-in closet, the bathroom and asking why there were two bathtubs. Naliaka groaned, still half asleep.

"Why are you sleeping in Queen's bed, anyway?" Julia demanded, finally settling down on the bed. "I hope you are not having sex with her. Is that why she favours you, because you two are lovers?"

That woke Naliaka up completely. "I am not gay!"

"Is she?" Julia quipped, poking Naliaka playfully.

"She has never tried anything with me." But she did remember the kiss a long time ago that had never been re-enacted, or spoken about.

Julia lifted one eyebrow. "So, why are you sleeping here?"

"You ask the weirdest questions."

"So shoot me. Anyway, her royal highness asked me to wake you up for your royal walk. I am your designated escort."

"Argh… what if I don't want to go?"

"She didn't sound like she was giving you a choice, or me, so I may have to drag you out."

After breakfast, Naliaka slipped into a pair of skin tights, a pair of boots and a long sweater. An umbrella dangled from one of her hands, while the other hand held her phone. Julia wore a pair of jeans and sneakers, and only a tee-shirt to protect her torso. Her head, covered by a hat, neck by a scarf and eyes by sunglasses, was more protected than her torso.

"I cannot risk running into you-know-who. This is for disguise, not for warmth."

"Are you not going to freeze, the rest of you?" Naliaka asked Julia.

"Skinny people worry about freezing," she retorted. "This layer of fat on me is there for moments like this."

Naliaka was a fast walker but had to slow down for a much slower Julia. When they stepped out of the gate, Naliaka looked around discreetly, expecting to see evidence of the supposed security. It was possible, she thought, that Boss had just told her about the security to keep her on edge, to discourage her from running away with his money. All the way to the road a few hundred metres from the gate, she saw nothing.

Then her phone vibrated in her hand. Boss.

"Where are you going?" he asked urgently.

Naliaka turned sharply, spun round, searching for someone, anyone, anything. She saw nothing.

"What's going on?" Julia asked with alarm, emulating Naliaka.

"Nothing," she assured Julia as she covered her mouth piece.

"Hey... sorry, Julia and I are just going for a walk." Her voice was calm, but her insides were anything but calm.

"Where to?"

Naliaka laughed unnecessarily, but for the benefit of Julia.

"Oh... I was bored in the house and I wanted to stretch my legs. So, how is Mombasa?" she asked with forced cheer, hoping Boss would catch on.

"You are sure you are fine? Not leaving for somewhere?"

Naliaka laughed again. "Oh no... perhaps I will buy a plate of chips for Julia... as for you, mister, make sure you bring back some seashells with you... bye bye, love you."

She turned to a confused Julia.

"John?"

"Yep. He is in Mombasa."

"Why did you look frightened?"

"Oh, that? I don't like maize plantations and when the wind beat against the stalks I freaked out."

For the rest of the walk, Naliaka's biggest effort was to try not to look around her.

"It's a good thing we have this time of our own."

They stopped by a bar in Ndenderu. Julia had a beer while Naliaka had water.

"I am serious about quitting this lifestyle," said Julia.

"I can imagine."

"My children... I have been thinking a lot about them lately. One is nearly twenty, the other one following closely behind. I want to see them so badly."

"What do you have in mind?"

"I need leverage against that fool."

"You could tell him you know he visits a whorehouse."

Julia shook her head. "Nah. That cannot work because nobody would believe me. I am the resident witch who abandoned her children."

"I wish I could help..."

"Malaika has agreed to poison him."

Naliaka spluttered her water on the table, some of it landed on Julia's hand. Julia didn't wipe it out and continued to look at Naliaka defiantly.

"What? It's a very nice way of dying, you know. He will not suffer, which is more than he deserves. The poison would take about two hours, meaning he would already be out of Queen's house."

"That's risky. Isn't there another way of...... I don't know,... doing things without killing him?"

"Any ideas? Because this is the only one I have."

* * *

Boss made an impromptu visit after dinner. Naliaka had just settled between Julia and Malaika in the television room so she could share the blanket with them, when Queen's call came through.

"Your boyfriend is outside."

"Where?"

"The parking lot."

She wriggled herself out and grabbed another blanket on the way out. There were three vehicles, she headed straight to the one Boss was in.

"What are you doing here this late?" she demanded, getting in the backseat with him and hugging him.

"I missed you."

"Are you not putting Queen in danger by coming here?"

"The last thing I would do is put you, or Queen, in danger."

"Where are your bodyguards?" She had just noticed they were alone in the car.

"In one of the other cars. I wanted us to be alone."

"Would you like to come in? It's warmer there."

"We can warm each other up here," he said, pulling her towards him, his mouth seeking hers and kissing it with urgency; each second of the kiss felt like offloading sadness.

"Now I am hot," she giggled when they stopped.

"Told you. Now we can talk."

"What about?"

"I didn't just come for a kiss, I have presented myself so you can ask me any question you may have, to give you another opportunity to pull out of my crazy scheme."

"I am not pulling out, but I may have a few questions... and perhaps a favour to ask."

He nodded. "Anything."

Naliaka cleared her throat and shifted uneasily.

"This is so, so hard."

"The kind of secrets we have exchanged, nothing should be hard to say."

"Would you kill someone for me?" she blurted out.

"I would kill for you," he said without hesitation.

Naliaka pulled her blanket closer to herself. "How does it feel to kill someone?" she whispered instead.

What did it feel like? He sat back against the car seat. He wanted to tell her the taste of the devil, that metallic one that flooded his taste buds whenever he felt murderous, precedes all else.

He thought about his first murder. How utterly relieved he felt as he drove the knife into Kimakia. How he had wanted to shout with joy when he cut off a piece of the repeatedly offending manhood. How orgasmic it had felt.

He thought about how he killed the rapist gang. He had lured them to him, one by one, over a stretch of time, pretending to be selling weed to them but instead punctured their lungs with Mato's dagger. How vindicated he felt as he watched life and blood drain out their evil bodies. Somewhere along the way, he lost count of the number of people he had killed. The ones he had ordered killed were even more.

Only one of his victims still haunted him. He had just started stealing cars, him and one of the other street boys. He still had the rookie fear that made one trigger-happy. He had not intended to shoot anyone, but when the woman passenger started screaming and punching, he pulled the trigger. The bullet went through the woman's throat, turning her screams into gurgles, then silence.

His partner ran off into the night, never to be seen again. Boss tried to run but his knees gave way, sinking him against the front wheel, feeling the vibrations because the engine was still running. He listened to the wailing husband, and their two children, over and over. Only when Boss spotted headlights approaching from a distance did he crawl away, into the woods, where he spent two cold nights, hungry. Only thirst had got him walking back to the city on the third night.

He thought about the greedy cop. Back then, he was still doing drug runs for Monde. He also used to be the one to give the street cops their cut, but there was a particular cop who kept robbing him, violently.

"One day, I will kill this fool," he complained to Monde, sitting by his wheelchair after having all his pockets turned inside out.

"Be careful about killing cops. The rest of them will hunt you down and make mincemeat out of you."

"Then you may have to find someone else to do this. I cannot keep losing all my money to him."

"You know, a little bird told me that he also takes a huge chunk off the other cops' cut."

"Greedy bastard. Why can't they kill him then?"

Two days later, Monde had a message from the greedy cop's boss.

"They said they don't care if he dies or not."

"Are you telling me I can kill him?"

"That's what I am telling you. He has several times threatened to rat on them whenever they challenge him. He has to go one way or another."

"So I can kill him?" He asked with a smile

"You want me to say it in French? Don't be stupid."

A week later, the rogue cop's body was found near Gikomba Market, inside a sack, with a single stab wound through the liver.

"Killing is not for everyone. You have to live with the ghosts for life," he told Naliaka.

"If I could, I would kill Kaggai and his brother."

"I can understand why you would want Kaggai dead, but why his brother?"

"He is… was married to Julia." Then she told him everything she knew.

"Tell me more about Kaggai."

"Married. Hates his wife. She hates him more. The two brothers are very wealthy. Tea plantation owners… And extremely vile."

"Why can't she just divorce him if she hates him so much?"

"It's always about money, isn't it? She probably would not end up with the money."

"Can't she get a good lawyer?"

"He could afford a better one I guess, and buy the judge."

"Killing is very final," he said gently.

Naliaka wanted to tell him she knew that, that it was the point, but also tell him that if she killed Kaggai a million times over, she would never feel guilty.

"Anyway, he is very fat and lives a very unhealthy life. He looks like someone who could die of a heart attack soon. Perhaps we will not have to kill him."

"What are you talking about?"

"Sometimes you do not have to kill people, they just die, or help them a little."

Chapter Seventeen

They were no longer suspecting trouble, it was imminent.

"The newspaper seller says the newbies are either not hiding anymore, or they are getting careless," Onyango had told Samuel. He, Samuel, needed to get back to the streets, but it was day two of living with a woman hell-bent on pretending the deaths had not affected her, of trying to act like the centre of her universe had not shifted. Samuel hated playing hide and seek, but he knew enough about grief to not try and manipulate it.

He sat alongside Kerubo on his balcony, sitting on the swinging chairs, watching the rain and the invisible mountain peak, each holding a beer.

"When is the burial?"

Kerubo shrugged and sipped beer straight from the can.

"The children arrive tomorrow," Kerubo answered. "Then they can plan."

"How many are they, again?"

"Three girls and one boy."

"Were you ever close to them?"

Kerubo remembered how, as a little scrawny kid, she would go to the Kamau's, and as soon as the children saw her, they would find something to do away from her. She shrugged.

"They were not interested in me. Also, they were much older, and probably didn't know what to do with me."

"What happens to their home, now that they all live away?"

"I have no clue."

"Why do you sound upset?"

Kerubo scoffed, then seemed to relax. "I am just projecting, I guess. I will be fine."

"I know you hate this question, but if I do not ask you, I don't know who will. How are you feeling? Like, really?"

Kerubo took a long swig of her beer, swallowed loudly, and remained silent.

"Kerubo?" Samuel repeated when no answer came forth.

Kerubo started swinging on the chair faster than before.

"I don't know, and that sucks. I should feel something! I mean, those two were practically my parents, and I think it is unfair to have the same reaction I had at my parents' deaths. I feel nothing. What is wrong with me, Samuel?" she looked at him pleadingly, eyes pregnant with tears.

Samuel held his breath, just for a moment, relieved, because he had finally detected emotion.

"You don't feel *nothing*, Kerubo," he said softly, reaching for her hand and squeezing it. "What you are doing though, is suppressing."

She let out a shaky breath.

"There is nothing wrong with you," he said gently.

"I want to cry for the Kamau's, but…"

"But you feel guilty because you did not cry for your parents," he finished the sentence for her when she hesitated.

She nodded. "Perhaps you should, perhaps you should not. I don't think tears particularly validate mourning. What is in here, " he stretched his hand, placing it on her left side of the chest.

"What is here is more important. Your parents were not nice people, they neglected you. I think it is perfectly fine not to have mourned them."

He felt her start to shake and quickly continued.

"I did not mourn for my father, because I had no reason to. In fact, I wanted to celebrate his death. Does that make me a bad person? I don't know, but I know my feelings were, and still are, valid."

And Kerubo finally broke down, starting with a howl that made Samuel pour a beer on himself. He put it on the floor, hers as well, then held her. For a long time, until she stopped crying.

"Right!" he finally said, disengaging himself. "I am hoping that has left you hungry, because I am going to the kitchen to make us some food. The last two days, you have been drinking like there's a void you are trying to fill. Time to change that!"

Kerubo sniffled and nodded. "I am starving, actually."

"That's such a coincidence, because I am starving too. I am hoping you are hungry for some pork ribs and *ugali*."

She had given him a sad smile. "Right now, I could eat you…"

"Ha! You are in luck, because I am well marinated."

* * *

Whenever Oti had at least twenty-four hours to himself, he spent them indoors doing pretty much nothing. The *nothing* included going to a nearby mall for two large-sized pizzas, many chicken wings from the same mall, *ugali* from a roadside kiosk, canned beer and a litre of cola. He would stop by his weed plug and buy enough to get a herd of elephants high.

He would place them, together with the remote-control gadgets, on the coffee table, and pull it close to the sofa. He would roll joints of weed and place them between the lighter and the ashtray. He would then turn on the television to a music station and listen loudly on the surround system to muff out the external sounds. Then he would lay on the sofa and consume his products in no particular order. On such days, the most exerting activity would be his walks to and from the toilet a few feet away.

Today was one of those days.

At six-thirty in the evening, he was as high as he had been at ten in the morning. On such days, he hardly checked his phone, but that was because the only person who ever called him was Jonte, and Jonte never called him unless there was a job happening that night. Sometimes he felt sad for himself, that he had an expensive phone, *legitimately* owned, yet he had nobody to call, or receive a call from. It was during such moments that the temptation to call his mother sneaked on him, but then again, he did not have his mother's phone number. He did not even know if she had a phone.

It was then by pure accident that he checked his phone and found six missed calls from Jonte.

He cursed and dialled back.

"Where have you been?" Jonte demanded, sounding pissed.

Oti hesitated, then looked at the phone screen to make sure he had called the right number. The only other numbers saved on his phone belonged to the slum broker and the weed plug. It was Jonte indeed, but his tone did not make sense. What Jonte should have said to him was '*vipi brathe*,' hi bro.

"In the house. Why?"

"You need to check your phone more often *bwana*. What if there was an emergency?"

There went the tone again. Oti came close to asking what the chances of an emergency were in their line of work, but he was still trying to work out Jonte's tone.

"*Si ni* sorry *basi... sema.*" I am sorry. What's up?

"I need to see you."

"Today?"

"Someone is waiting for you outside that pub you took me to sometime back. Half an hour."

"Why can't it wait until tomorrow? I am so stoned," Oti protested. He had already smoked four joints, was about to light the fifth one and that was on top of the beer.

"Because it has to be today. Be there. Thirty minutes."

"Is it a job? Because if it is, I am too stoned to do it."

"Thirty minutes, Oti."

"Hello?" but Jonte was gone.

Jonte disconnected the line quickly because he had started feeling like an ass. Listening to Oti answering him, using the same tone of voice as ever, the friend's tone while he cringed at his own tone, got to him. But what was he supposed to do? Boss was there, staring at him unblinkingly. He was being tested. Besides, his loyalty lay more with Boss than with Oti, as much as he liked the latter.

Oti stared at his phone in confusion. "Am I that stoned?"

Once in a while, weed did things to his head. One time he had been sure his mother was in the room, having a conversation with him, as she tidied up for him. How about that time his table had turned into a giant locust? Yes, that could be it, because otherwise it would not make sense for Jonte to order him around, like he was Boss. It was even possible that he had imagined the call, but he decided to go anyway.

He took another slice of pizza and chewed on it slowly, bit by bit, while staring at the television, wondering if he should shower before leaving. He could smell his own sweat, but the bus stop was fifteen minutes away, and Jonte did not sound like he was in a mood to be delayed.

He turned off the television and the surround system, letting in the ghetto noises of drunks, unruly children and laughing women. How the women still managed to laugh all day, in the midst of all their troubles, was beyond him. The men never seemed to laugh. Their voices were only heard through loud drunken monologues, or during fights.

Oti slipped into a pair of jeans on top of the boxer shorts he had worn all day, covered the vest with a tee-shirt and a jacket, tucked his empty gun and walked into the approaching night.

* * *

As Oti entered the house, his heart was racing erratically as it had been since he was picked up by two men. The men could have been the same ones who had picked him and Jonte from jail, in a big, black car, which could have been the same car that had picked them from the said jail. The men had spotted him before he spotted them, something that should have been impossible because as far as he was concerned, he had the best night vision, and had a knack to spot trouble from far. A more bothersome thought was how they could recognise him so easily at night, like they knew him?

One of them had walked to him from behind, poked him with something that could have been a gun or finger and roughly whispered, "get into that car." He did, in silence, touching his gun then cursing silently because it had no bullets. Perhaps he should talk to his guy in the slums to see if he could get bullets for him. What use was a gun without bullets?

They drove in silence. Oti, along the short drive, considered jumping out of the moving car. He let his fingers feel the door but could not locate the lock, so he sat back and tried to guess why Jonte was sending scary people to pick him up, the kind of thing Boss would do.

It was now completely dark, but he remembered the house they drove into. "Jonte is waiting for you inside," one of the men said to him after opening the door from outside.

There were four figures in the dimmed room, and he was sure none of them was Jonte. Three of them were huge, like the ones who had driven him here. One of them was Boss. He had only met him once before, but he could never forget him because his memory was as good as his night vision.

"Oti, have a seat." Boss was sitting in the same position he had occupied during their first meeting, the top seat at the dining table. The other men were sprawled on the sofa, their long legs sprawled in front of them. He hesitated, wondering where to sit.

"Anywhere?"

"Anywhere."

Oti sat on the floor. He was sober by now and his instinct told him this was not exactly a social call. He rummaged through his memory, wondering what it was he may have done wrong. He couldn't think of a thing, unless Jonte had told him about his suggestion to go independent.

"I guess you like the floor. Suit yourself. How are you?"

"Fine. Fine, Boss."

"That's good. How is work?"

"Fine, Boss."

"Jonte will be here in a bit, then we can start off. Would you like something to drink?"

Oti shook his head. "I am fine, thank you."

For minutes, nobody spoke. Oti did not look up, instead he concentrated on his toes, but he could tell the four pairs of eyes were watching him from both directions. He had an urge to cough but he fought it down. It was a cold evening but he was sweating and his unwashed body had doubled its odour. If he survived this, he promised himself never again to think of going against Boss.

Jonte had been waiting in his new bedroom, like Boss had instructed him. The idea was for Boss and the other three to observe Oti's body language. To see if Oti would exhibit fear or stubbornness. If he exhibited the former, he had a chance of survival. The latter would send him straight to hell. Jonte spent the whole five minutes crossing his fingers for Oti.

"Oti," Jonte called, standing a few feet away from Oti. Oti looked up in confusion. "Won't you take a seat?" Oti shook his head, not because he did not want to take a seat but because Jonte did not sound afraid of Boss. Jonte, the same man who told Oti over and over about how to behave in front of Boss, the one who never let him forget that Boss was capable of cutting off a finger for a misdemeanour of not saying please, was behaving like Boss was his equal. He stole a quick glance at Boss, but Boss was doing something on the phone, unbothered.

"Take a seat." He pointed at the dining table. Oti slowly got up and selected the seat farthest from Boss. Jonte took the one closest to Oti. "Relax. You haven't done anything wrong... yet."

Oti's head almost snapped as he looked at Jonte. He went to say something but Jonte put up his hand.

"You and I will no longer be working together, not like we used to. Boss has asked me if you can work alongside someone else, I said you could. Do you think you can?"

Oti, in both relief but more confusion, nodded in quick succession.

"You cannot do the night duties for now, but I have a proposition for you." Jonte cleared his throat and turned towards the men on the sofa. "If you are okay with it, you will be working alongside those gentlemen."

"What is it they do?"

"They are in charge of making sure all turncoats are taken care of..."

"You mean, kill?"

"They keep the Boss safe. They keep everyone else in line... really, they are nice people, unless they do not have to be nice."

Boss, from his corner, was fighting a satisfied smile. The more he listened to Jonte, the more he was sure he had made the right decision with him. Listening to him talk to Oti, giving him options that were really not options, something he, Boss, excelled in, was like looking into the mirror. He hoped Oti would say no to the proposal, just to see if Jonte would have the guts to kill his own friend.

"I... I have never killed anyone..."

"I hope it stays that way," Jonte answered, hoping so because he remembered the first time a man died in his hands. It had taken him months to stop having nightmares.

"If I say no?"

Jonte shrugged, eyeballing Oti. "I would be disappointed. We would all be disappointed, but we cannot force you."

Oti shivered, not from the cold temperature but from the chill that went down his spine. Right at that moment, he remembered his time in the cell with Jonte. How Jonte had been the alpha of the cell, yet never got into fights like the rest. The food and cigarettes he dished out to other prisoners had helped, but Oti could bet that even without the freebies, Jonte would still have been the alpha. There was a quiet coldness about him, a calm air of debauchery. It was possible their one-year-old friendship had crowded Oti's vision of Jonte, but it was there, and he was looking at it right at that moment.

"Can I… can I think about it?"

"You have twenty-four hours."

"Thank you."

"Hungry?"

Oti shook his head. Jonte shrugged and stood up.

"Alright. You can leave whenever you want. The same people will drive you back to the same spot they picked you from." Jonte walked to the bedroom.

Only when he softly shut the door behind him did he start shaking, no longer sure he was suited for the role.

* * *

When Oti alighted from the vehicle a few minutes past nine, he fought the urge to run. Expecting to be shot at any moment, he walked, in reverse, watching the car's tail lights disappear. He still did not run, but he walked fast, not towards his house but towards his mother's house.

The scary and confusing episode with Jonte had given him a sudden urge to be near his mother. He stepped over what could have been poop or mud puddles, rubbed shoulders with people who could have been fellow criminals or just ghetto residents walking home.

He stood outside the door, went to knock it, then changed his mind. He leaned on it, it creaked and for a moment feared he had been heard. He could hear a muffled conversation from the inside. With all their children out of the nest, his parents now lived on their own.

He heard them laugh. When he lived here, they were always shouting or moaning about something one of the children had done, or not done. He allowed himself a smile, genuinely happy that they could finally have time to themselves, time to laugh, time to enjoy some meat dish—and he could tell they were cooking meat. A few days earlier, he had done his night deliveries and he had put money in the bag.

Slowly, feeling better, he walked back to his house.

He was sure he had turned off the lights but he found them on. Again, he blamed the weed. He took a step inside and paused. He was not the neatest person, in fact, he hardly cleared up stuff, unless they became a health hazard, and no wonder the pizza and chicken boxes neatly piled on each other was something that caught his attention. He opened the boxes—empty. So was the soda bottle.

With his heart beating so hard that he could hear it, he looked around the room. If somebody had broken into his house, his electronics would have been missing. Nothing was missing. If somebody had broken into his house, there would have been clues at the door—like a broken padlock. Even with a master key, they would have been in too much of a hurry to bother locking the padlock. The padlock was intact.

As much as he blamed weed, because it was the only rational explanation, he tiptoed to his bedroom. He gasped and took several steps back. He never made his bed, yet what he was looking at was a bed made the way they made them at the hotels he took prostitutes to. By this time, his heart was nearly beating out of his mouth as he checked his house bank located in a box under the bed. The padlock was intact. He opened it—no money seemed to be missing, but there was something new, a wad of dollar bills on top of the Kenya shillings.

That was when his body turned into liquid, and if he had not stopped to take a piss outside his house, he would have peed on himself. Whoever was here had not come to rob him, they had come to leave him a subtle warning.

He sat on the floor against the bed and looked up at the ceiling, for the first time noticing the cobwebs gracing it. On his walk back from his mother's house, he had made a decision to run away to another town, perhaps Kisumu. He had enough money to start him off in a business. Surely, nobody could find him in Kisumu. He did not consider himself to be a good man, but he had never had the killer instinct.

Jonte and Boss, now that he was starting to think of them as the same person, wanted to turn him into a killer. Looking at his house, knowing Jonte and Boss had sent their goons here, he knew running away was not an option. They would know, they would kill him before he boarded the bus.

Ten minutes later, still sitting on the floor, he dialled Jonte's number.

"Jonte, who was in my house?"

"I don't know what you are talking about."

That was all Jonte said before disconnecting.

And Oti wept.

*   *   *

Jonte was finally alone in his new house; alone, if he didn't count the security men lurking outside. He was physically ready for bed in his sleeping boxer shorts and tee-shirt. Mentally, he was nowhere near ready. He sat on the most comfortable king size bed he did not know existed until earlier that day, and wondered what use the bed was if he could not have sex on it.

He was thinking about Oti, if he would see him again alive. He was aware a couple of men had gone to Oti's house. What Oti would do thereafter would determine if he lived, or *disappeared*.

Jonte entered the bed, positioned three pillows under his head and faced the white ceiling. He reached for the bed switch and turned it off. He shut his eyes and willed himself to sleep. It would be two hours before his brain finally succumbed to fatigue. Those two hours would be spent thinking about the new direction his life was about to take. Nobody had told him directly, but he did not need anyone to tell him that he was about to become a crime boss. Nobody had asked him if he wanted the position or not, but he knew, if he wanted to live, he had no choice. The question was, where was Boss going?

Would he be okay to run the crime world? He was starting to warm up to the idea of calling the shots, although his ambitions had never been that high. He had never desired Boss's job. He was satisfied to be the teacher's pet, but now he wondered if he had been groomed right from the start. Now it made sense why Boss forgave him for a misdemeanour that saw his fellow thieves fed to the lions of Amboseli.

* * *

Naliaka's view from Queen's bedroom was better than her view from her room on the first floor. She saw farther. It was just past ten in the morning, and she would have preferred to be outside enjoying the sun that had decided to surprise the rain, but Kaggai was around. From the balcony, she watched him waddle in. He looked fatter than she remembered him. An hour later, she watched him waddle out, a smug smile on his face.

She looked around Queen's balcony that had several potted plants, selected the one closest to her and spat the bile into the plant, apologising to it immediately. Boss's call came through just as Kaggai's car disappeared out of the gate.

"Hey!"

"Why do you sound like that?"

"Like how?"

"I don't know… angry, perhaps?"

"I am fine. Just bored."

Boss cleared his throat. "I am about ninety-eight per cent sure that my enemies do not know about you. I suppose it is okay to go back to your house if you want to."

"Are you sure?"

"Besides, I have information that they were asking around if anybody knows my girlfriend. If they knew about you, they wouldn't have been asking that."

Naliaka felt her earlier happiness ebb away, replaced by dread and some bile. She spat on the plant once more. "So they can still find me?"

"If someone talked. But... the people who know about you are unlikely to talk. Also, I am retaining your security, but you can go out if you like."

"Okay."

"I have a few people operating taxis. I will send you two contacts. Use only them, please."

"So they can report back to you?"

"How dare you?" Boss retorted.

"Sorry."

"It's for your security, and my own peace of mind."

"Thank you... I... I can go and see your parents?" It was her way of apologising.

Boss was about to say he wasn't dead yet, but instead he asked, "When?"

"Day after tomorrow? Today, however, I would like to go out."

"Oh?" She could almost taste the disappointment in his voice.

"I will stay away from the usual joints. I want to go out with the priest."

"Oh... okay. Just be careful."

"I will. The priest, if he is available, will be driving. What will happen to my taxi guy?"

"He will follow you discreetly from a distance."

"And wait all night?"

"And day, if necessary. You must not be out of his sight."

* * *

Naliaka did not own a black wig, but Malaika did. She wore makeup, but the fake eyelashes were missing, so did the red lipstick which was replaced by a peach one. Instead of the tiny clothes, she wore a pair of skinny jeans, ankle boots and a sleeveless black top. The rain had brought with it its cold cousin so she wore a beige trench coat.

She picked a random pub in Ngara. When she was starting out on her own, she had tried Ngara, but the patrons were more interested in drinking than sex.

The middle-aged men, however, would walk up to her and touch her buttocks, or boobs. They reminded her of Kaggai, and that had been enough reason for her to write off Ngara.

Earlier, she had called Father Joshua.

"Kiki, is that really you calling me?" he asked in excitement.

"Hi Father. What are you up to later on?"

"Why?" he had asked cautiously.

"Obviously, because I want to see you, though it's okay if you were not planning to come to town."

"I was," he said quickly. It was a lie. He had gone out the previous night.

"Alright. I should be in town by seven. Let me know when you start driving down, then I can tell you where I will be."

"Not in the same place?"

"No. I feel like a change of scenery. Ngara okay with you?"

"Ngara?" He knew enough about Ngara clientele to know that if any of his congregants, mainly made out of middle-aged people, decided to go out, they would most likely pick Ngara.

"Is there a problem?"

"No… no. Let me know."

* * *

Naliaka selected a seat at the counter where she could observe a huge section of the crowd without having to turn this way or that way. She smiled at the barman before making her order, and asked him to charge her for whatever he was drinking. Bar people, she knew, were important to befriend. They knew everyone, all the trouble spots. They also came in handy for chats.

The barman was too busy to chat, and getting busier by the second, so apart from Googling random stuff on her phone, she watched the crowd, relishing the moment because for the first time, she was not vetting men to go home with, or rob. She was, she thought with a smile, waiting for a date. The crowd she was watching had not changed; pot-bellied men, loud older women drinking away from the men. One man-guitar musician *murdering* words of songs, nobody dancing on the floor, but everybody dancing from their seat.

A few minutes into her vigil, her interest was captured by four women sharing a table. If she had wanted to ignore the women, she would have miserably failed because apart from being in her direct eye line, they stuck out like sore thumbs. They looked well into their fifties. Naliaka momentarily thought of her mother, who would be more or less their age, but she quickly blocked out the line of thought. The women were uniformly overweight. A quick glance would mislead anyone into thinking they were deliberately sitting with their legs apart, but a deeper look revealed that the weight between their collective thighs made it impossible to sit any other way.

They were not using glasses to drink their beer, and hardly any of them put their bottles down. They were also laughing very loudly, their deep laughter carrying through the loud music. They were also flirting with two younger men at the next table.

She let her eyes wander to the rest of the crowd, and that was when she spotted him. He wore a hat pulled down to his forehead, but she knew he was looking straight at her, that he had been looking at her for a while. He sat alone on a high stool at the second counter directly behind the four women. Like the four women, he was drinking straight from the bottle. He raised the bottle at her, she acknowledged.

Her eyes went back to the women. The two men taking seats on the table the women occupied. To Naliaka, the men could have passed for their sons, or much younger brothers, but it was the new world order. Naliaka watched the women pause their laughter to watch the two men, and exchange knowing looks.

For the first time since she started watching them, two of the women put their beers on the table, reached for their bags and started fumbling inside. The other two got busy with the two men, touching and chatting. Naliaka felt attacked on the men's behalf, but then again, they didn't seem to mind.

"Those two men are in so much trouble." It was the barman. He was watching the activities on the same table.

"What do you mean?"

"The number of men who have almost died because of them… tsk tsk tsk…" he was shaking his head, but before he could finish up the story, he had to serve other customers. Naliaka turned to look back at the group.

Two of the women were already kissing the two men, the other two pulled the men's drinks. At first, Naliaka wondered why they were caressing the bottles, then it hit her.

"Oh my goodness!" she gasped, looking at the barman who shrugged and continued serving the customers. She knew what just happened because even though she had always been a lone operator, she knew other prostitutes because it was always important to avoid bloody territorial wars. She knew girls who posed as prostitutes but they were thieves who drugged men by kissing them, letting them smell their boobs or by doing what she had just seen happen.

What shocked her was the age of the women. They looked like somebody's mother—like Julia. Naliaka looked at the man who had waved at her earlier. He seemed to be watching the women, but he did not look that bothered, neither did the people in surrounding tables.

And she watched, until the men slumped on the table; the women emptied their pockets, took their phones, then walked away.

"Some end up in hospital, others are woken up in the morning by the cleaners," the barman said.

She jumped when somebody tapped her shoulder.

"Hi, I have been watching you." It was the man she had exchanged looks with and both of them had witnessed the robbery.

"Father Joshua!" She nearly screamed. "What's with the hat? You look so different!"

"Look who's talking!" Father Joshua answered as he hugged her. "It took me almost half an hour to be sure it was you. You look... what can I say?" He was studying her from an arm's length.

"Normal?" she asked with a giggle.

"Your words, not mine. But I like what I am looking at."

"So, why are you hiding under the hat?"

"Because, my dear, my congregants are the sort of people who would come here. In fact, I could swear I give Holy Communion to one of the women we were just watching."

They both laughed as he settled next to her.

Chapter Eighteen

A week had gone since the Kamau's died.

Samuel was back on the streets, and Kerubo took the week off, which messed with Samuel's diet as she only delivered food under the cover of darkness.

On the eve of the burial, Samuel defied Onyango and went to his house to be ready to accompany Kerubo to the burial. He made her sleep in his house and in the morning, as they left for the mortuary, they both dressed in black jeans trousers and tee-shirts, topped with dark sunglasses.

They joined the small procession, with Samuel one step behind Kerubo when she was shaking hands with the aloof Kamau children. The daughters barely nodded at her, but the son was friendlier, even excited as he hugged Kerubo and asked how she was doing.

The drive to the cemetery was a silent one. Kerubo and Samuel stood a respectable distance as the body was lowered.

"Let's go!" she whispered to Samuel as soon as the first soil hit the casket.

"Aren't you going to stay to the end?"

"The end happened a week ago."

"I think the son actually wanted to talk to you."

"Not interested," she answered, but peered at the tall man who was solemnly looking at the double grave.

"Did you see them earlier? I refuse to be looked at as an imposter."

"The son does not."

"Why are you insisting?"

"Because, Kerubo, I believe speaking to him will be a closure for you."

She looked thoughtful for a moment. "I will think about it."

Kerubo broke down as soon as they entered the car. She was not crying loudly, but she was heaving and using tissue back-to-back to wipe her eyes. She cried all the way to her house, because she said she wanted to be alone.

"Are you going to be okay?" he asked as he pulled over at her gate.

"I will be fine, I promise."

"Will you go back to work tomorrow?"

She nodded. "I need the distraction."

"Will see you in the morning, then. Oh, and I like my breakfast with bacon."

"Piss off."

He watched her until she disappeared, then he drove away.

Kerubo waited until she was sure Samuel was gone, before summoning a taxi.

Selina opened the door wearing a *dera*, hair unkempt, like she had just woken up.

"Really, Selina? You need to first ask who is at the door before opening," Kerubo reprimanded before inviting herself in.

"Yes, mother," Selina said with an eye roll, shutting the door. "What the hell are you doing here?"

"Visiting. Do you have food? I haven't eaten all day."

"Chica, you cannot just turn up *fwaaaa*. What if I had my boyfriend here?"

"You don't have a boyfriend."

"It doesn't mean I don't have sex."

"Oh, well," Kerubo was already in the kitchen, checking what was in the cooking pots.

"Ooh... nice. Chicken and rice, like you knew I would turn up."

"Seriously? Anyway, where have you been sick?"

Kerubo looked at her friend in confusion. "What do you mean?"

"You told me you were taking the week off work because you were sick."

"Oh, sorry, that was a lie. My adoptive parents died. Burial was today."

* * *

An hour later, Selina had cried more than Kerubo had done in a week, and that had been a lot of crying she had done in a week.

"I am so sorry..."

"I am sorry I didn't tell you. It is all so complicated."

"I wish you told me. I could have come to support you at the burial."

"Sam... eem... Samantha was there," she said, regretting immediately.

"Who is Samantha?"

"Oh... erm... she is a girl I knew in college. She heard about the deaths and looked for me."

311

"That's good, then. I thought I had a rough life but shit… you sound cursed."

"Thanks," Kerubo said with a giggle. "That's why you have trust issues."

"What do you mean?"

"I have known you for years, I can swear I am your closest friend, yet only after your adoptive parents are dead and buried do I find out about them. You, the same person who prefers one-night stands… trust issues right there."

"I just hate burdening people with my problems."

"Trust. Issues. Anyway, are you still hungry? Let me warm some food. I have enough wine for the night."

The two girls sat late into the night, talking. Selina talked more, about her father who had his operation, but was not doing very well. About Jonte, who kept sending money to Selina's phone.

"A couple of times I returned the money, but he would send it back with extra money. I don't know what to do with it."

"Use it."

"For what?"

"Your younger siblings. You keep telling me they haven't joined college because there is no money. Use it."

"Two problems with that. One, I would have to explain the money to father and two, I am not sure I actually want money from him."

"He could be a car salesman, you know." Kerubo could not bring herself to face Selina as she said that.

"I don't know, actually. There is just a sinister aura about him."

"So ask him to take you to his workplace."

"I just might."

"He doesn't look like a thug to me," Kerubo was trying to keep the conversation going.

"That's because he is a good-looking man, and nobody expects a good-looking man to be a criminal."

"Yeah, you are right," Kerubo thought of Boss. "Traitor..." she muttered to herself.

"What's that?"

"Nothing. Is there more wine?"

* * *

The alarm went off at two in the morning.

As Samuel put on his white vest and white underwear, as he packed the dirty-looking clothes, and put them in a disposable bag, he felt a certain kind of sadness overwhelm him. This was always the hardest part, saying goodbye to comfort. This one was almost worse because it had lasted only a night.

He turned off all sockets and light switches, grabbed his car keys and walked out.

Forty minutes later, he parked the car on a random street where Kerubo would pick it up and return it to the car hire company. He hoped by the time he took his next break, he would have his car back. He looked around to make sure there were no people, and when he came out of the car, he had transformed back to Chizi Samuel.

It was cold, but the rains that had been beating the streets earlier had subsided. He cursed, because instead of wearing a pair of old boots that would protect him from the mud puddles and goodness knew what else was mixed with the rain water, he wore sneakers. He would send a message to Kerubo to bring a pair of boots for him.

He shivered and pulled his sack coat closer to his body. When it was not raining, he enjoyed this quietness in the city. It was four in the morning, the quietest time of the city. It was a pregnant kind of silence because in less than an hour, the city would burst with noise from the early risers.

Ten minutes later found him on Kirinyaga Road. He did not stop by his booth. Instead, he walked on to the end of the street, right outside Boss's house. It was quiet, except for the usual street boys. They called his name in greeting and offered him hot *mandazi*. He ignored them and walked to the end of the street then retraced his steps to the booth.

* * *

Chizi Samuel sniggered as he watched Kerubo walk towards the booth in the morning. He was however glad because instead of the dejected girl he had expected to see, she walked towards him with a smile and a bounce.

"Don't smile so much. People may suspect you are in love with a mad man."

"The horror!" She feigned shock, taking a seat next to him.

"You are late."

"Shoot me."

"Where are my boots?"

"I will get you a pair when the hawkers come in. I refuse to spend money on new boots for a mad man."

"You have a hangover?"

"Brrrr… What's your problem, mother?" She removed an unfamiliar flask and food warmer.

"I would congratulate you for buying new utensils, but they don't look new." He pointed at them with his mouth.

"I did not sleep at home."

"I drove you home!"

"You also left my legs with me," she said with an eye roll.

"Gosh, glad to have your salty self back. Where did you sleep?"

"Selina's. I felt lonely when you left."

"Can she give it as good as I can?"

"You rate yourself too highly, mister, "she laughed. "But she and I have something in common—we like our men rough around the edges."

"Well, they don't come rougher than me… feeling better, though?"

"Oh yeah, and then on some other news, I convinced her to ask Jonte to let her visit his workplace."

"Impressive."

* * *

Half an hour later, Samuel walked towards Boss's building.

If he did not know *who* Cecilia was, he would have been as convinced as everyone else, that she was a *Mama Mboga*, but he would have wondered why a *Mama Mboga* was in the city so early. Everybody knew, or should know, that home time was the peak. People did not buy vegetables on the way to the office, they bought them on the way home.

Cecilia sat on the pavement, protected from the wetness of the night before by a sack. In front of her on another sack were onions, tomatoes and garlic. She was dressed in a heavy coat and a *leso* around her small waistline. He could see her jeans and sneakers. It may have been a cold morning but Samuel knew the heavy coat was there not to protect her from the cold, but to hide her gun. On her head was a woollen hat.

He dropped some of his paraphernalia when he got to her, mumbled a sorry and went down to collect them. "Hey there. Reporting for duty."

Cecilia did not turn to look at Samuel as she spoke. "Let's kick some ass, handsome."

"I like you," he mumbled back. "Kerubo will come to buy some vegetables later."

"Tell her to hurry. Stock is running out fast."

He chuckled and moved on.

He could not be sure, but there was something about the street boys, the same ones who had offered him a hot *mandazi* earlier, still in the same spot, holding on to their glue bottles, but not sniffing it. They were looking at something across the streets, and their heads were huddled together.

Samuel followed their eye line. It should not have bothered him, especially because the street boys co-owned the street with him. They were part of the landmark. But his heightened instinct made him stop. Perhaps, like him, they had noticed something on the streets.

A few feet from them, Samuel sat on the pavement, leaned against the wall and pretended to nod off.

"… *mfwate peke yako sisi tutabaki hapa*." Follow him as we remain here, one of them said. Samuel opened his eyes an inch and watched one street boy cross over in a hurry.

"… another one will…"

"… something is going…"

"I heard they want to kill…"

The more he listened to the disjointed conversation, the more frustrated Samuel felt. The more he listened to them, however, the more convinced he was that he should have paid attention to them a long time ago.

"He's coming back."

Samuel shifted and adjusted his ears. If he could catch what the returnee had to say, he would know if he was wasting his time here or not.

"You see that one… the tall one wearing a long coat."

"Half the people have long coats," the bigger of them protested.

"The one with the longest." Samuel opened his eyes again and looked across the street and nearly gasped because it was one of the men he had spotted two weeks ago.

They met just up the road, spoke for a few minutes then…

"Is Boss in?"

Samuel nearly screamed. He had heard enough. Resisting the temptation to run, he stood up slowly and stopped by Cecilia. He bent down to scratch his ankle.

"You need to move your market closer to the building. There is activity. Kerubo will give you details…"

NaiRobbery Cocktail

Chapter Nineteen

If anyone had bothered to look, they would have noticed that Chizi Samuel was taking bigger strides than usual, the type of strides somebody with purpose would take. If they would have looked at his face, they would have seen a deep-set concentration and perhaps think it was a strange look for a supposedly insane person, but as he made his way back from Cecilia, he did not care about the little details. There were too many things he was trying to work out. One of them was figuring how much time they had as it looked like the clock had started ticking backwards.

By the time he made it back to the shed, Cecilia had already moved her groceries right to the edge of Boss's building, only a few metres away from where the street boys were. They would probably have paid attention to her if they had not been unblinkingly looking across the street. Being her first day on the street, she was not sure what she was looking for, but she hoped her experience would help her pick on stuff that did not look ordinary—if only she knew what was ordinary on Kirinyaga Road.

Samuel's heart was thumping, and when he sat down on the bench to gather his thoughts, it was because there was a genuine need to do so. He sat back and took a few gasps, and thought about what he had just learned. His thoughts were jumbled, yet there was little time.

Rumour had it that Boss was once a street boy, and Chizi Samuel always took it as just that—a rumour. It was like he had just sprouted from the ground, like an unwanted weed, and matured to become the most feared thug in the Nairobi metropolis. Now that he was sure the street boys were connected to Boss, the rumours made sense. The pieces of how Boss had a tight grip on everything fell into place. Samuel's admiration of Boss went a notch higher.

The street boys were watching more than one man, they had mentioned killing, and they had mentioned Boss... the questions bugging him were, who was going to be killed?

"Cecilia told me you had something to tell me?" Samuel was a little startled. He had not seen Kerubo approach. "You are jumpy! What's happening?"

"Not sure. But you need to go and see Cecilia, like right about now."

By the time Samuel finished narrating what he had witnessed and heard, Kerubo was already heading towards Cecilia.

Cecilia was still sitting on the ground, discreetly looking around her, still wondering what it was she was supposed to be looking at. Kerubo squatted in front of her and started selecting groceries, turning tomatoes slowly in her hands.

"What am I supposed to be looking at?" Cecilia asked.

"You see the street boys behind you?"

"What about them?" Cecilia whispered back.

"Samuel is sure they are connected to Boss. They are watching something, someone, or two, across the street. Keep an eye on them, and across the street."

"Right."

"Has *you-know-who* left the building yet?"

"I haven't seen him." Cecilia, who had never seen Boss face-to-face, had spent the last one week studying different photos of him. If he had passed by dressed in rags, she would have recognised him.

Kerubo stood up and turned around casually, scratching her head as she did so. It did not take long for her to spot the man Chizi Samuel had described. He was sitting on a kerb against a building, alone, and he was stoically looking across the street.

"A cop," Kerubo said to Cecilia.

Kerubo turned to look at the street boys. They were looking at the same man, unblinkingly.

She squatted again. "If you look across the street, a slight angle to the left from where we are. There is a man…"

"He's wearing a long brown coat," Cecilia cut in. She had seen him and noticed him for just sitting on the same spot, doing nothing. "I noticed him. One would think they would send people who try to be less conspicuous."

"Perhaps they want to be conspicuous. It's game on, I am sure about that. Keep an eye on him, and your gun cocked. I need to call Onyango and update him. Please call me if anything happens."

Cecilia chuckled. "By the time you get here I will either be dead or have killed them all. You guys are all so far. Samuel should spend more time on this end of the street… oh, and you are looking delicious."

Kerubo blushed but just before she thought of something to say, there was a commotion. The street boys were the first to stand up quickly, then she saw the two burly men, and behind them Boss. The three of them paused at the door, looked around, then walked to the opposite direction of where Kerubo and Cecilia were.

When Boss suddenly turned with his eye line straight at Kerubo, she was about to stand up. She stayed put, returned his glare for a moment then started selecting her groceries again, heart in mouth.

"The statue just breathed life into himself," Cecilia said, pointing across the street with the mouth. "He is following our man."

At the same moment, one of the boys left in a hurry.

"This is getting very interesting…"

* * *

Midday found Cecilia noisily chewing on an apple and staring across the street at the empty spot where the watcher had vacated. Only one street boy remained, and he was dozing behind her. But she was also worried that her vegetables would run out. When she set up camp, she had not expected to sell anything, but people kept stopping by and buying stuff. The customers took away the boredom, but they were also an obstruction.

Then Boss returned and with him, life on the street seemed to return as well. His first stop was right in front of Cecilia, and at that moment, her heart almost gave up beating. The sun that had gifted itself to a rainy day was directly above them, and when she looked up at him, she squinted.

She greeted him. "Hello sir. Do you want vegetables?"

He let his eyes linger on her for a few seconds before he nodded. "I do. They look very fresh."

She nodded enthusiastically. "Fresh, fresh *kabisa*. Onions? Tomatoes?"

"How about those two? For a hundred shillings each. "

Cecilia stood up then bent down to select. "You are a good man… your wife is lucky to have a husband who can buy vegetables for her."

He chuckled. "I am not married."

"Oh…" She said, standing up and holding out the stuff she had put in a bag. "Such a fine-looking man without a wife? What do girls want? Oh, you must be the one who is refusing to get married."

Boss gave a genuine laugh. The tomatoes and the onions would end up with his street family because his cook did all his shopping. He had stopped by because he liked to know who was new on the street, especially if the new person decided to pitch camp outside his residence, more so during uncertain times. Looking at her, listening to her, he didn't think she was one of the bad guys, but one could never be too sure. With her headscarf and *leso* and a jacket, she looked like any other *Mama Mboga*, but for his own peace of mind, he would ask his boys to keep an eye on her. If he could be honest, he had stopped by hoping to find the tall woman who had been chatting to her earlier.

"Are you married?" he asked, selecting notes from his wallet.

"Yes. Ten years and four children later and counting."

"Too bad," he laughed and walked away, waving at her.

She watched him until he disappeared into the building, wondering if making contact with him was a good or a bad thing, wondering if his stopping by was planned or a mere coincidence. She sat down slowly then turned to the parking boys. The other two had returned only seconds after Boss returned.

"Are you hungry?" she asked them.

"Yes…" they answered in unison even though they looked anything but hungry.

"I am hungry too, but I do not want to leave my vegetables. Can I send one of you to buy me food?"

The boys looked at each other in confusion, then back at her in silence. "It's okay. I know people do not trust you a lot, but I usually trust people unless they give me a reason not to. Come on, if you can get me *chips karai*, I will buy you two packets to share among yourselves…"

"Why would you use so much money? You are just a *mama mboga*."

Cecilia wanted to slap herself. That was something she had not thought about. The profit margin in what she was doing did not allow her to go around buying extra lunches. She smiled. "I won a little money in the lottery last week." They gave her a blank stare. "Don't expect me to be buying you lunch every day. In fact, after today, I cannot afford lunch for a week so I will have to bring my own lunch…"

They laughed at her. But it seemed to work because the biggest boy turned to the smallest one and nudged him towards Cecilia.

"Thank you. You are good boys…"

She ate her chips, unbothered about their origin. She had had worse in the line of duty. She watched them share the two packets, their eyes constantly on the watcher who had returned only minutes after Boss. Next to the man was Chizi Samuel, dozing on and off.

Samuel watched, through half closed eyes, what was happening across the street. He saw Boss stop by. He watched Cecilia engage the boys, watched her and the boys eat her fries. It all made him edgy, because none of it was a part of the script, but Onyango had told him to trust Cecilia.

One of the boys disappeared after lunch, but returned half an hour later. It may have been her imagination, but the three boys seemed to take more interest in her. They were watching her almost as much as they were watching the man across the road. She spent most of the time pretending not to notice them. There was a possibility she had piqued their interest because of the free lunch, but something had changed.

By six, it was obvious to both Cecilia and Chizi Samuel that nothing else was going to happen. Besides, Cecilia was out of stuff to sell and no longer had an excuse to stick around. She gathered her empty *kiondo* and sack and walked away, intending to stop by Kerubo's for a chat. Halfway, she changed her mind because she noticed that she was being followed by one of the parking boys.

* * *

Oti had four hours to make up his mind. He was torn between his desire to stay alive and disgust for possibly taking another life.

For the umpteenth time, he went to the toilet and threw up bile, trying to control shakes of fear and hunger. He had not eaten, or slept, since meeting Jonte.

Wiping his mouth with the back of his hand, he smelled his own sweat and remembered he had not had a bath for two days. He warmed the water and bathed, taking unnecessarily long. It was during the bath that he made a decision.

An hour later, he knocked on his parents' door.

"Who is it?"

"Me."

"Who is *me*?"

"Oti…"

There was silence from the other end. It may have gone for three seconds or three minutes. Time stopped to matter, because he was more bothered about what he was going to say.

His mother flung the door open, and for the first time in close to ten years, mother and son faced each other. For the length of time they stared at each other, Oti was slowly being consumed with shame from realising that he had never really looked at his mother's face. It was like he was seeing her nose, one that resembled his, for the first time. He had no memory of the scar on her neck, and it looked old.

"Mom…" he whispered.

"Come in, Oti." She waited for him to enter before shutting the door behind her.

He stood inside, looking around at the small space he had grown up in. It nauseated him to think of the number of children and two adults who had to fit in the space.

"Won't you sit down?"

Oti looked for a seat but could not find one. He looked at her questioningly.

"You forgot how to sit on the floor? Or are you afraid of making your nice clothes dirty? Okay, I will give you something to sit on."

"No… no mom. I will sit."

He sat down, immediately feeling like the cornered child he always was.

"Where is dad?"

She shrugged and sat on the only available stool. "Who knows? Kibera is big."

He stared at his own shoes, suddenly thinking how wrong it felt to wear shoes inside a house. He could also feel his mother's eyes boring into his temple.

"*Ni nini,* Oti? Why are you here?"

"Am I not allowed to come here?"

She laughed. One short sharp laughter that made him feel stupid. "After nearly ten years you just realised you are still allowed here? *Maajabu.*"

"Sorry."

"Sorry? Do you realise how many times I have stayed up all night, wondering if you were dead or alive? Do you? Even your siblings no longer spot you like they used to."

The last sentence was choked. He was having his own battle of tears. "Why do you hate your mother so much, Oti?"

"I... do not hate you."

Only when he uttered those words did he realise it was true. He did not hate his mother, he just did not know how to love her.

"I thought you hated me. All of you hated me!" he blurted.

It surprised him as much as it surprised his mother, because the last time he had worried about being liked, he was not even ten.

"Are you stupid?" she asked incredulously. "You think I gave birth to you because I hated you?"

Oti shook his head, but he squared up to her.

"Why did you? I mean, give birth to so many children you couldn't take care of?"

"Children are a blessing..."

It was Oti's turn to laugh. "How have we blessed you?"

Oti's mother had looked and sounded vicious a few seconds before. Now, as she answered her son, she looked anything but unfriendly.

"Children are supposed to be a blessing," she said, almost to herself. "We thought if we had many of you, there were chances that one or two of you would make it. *Mchezo wa pata potea*."

She suddenly looked up at him. "But you look like you are doing better than them all. It is you who has been leaving stuff outside the house, isn't it?" He nodded.

"I knew it. I told your father I knew it was you."

"You are not upset, are you?"

"Why would I be? That food has been enough to feed us, two of your sisters and their children."

"I thought they were married?"

"They still are, to idiots. Your sisters spend their days looking for their husbands in the ghetto ditches... stupid drunks." She clicked her tongue. "What do you do for a living?"

"I am a driver." This lie was premeditated.

"Oh, that's good. I did not know drivers get paid that well."

"My boss is a rich man and he is generous too."

"God bless him."

"I came to ask if there is anything you need... I have some money saved up, and would like to give it to you. You could start a business."

She sat up straight, her face brightening up. For a few seconds, Oti saw a potentially beautiful woman, or a woman who could have been beautiful if life had been kinder.

"But, should you not be saving the money for your children? Are you married?"

Oti chortled involuntarily. "I don't have children. I am not married."

"But you will be." It was not a question.

He shook his head. "No, I do not want to get married and I do not want to have children."

"Why not? Children are a…"

"… blessing," he cut in. "We never made you smile. You were always shouting and threatening and whipping us. We made you and dad miserable. My sisters have children they cannot feed! Again, I ask, how are they a blessing?"

"You want to die without children?"

"When my time comes, I shall have no regrets. But that's not why I am here."

Oti's mother looked at him long and hard, then sighed as long and as hard.

"Anyway, you know very well we are always in need of money… your sisters and I…"

Oti stopped himself in time before he told her he had no intention of feeding his sisters, then he thought about the box of money in his house and decided he could afford them too. He could afford to feed his whole family for a very long time. He reached for his trouser pocket and removed a stuffed A4 envelope and handed it to her. "Here. You could use it to stock up a shop."

She took the envelope, clutched it to her chest, and smiled at Oti.

"You were always the most difficult one, but I knew you would be the one to make something of his life."

* * *

Oti was not the only one having an awkward meeting that evening.

The day had started on a high note but by midday, the promising action had hit a plateau, and Kerubo spent the day chewing on her nails, staring at the door and checking on her phone over and over. Selina noticed. "I am expecting a call from my adopted brother," she told Selina.

"Why is that making you nervous?"

"Because we were never close. I don't know what he wants to talk about."

"Is he cute?" Selina asked, nudging Kerubo with her elbow.

"Really, Selina?"

"It's okay to think your brother is cute. I think Jonte is cute."

"He is your brother," Kerubo agreed.

"So, is your brother any good-looking?"

Kerubo considered the question. She would not classify Joe in the same handsome section as Samuel, Boss or even Jonte. He was an average-looking man whose best features were his confidence and smile. He was a little beefier than the kind of man she went for, but he was not fat. He was the only tall member of the Kamau family.

"He is an attractive man, I guess," Kerubo answered.

"That's a good start. Is he married?"

"How about I introduce you to him, then you can ask all the questions you want."

"You do that. I will appreciate it. I am looking for a boyfriend, possibly a husband.

Kerubo was still smiling as she took Samuel his lunch. Then they started talking about Boss stopping by Cecilia's.

"You know, yesterday, Boss saw me. Like, stopped, turned and eyeballed me."

"You think he recognised you?"

She shook her head. "I don't know."

"Perhaps we are just overreacting."

Neither looked convinced.

* * *

Ngara was a five to ten-minute walk from the shop, depending on how fast or slow she walked. Just at the corner of the street connecting Globe Roundabout, Kerubo saw the evening hawkers selling shoes, and remembered she had promised Samuel a pair. Her phone rang as she was going through the shoes.

"Hi Joe."

"Kerubo!" He sounded cheerful. "Sorry, I didn't call earlier. I didn't realise there was so much to do about our parents' estate."

"I can imagine." She had her phone trapped between her shoulder and ear as she used her hands to turn over the boots.

"What are you up to this evening? I was hoping to take you out for dinner."

"Dinner?"

"You don't mind, do you? It would be a perfect time to talk about stuff, and it is a lot."

"No... I don't mind—just the short notice."

"Did you have something else planned?"

She shook her head. "Pick me up at eight."

* * *

Early in the evening, Oti walked with a confident bounce. Talking to his mother had taken some of his fear away. Even Jonte's call did nothing to unnerve him, not even when he told him to be ready to be picked up by the same men at the same time.

This time round, he spotted the men before they spotted him. He walked towards the car willingly, opened the door himself and entered. Like the day before, he had butterflies in his stomach, but unlike the day before, they were not agitated butterflies.

Oti had expected the same delegation as the day before, but there was only Jonte, sitting on the same spot as Boss had the day before.

"Oti, come in. Please take a seat." He was still not his usual Jonte, but he was not the Jonte of the day before. Oti even detected a hint of a smile.

"Thank you," Oti took the farthest seat.

"How are you?"

Oti shrugged. "Confused."

"Have you made your decision?"

"I did not think I had a choice."

"What's your decision?" Jonte asked, ignoring the dig.

"I will do whatever you want, but I have conditions."

"Are you giving me conditions?" It was a question asked softly, but when Oti looked at him, he saw fiery eyes. He looked away quickly.

"No."

"But you just said that."

"I meant to say a favour."

"I think we should eat as we talk."

Oti saw the bowls and the cutlery for the first time. He had been too focused on Jonte to even smell the food.

"So…" Jonte said in between chews. "The conditions, also known as favour, I am listening."

"My money. You know where it is kept?" Jonte nodded. "If something happened to me, could you please make sure that it gets to mom? I will give you her number."

"Are you expecting something to happen to you?"

"I am hoping nothing does, but these are dangerous times."

Jonte chewed thoughtfully as Oti tried not to stare at him. Oti considered his former friend, now boss, as fascinating to watch. It was like something had happened to his being, his whole demeanour. Like some calm evil spirit had taken over. It was Jonte, yet it was not.

"I am just wondering—didn't you tell me that you are not in touch with your family?"

"I went to see my mother today."

"Right... what did you tell her you do for a living?"

"I told her I am a driver for a wealthy man who pays me well."

"That's very clever."

"So... when do I... start?"

"How about tomorrow?"

* * *

Just past eight o'clock, Joe called to say he was waiting at the parking lot.

Kerubo had settled on a pair of black skinny jeans trousers, a red sleeveless top and a matching blazer. On her feet were a pair of two-inch-long boots.

"Gorgeous," Joe remarked as he opened the passenger door for her, surprising her with a kiss on her cheek. He was also casually dressed, in blue jeans trousers, and a blue polo shirt, his feet inside loafers.

"Thank you." Her cheeks burned, horrifying her because they were burning with shyness. She had feared this might happen, that Joe would bring out unfamiliar feelings, effortlessly unearthing her vulnerable self. With Samuel and everyone else she knew, it was easy to be the tough Kerubo who never let much bother her. Joe, on the other hand, had known her since she was a scrawny, dirty and sometimes snot-nosed near-homeless girl. That was, she knew how she would always feel with him, with the Kamau children.

One of the few memories she had of Joe was when she was in high school, over the holidays, and she was making *chapatis* in their kitchen. She had turned and caught him leaning on the door frame, staring at her, a sly smile on his face, and then he had disappeared without talking to her.

It was a silent drive to the restaurant, but the radio stereo was playing reggae music. From the corner of her eye, she could see him nodding to the beats, sometimes singing or whistling along.

"I thought a nice, quiet place would be perfect."

"Okay," she said submissively, allowing him to place his hand on her waistline, nudging her towards the restaurant.

It was the type of restaurant that had menu-carrying waiters arriving at the table at the same time with the guests. The kind of restaurants where waiters were taught chivalry because they pulled seats for ladies. It was the type of restaurant that had waiters bow and smile at the guests. The kind of restaurant that Samuel and Kerubo avoided because they could not be bothered with fine dining and they never served enough food.

"Thank you for coming," Joe said from across her as he studied the menu. She was doing the same. "I wasn't sure you would accept the invitation," He continued as he ran his finger over the list of food.

She cleared her throat. "Why would you think so?"

He paused to look at her, even managed to look surprised. "You know…"

She shook her head. "Know what?"

He shut his menu to look at her, and she held his gaze, unfazed, for the first time ever. "We ostracised you as a kid. If that were me, I wouldn't agree to meet. I hold grudges," he chuckled. She cleared her throat again.

Kerubo looked back at her menu. "I was just glad to have your mother support me," she lied.

"Either way, I want to apologise, and to thank you," Joe continued when their order was taken.

"Whatever for?"

"Apologise for not being a better person to you. I lost the opportunity to be a good big brother. You were just a kid and scared. My sisters and I should have been better people."

"Your mom did a good job."

"She did," he swallowed hard. "Also, to thank you for being the daughter, the child that we, the kids, could not be, from so far. Mom and dad could not stop talking about you whenever we spoke on the phone. You made their last days bearable. Thank you."

Kerubo fought back tears. "It was the least I could do, and I enjoyed looking after them when I could. If it wasn't for her, I don't know where I would be. Probably dead."

"I am sorry," he said as he reached across to her, squeezed and rubbed her hands. She shivered and pulled away.

With the hard stuff out of the way and with the help of the wine, the rest of the dinner eased up. He spoke about his life in America; she laughed mostly because his life sounded like a tragicomedy. He was going through his third divorce in ten years.

"Would you move back to Kenya?"

He took time to answer, chewing on his meat.

"I guess I would. I mean, there is nothing to keep me there anymore. I went to university, I graduated, got married, divorced and repeated that two more times… there are no children to keep me tied there. I think I already paid for any sins I may have committed," he laughed.

She smiled.

"But it is not something I had ever thought about. Are you dating?"

The question was so out of the blue, she nearly choked on her wine.

"Kind of…"

"Kind of, meaning?"

She shrugged. "Meaning he and I are awesome friends but I can't be bothered if I caught him with another woman."

Joe chuckled. "Would he be bothered if he caught you with another man?"

She laughed. "Certainly not."

"Open relationship? Just the kind of relationship everybody should have. It makes life less complicated."

Kerubo nodded. "Would you get married again?"

"I would. Three times later I should be very good at getting married."

She laughed. "Aren't you heartbroken?"

He shook his head. "Nope. By the time the divorces happen, I am ready to jump off the highest cliff." He chewed a piece of meat thoughtfully. "Of course, deep down you feel like a sucker… I mean, what else would you need to know you are an utter failure, than three divorces on your CV? One thing is for sure, though. I am not getting married to another American."

"They were all Americans?"

He nodded and smiled. "I don't think they loved me. I doubt I loved them, but there is this thing of being looked at as a novelty— you know, the African prince and stuff? Shock on them when they realised I was just another man with a foreign accent," he laughed, but didn't sound happy.

"My friend wants to meet you."

"Who is your friend? Why does she want to meet me?" he asked looking suspicious.

Kerubo shrugged. "I was just telling her that I was meeting up with you, and she asked me if you were cute."

"Do you think I am cute?"

She nodded shyly.

"That restores some confidence after the divorces." He winked at her.

"I think you are an absolutely drop-dead gorgeous woman. I always thought that. I always wanted to ask for permission to stare into your brown eyes."

She took a gulp of her wine. So much for fine dining.

Two hours later, he settled the bill and led her out of the restaurant.

"I brought you something from America." he said as he opened the car door for her.

"What is it?"

"I have it in the hotel room. Is it okay if we go for it?"

She hesitated, just to be sure she was not misinterpreting him. Over dinner, she had seen the lust in his eyes, smelled it. The lust had rubbed off on her whenever he touched her across the table. If she went to the hotel, something was bound to happen.

"I love presents."

* * *

It was a déjà vu moment for Kerubo. In that same hotel while in college, she had lost her virginity to Daktari, a college drug dealer she had helped trap. It was also her first job as a honey-trap. For a moment, she wondered where Daktari was, if he had done his time in jail.

She stood awkwardly at the centre of the room, even though her head was whooshing with too much alcohol and too much laughter. With her back on Joe and hands in her jeans pockets, she looked at the television set mounted on the wall. Then he was standing behind her, helping her off her blazer. She shook it off. He hung it on a seat and returned to her, hugging her from behind, pressing his excited manhood against her bottoms, breathing lust into her neck before kissing it. Slowly, he turned her to face him.

She had never realised how huge his hands really were until he cupped her face with them.

"Look at me," he commanded with a whisper.

She did, but her eyes, intoxicated with alcohol and desire, refused to focus. When he kissed her, her eyes shut completely. He held her hairpiece in one knot and pulled it gently, several times, his other hand working on her breasts, then both hands went for her jeans.

"You are sure?" he whispered.

She nodded.

Joe effortlessly lifted her long frame onto the bed.

* * *

"I actually believe heaven is something close to what just happened," Joe said.

They lay in bed, naked, sweaty and still a little out of breath, her head on his hairy chest, listening to his erratic heartbeat.

Kerubo cackled. "What do you think your mom would say about this?"

He groaned. "On any other day, I would call you a party pooper for bringing her up at this naughty moment," he laughed. "But somehow, I think she would actually be happy… only she would hope more happened?"

"More… how?"

"Mom was not stupid. She knew I had the 'hots' for you since I was a teenager."

Kerubo gasped. "But you didn't!"

He laughed. "I used to love watching you but you always had this frightened look whenever we bumped into each other. And you were just a kid."

"Can you blame me? You guys looked scary."

"I didn't look scary. I was handsome. Anyway, I often watched you through the window as you did your work outside."

"That makes me feel uncomfortable. What if you caught me scratching my nether areas?"

"I caught you scratching your boobies a couple of times," he chuckled. She slapped him lightly. "You were in high school. I knew you were going to be a hot number but… I don't know. I was so used to hearing my sisters being all negative about your relationship with mom, how mom was bringing street children at home. I was afraid of offending them."

"Ouch! That actually hurts."

He shrugged. "I probably shouldn't tell you this, but it may help you understand their attitude. We didn't really hate you. We just did not understand you, your presence. We were hormonal teenagers, moody and entitled. I think my sisters, especially, thought you were getting too much attention from mom. I, on the other hand, was siding with my team, so to speak. Sorry about that."

She pulled the duvet to cover herself, suddenly feeling vulnerable and speechless.

"I may not be able to apologise for my sisters, but I can do it for myself. I was a coward."

She sat up and took a deep breath. "Don't beat yourself too hard. You were the youngest of them."

"… and the man."

"Did your sisters know that you were coming to see me?"

He nodded.

"What do they think?"

"I doubt they care, really."

Kerubo laughed, for nothing better to do. "I need to go. I have to work tomorrow."

"Was it something I said?"

She shook her head as she disengaged herself from him. "No. It's getting late and I have to work tomorrow."

"But we just got warmed up."

His boyish protests made her laugh loudly. "Perhaps next time we can do a repeat."

"Can I see you tomorrow?"

"Perhaps. Who knows what will happen tomorrow? I can't promise, though."

His shoulders fell with disappointment. "It would be awesome to see you before I leave... it doesn't have to be for sex, but it would be awesome if it included sex as well."

"You are pretty good at it so..." she winked, disappearing into the bathroom.

When she came out, he was holding a gold chain.

"I got this for you," he said. "I even have your name in tiny letters on the amulet."

"Oh, here I thought the sex was the present!"

*　*　*

Midnight found Boss pacing the rooftop, like somebody had injected adrenaline directly into his veins, or like the alcohol he was drinking was laced with energy tablets. He knew he needed to sleep, but his brain refused to slow down.

It was raining. The last time he was rained on, was as a little boy, way before Kimakia ruined him. Back then, rain was never a reason to stop kicking the ball with his friends. They would kick it until the ball, made of plastic and cloth materials, was too heavy with water to kick around.

Now, the rain was giving him a sense of security, like the raindrops were a shield against evil. And there was evil around, so much that it was tangible. Most of the evil was from him.

He missed Naliaka because she made him feel like a good person. Like he always did when he thought about her while on his own, he touched his groin and willed himself to picture Naliaka naked.

341

NaiRobbery Cocktail

It responded. The last one week had been a strange one, because he had been preparing for his biggest fight so far and also, he had held a hard-on the longest. He played with himself, and although an orgasm had remained elusive, he patted himself on the back.

The day before, he even looked at another woman, and wondered how it would be to have sex with her.

But there were bigger issues. He was tired of living on the sharp edge. The question was, would he walk out with his life? Would he go home with the girl? The possibilities were pretty slim knowing how things worked. He was working at laying down his insurance by having his own person, Jonte, on the mantle. He was working on eliminating people who were hell-bent on getting rid of him, but he knew better than to underestimate them. The possibility of them killing him before he killed them was fifty, fifty.

Chapter Twenty

B oss stayed up on the rooftop, drank beer and made many calls,
only going inside the house when the rain ceased at three in
the morning. He had a long, hot shower, and black coffee. He then
slipped under the duvet and stared at nothing until morning came.
He took another shower, another cup of coffee with his breakfast,
then followed his bodyguards out of the building at mid-morning.

The one who had become known as Watcher One was on duty.

Chizi Samuel was sitting a few metres from Watcher One. Nobody
paid attention to him. Cecilia was just setting up her makeshift
market. Boss nodded and waved at her. She waved back.

It was a niggling feeling that made him order for surveillance
on *Mama Mboga*. Since Boss ordered Cecilia to be followed, no
suspicious activity from her had reached him, but his sixth sense
refused to believe she was there to sell vegetables.

As casually as he could, one bodyguard in front and the other one
behind, he walked down the road where his car was parked.

"We are heading there." He was using a different phone line. Not the one Naliaka had. Not the one his contacts had. A third one he only used when he and his people were on high alert. Once in a while, he used the registered line, just to keep the listeners confused.

They were in Westlands within minutes. "Let's give the bugger time to find parking," Boss instructed. Occupants of his own trail car reported Watcher One had hopped on a motorbike, just like he had the day before. Boss did not understand how careless the other party was. If he had wanted the watchers dead, they would already be minced.

Minutes later, they entered a restaurant and ordered coffee. Forty-five minutes later, Boss went into the toilet. The Boss who came out and went to the car, followed by the bodyguards, looked like the Boss who had gone in, even wore the same clothes, only he was a skin tone or two lighter.

Ten minutes later, the original Boss came out and entered a different car with a different set of bodyguards.

Boss and his new entourage headed back to town, back to his house. There was one more thing to do before heading to the undisclosed location.

* * *

For Jonte and Boss, theirs was criminal love at first sight. When Jonte had tried and failed to pick Boss's pockets, Boss had been more amused than angry at the audacity. His was an aura that scared off people and enough times, he had occupied a table on his own while people around him stood, or looked for other tables. That Jonte had got as close as he had, deserved an award.

He, Boss, could have let his bodyguards beat Jonte to a pulp, but there was something about Jonte. The same thing that had made him want to talk to him, know him better and then offer him a job. He never regretted that decision. That first night, Jonte, injured, cold and scared, was transported inside the boot of a car to an undisclosed location.

It was an old house in a busy neighbourhood, with snake-like plants crawling up its walls. It stood on its own, had a high electric fence and security cameras and dogs, for obvious reasons. Two of Boss's high-ranking employees lived in the four-bedroom house. The two were the same ones in charge of surveillance and interrogations.

Only the privileged few knew details of what happened inside. Other unauthorised guests were hauled in, blindfolded or comatose. Sometimes both. Most of the unauthorised guests left with psychological and physical trauma. Some of the guests left in sacks, cheap versions of body bags.

It was a perpetually cold house, the weather notwithstanding. The almighty sun passed round and over it, avoiding the ghosts that lurked within and vile characters who lived there. The inside of the house was dark, too, and not for lack of windows. In fact, French windows dominated three sides of the living room, but the trees and bushes of flowers surrounding the house kept out natural light.

Several groups headed there.

* * *

Jonte took deep breaths in an attempt to calm down. It was cold, but his palms were wet with cold sweat. He had just used the public toilet at GPO, but five minutes later he was tempted to walk back and use the same toilet.

345

What he was about to do was the equivalent of a final exam, one that would decide if he moved on to the next level, or got kicked the hell out. Mentally, he rubbed his palms together in readiness. He was just a lone figure in the midst of hundreds walking in and out of Uhuru Park.

In measured steps, he walked into Uhuru Park, alone. But he was not alone. Keeping an eye on him were about fifteen people from the age of ten to twenty five years, some in tattered clothes, all spread out in well synchronised formations, all doing their best to remain inconspicuous.

He was going to meet the police contact, Judas. Judas did not know that it would not be Boss turning up. Jonte had discussed with Boss and agreed to take advantage of the element of surprise by ambushing Judas. That way, he would have no time to call anyone to warn about the change of guard.

There was a risky chance that Judas would refuse to play ball. There was even a chance of a physical confrontation, and even worse, a gun fight. They were ready.

Jonte walked as near to the cash booth as possible, then made a call to Boss. He spotted Judas, standing a few metres from him, unable to hide his impatience. He kept shifting his weight from leg to leg, looking at his watch and clicking his mouth.

"I am a few metres from him," he mumbled on the phone to Boss.

"I am going to call him immediately. When he looks at you, nod at him and tip your hat."

Ignoring the shoving and pushing from people making their way to and from the boats, he watched Judas. He saw him pick a call, tense up, and look around him in surprise. Their eyes met, Jonte nodded and tipped his hat. He, Jonte, continued to watch Judas, ready to bolt depending on what happened next. He watched Judas make angry gestures, still on the phone. Jonte stopped breathing, just for a few seconds, when Judas disconnected the line. He resumed breathing when Judas beckoned at him to join him in the boat.

He entered the boat next to Judas, and they started cycling away towards the centre of the lake without looking at each other.

They were a few metres from where they set off when Judas said in an accusing tone, "You are short."

"You are a tall asshole," Jonte retorted.

Judas laughed. "At least your sense of humour is better than Boss's," he said, removing his sunglasses and rubbing his eyes. "The hell is wrong with you guys? You don't run the show. How dare you change things?"

They stopped in the middle of the lake and let the boat tread.

"I thought Boss told you about the impending changes the last time you met?"

"He did not get our greenlight."

"He doesn't need your green light. Besides, nothing has changed except the messenger."

Judas humph'd. "Like we can trust you after this!"

"I don't think this is the time to worry about who is in charge. We have a common enemy we need to deal with."

Judas, in frustration and acceptance of the situation, growled. That the new guy sounded confident made him feel less worried, and he had been worried a lot of late. "Anyway, what's happening on your end?"

Jonte cleared his throat, then told him about the watchers.

"They haven't done anything, but we know they are not there to give Boss security. What we would like to know is what they are waiting for."

The contact cleared his throat as well.

"They haven't attacked because they are still looking for leverage. Your operation has proved too tight for them, and he doesn't have enough to try and hang Boss. Nobody is talking." He rubbed his nose noisily. "He could just have Boss killed, but that would be pure malice. No winners. From sources, they had recruited someone who would have become the new kingpin. It has been a week since they heard from him. What did you guys do with him?"

"I don't know what you are talking about." Jonte did not really know anything about that, but even if he did, he would still have given the same answer.

"You know, I always wanted to ask, is Boss actually a good man worth the kind of loyalty he has, or is there something about him we don't know?"

"Surely, you are not trying to get inside information from me?"

Judas chuckled and shrugged. "One's got to try. I can't wait for the day somebody actually betrays him."

"What can I say? He is a good boss."

He nodded. "I feel weird agreeing with you, but out of all the criminals I have worked with, he is the most honest. Never tries to undercut. Anyway, what happens now? The egotistic tension between my two bosses at work is like a time bomb. If you guys do not sort it soon, we are all screwed. We cannot make a move, for obvious reasons. Only you can."

Jonte cleared his throat. "Foot soldiers, we know our place. Something is up. Today."

"What are you planning?" Jonte could feel Judas's glare.

"We are sending a message. How they receive the message will determine what happens next."

"So nobody dies today?"

"No plans to kill anyone, but accidents happen," Jonte answered with a shrug. "A piece of advice for you and your people: have good alibis for today and tomorrow. It is likely to get dirty."

"You should have warned us."

Jonte chuckled. "Don't look so hurt. It's not like you trust us either. The only thing between us is honour among thieves. We deliver on our promise."

The two figures cycled back in silence. Judas hardly waited for the boat to stop before jumping off, rocking it so violently that Jonte nearly fell in the water. Jonte took time to stretch. He was proud of himself, of how he had handled it.

He had relished it.

* * *

Naliaka woke up with more energy than she had woken up with for a week. Since moving to Queen's house, the feeling of being useless was the only achievement, and drinking, because drinking took her mind off her problems, and shortened the days.

She may have been feeling useless, but she had managed to make two major decisions—to no longer sell herself, and to no longer rob. That decision led to another problem: what she would be doing for a living.

She considered marriage—catching a man would be the easy bit. She did not know any happily-married people and in fact, the only married people she knew were her clients, and that they went to her was bad PR. But being married and having children would be something to keep her busy, and she could go in with zero expectations.

Today, however, she would not worry about her future. She would worry about settling old scores for herself, and for Julia. And she would search for Boss's parents.

It was way past nine in the morning when she finally dragged herself out of Queen's bed, showered, and slipped into a pair of jeans, a light sweater top and sneakers. She grabbed some dollar bills, without counting, from the backpack, and stuffed them in her handbag.

With a bounce, and a smile on her face, Naliaka joined Julia, Malaika and three other girls for breakfast. "Lazy bone," Malaika called as a good morning. "What are you so happy about?"

"Morning, ladies."

A preoccupied Julia nodded her greeting, her eyes on the half-eaten sausage on her plate. For several days, Julia had gone into a pensive mood. She spoke little, and was often spaced out. The other girls would exchange knowing looks, and let her be.

"I think Julia is going through menopause. The mood swings of this woman!" Malaika declared in exasperation before excusing herself to leave the table.

The other girls followed, and only when it was just Julia and Naliaka, did Naliaka whisper, "I am going out today.

"Why are you whispering?" Julia asked, furrowing her brow.

Naliaka smiled, undeterred. "Can you tell me where your house is?"

Julia paused then glared at Naliaka before dropping the fork on the plate.

"What are you on about?"

"Directions to your house, please?"

The two women eyed each other in silent communication. A minute passed before Julia sighed. "Naliaka, you must not give me hope if you will not do anything about it."

"Trust me, please."

When Julia left the table, Naliaka thought she was storming out. She shrugged and continued to eat, but a few minutes later, Julia returned with a pen and a paper.

"I will write it down for you. Also, the two hideous brothers don't live far from each other."

She winked and smiled.

"Great."

"Also, don't do anything stupid. I know it is weird for me to tell you that, but please do not take a bullet for me."

"I will be careful. Where do your children live?"

Julia snapped her head, looking alarmed.

"Why?"

Naliaka shifted on her seat and took a deep breath. "Because it would be good to know where your children stand with you."

"They live with him. Listen, Naliaka, that man hated me. I doubt anything has changed. But apparently, he still dots on them, and I suppose I should be thankful for that. They have not only one present parent, but one who loves them."

"What if I can talk to them?

Julia sat up, alarmed. "How the hell would you do that?"

Naliaka shrugged. "There is always a way. If I can find that way, would you be okay if I spoke to them? I would be discreet."

"I suppose it is okay."

"Write down their phone numbers for me, please."

* * *

"You know, there doesn't have to be tension between us," Jonte said, unwrapping a pack of chewing gums and offering one to Oti. Oti accepted it and popped it inside his mouth, sucking at it and savouring the taste before starting to chew. It took both of them right back to the first time they met, when Oti had outsmarted Jonte on the streets of Nairobi.

The two men occupied the backseat of a V8 engine car, similar to the ones that ferried Boss around. Behind the dark wound up windows, Jonte studied Oti, whose body language was of a cornered meerkat. Jonte allowed himself, just for a few seconds, to feel like a jerk, but that did not last long.

They were on a dangerous path, and he, Jonte, hated how he was playing with his friend's emotions, and life. There was the possibility that Oti would be collateral damage just so he, Jonte, could prove his allegiance to Boss. It broke his heart because Oti was his only friend.

Before his life of crime, he had a friend for every occasion. He had since dropped all of them, because friendship and crime did not mix well. Now here he was, about to sacrifice the only friend he had made in adulthood. Again, he allowed himself to feel guilty, and this time round he resolved to fight for Oti.

He turned again to study Oti, who had pushed himself against the car door, a trickle of sweat on his temple.

"I know this is confusing," he said. "But, if it helps, I did not know about the changes until a few days ago."

Oti nodded in his stoic state.

"It's largely up to you how this ends."

He popped another gum in his mouth. He offered the remaining one to Oti.

"If it makes you feel better, I do not have a choice either. Actually, I do have a choice—I can stay on and make it work for me, or I can choose to die."

"B… but, kill people?"

Jonte sneered. "Oti, you are a thug. A thief. You are scum!" He said with more force than he meant to. Oti cringed. "Every criminal knows that there is always a risk that somebody may die in their hands. Why do you think we do not have bullets in our guns? Do you think it is because we cannot afford them?"

Oti looked thoughtful, then shook his head.

"Exactly. You may want to convince yourself that you are a good guy, but remember, I have worked with you. I have seen how excited you get when we make a hit. I have seen you use the gun to injure victims." Jonte paused, letting his statement sink. "You, Oti, would have already shot someone dead, if you had bullets in your gun. You are trigger-happy. Deal with it."

Oti reacted like someone who had been slapped. He had been slapped with the truth. He thought about all those times he had cursed for not having bullets in his gun, the most recent one being only a couple of days earlier.

The rest of the drive was in silence.

* * *

In another vehicle. The journey started somewhere on Koinange street, in a pub. Conspicuously, a woman was among several lone, middle-aged women. Several young men sat on other tables. Once in a while, the men turned to chat with one another. The women avoided one another's gaze. The pub was popular for being a favourite spot for older women who liked to pick young men for sex.

For three days a week, she went to this pub to eat, drink, and to have sex. She was in her forties, with a potbelly she was perpetually trying to reduce. When she was half her age, she had been a petite girl, but three children later, and a husband who seemed to lose interest in her with every child, she had turned to the fridge for comfort. And ate. And got fat, then watched her husband go for younger versions of her.

He was a Kiganjo Police Academy rookie when they met. With every promotion, he got crueller to her, and the number of women increased. She could have just walked out, especially because her hardware business was minting more money than her husband could ever earn even if he became the country's top cop, but she loved the comfort of having a husband, and she loved the family house. Besides, he was hardly ever in the house because he was either working or visiting his women.

She had lived years being celibate, and not out of choice; she had largely been okay with that. However, when she turned forty, something happened with her libido, something that got her embarrassing herself with him as she unsuccessfully begged for sex. She bought sex toys. Then, during one chama meeting, a woman told them about the pub. And her life improved.

For four years, she had done it, every second day on weekdays. She knew all the faces of the male regulars. Today, there was a new face; it was nothing new—it happened once in a while.

When she walked in, huge sunglasses on her eyes, the barman delivered a cold beer and took her food order of fish and *ugali*.

Then she started window-shopping for the men from behind her sunglasses. She noticed the new guy and smiled to herself.

The new guy had clearly not read the rules of "no approach", because as soon as the waiter walked away, he walked up to her. She considered telling him off, because she preferred to have the power from the outset, but when she studied him closely, she decided one day of rule-breaking would not do any harm.

He was exactly what she liked: tall, chocolate brown, and muscular. She loved the blend of his skin against her own caramel skin colour.

When he stopped in front of her, she gave him a once-over, taking time to look at his strained crotch, then nodded in approval. With her mouth, she pointed at the seat next to her.

"You are new around here?" she said as her way of greeting.

"I come in the evening."

She could not have known, but the man already knew that she never went to the pub in the evening. It was his first time in the pub.

"No wonder. So are you as good as you look?"

"Better."

She laughed, liking him even more. And he was interesting to talk to. Often, the men she chose would sit quietly next to her and smile, eat quietly and smile, drink quietly and smile. They only found their voices when they went up to a room. Not this one. He was funny, and when the food was brought to the table, she almost regretted that their chat was about to come to an end.

She paid the bill and they got up to go to the room, but never made it upstairs because she started feeling woozy and she could not focus on anything.

"She needs a doctor!" The young man shouted, supporting her to the exit, a waiter helping her to a *taxi*.

Now, delirious with the drug he had sprayed on her face, she was in a car with three strange men. One of them was the same young man who had serenaded her earlier. She was sandwiched between him and another unsmiling man. Then there was the unsmiling driver. She knew something was very wrong, but she had lost her ability to resist, or ask questions.

They pulled into the compound and she was helped out of the car, into the house.

* * *

When Watcher One earlier followed Boss to Westlands, he also followed the body-double on a wild goose chase on Thika Road. Boss returned to Kirinyaga Street, catching Watcher Two off-guard. He was busy browsing on his phone, the reason Boss stopped to chat to the new *Mama Mboga* long enough for Watcher Two to notice him.

"Good morning, *mama.* How is your day?" he greeted Cecilia cheerfully.

"Morning, sir. Did you finish the tomatoes already?"

He chuckled. "Certainly not, but I just noticed you have lemons and garlic."

"I do. How many do I pack for you?" Cecilia was having a hard time keeping calm. She was multitasking by packing stuff for Boss and watching the man across the road. Something had set him off, and it had something to do with Boss's return. On spotting Boss, Watcher Two shot up, dropping his phone in the process. With some confusion, he looked around him, like someone who had woken up from slumber.

Then he made not just one, but two frantic calls. When done with the calls, he stood up, sat down, then stood up again, scratched his head, looking across the road thoughtfully.

"What a hardworking woman you are," Boss said as he paid her.

"Thank you."

She watched him disappear into the building, then discreetly looked at the street boys. They were intensely looking at Watcher Two across the road. Cecilia relaxed when she spotted Chizi Samuel, sitting close to Watcher Two, pretending to be asleep.

Chizi Samuel got up slowly, like a creaky old man would do, and walked away towards Kerubo.

* * *

When his door shut behind him, Boss went straight to the fridge and picked a canned beer, opening it with a loud gassy pop. By the time the fridge door shut, he had downed a quarter of it.

This was the day that would decide who between him and his current enemy had the edge. It could even be the day that his empire came down. The day he would die.

He dialled Naliaka's number. She picked it after a single ring.

"Hey!" Naliaka answered cheerfully.

"You are very cheerful!"

"I am being useful today, that's why. I will hopefully get to see your parents, and I also have another stop to make."

"What other stop?"

"Remember I told you about Julia, and her husband?"

"Right..."

"I am going to try and contact the children."

"Don't do anything stupid."

"Julia told me the same thing. I am not going to try and kill anyone, I just want to try and see the kids, and the worst they can do is refuse to see me."

He took a deep breath. "Just remember to depend on the taxi driver if you need to."

"I understand." She did.

"He is under instructions to keep you safe, at whatever cost."

"Thank you. He should be here any moment now."

"Remember though, he must not know it is my parents you are visiting."

"I understand."

"Take care of yourself, Naliaka."

He looked at his watch. About an hour had passed since he returned to the house. It was time to go to the next phase.

* * *

Kerubo's phone vibrated. Samuel's name flashed on the screen for just a second before it was disconnected. It was lunchtime, no need to cook any excuse to see him. Chizi Samuel's kept a phone on him, a basic one for emergencies. He had never had to use it before, and Kerubo knew it was an absolute emergency when she saw his name flashing on her screen.

"Something intense is going on, on the other end," he started, taking the dish from Kerubo but instead of attacking the food, he placed the dish by his side.

"In the morning, Boss left, Watcher One followed, replaced by Watcher Two. When Boss returned, I was sitting close to Watcher Two who looked like he had seen a ghost at the sight of Boss. He made very frantic phone calls—he, Boss, was apparently supposed to be on his way to Thika. Boss stopped to chat with Cecilia to find out if she knows anything."

"So, maybe he shook off the trailer."

"Maybe he did," Samuel answered, not looking convinced. "If I had not listened to the conversation, I would have gone with the shake-off theory, but Watcher Two kept asking the person on the other end, and I am pretty sure it was Watcher One, if he was sure he had not lost track of Boss, if he was sure it was him he had followed. He kept telling him that he was looking at Boss across the road."

"Sorcery," Kerubo quipped.

"Or a double." When Boss said that, he realised he had thought it all along.

"Huh?"

"Body double. Political decoys, they are called. Saddam Hussein reportedly had several. Stalin and Fidel Castro and many others had them. All these figures had one thing in common; they had people who wanted to kill them. In Happy Valley they are called celebrity lookalikes, or doppelgängers."

"How do you even know these things?" Kerubo asked in fascination.

"I was in the army, remember. It was our business to know," he said smugly.

"Imagine two of *him*."

Samuel shrugged. "It's the only explanation."

"Where would he get somebody who looks like him so much that he could pass as him?"

"He would be a very lucky bastard, and we know he is a lucky bastard. They say that out there, there is someone who looks exactly like you, head to toe."

* * *

When Boss walked out of the building, Cecilia was on the phone with Kerubo, trying to keep calm about the information she was being fed. She discreetly looked at him disappearing into the crowd, his bodyguards surrounding him, and wondered if the man she had sold to yesterday was the same man she had sold to earlier on.

Watcher Two followed Boss's entourage.

* * *

Traffic out of the city was slow; perfect conditions because Boss needed Watcher Two to catch up. They already knew he was on his bike, one he had shamelessly parked next to Boss's car. He followed them, out of the city and into faster moving traffic on Mombasa Road.

They didn't get far. A kilometre into Mombasa Road, an accident happened. The accident involved a 4x4 and a motorbike. The vehicle hit the motorbike from behind, sending the rider and his bike sprawling on the tarmac. The driver of the 4x4 and his passenger came out of the car quickly, and started helping the rider up. The rider, who knew what was happening, protested weakly, insisting he was not hurt.

"No, we have to take you to the hospital."

"I am fine. Leave me alone!" He had a broken leg, and although the helmet had cushioned his head from serious injuries, there was blood trickling down. He had bruises on his arms, bruises that could be seen through the shredded shirt.

"Your leg is broken, and you are bleeding," the driver of the car insisted, ignoring the protests, the two car passengers hauling him up. The rider screamed in pain, and then passed out. They carried his limp body to the backseat of the car, and headed to the house.

* * *

There were ten people in the room.

Two of them were there unwillingly.

Oti stood at the back of the room, behind everyone, fighting fascination and fear of what he knew was likely to happen. The two people on the floor looked half dead already. When they had driven into the compound, a chill had gone down his spine. Now he was a little relaxed, because he knew he was not the victim.

Boss and Jonte were the only ones seated. The others were standing at different positions, menacingly looking down at the two figures, one of a man and one of a woman, both still passed out.

The man came round, immediately cringing and groaning in pain. It took him a few seconds for his eyes to adjust to the room. He saw the figures and remembered why and how he was here. He sat up quickly, surprised that they had not tied him up, but the pain in his broken leg reminded him why.

"Welcome back," Boss broke the silence.

"You will regret this..." he threatened, voice barely audible.

"That is so unoriginal," Boss said with a yawn.

"You don't know who you are dealing with.'

"Jonte, tell the man who he is, his rank in the police, his wife's name, his girlfriend's name, where his children go to school..."

"The hell!" Watcher Two shouted, genuinely shocked after Jonte answered everything correctly. When he had been put out there to watch Boss, he had suspected it was not official business, but he was a lowly-ranked policeman with no authority to question. Nobody

361

had told him that he would be investigated. He had believed his boss when he had told him he was keeping an eye on pesky criminals. Over time, he had started wondering if pesky was the right description.

Jonte cleared his throat, ignoring the man's groans. They were no longer groans of pain but groans of fear.

"Do you still think we do not know who we are dealing with?"

The man wimpered and shook his head.

"I... you... my colleague followed you. How did you..."

"Shake him off? Oh, that was easy."

Watcher Two's shoulders dropped and he let himself sink to the floor, his head resting on the woman's thighs.

"Careful where you rest your head! Your boss may not be very happy to know you put your head on his wife's thighs."

"Oh lord... oh lord..." He was up again, looking behind him at the sleeping woman. "Is... is she dead?"

Jonte spoke. "Not yet."

"Why is she here? My boss will kill you all."

"Argh! There you go again, underestimating us," Boss said in disgust.

"She will walk out of here, alive," Jonte said. "As for you, that is up to you."

"What do you want with me?"

"You are going to tell us exactly what we want to know."

Somebody squeaked. It was Oti. He was trying to shrink to nothingness. If anybody had heard his squeak, they did not acknowledge it.

"What do you want to know?"

"How about everything?"

"I don't know much."

"… two broken legs, two broken arms…" Boss interrupted. One of his guys approached Watcher Two as he cracked his knuckles, and gently kicked him, but on the broken leg.

He screamed.

"My new boss told us to watch your house, to watch you and report everything that happens. I swear, that is all I know!"

Boss put up his hand to stop the torturer who was about to kick again.

"Did he tell you why you were watching us?"

He shook his head. He was crying and snorting at the same time.

"He said you are a wanted criminal and needed to be eliminated."

"Mh… did he ask you to kill me?"

The man shook his head. "No." He looked thoughtful. "No. But I did think it was strange that I did not fill up any reports and he warned us not to tell anybody else."

Jonte and Boss exchanged glances, they nodded.

"How many of you have been watching me?"

"Two of us."

"Are you sure? He has not planted other people on the street?" He was thinking about *Mama Mboga*.

Watcher Two shook his head emphatically. "Not that I know of. I swear."

"If he has, and we find out about it, you know we will come for you, right?"

"I swear I don't know about anyone else."

Boss nodded. "We believe you."

"You do?" the man asked in disbelief.

"Should we not?"

"No… no, no, please. I am telling the truth… does… does this mean I will survive?"

"We keep our word. Now, you see the woman next to you? I told you it is his wife. We know he doesn't love her, that he probably would not care if she was dead or alive, so we will not kill her. She will be okay once she sleeps off the drug. We will take you to the hospital and when you see your boss, tell him about it. That the same way we had his wife is the same way we can have his children, or him, or his pregnant girlfriend. Also, tell him the man he had picked as his puppet is resting somewhere in Karura Forest. Hopefully the wild animals have left something for him to be identified from."

* * *

After much confusion and eventually being unable to contact Watcher Two on the phone, Watcher One drove back to the station where he found his boss frantic.

"What the hell happened?"

"Sir?"

"I just received a call from the hospital that your friend was involved in a bike accident."

"I didn't know about that, sir!"

"I thought you were following the target and he was watching his house. Why was he on the road?"

He took a deep breath. "Sir, I followed the target…"

His boss, a man with a potbelly hanging over his uniform, one whose buttons threatened to pop and should never have been anywhere near the disciplined forces, did not let him finish.

"You are a bunch of losers! Losers! You cannot take care of one small criminal. What kind of cops are you? Useless. Useless!"

At that moment, his phone rang. He listened for a few seconds then punched the wall. He turned to his subordinate, eyes red with fury, and shouted, "Get the hell out. Get out!"

Chapter Twenty-one

As Boss was raising the stakes, Naliaka was at the periphery of the shopping centre that many years ago was home to a young Boss. It had all the characteristics of a sleepy town whose reserve energies had been sucked out, drop by drop, by repeated failed attempts to develop it, leaving a collage of tangible failures.

Buildings, some dating back to the colonial era, were covered by a thin layer of red soil. The newer ones, only differentiated from the older ones by the two-storey design, looked like haunted houses, with plants growing from inside to heights higher than the houses.

The road had patches of tarmac that looked out of place in the midst of red dust and potholes deep enough to swallow the wheels of a small car. The trees paving both sides of the avenue were a mix of green and red soil, as though desperately seeking the rains.

"Please pull over," she instructed the driver. She was fighting excitement and fear, and she needed time to reconcile this neighbourhood with the Boss of today.

From inside the car, behind her dark sunglasses, Naliaka studied the passers-by. All of them, with feet covered in red dust, were curiously looking at the car. She understood why—there did not seem to be many cars around. Any car would pique interest. She saw tired farm workers dragging overworked *jembes* behind them, too tired to lift them to their shoulders.

Everything there reminded her of the life she led as a little girl, a life in which dejection and dirt were part of the daily attire. She took in a sharp breath and blinked several times to travel back to the present.

Naliaka considered asking a passer-by if they knew Mama Kanja but instead, she removed a piece of paper from her bag, on which Boss had drawn directions to his parents' house. "Okay, according to the directions, we need to take a left turn here and drive to the end at a T-junction. From there, go left. Take a right, then look for a wooden stream of houses…"

The driver nodded and eased onto the road. Within minutes, they were outside the stream of houses. With feigned bravado, Naliaka stepped out of the car and walked towards the compound.

The gate was made of iron-sheets so rusted, she didn't have to open it to step into the compound because there were holes big enough for her to just bend a little to fit through. The compound was empty, except for washing basins and hung clothes flapping against the wind. There was a house with a slightly open door. She started calling out, "*Hodi! Kuna mtu? Hodi?*" Hello! Is anyone there?

A woman holding a sugarcane emerged from the open door, shielding her eyes from the bright sun with the free hand. She sucked in the cane juice and spit some remnants before speaking. "Are you lost?"

Naliaka shook her head and stepped closer. "I am looking for Mama and Baba Kanja... do you know them?"

The woman bit off a small piece of the sugarcane, chewed for a few seconds, spit more remnants, then stepped closer, shamelessly studying Naliaka from toe to head, stopping at the face. When the woman shook her head, Naliaka dropped her shoulders in disappointment, thinking she meant that Kanja's parents no longer lived there.

"Do you know where they moved to?"

"They haven't moved, and it doesn't make sense why they have not. If I was doing as well as they are, I would already have built myself a house far, far away from this dump." She swept the hand with the sugarcane randomly at the compound but her eyes remained fixed on Naliaka.

Naliaka smiled.

"Would you know where they are right now?"

"Are you driving?" She was peeping behind Naliaka. "Of course you are driving. A girl who looks like you would have to be driving, plus there is no red dust on your feet."

Naliaka flashed a smile. "I have a driver."

"Even better. I bet you are married to a rich man..." She laughed very loudly, threw down her sugarcane, used her *leso* to wipe her hands and mouth then tightened the *leso* back. Naliaka faked a smile.

"Could you give me directions?"

"I can take you to their shop," she offered, pulling her door shut and walking towards the gate.

"How far is it?"

369

"Not far. But I can save you the trouble of searching. Also," she added with a mischievous laugh. "I have not been in a car for so long and opportunities like these do not come often."

Naliaka indulged her with a smile. The more things changed, the more they remained the same. This same scene could have been in her own village, with a similar borderline malicious village woman. In fact, this enthusiastic woman reminded her of a neighbour in another life, a woman who grated on Naliaka's mother. She talked too much about other people, offering information without being probed. *"Don't be deceived,"* her mother would say. *"The same way she talks about other people to you is the same way she will talk about you to other people."*

"She is going to take us to the person I am looking for," Naliaka explained to the baffled driver. The woman had walked in front of Naliaka, entering the front seat. And she was chatty. Naliaka worried she would start talking about Boss, then she relaxed because the driver did not know Boss and Kanja were one and the same person.

"You must be a relative... are you a relative?" the woman turned to Naliaka when the car started moving.

"I am the daughter of their long-lost sister."

"Oh... how happy they will be to see you. That family seems to lose people a lot. They lost a son as well."

"That's sad. How many children do you have? I could give you some money so you can buy presents for them," Naliaka said to digress her from talking about a boy who disappeared to the city. It would be easy to put two and two together for anyone who knew Boss.

370

"Haiyaaa. Such a nice lady. *Anything* will be fine," She beamed, turning to the front and directing the driver to take a left turn. She turned again to Naliaka.

"Are you married?" Naliaka asked.

"No. Single mother."

"Aha… so if I shop for you, there will be no man to accuse you of taking money from other men."

They laughed. And thankfully arrived at the destination.

"That shop over there," the woman pointed at the building with her mouth, easing back into the seat like she intended to remain in the car.

"The cereal shop," she tucked herself further on the seat.

With a racing heart and shaky legs, Naliaka followed and for a misguided second considered bolting, changing her mind. Suddenly, it felt like a burden too heavy to carry. She had not even thought about what she was going to say to them.

"Mama Kanja!" the enthusiastic woman called out at a petite woman weighing beans, her back on them. "Mama Kanja. You owe me much. I have brought your niece to you."

Mama Kanja paused for a few seconds before straightening up then slowly turned towards the newcomers. First, she looked at her neighbour in confusion, then at Naliaka in more confusion. "What do you mean?"

"Your sister…the long-lost sister, remember? This is her daughter!" The woman patted Naliaka's shoulder.

"What?"

Mama Kanja dropped something on the floor. She slowly bent down to pick it and when she straightened up again, there was a knowing look on her face.

"Wow, thank you so much Mama Junior. You can go, I will pick it from here." She turned to Naliaka, "My niece, welcome. I am so happy to see you. Give me a moment."

Naliaka nodded and folded her arms across her chest, then turned to Mama Junior who was still standing next to her expectantly. Naliaka stared at her in a moment of confusion before digging into her jeans pocket for money, handing it to Mama Junior without counting.

"*Haiyaaa…* you didn't even count the money?" Mama Junior asked, nearly grabbing the notes from Naliaka and counting them.

"Heh! I have not held so much money at a go in a long time. Today we shall eat meat…" She started walking to the door before pausing halfway. "Mama Kanja, enjoy the reunion with your niece."

Naliaka sort of waved her off, then stood awkwardly, watching Mama Kanja serve the customer. The older woman was looking everywhere but towards Naliaka's direction. It left Naliaka with the freedom to study her, looking for traces of Kanja. His mother was petite and caramel skin colour with a round-face. Kanja's square jaw and dark chocolate skin colour must be from the father. She looked around the shop, wondering where the father was.

Finally, they were alone. A long minute of silence followed, one the two women spent in a silent stare down. Naliaka blinked first.

"Erm…"

"He sent you, didn't he?"

"Erm… who?"

The older woman clicked her tongue. "Don't play with me, young lady. I do not have a lost sister, nor does my husband. Kanja sent you, didn't he?"

Naliaka nodded, feeling the shame that should have been Kanja's.

And the crying started, preceded by the older woman bending forward, hands on her knees. At first, it sounded like Kanja's mother was choking. Naliaka took a step towards her then stopped when she realised she was holding herself from breaking down. She watched her heave violently and when the wailing started, Naliaka jumped in panic. She looked behind her, hoping no customers were lurking outside.

"Can I shut the door? Just for a while?"

The older woman, now sitting on a sack full of rice, nodded. Her head was on her knees and trapped in her palms, body shaking so hard it looked like a seizure.

Naliaka shut the door, bringing the shop into total darkness. She traced her fingers on the wall where she thought the light switch would be and clicked it on. Showing more courage than she felt, she walked to Kanja's mother, sat on a sack, took Mama Kanja's skinny fingers and gently pressed them with her own.

"He is fine," she whispered, then hoped that he really would be fine.

"I know," she sobbed. "I know he is fine. If he were dead, I would know it here," she placed her hand on her heart. "I have prayed for this moment. I wanted him to be where you were standing a moment ago, sit where you are sitting right now. Do you know we have refused to move because we did not want him to wonder where we went?"

Kanja's mother gave another long howl. Naliaka pressed the fingers again.

"Tell him not to be afraid of coming home, tell him the money he gives us has helped us buy land and build a home and start a business. Tell him to come home, so we can move to our new home."

Naliaka swallowed her own tears and squeezed her fingers into her palms. "I will," she whispered, and took a deep breath. "Where is… where is his father?"

"At the hospital. He has issues with his blood pressure; it needs regular monitoring."

Naliaka swallowed hard.

"I have a phone. He can call me. Will you give him my phone number?"

Naliaka nodded, and as unreligious as she was, she prayed that Kanja would come out alive.

Mama Kanja regained some of her control, even managed to look a little embarrassed. She stood up, rubbed her eyes and straightened her flowery dress. "Are you his wife?"

Naliaka chuckled, "No."

"His girlfriend, then." It was a statement. "You are a beautiful girl… What's your name?"

"Naliaka."

A knock at the door interrupted their next session of silence. It was Naliaka's cue to stand up.

"Erm… I have to go, but," Naliaka reached for her bag and fished out wads of cash. "He wanted you to have this."

She hesitated, then whispered. "It looks a lot."

"He wants you to have it."

Mama Kanja shook her head. "I… we don't need any more money. We have enough. We want to see him. Tell him we want to see him, please…"

Naliaka heard panic in the older woman's voice. It was her turn to want to cry.

"And he will come."

"When?"

"Soon… very soon," she whispered, like she didn't want the older woman to detect the hesitation in her voice. At that point, she wanted to slap Boss for making her give possible false hope to his parents.

"Please take the money. He would be upset if you did not."

"What does he do?"

"Oh, he sells cars. He owns a big car business."

"That's good. Tell him to come home. If he does not want to come here, we can come to him… tell him."

Naliaka nodded, "I will." She had not planned to, but Naliaka bent down to hug the older woman, then realised she needed a hug more than Kanja's mother needed it.

Naliaka was on a high when she opened the shop door to let in the customer, and let herself out, waving at Kanja's mom. She, Kanja's mother, was red-eyed, but she was smiling.

"You better not die on me, dude!" she muttered under her breath, and did not realise she had crossed her fingers.

* * *

While holed inside Mama Kanja's shop, Naliaka dreaded the possibility of Mama Junior stopping by to chat to the driver. She had worked out that Mama Junior was the type to fish for information, but the money must have excited her because the driver was on his own. He was leaning on the car while talking on the phone, cigarette dangling from the fingers of the free hand. When he spotted Naliaka, he disconnected the call and dropped the cigarette, stomping on it with his foot until it blended with the red soil.

"We just have one more stop to make. I hope the rain does not come down," she looked up at the sky, surprised to see dark rain clouds that were not there earlier.

He nodded. "Boss told me about the next stop. Which way?"

"It's on our way back."

"Boss tells me it may turn… strange?"

Naliaka, from the back seat, looked up and found him looking at her through the rear view mirror.

She nodded. "Hopefully not."

"How do you want to do this?" He pulled over and turned to face her. While earlier he looked like any taxi driver, the man she was looking at was giving her chills. His eyes were dilated, like a predator's.

"Erm… I need to make a call first."

"You do that before we leave. I would like to know the plan."

With shaky hands, Naliaka scrolled down her phone, ignoring the driver's gaze. She finally found the name she was looking for. Jamie was Julia's son, nineteen years old. At first, she had thought Judy, the girl, would be easier to talk to, then she remembered teenage girls were more unpredictable.

Her heart beat faster with every ring of the phone. Five rings, then there was a groggy hello. Jamie sounded like someone who had come out of sleep.

"Jamie?"

"Who is this?"

"I am… I am your mom's friend…"

There was a pause and ruffling.

"Is this a joke?"

"It's not. Can I… are you at home?"

"Why?"

"Because I would like to see you, if you don't mind." Naliaka was aware she was being too abrupt, but she was too scared of him disconnecting the line before she said anything interesting enough to keep him on the line.

"Who is this?"

"Your mom's friend, I already told you that!"

"My mom is dead."

Naliaka choked. Then quickly recovered.

"Your mom is not dead," she whispered, choking tears. "I was with her this morning."

"You are lying!" he was crying. She felt like a legitimate angel of tears. "Where are you?"

"I am near your home. If you can, meet me at the shopping centre in twenty minutes, and I can prove to you that she is not dead."

"How can I trust you? You could be a kidnapper."

"If I was one, would I be asking you to meet me at your shopping centre where everyone knows you?"

Pause. "I guess not."

"So, can we meet?"

"I guess…"

"Jamie, please, do not tell your dad. Please…"

"Why not?"

"Are you sure you want me to answer that?"

Pause. "See you in twenty minutes. How will I recognise you?"

* * *

The afternoon was too quiet for Kerubo's comfort, especially after a morning of high voltage activity. There was no doubt it was "the calm" before the storm. What was undebatable was that there would be casualties. She could become a casualty, and that made her edgy.

It made her think about her life, about what her legacy would be if she were to die. No family. Her real job was a secret and the most interesting thing anyone would engrave on her gravestone was that "she was a good shopkeeper". If she died now, she would have nobody to mourn her, except Samuel. But Samuel was also a frontline soldier who may be collateral damage. Selina would possibly mourn her, but Selina would be trying to process that her boss and friend had lived a secret life.

All morning, and part of the early afternoon, she was constantly on the phone with Cecilia and Onyango. In between she had made excuses to go and see Samuel. She had just finished a call with Onyango, who unfortunately did not seem to know what was happening either, when Selina returned from her lunch break with a toothpick stuck at the side of her mouth.

"Is it me or are you constantly on the phone today? And do not even get me started on the visits to Chizi Samuel. What's that about?" Selina asked, glaring at Kerubo as if daring her to negate her observations.

"Did you know toothpicks are bad for your teeth? Use dental floss."

"Don't change the topic."

Kerubo sighed and put on an innocent face. "I think I am finally mourning. I feel very restless," she lied. But the lie worked somewhat, because she saw Selina's features soften. Nothing like evoking pity to deflect suspicion.

"What does Chizi have to do with it, though?"

Kerubo shrugged. "Sometimes, mad men understand you better."

"I am so insulted!" Selina had feigned fake horror. "What about the phone calls? I have never seen you making so many calls."

"There is a lot going on in my life, Selina. I will talk about it when I am ready."

"Touché, much. Talking about phone calls, I intend to call my brother today."

Kerubo straightened up. "Oh, you are going to ask him to let you visit him at work?"

She nodded. "Dad is not doing very well, and if I can reconcile the two before… you know, in case he dies, I would be very happy."

"Call him now before you lose your nerve," Kerubo urged Selina. She wanted to know if Jonte was as busy as Boss was.

"Now?"

"Now."

Selina dialled her brother's phone. It rang to exhaustion. "Perhaps he is busy."

"Perhaps," Kerubo answered thoughtfully.

"I have done my part. *Haya basi*, I am off to the back to arrange files. These useless boys wait for me to take my lunch break, then throw the office into disarray."

Selina disappeared into the back office, leaving Kerubo in her own thoughts. She sat behind the counter, uneasy and anxious, wondering if the action down the road was over for the day, or if they were all regrouping.

She called Cecilia.

"It's gone quiet," she said. "Even the boys behind me disappeared, it's like I imagined the whole thing."

"Yet we know you did not."

* * *

When Selina's name flashed on Jonte's phone, he was sitting next to Boss in the parking lot.

"Who is calling?" Boss asked when he noticed Jonte frown.

"My sister. She never calls me."

"The one who works at the shop?"

Jonte's instinct was to ask how Boss knew where she worked, then he swallowed his questions. Of course he knew where all his siblings were.

"Yes. Dad has been unwell so…"

"You are wondering if she is calling to tell you he is dead." Jonte nodded.

"Call her back."

"What if he is dead?"

"Then you bury him. That is what you do with dead people."

Jonte cringed internally, but remained calm externally. He was sure he would never be as detached from human feelings as Boss.

"So you wouldn't mind if I attended his burial?"

Boss shrugged dismissively. "Why would I? He is your father."

Jonte called his sister back.

"Selina, is everything okay?"

"Hello to you too." She cleared her throat and prepared her mind for disappointment. "I just realised that I do not know where you work."

Jonte shifted on the seat and looked at Boss. There was no way of telling if Boss could follow the conversation.

"You never were that interested."

"I know. I am sorry… I want to come visit you at work." There was silence from Jonte. "If you do not mind."

"You want to come and see me at work?" Jonte asked unnecessarily, looking at Boss. Boss lifted one brow and shrugged.

"Is there a problem with that?"

"No. Not at all. When would you like to do that?"

"How about tomorrow?"

"Tomorrow? I may be going out of town. Can I get back to you in the morning?"

"That's fine."

"How is dad?"

"Not good."

"Should I go and see him?"

"Not a good idea. We will talk about this when we meet."

"So… your sister wants to prove that you actually work?" Boss asked with borderline amusement.

"Where am I supposed to take her?"

Boss chuckled. "Jonte, you do have an office on Ngong Road."

* * *

Kerubo sat behind the counter, face cupped in her palms, staring at nothing through the door. Her phone was on the counter surface, and it was ringing. She side-eyed it and cringed a little when she saw the caller ID. Joe. The day had been too exciting for her to think much about him, but she had, just a little. She had had better sex, but it had been good. Only after she had arrived home had she realised that Joe had been something like an item on her bucket list and now that it was ticked, the excitement was gone.

Reluctantly, she picked the call, summoning some cheer to her voice. "Joe!"

"Hello there. How are you?"

"I am well. Still at work. How was your day?"

"I spent the better part of it thinking about last night."

"Oh…"

Joe laughed.

And she said, "Oh ouch, that hurt."

Kerubo swallowed.

"So… what are you up to tonight?" Joe ventured to ask.

"Tonight?"

"I was hoping you would be free. I am leaving soon."

"My friend, Selina, and I had dinner plans."

"Dang! Can't you cancel her?"

"If you knew Selina, you wouldn't make that suggestion.'

"Bring her with you, then?"

"What?"

"If I cannot have you alone, I am willing to share you with your friend."

"Can I ask her if she is alright with it, then I get back to you?"

"If you do not call in two minutes I will call you back."

She disconnected the call and put the phone back on the counter, rubbing her face vigorously. One of the other workers was walking to the back office and she sent him to call Selina.

"What's up?" Selina asked, looking ruffled. She always looked so ruffled whenever she was arranging the office, something she did about seven times a day.

"Dinner is at eight."

"What dinner?"

"You, Joe and I are having dinner."

"Joe? Who is Joe?... oh!" her face brightened.

"Are you on?"

"Why would he invite me?" Selina challenged, looking sceptical.

"You are the one who wanted to meet him, no?"

* * *

For over an hour, Naliaka sat in the car, mostly fighting nerves. It was past four o'clock and the sunset was beckoning, and with it came the doubts about the wisdom of it all.

When her phone rang, she jumped and nearly dropped it.

"Are you here?" Jamie, sounding very nervous, asked.

"I am. Where are you?"

"Erm... I am in a pub called The Dirinkingi Deni."

"Are you alone?" Affirmative. "What are you wearing?"

"I am in a white polo shirt, blue jeans and a black baseball hat. What are you wearing?"

"I will find you."

She went to open the car door but the driver stopped her. She didn't know his name, and on her phone he was saved as Taxi Driver, and it felt too late to ask his name. She put a note to herself to ask Boss.

"I need to make sure he is alone and stuff?"

Naliaka sat back, relieved. She was feeling uneasy, and she was beginning to think it was not because of talking to a man-boy who had not seen his mother for ten years. So she told him where Jamie was, and what he was wearing. She watched him walk away, stopping a random person who pointed at a direction and the driver nodded.

And she wanted to pee. Badly.

Many minutes ticked by, too slowly. She exhaled deeply when she saw the driver return—his body language gave no clue.

"He's not alone," he said as he entered the car.

"What?" Naliaka asked, feeling betrayed. "Who is he with?"

"Two older men, at least. They were not sitting together, but he kept looking towards them, and they kept nodding at him, I guess in encouragement."

Naliaka dialled Jamie. "I told you to come alone."

"I am alone."

"Now I am going to have to disappoint your mother." She felt awful about that statement. It was unfair of her to make him feel bad about taking precautions. "Who are you with?"

"Erm… dad and my uncle."

"Kaggai?"

"How do you know him?"

"I thought they hated one another," Naliaka said instead.

"Well, yes… who the hell are you? How do you know so much?"

"I am your mother's friend, so I know a lot." She inhaled deeply. "We will have to do this another time."

"No! Wait!" It was a desperate call. "Please…" It turned to pleading. "Please, I need to know where my mother is. I thought she was dead… please. I am sorry. I can shake off the old men."

"How can I trust you?"

"Please…"

"I will call you back," she disconnected and looked at the taxi driver. "What do you think?"

He shrugged. "I wouldn't trust him, but I will go with whatever you decide."

Naliaka chewed on her lower lip until a pain jabbed it and she tasted her own blood. If she walked, she would be letting Julia down, but then again, she could just tell Julia she had made contact and that her son sounded excited. If she stayed, she risked being sassed out, and there was no way of knowing how badly her driver/bodyguard would react.

"Check him out again… when you go inside, I will call him and ask him to leave, then see if the two men will follow."

The driver nodded and walked out, back towards the pub. A minute later, he called her. There was now one man, he thought the second one might have gone to the toilet. Naliaka called Jamie. "Walk out now."

"My dad walked out," Jamie whispered into the phone. "My uncle is still here."

"Walk out." Naliaka repeated. "Keep walking to the main road. Make sure you shake him off, and when I am sure we are safe, I will drive towards you."

"Please promise you will not harm me."

"I swear."

"Okay."

"Well, well, well… look who is here!" When Naliaka heard the voice, she first assumed somebody outside the car was talking to somebody else outside the car. Until somebody tapped the car window, and she wanted the ground to open up and swallow her together with the car. Julia's husband was glaring at her, in confusion and anger. "It's you, isn't it?"

When she still worked for Queen, she never slept with him. She had however bumped into him several times, nodded at him like she nodded at other clients in greeting. This was the first time she was studying him closely. She cringed, thinking he looked as hideous as his brother. His saving grace was the absence of too much gold and patched jeans, the scar and that he still had all his teeth intact.

"What are you talking about?" she asked, desperately trying to regain the composure she had lost during the shock of seeing him.

"Don't take me for a fool, little girl. You are the one calling my son, claiming to know where his mother is."

"What are you talking about?"

"This is a village. Everybody knows everybody. New people are noticed faster than lightning. I saw your boyfriend in the pub 'studying' my son, and I followed him. Where the hell is my wife? I am sure she is dead so the question is, why are you lying to my son? Are you trying to kidnap him?" He was frothing from the mouth, looking more excited by the second.

Her phone was ringing. It was the driver. She was torn. If she told him there was trouble, the likely thing would be him running outside and shooting at the trouble. She didn't want that. If she didn't pick, he would come running out anyway. She needed to get rid of Julia's husband.

"Why don't you ask your loving brother?"

He took a step back. "What does that even mean?"

"Your brother has been shagging your wife for years." She pointed at the direction of the pub with her mouth, "Go in there and ask him."

The shock was so real and great, Naliaka was sure she was about to witness a heart attack. Within seconds, he seemed to age twenty years. For a moment, Naliaka felt sorry, until she remembered he was a wife batterer.

With robot-like movements, he turned around. Slowly, he dragged his feet towards the pub. From a distance, she saw the driver returning, walking quickly, looking alarmed, but he had not seen Julia's husband talking to her.

"You are not picking up your phone?" he asked accusingly.

"Sorry. Can we follow Jamie?" She found no need to update him about what just happened in his absence. "He went that way... is the other man still in the pub?"

The driver nodded. "He is. He has a beer in front of him."

She called Jamie.

He was easy to find. A smartly dressed, tall young man in the midst of scruffy people, and he looked extremely nervous. They stopped. She opened the back door and called him. Without a second thought, Jamie jumped into the car and they drove off.

"Where are we going?" he asked nervously.

"Away from prying eyes," she saw him breathe in relief. "But really, you should be weary of strangers."

"What?" he looked at her with big alarmed eyes. "You said..."

"I know what I said, and you are lucky we are the good guys, but bad guys would use the same tactics. Do not ever, ever get into a car with strangers. You are a rich kid, a lot of people would be interested in your father's money." Naliaka saw the sweat on his forehead. "We can stop here." It was more of a highway pub, one of those that did not have regular patrons, relying on tired, hungry and thirsty travellers. It provided anonymity, and she had no intention of going inside with Jamie, but she needed to pee. She excused herself, rushed to the toilet. When she returned, Jamie was sitting in the car like a statue. The driver was outside with a cigarette, and on the phone.

"Could you please give us a few minutes?" she asked the driver, he moved farther from the car.

"You are so beautiful..." If he did not sound so shy, Naliaka would have considered it a bold statement.

"Thank you. And you are a very handsome young man." Jamie removed his baseball hat, revealing a shaggy mane, one he shyly rubbed.

"People say that I look like mom a lot. So, you really do know my mother."

"She asked me to find you."

"Dad told us she was dead."

Naliaka shrugged. "Perhaps it was his way of closure, and to stop you from asking questions he did not have answers for, but your mother is alive and well."

"Why send you?"

"She did not want to risk rejection, or bumping into your dad. She was not sure if you understood why she left."

"I know why she left. I was not that young to see what used to happen." He looked angry, but just for a moment. "But she could have called me..."

"With what number? You and Judy only got phones a few months ago."

"How do you know that?"

"Because a little bird used to keep her updated on how you two were doing. She is very proud of you. She even has your current photos."

"Your mom is tired of running, hiding from... you know..."

"From dad. He is a prick."

Naliaka chuckled, "Your words. How is Judy?"

"Judy doesn't like to talk about mom. She was younger, but I am sure she will come round if I talk to her."

Naliaka nodded, happy that she had picked Jamie to talk to.

"Can I talk to mom?"

Naliaka nodded and dialled Julia's number. It rang once.

"What's happening? Did you find them? What did they say?"

Naliaka laughed. "How about one question at a time? Even better, somebody wants to talk to you."

"Who?" Julia screeched.

She handed the phone to Jamie. Jamie looked at it, Naliaka nodded at him. He took it, slowly raising it against his ear.

"Mom... is that really you?"

* * *

Kaggai was home alone, enjoying the rare peace of having the house to himself. From his vantage point in his office, only two hundred metres from the house separated by tea plantations, he had seen his wife driving out.

He walked to the house with the intention of doing nothing but enjoying the peace and checking out the changes she had made. She was always redecorating and often he walked into a house that did not resemble one he had left in the morning.

Then his brother called. He ignored the first call, sure that his brother had misdialled. They were partners in the company, their offices next to each other, but all their official liaisons were handled by their personal assistants.

He let the second call ring six times. When he picked it, he did not say hello. Instead he cleared his throat.

"Are you at home?" his brother asked.

"Why?" his voice was full of suspicion.

"I need your help."

"What?" he asked and laughed in disbelief.

"I… somebody called my son, claiming to know where my wife is."

"What?" Kaggai asked in genuine shock. If he had not been sitting down, his knees would have given way. As far as he was concerned, he was the only person who knew where Julia was holed up. As far as he knew, Julia never left the confines of Queen's house and the only person who would know her whereabouts would have to be a customer, or a member of Queen's lair.

"I know! Ridiculous. I am sure Julia is dead."

"Why? Did you have her killed?" He wouldn't put it past his brother to have tried.

"Of course not, but if she was not dead, where would she have been hiding for all those years?"

"So what do you want of me?"

"Whoever it is wants to meet Jamie at the shopping centre. I need someone to sit with me in case… you know…"

"Kidnapper?"

"Yes."

* * *

Dusk was fast approaching.

Kaggai was in the middle of pouring himself a beer when his brother walked in, dragging his feet and shoulders, like a man dragging bags of cement. He felt his heart skip several bits and he noisily put the bottle back on the table, touched his gun for assurance.

For minutes, Kaggai looked at his brother who sat quietly opposite him, staring at Kaggai, but seemingly not seeing him. Kaggai was torn—he wanted to walk away because every sense in him screamed at him to walk away, but he was afraid of being shot in the back, and his brother could.

Then he suddenly walked away. Kaggai asked for another beer and called Queen.

* * *

Kaggai was the only one who knew that Queen was in hospital. When his name flashed on her phone screen, she thought he was checking up on her.

Dressed in a characterless blue gown open at the back, Queen lay on her back, facing the ceiling. Once in a while, she turned her eyes towards the drip that was administering medication into her body.

Three years earlier, Queen was diagnosed with stage two ovarian cancer. The diagnosis had shocked her, not because it was cancer, but because it was ovarian. She, still a virgin, suffering from ovarian cancer was similar to someone who had never smoked getting lung cancer. It had been managed without much fuss, quietly.

Then it made a vicious comeback with stage four—like it had never left.

She was dying. Even the doctors had stopped giving her hope. She was opting for palliative care, not treatment. She was absent from home for longer, and often. She knew it would just be a matter of time before the girls suspected something was gravely wrong. Her skin was pale, she had no energy, and the weight loss could no longer be explained with diet.

In the hospital bed, she finally wrote her will and left everything to Naliaka. Her own mother was dead, just like Naliaka's, and like Naliaka, she too had been an only child. She had no friends to speak of. Naliaka was a natural choice because she knew Naliaka would be kind to the other girls.

Queen carried guilt about Naliaka for years. She was the first to admit that she could have done so much better, offered her a life out of prostitution, but she had not, because she had not been familiar with empathy. The money would not give Naliaka another chance, it would not erase what Kaggai had done to her, and it would not make her forget about the men she had slept with, but it would make Queen feel better about herself.

Naliaka was the daughter she never attempted to have. The girl who had taught her how to love.

When Kaggai told her that somebody was looking for Julia's son, she knew that Naliaka was responsible. Naliaka and Julia were close, and although she could not imagine how they had done it, there was no doubt in her mind that the two had colluded. She had her misgivings, that Julia's husband knowing where his wife had been all along would stir a hornet's nest that may end up exposing her operation. Then again, it was an operation she no longer had passion for. Since the doctor had announced the return of her cancer, she had not taken in new girls. She had been flirting with the idea of kicking out all the girls, except she did not want to leave them homeless.

She called Naliaka.

"Queen! I feel like I haven't seen you for years!" Naliaka was at the back of the taxi heading back to the house.

Queen gave a short laugh and coughed. "I know. What have you been up to today?"

Naliaka paused, wondering if it was possible that one of the two brothers had already updated her. "This and that..."

"Oh?"

"Long story. I will tell you about it over a glass of wine," she paused and took a deep breath. "I also went to see Julia's son... he is very handsome."

"Oh," she said with relief, glad Naliaka was forthright. "That's interesting." She took a deep breath "You and I need to sit and talk. Tomorrow, my driver will pick you up and bring you to where I am."

"Where are you?"

"Not far..."

"Erm... are you upset with me? You sound... strange."

"No, I am not. Far from it. We just need to have a talk we should have had a long time ago."

* * *

If his flab did not threaten to pour out of his uniform, he would be proud of it, but he spent his uniform days as a police boss, embarrassed about his weight, angry at how people looked at him in disapproval and jealous of his peers who fit in their uniform. He could no longer see his feet while upright, or scratch his back, because several layers of fat got in the way. Every time he had to get a larger uniform, he promised himself to watch his weight but as soon as he saw fatty meat and downed it with several beers, he would forget his resolve.

He could remember when his morals took a nosedive, when he bribed for his first promotion, and every other that followed, to his current rank. He knew of officers who got promotions by merit, some because they excelled at their duty stations or had good education to back them. He had neither. If he had not often dug into his pockets, he would still be a lowly officer, walking the streets of Nairobi directing traffic, or even worse, Turkana, chasing cattle rustlers.

The more promotions he got, the greedier he got. He hated that his wife questioned his morality, which was laughable because her business capital was sponsored by his corrupt activities. To get back at her, he started sleeping around. His excuse was that she had grown fat, a self-defeating excuse because his fat matched hers layer for layer.

Along his career path, he befriended criminals and promised them protection in exchange for money. This was always easy, until his current posting. The top criminal, Boss, was too powerful and was liked by enough powerful cops from different stations. Really liked, and not just because he gave Caesar what was his, but because he was keeping crime rates in the city at manageable levels.

He hated that he was not able to speak to Boss. He knew where he lived and could have just stormed there, but Boss was shielded by enough security. It would be bloody, so he needed what looked like a legitimate reason to storm in. His first idea was to frame him for a crime, but none of his colleagues was willing to help.

He tried to gather information on the streets, something that had always been easy, but with Boss, nobody was talking. He could have just killed him, but his own colleagues had threatened dire consequences.

"Find out what happened to the last person who tried to do what you want to do", they had told him.

He did not want to die, he just wanted to have more say in the amount of money that came to him. He tried to plant his own person as the crime boss, but the one guy who had been willing to take on Boss had disappeared mysteriously before his decomposing body was discovered in a forest.

Now, he was heading to a hospital to visit one of his watchers. He already knew it was not an accident before he got there, and on his way, kept expecting something similar to happen to him.

* * *

His watcher was in a private hospital, in a private room, one the police medical cover did not provide for that rank. The OCS walked in cautiously, looking around the room before his eyes settled on the officer, whose face was heavily bandaged, and a plastered leg elevated. His eyes settled last on the drips.

"You need to go to a government-approved hospital. Your insurance cannot afford a private room in a private hospital."

Watcher Two cringed.

"It is paid for." He deliberately left out the word "*afande*".

"By whom?"

"I don't know, but a hospital accountant was just here to tell me that my bill would be fully covered as long as I am here."

"Boss?"

Watcher Two rolled up his eyes.

"Did he do this to you?"

"It wasn't an accident."

"I am going to order for his arrest! He doesn't know who he is messing with." The inspector was breathing hard even though he was seated on the available chair.

Watcher Two shook his head. "No, sir. I think you are the one who has no idea who you are messing with."

"How dare you!"

"With all due respect, sir!" Watcher Two shouted; it caused him pain, but he did not care. "Sir, you used me for unofficial business. I want nothing to do with it anymore. I am done."

"That is insubordination!"

"I am beyond caring. I nearly died today, and not in the line of duty. If Boss had wanted me dead, I would be dead. I am done. You sort your own mess without involving me."

The OCS took several deep breaths, sweat trickling down his temple, glaring at Watcher Two. He glared back, unblinking.

"What happened?" he finally asked in a more controlled voice.

"A lot," he told him. "Finally," he concluded, "You better check if your wife is alright. She was lying next to me, unconscious."

He stood up so fast he even shocked himself. "What? If they have hurt her…"

"They haven't. She probably doesn't remember she was there. They just took her to show you what they are capable of." Watcher Two studied his boss as he walked up and down the room, watched his cavalier attitude diminishing fast, as it hit him that he was not as powerful as he thought he was. If he was not in so much pain, pain he was blaming his boss for, he would have felt sorry for him."

* * *

"I feel so drab just walking next to you," Kerubo remarked with a giggle. They just alighted from a taxi, her and Selina, and walked to the restaurant where Joe was waiting for them.

"If I wasn't feeling so damn hot and sexy, I would be upset with you for not telling me the dress code was casual." Selina was nowhere near as tall as Kerubo, nor as slim or stealthy, but she was effortlessly sexy. Every man they met on the way stared at Selina. She, Kerubo, was the taller one, but she felt invisible.

Selina wore a black short dress that left her wide hips and shapely legs for all to see. On her feet was a pair of red heels. Her hair was held in a high bun, face carefully made up.

"Sexy suits you totally," Kerubo said, hoping that Selina's look would take Joe's attention away from her. She had deliberately dressed down, knowing Selina would be her usual self and dress up. She had on a pair of blue jeans, a blue sleeveless top and sneakers, but no handbag. Her phone, money and house keys were in her jeans pockets. Her gun was tucked in her sock.

Her dressing had not only been inspired by her need to deflect attention from herself, but also by the possibility that she could be summoned any time if things started happening on Kirinyaga Road.

"Well, thank you," Selina said, flipping imaginary hair from her forehead.

Selina was the first to go through the security booth. She was clean off metals. This would not be the first time Kerubo had gone through security while carrying a gun, but it always made her heart rate go up. She went through the first time and the metal detector went crazy. She reversed and removed her keys and phone, passed them to the security. Second time the detector went crazy. She pointed at her navel and lifted her shirt to expose a navel ring.

"The belt too. You want me to remove them?" she asked innocently.

The security woman shook her head, instead passing the gadget up and down Kerubo but never getting to her legs. She was ushered in.

"You wear a lot of metals." Selina remarked casually.

"Goes with the territory."

"Tomboy territory. You could pass as my bodyguard, the way you are dressed."

"That's not such a bad thing, is it?"

Selina laughed.

Kerubo spotted Joe's lone figure waving at them from a corner.

* * *

Kaggai paced in and outside the house, at some point walking up to the edge of his brother's compound only a hundred metres away, then back. He removed an aged bottle of whisky he had been keeping for an opportune time. He sat on the sofa, one that during happier times he used to frequent. It was just about the only thing that his wife had left in place.

He was halfway through the bottle when there was a bang at the door. Then another one and with each bang, it got louder. He stood up, taking his time because not only were his knees wobbly from his body weight, but also from the alcohol. It was a deranged brother he opened the door for, and it was a deranged brother who greeted him with a punch, one that landed on the very scar that his father had left on him so many years ago. The second punch removed the tooth next to the same one his father had removed so many years ago. He staggered back, landing on his knees with a thud. He was sure his hip bone was broken from the impact, among other bones.

He groaned in pain.

"You bastard!" his brother screamed, kicking him in the ribs and ending up on the floor. He had also been drinking, and he was as heavy. "You have been screwing my wife! What kind of a brother are you?"

Kaggai looked at his brother and laughed, blood trickling from his mouth and nose. He laughed at the absurdity of the situation, laughed that deep down he felt relief, that he no longer had to keep the secret about Julia.

"Clearly, I am a better lover than you are," he slurred.

The loss of the second tooth had given him a more pronounced lisp. He made a snap decision to have both teeth fixed after this.

"Bastard!"

The insult was followed by a weak punch.

"Bastard...Look who's talking. Do not pretend to be the offended party. You hate your wife, and she hates you!"

"Like yours does?"

"At least mine is still with me, and not selling herself to every Tom, Dick and Harry."

"What the hell do you mean?"

Kaggai laughed again. "Oh, you don't know the half of it. Your wife sells her body in a house belonging to a woman called Queen..."

"Queen? The Queen?"

"You know Queen?"

He did not answer. Instead, he removed a sound that made Kaggai think of a lion in agony. It did not even matter, that he had never seen a lion, in agony or otherwise. A sound that made Kaggai cringe then see his life in slow motion.

There was another familiar sound. A pop. He, Kaggai, only heard the pop after the impact. He did not feel the pain either, but when he looked down at where the centre of the impact was, which happened to be the left side of his chest, he saw a hole through his white vest, then the vest started turning red, then he lost both his vision and hearing.

* * *

The phone alarm shrilled at six thirty in the morning, waking Naliaka from a drowning dream. She snoozed it three times within thirty minutes before eventually forcing her eyes open, but continued to lay on her back. Even without lifting it, she knew her head was heavy, the pain just waiting for the slightest movement to ignite. She had a hangover because she, Julia and Malaika had stayed up late, repeatedly raiding Queen's drinks cellar, laughing about this and that.

Naliaka, keeping a safe distance from Julia, had narrated that part of the story with bated breath, afraid that Julia would hit the roof over the exposure, but Julia laughed hard and long, a new kind of laughter that came with the joy of speaking to her son after ten years. Only after the laughter did Naliaka move closer to Julia.

"If I do not have another payback, this will be enough," Julia said. "You awesomely malicious woman. Who would have thought you had it in you? It is always the quiet ones you have to worry about." They clicked their glasses and continued laughing and drinking.

Now, at a snail's speed, she sat up against the headboard for a moment to let the brain settle. The only reason she was getting out of bed was Queen, who had sounded strange on the phone and she, Naliaka, needed to know why. Slowly, she eased her legs out of the bed and let her feet sink into the thick soft bedside carpet. With half-closed eyes and half the will to live, she dragged her feet to the bathroom.

From Queen's medicine cabinet she got two painkillers, swallowed them with tap water, then brushed her teeth as she studied her red eyes in the mirror, wondering when she had become a regular drinker; she decided she needed to get back to her near-teetotaller days. What she really wanted to do was fill Queen's under-used Jacuzzi with water, and dip herself in it for an hour. What she did was have a cold shower.

She found all the girls around the table, having breakfast and chatting in low tones. They chorused a good morning. The painkillers had not worked fully, so she smiled painfully and waved at them, taking the only available seat between Malaika and Julia.

"The best cure for hangover," Malaika offered her usually unsolicited advice. "Is this…" She picked a half-full glass of wine from the table and gulped some, washing down the bacon she was chewing.

"If I smell another drink for three years I will throw up." She meant it.

"What you should worry about is that she thinks it is okay to eat bacon and wash it down with wine," Julia said with an eye roll.

"If you are a normal human being, pop down a couple of painkillers and wash them down with a lot of water."

"Why are you up so early, anyway? You do not have to work like the rest of us?" Malaika asked.

"I am going to see Queen."

The whole table went quiet and everybody turned to Naliaka, even those who were having cluster conversations.

"Where is she?"

Naliaka shrugged. "I don't know. She is sending the driver to pick me up."

"Perhaps she is in hospital," Malaika suggested, digging out for a cigarette and holding it unlit between her fingers.

"Why would she be in the hospital?"

Malaika shrugged with near nonchalance. "I don't know... but she has this sickly look of late. I grew up with a lot of sick people around me and I know how they smell and look... and she has lost weight."

"She did tell us she was dieting."

Malaika shrugged. "Perhaps you should also ask her why the client booking has gone down. Today, I only have two."

Naliaka looked around at the table, the other girls nodded. The rest of the breakfast was consumed in silence.

* * *

For the entire forty-five-minute drive, Naliaka sat back-right, staring out of the window, thinking about everything and nothing, afraid to settle on any thought for long.

The hospital sign at the gate caught Naliaka off-guard. She jerked involuntarily, for a moment thinking, hoping, that she was hallucinating.

"She's at the hospital?"

The driver nodded, looking at her strangely through the rear-view mirror.

"Why?"

He shrugged. "She is in room number six, third floor" Suddenly, Naliaka felt nauseous. She burped an alcohol smelling burp. Her headache was back, so was the thin sweat.

On her walk to the hospital reception, up to the third floor room indicated on the paper, she started hoping that Queen was not the patient, that she was just there giving moral support to someone else—like a relative, or a friend, an unlikely thing because Queen had no such attachments.

Queen, without her wig, a visible bald head, face without a trace of makeup, or smile, or the hardness that often scared off people, looked vulnerable. In one instant, Naliaka's world crumbled. She howled and burst into tears. Queen, who was asleep when Naliaka walked in, woke up with a start and nearly dislodged the tubes going into her hands.

"Shhhhh…" Queen hushed, beckoning Naliaka to approach. "Stop crying like a little girl." Naliaka cried harder. "Come here and give me a hug…" Naliaka did and for minutes on end sat on the edge of the bed, buried in Queen's ample bosom.

When she finally sat up, her face was puffy and wet with a mix of tears, sweat and possibly snort. She picked a tissue from the side table and blew her nose, throwing it in the bin.

"There is a sink over there," Queen pointed at the sink with her mouth. "Wash your face. You look as terrible as I do."

Naliaka forced a smile and did as she was told.

"What's going on?" she asked when she returned to the bed, her face undried. She took another tissue and blew her nose noisily.

"Life."

"Why are you here? I saw you three days ago and you were fine… I thought you travelled."

"Then let this count as travelling."

"Is it food poisoning?"

"I wish."

"Are you going to be okay?"

Queen shrugged. "Only God knows."

"You don't believe in God," Naliaka said accusingly.

"Says who? Anyway, when mortality looks so within touching distance, you start believing in anything that gives you hope, like God." Queen laughed. Naliaka did not.

"You are not dying though, are you?"

Queen shrugged. "Aren't we all? It's just a matter of when."

"Stop talking nonsense!"

"I did not call you here to discuss my mortality. It is such a drag topic."

"Why did you call me?"

"To tell you I am sorry."

"For what?"

"For everything. So much I did wrong. For anything I could have done differently." Naliaka swallowed salty tears. "I could have done so much for you, Naliaka, but I threw you to the hyenas and they devoured you."

Naliaka blew her nose again.

"I could have turned you into a respectable member of society."

"That is not entirely true. I think you do great for a lot of women…"

Queen sneered. "By making money out of their vaginas?"

Naliaka shrugged dismissively. "The women come to you, willingly. They come because they know they can be safe with you."

"Except you…"

"I… well, yeah. But it is different now. I am happy."

"Because you have learned to be happy, not because I made you happy."

"Debatable. I think you have been part of many of my happy moments."

"… sad moments, too…"

"Isn't that life? Why are we talking about this? It is making me uncomfortable, especially when you are lying there with things attached to you…" Naliaka walked to the window, arms crossed, holding back tears.

"Because, my dear Naliaka, I would feel better if you let it out… let out all the anger and bitterness you surely hold against me. I feel like shit whenever you are so nice to me."

Naliaka turned briefly to look at Queen. Queen was right—she hated her, intensely, but only once in a while. Most of the time, she loved her, as intensely. She turned back to look through the window at the dreary weather.

"I wished you dead," Naliaka said in a low tone. "I really wished you dead." She paused, expecting Queen to interrupt. Queen was silent. When Naliaka turned to look at her, she expected to see a shocked face, but Queen had no particular expression on her face. She nodded at Naliaka in encouragement. Naliaka turned back to the window.

"I don't wish you dead anymore." Queen sighed deeply. "Now, I have nothing but love for you. You fed me, housed me, hugged me when I needed a hug. I honestly do not know where I would be without you."

"Even though I could have taken you through school?" Queen asked in a whisper.

Naliaka shrugged again. "It was not your prerogative. I was a stranger, not your relative. You could have, but you didn't, but you still turned out to be the one person who has stood by me at my lowest moments."

Queen finally let out a tear. "You really mean that?"

Naliaka nodded, walking back to Queen and kneeling beside the bed, taking her hand into hers, careful not to interfere with the tubes. "I forgave you." She took a deep breath, at the same time blinking back tears. "Do you remember when you gave me the speech of men using me anyway, and it would be better if I had a say in how they would use me?" Queen nodded. "The times I have ignored that advice, I have been fleeced…" Naliaka laughed. Queen laughed, then took a deep breath. "So when are you getting out of here?"

"Who said I am?"

"Why wouldn't you? They are treating you, aren't they?"

Queen shrugged and cringed with pain. The talk with Naliaka was draining her. "They are trying but… listen, let's not talk about that right now. There is something else I need to talk to you about."

Naliaka released Queen's hands and sat on the bed, looking down at Queen, like someone seeing something for the first time.

"The house. I want to close it."

"What? Why? What happens to the girls?"

"That's where you come in."

"Me?" Naliaka stood up again, but instead of going to the window, she started pacing up and down the room.

"I am asking you what you think we should do with the girls."

"We? Like what?"

"I do not want to kick anybody out. You could run it if you wanted to. I am not asking you to, though."

Naliaka thought of Malaika's observations.

"Erm… have you by any chance reduced the bookings?"

"More than that. I am not making any more bookings. The men who are still coming in have been booked already."

"How will the girls earn their living?"

"They will get paid, more or less what they were earning per month, but only for three months. After that, they are free to stay on. I am happy to keep feeding them, but I cannot pay them after three months. Also, they cannot bring men into the house."

"I don't understand."

"You do not have to give me an answer right now but, if you had such a house, if you did not want to kick the women out, what would you do?"

Naliaka shook her head. "Everything, including you being here and talking like that…"

They were interrupted by a nurse who walked in carrying a tray with bottled water and pills in a saucer. She smiled and said good morning. Naliaka nodded and continued to watch in fascination as the nurse took Queen's vitals, noting them down. She watched Queen accept what seemed like dozens of pills, and swallow them. By the time the nurse walked out, Naliaka was leaning on a wall and crying silently.

"Tell me about Kaggai and Julia's husband," Queen said in a sudden change of topic.   Naliaka chuckled involuntarily in between tears. She still did not know what was ailing Queen, but she was afraid to ask, sure that it could not be good at all. The hints were in their conversation.

"That was almost funny. He is your friend though, Kaggai, I mean. Are you sure you are okay with what I did?"

Queen shrugged. "He is a sanctimonious bastard. I have no particular feelings of love towards him. He is a friend quote unquote, because he is the oldest customer I have. That does not change the fact that he is a creep."

Naliaka chuckled again. "His brother?"

"Violent misogynist... it's an unfortunate family they come from."

"Are you not afraid of being exposed?"

"Let them try. I have interesting files on them," Queen smiled. "But even if they did, they would not have any proof. The only records I keep are from the clients doing what they shouldn't be doing."

"What sort of records?"

"Visuals."

Naliaka gasped and covered her mouth with her palm. "Like, you have cameras in the rooms?"

"Don't look at me like that! I only record their first day purely for insurance, not entertainment."

"Have you ever recorded me?"

Queen nodded. "Of course... but I destroyed yours."

"Recording people is terrible!"

"I am a sleaze, I know, but I am in a sleazy business, so it comes with the territory."

"The police could raid the house though."

"And find what? Many women together? That is hardly illegal."

Naliaka shot up so fast, shocking Queen and nearly sending her off the bed.

"What's wrong?"

"That's it! We could turn it into a rescue centre for women."

Queen opened her mouth to respond, but Naliaka's phone shrilled in her pocket. She fished it out, hoping to see Boss's number. It was not, and she frowned at the caller ID.

"Boyfriend?" Queen asked.

"No...Julia's son. I don't know why he is calling me while he now has Julia's number." She picked the call. "Jamie?"

"Naliaka... sorry... I... I didn't know how to tell mom. Please tell her that dad and uncle Kaggai are both dead."

* * *

Globe Roundabout, early morning.

It was a misty morning.

A tall, lone figure covering herself with an umbrella, wearing a trench coat over skinny jeans tucked inside a pair of brown leather boots, walked in quick and deliberate steps from Ngara to Kirinyaga Road. The mist water had enough power to form small tributaries on the tarmac. Once in a while, vehicles ran over the tributaries, splashing the water to twenty different directions. The same tributaries would recreate immediately.

Kerubo was an hour earlier than her usual time, and it was no wonder she was nearly alone on the walk. Globe Roundabout was popular with thugs, Samuel had heard all sorts of stories about the things that happened around Globe roundabout. Lone walkers avoided the route. Not Kerubo. She had confidence in her fighting skills, and if they were not enough, she could always shoot them. She had never had to test her combat or sharpshooter skills, and she was confident the resident thugs were now too familiar with her.

She stopped a few metres from the shed to catch her breath, and to watch Samuel.

He lay on the hard, metal seat under the shed, with a carton as his mattress. She could see his body rising up and down in regular breathing. He was covered head to toe by a blanket, but Kerubo still felt uncomfortable on his behalf. Over the years, she had made peace with Samuel's choice of lifestyle. A wealthy person's choice to live like a pauper for three weeks every month. Once in a while, like now, just when less than an hour ago she had woken up in a comfortable and warm bed, and had taken a hot shower, she wondered and worried about his choice.

In a sudden movement, Samuel sat up.

Kerubo chuckled involuntarily. "Did you feel me watching you?"

Samuel yawned and stretched his arms. "Of course I did." He swung his legs down. "You looked wet and ready to eat". He winked. The reason he had woken up had nothing to do with feeling Kerubo's eyes on him, but a graphic sex dream about the two of them.

"Shut up!" She rolled her eyes and walked towards him.

"What's your problem?" he asked, adjusting himself on the cold metal seat. "A moment ago you almost looked like you felt sorry for me."

She smiled, handing him a bag that had his breakfast. Tea, two sausages and toast. "I actually do. Are you really okay doing this?"

"What? Sleeping on the streets? Easy peasy. Besides, what else is there to do with my life?" He accepted wet wipes from her.

"So this is merely out of boredom?"

He shrugged, pouring the steaming hot tea in a plastic cup.

"Or perhaps you are just running away from something?"

"Like what, oh dear shrink?" He took a bite that took half his sausage.

"Like happiness?"

"I am very happy."

"Liar. When I looked at you a moment ago, I couldn't help thinking how dumb all this is. You should consider quitting."

"And do what?"

"Anything that does not involve living on the streets."

He chewed thoughtfully before talking. "Your wish for me may come true if this thing blows up, which it will. Our covers will be blown, and we may both be jobless for a while. Have you thought about what you would like to do?"

Kerubo shrugged. "I think I will retire to Nyeri and farm. It would be awesome to wake up and look at Mount Kenya every morning."

He sniggered. "You don't have enough money to retire."

She sniggered. "Money is not everything, but I guess you wouldn't know that, seeing you are wealthy."

"Why Nyeri?"

"It would appear that I inherited land from the Kamau's."

"And the kids are alright with that?"

"I don't think they have any use for it, seeing they all live in America. Besides, there is enough for everyone."

"There is never enough land for some people. Is it in writing?"

"It is. Joe gave me a copy of the will last night."

"You saw him last night?"

"Mh-h. I took Selina with me," she said and giggled.

"What?"

"It was love at first sight for them. I left them together."

"Are you okay with that?"

"Why wouldn't I be?" she snapped, feeling defensive. "Anyway, I wasn't drinking, because I was expecting to be summoned to shoot someone anytime. They were both drinking and I didn't want to be the party pooper. So, I faked a headache and called a taxi."

"Right. Anyway, why are you in so early?"

"Because I wanted to find out if anything happened."

Samuel shook his head. "Nothing. Zilch. I walked that way several times and nothing, except for the street kids. It's weird."

"I found a text from Onyango. '*Enemy appears to have been neutralised,*' it said."

"That's a good thing, right?"

Kerubo shrugged. "Perhaps the enemy is regrouping. I feel like this thing should just blow up already. I hate waiting for something to happen. It is stressful."

"I know what you mean."

* * *

That Boss managed to catch several decent hours of sleep pleasantly surprised him. Even the nightmares that had been shadowing his dreams for days were absent. That he had taken copious amounts of alcohol, and woken up without a hangover, was to him a sign for good things ahead. He woke up at ten, and because he did not want to take chances with a delayed hangover, decided to prepare an elaborate and greasy breakfast. He had the appetite, and he had the time, because there was nothing particularly planned for the day. Just waiting.

As he beat the eggs, as he cut the onions, tomatoes and *hoho*, as he separated the bacon, as he defrosted two sausages and warmed *ugali* in the microwave, as he boiled water and milk to make tea, he thought about his jaded life, one that had so far involved chasing rainbows and running from the *kínyunjurí*, the bogeyman. All he had ever wanted was to be happy, happiness had been constantly elusive, and when available, it was in small bursts, like chewing gum that lost its taste within minutes. He was tired of running, of looking over his shoulder. Of being the absolute bad guy.

412

He thought about his dream of getting a good job in Industrial Area all those years ago, about the drugging and the mugging and the gang rape that had quickly turned his life upside down and all ways. He thought about Mato, and only realised he was crying when he tasted the tears. He thought about his short career as Monde's drug mule, and about Monde's death. How Mato and Monde had been his stepping stones to being the all-powerful crime boss.

He thought about Naliaka. He frowned, worried that it may not be a happily ever after with her, for two reasons. One, that he may not live long enough, and if he did, he may never be able to make her truly his because, how would he do that if he could not do the most basic thing?

* * *

Cecilia pitched the station at her usual spot at nine in the morning.

She looked across the street and spotted Samuel faking sleep. There was no trace of a watcher. She had not expected to see any.

And so, with her coriander and *hoho* and tomatoes and onions and lemons and a gun, she sat down, mentally prepared to be bored out of her mind, but open to street excitement. In the few days she had been around, she had managed to make a few friends. Perhaps today would be a good day to ask seemingly innocent questions.

All day, there was no sighting of Boss, and by the time Boss left the building in a hurry, Cecilia was long gone, having run out of stuff to sell. Samuel was on the other end of the street and did not see Boss leave the building. But the night was quiet.

* * *

413

Selina walked into the shop, red-eyed, wearing clothes Kerubo did not recognise, and looking a tad embarrassed. She paused at the door and glared at Kerubo. In return, Kerubo giggled before bursting into laughter. "Busy night?"

Selina grunted and entered the shop. She did not talk until she was standing next to Kerubo, first elbowing her gently. "I have never had sex on the first date," she whispered to Kerubo, covering her mouth in embarrassment.

Kerubo laughed loudly

"I feel so naughty," Selina said, covering her face with her palms. "He had to have the hotel boutique open earlier than usual to get me these clothes."

"You bad girl!" Kerubo giggled and playfully poked Selina's shoulder with a finger. "You have matured."

"He is a beast," Selina declared. "I want him for keeps, but only if he promises to keep his game up."

"He is leaving tonight."

"No, he is not. He postponed the flight by a week!"

"Why?"

"You wouldn't know this, but I am a pretty amazing woman in and out of bed." She bent closer to Kerubo. "I am moving into his hotel room for the week," she whispered. Kerubo gasped. "He is also coming to pick me up at lunchtime to take me to see Jonte."

"You guys move fast!" Kerubo felt more jealousy than shock. Jealous that it seemed so easy for everyone but her to just get together and make such grand plans while all she successfully managed were one-night stands. Then again, she was good at sabotaging herself and how she had treated Joe was a typical example of how she treated men who were not Samuel.

414

"Life moves fast, you have to move with its speed. He loves you, by the way."

"What do you mean?" she was searching Selina's eyes.

"He told me you are the little sister he never had."

"Oh. What else did he tell you about me?"

"He wishes you happiness."

"Right... all the best to the two of you." And she meant it. Jealousy couldn't stop her from being happy for Selina. "So, you are going to see Jonte today?"

Selina's face brightened up more. "Yes. He called me when I was still at the hotel. His office is on Ngong Road. It would seem that he really does sell cars."

Kerubo twisted her mouth thoughtfully. "I wish I could come with you..."

"Why don't you?"

"Because, for starters, somebody needs to man the counter so we both cannot disappear, and second, I do not like being a third wheel."

"Is that why you faked a headache last night?"

"You guys were giving me a headache with all the lovey-dovey behaviour. It was disgusting." They both laughed.

* * *

Besides feeling like an imposter, Jonte was extremely nervous. He had been to this particular car yard to run errands for Boss. Sometimes he stayed around, admiring the cars, wondering if he would one day steal the same cars once they were sold. A couple of times he attempted to be a salesman. He was not good with persuasion that did not involve an empty gun, and no wonder he never made any sale.

He walked in wearing not his usual jeans and a tee-shirt, but in a suit, shirt, tie and leather shoes, all of them bought earlier that morning. The tie was strangling him. The leather shoes felt too hard to his sneaker-feet, and he hated how they looked. The suit and shirt, as well as they fit him, made him feel ridiculous.

That Oti was laughing at him as he sat across the table did not make it any better.

"Keep laughing like that, and I will shoot your stupid mouth!" Jonte threatened, but it only made Oti laugh louder. They were in an office usually preserved for Boss whenever he visited. It was wiped and dusted every day. The only thing Jonte had brought with him to complete the look of a legitimate office was the laptop.

"You look ridiculous," Oti said in between laughter.

Earlier on, when Oti had entered the car beside Jonte, he was nervous. Not anymore, because during the ride, Jonte had been his old self.

"Why are you looking like that?" Oti had asked between laughter, referring to Jonte's suit.

And Jonte explained.

"So why am I coming?"

"Quite honestly, I just need a familiar face, and you came to mind."

* * *

With sweaty hands and shaky feet, Selina stepped out of the car and leaned on the door for a few seconds. She was nervous, and not because she was about to see, for the first time, where her brother worked, but because she wanted to believe that Jonte was not what everyone thought he was.

There was another reason she was nervous; Joe proposed, less than twenty-four hours after they met, when he went to pick her up. Kerubo had walked out to say hello to Joe and after greeting each other, Joe held Selina at arm's length to admire her then hugged her.

"We should just get married," he said.

Kerubo took a step back.

"Yeah. Why not?" Selina answered casually before giggling at Kerubo.

Kerubo started to laugh, because she was sure they were playing a joke on her, until Joe turned and produced a ring, and slipped in on Selina's finger, and they kissed.

When they drove off, Kerubo stood on the same spot for minutes on end.

* * *

Selina shook off a load of nerves.

She paused at the entrance of the car yard and marvelled at the rows upon rows of expensive-looking vehicles. She spotted two men leaning on one of the vehicles, men she assumed were salesmen. She waved at them and walked towards the only structure, a large container at the end of the yard. It had two doors, and she stood in front of them to see which one had life. She was about to knock on one door, when somebody emerged from the other door and called her name.

"Selina?" She peered at him. He seemed like he was trying to smile, but it looked more like a grimace. She smiled back and nodded. "Jonte is in here."

Oti stepped aside to let her pass.

She found Jonte sitting on the wooden table, nervously smiling at her.

"Selina... so good to see you."

She smiled and approached him, giving him a long hug.

"Since when did you start wearing suits?" she asked when he released her. She did not realise she was crying until Jonte used his thumbs to wipe off her tears.

"Comes with the job," he said, pulling a seat for her. He then took the one opposite.

Selina studied her brother across the table, hand on her chin. She missed him. They were many siblings, but they were always closer to each other than they were with all the other eight siblings. Jonte was the first born while Selina was born first among the girls. They often conspired against their parents, or other siblings, against the world, but that was until Jonte changed.

"What happened to us?' she asked with a deep sigh.

Jonte shrugged. "I don't know. I guess people change." He was looking beyond her.

"But why? You just... you just stopped being you."

Jonte shrugged. "Life can change you. You are not the same person you were five years ago."

I am not the same person I was less than twelve hours ago, she thought. "But siblings should not change. Look, you and I have always been straight with each other so I will not beat around the bush. Are you a criminal?"

Jonte chuckled, looking beyond his sister again, and wondering why Oti was taking too long with the coffee. "Does this look like a criminal activity to you?" His inside was in turmoil but on the outside, he was calm and smiley, and even managed to look hurt by the question.

Selina turned around and looked outside at the cars. "Well, no... but the rumours..."

"So you would rather believe rumours than me?"

"No!" It was a guilty no. "No... it's... so, you want to tell me that you have never done anything criminal?" she challenged, to hide her guilt.

Jonte shook his head. "Selina, do not be naïve. I challenge you to bring me anyone who has never done a shady deal in his life. We cut deals left, right and centre to survive. Now, if you are asking me if I have never cut a deal in my life, the answer is no, I cut deals all the time. I am as criminal as the next person... Look, can we talk about something else? I feel like I am in a court of law. How is dad?"

Selina sat up in relief. "Dad is not well. I think they sent him home so he could die there."

"Who is looking after him?"

"A nurse we hired with the money you are giving. He is as comfortable as he is ever going to be."

"Is he not wondering where the money is coming from?"

"He is too sick to care," Selina shrugged.

Jonte reached for his back pocket and retrieved his wallet. Among several bank cards, he selected one and handed it to Selina. "Here... take this. Please do not hesitate to use it for dad, or for other needs for that matter."

Selina hesitated. "How much is there?"

"Enough."

She took the card. "So you really are not a criminal?"

"I thought we went through all that!"

"I am getting married." She blurted out, studying her finger with the ring.

"What? Who is the lucky guy?"

"His name is Joe. He lives in America."

"You are moving to America?"

"Maybe."

"When is the wedding?"

"We haven't decided. He is outside waiting."

"Let's all have lunch together," Jonte said enthusiastically, happy to get out of the office that was slowly closing in on him, wishing he could get out of the suit as well. "Oti was supposed to get us some coffee, but clearly we shall have dry bones as we wait."

Oti walked in, carrying.

"Sir, are you going already?"

"Sorry, Oti. My sister and I are going for lunch. Please wait for me, we need to go through a few things. Try and sell some cars, will you?"

"Yes, boss."

* * *

Joe saw the two siblings approach and came out of the car to greet them, his figure towering over both of them. With a nervous smile, he stretched his hand to Jonte, taking in the resemblance between them. "So good to meet you."

Jonte took a few seconds to answer, using the seconds to study Joe. "Good to meet you, too. I hear you are about to become my brother-in-law. This obviously calls for a celebration. Lunch is on me."

420

"Absolutely not. I cannot be seen to be a man who cannot pay his bills."

They all laughed. "Alright. But we use my car…" Jonte said firmly, signalling a man standing beside his big car. He took the front passenger seat as the lovers sat at the back.

A few metres away was another big car similar to Jonte's. The darkened windows kept the three men inside from view, but they could see everything going on around them. As soon as Jonte's group drove off, two of the men came out of the car and headed straight into the car yard.

Oti accidentally knocked off the coffee on the table as he vacated the seat that Jonte had sat on earlier when the men walked in. He used his tee-shirt to wipe the table, then picked the tray, coming face to face with Boss and a bodyguard.

"Boss, welcome, sir!"

Boss looked at Oti in a moment of confusion before nodding. "Oh, hello there. You are still working here I see?"

"Sir?" Oti asked in confusion.

"Who else is here?"

Oti nodded towards the gate. "Jonte just left, but there are two men in the next office."

"Right. Where has Jonte gone?"

"I don't know, sir." A feeling to defend Jonte kicked in. Already, Oti was regretting why he mentioned him.

"Right. I need to be updated on the account books. Who can do that?"

Oti tensed, then pointed to the next office. Boss huffed and walked into the office. Oti was left, still holding on the tray, staring at the door that Boss disappeared into.

* * *

Boss, looking flustered, walked into the hospital room where Naliaka was. She was asleep, her chest was moving in regular up-and-down movements. He studied her face, looking so peaceful and beautiful, nothing to show she had just had a concussion. He resisted the temptation to wake her up and instead walked to the next room where Queen was.

He found Queen sitting up, looking worried. She sat up straighter when Boss walked in.

"How is she?"

"She looks fine," he answered, shutting the door behind him. He sat on the bed, facing Queen. "What happened?"

Queen shook her head. "She received a call from Julia's son, and the next thing she went down and hit her head on the edge of the bed." Queen cringed as she pointed at the part where Naliaka had hit.

"Julia is…"

"I know who Julia is. Where is the phone?"

Queen turned to the bedside table. "It's broken, and off."

"You have Julia's number though?"

Queen nodded.

Boss nodded. "How did you get my number, anyway?" It was Queen who had made a frantic call to Boss. At first, three of her calls had gone unanswered. She had texted him and when she called the fourth time, he had answered.

"I demanded it from Naliaka when she brought you home on my birthday."

Boss smiled. "I am glad you did." Boss studied the tubes running through Queen, like he had not seen them before. "Why are you here, anyway? Naliaka never told me you were unwell."

"That's because she did not know, until today. I am dying."

"The heck!"

"We all will!" Queen's attempt to joke worked on Boss. He gave her a half smile.

"What's wrong with you?"

"The big C and it is advanced enough to make me call hell in advance to ask if they have the presidential suite," Queen giggled.

Boss smiled and shook his head. "Tell them to reserve the other presidential suite for me."

* * *

The OCS had a terrible twenty-four hours both at home and at work. He considered escaping to his girlfriend's, but the humiliation of the day had taken away his energy.

After his hospital session with Watcher Two the previous day, he drove straight home and found his wife alone, with no trace of the children. He did not ask where they were. Either she did not hear him come in, or she simply ignored him, but for a minute or so, he stood leaning on the kitchen door, watching her buttocks shake in rhythm as she made *ugali*.

She paused her *ugali* pounding and turned to look at him with a flat expression. Without a word, he went to the bedroom, showered and went to bed on an empty stomach, but spent the whole night listening to his tummy rumble and his wife's snores and farts.

How she could sleep after such an ordeal was a mystery to him, but then again, she was probably suffering the effects of what they had drugged her with. At four in the morning, he left for the office, ignoring the officer on desk duty who was asleep. He sat behind his desk, mostly staring at nothing, plotting and un-plotting, scratching his head and beard; he had forgotten to shave in his hurry to leave the house.

At eight, he walked to the police canteen and had a breakfast of two mandazis, two sausages and tea. It was on his way back that he bumped into Judas, who was talking to another officer. "Would you please come to my office when you are done here?"

"Sir, you called me?" Judas asked, standing to attention at the door.

"Shut the door and sit down."

Judas did.

"What the hell happened yesterday?" It was not a demand, rather an appeal from somebody who was totally confused. For a moment, Judas felt sorry for his senior, thinking that no man in authority deserved such humiliation, but then he remembered he had asked for it.

"About what, *afande*?"

"Please, don't take me for an idiot."

Judas shrugged. "I really do not know what you are talking about."

OCS sighed in frustration, running a hand over his face. "Alright, I get it. I get that I have not been cooperative, but I think you are making a mistake by supporting this Boss. We in authority should stick together. You cannot collude with criminals against your own."

Judas stared at his boss unblinkingly, fighting the temptation to laugh.

"You people will regret this. I promise you that," OCS declared, unable to hold his pleading attitude.

"We have nothing to regret, sir."

"You think you have your tracks covered, but I will find a crack somewhere. That's a promise."

"Can I go, sir?"

"Get out!"

* * *

OCS, driven by a dented ego, spent his day making calls, begging and blackmailing people into agreeing to work with him. By evening, his dignity was slightly injured. To wind down, he went to his favourite *nyama choma* and beer joint on Waiyaki Way. It was past seven when he parked his car in the car-crowded, well-lit parking lot, alone.

Something piqued his sixth sense, but by the time he reached for his gun, there was another one pressing on his neck.

"Relax, *afande*. We don't mean you harm, unless we have to. Just walk with us. We will not take much of your time."

"Do I have a choice?"

"Not really, but you could choose to walk peacefully or otherwise."

NaiRobbery Cocktail

Chapter Twenty-two

The last time Jonte laughed as hard as he laughed during his lunch date with Selina and Joe, he had not started his life of crime.

For hours, they reminisced about their childhood escapades, avoiding the moment things went south, and by the time he returned to the yard just before five in the evening, he was euphoric, tipsy and giggly. He did not expect Oti to be still around, so when he left the car and headed straight to the makeshift toilet to empty his pressing bladder, he assumed the man sitting on a car bonnet was one of the salesmen.

Until he looked again. And his euphoria dipped with every other feeling he had.

Oti sat on the bonnet, feet on the fender of a big car, shaking one leg nervously and furiously, chewing his nails intermittently, totally lost in his thoughts.

Pressing the bladder forgotten for a while, Jonte walked to him.

"Oti? I didn't know you chewed nails."

Oti turned slowly to look at Jonte, although Jonte felt like he was looking through him. A few seconds of silent stare and Jonte poked him on the shoulder.

"How was your lunch?" Oti asked while he stretched, rubbed his eyes and then yawned, like one would do after waking up from a long nap.

"Lunch was good. What's wrong? You look like shit."

Oti shook his head and jumped off from the bonnet, looked around him nervously, like to ensure there was nobody within earshot, before bending close to Jonte.

"Boss was here…" he whispered.

Jonte took a step back. "When?"

"Just after you left."

"What did he want?"

Oti shook his head, still looking around him nervously. "To look at the accounts."

Jonte loosened the already loose tie, then put his hand in the pockets.

"Nothing wrong with that. It's his company."

"Yes, true. But he looked *funny*."

"What do you mean, *funny*?"

Oti shook his head again. He was struggling with words. He was still trying to understand why he had found Boss's visit weird. "I don't know how to describe it but… he was… for starters, he did not remember me."

Jonte laughed. "That's ridiculous. Boss never forgets a face."

"He also seemed to think I work here."

"That's impossible."

"They went to that other office and stayed for about an hour. Then they just walked away, then entered the vehicle and left."

"Who was he with?"

"His bodyguard."

"You mean, bodyguards?"

"One."

"Boss always has two bodyguards with him, and there is always another vehicle with more of them…"

Oti shrugged. "There was one with him, and I am sure there was only one car."

"Why didn't he tell me?"

That question bothered him all evening. Even more because while still at the yard, with Oti looking on, Jonte called Boss to update him on the lunch, and to ask if there was anything he needed done.

"Keep your eyes open. We cannot relax, just because we scared off the OCS. I am certain he is planning something, but now that we have Watcher One on our side, hopefully, we can keep tabs.

"Is it okay if I invite Oti over to the house?"

Boss did not hesitate. "Oti is good. You trust him, I do too. But always remember, fear everyone. Trust nobody."

Boss said nothing about the yard visit.

Jonte and Oti did not say a word to each other on the way to Ngumo, both of them faced their side of the window, deep in thought.

By nine, they were done with dinner and were at the balcony that faced a high wall full of the uninteresting nothingness of a Nairobi night. They were ten minutes into sharing a joint, when Jonte suddenly asked, "Do you have your gun?"

Oti chuckled, taking three quick puffs, holding them in for a few seconds then blowing them out as one long smoke that disappeared into the nothingness. He passed the joint to Jonte. "As useless as it is, I never leave it behind. It is like having a security alarm that does not work, but still gives you some sort of comfort. Why do you ask?"

"Can you use a gun?"

"Of course I can. I know how to hit people's heads with the muzzle... you have seen me do it many times," Oti said with a chuckle, louder than the one before. Jonte emulated him as he took the weed and took a drag.

"You are foolish..."

"Oti's chuckles were breaking into guffaws. "I have watched enough movies to know how it is done... just hold it like this..." he stretched his right hand, index and middle fingers facing forward and thumb facing up.

They laughed long and hard. Laughter that was followed by a long episode of silence.

Jonte cleared his throat. "I have bullets. I want you to be part of my security."

"Dude, I may end up shooting you instead of at the enemy."

They laughed again.

"Then we have to make sure you get some shooting lessons. Tomorrow morning when you are not making stupid jokes, I will show you how to load bullets. We can pay for shooting lessons later."

"Are you okay?"

Jonte shrugged. "I don't know. But why did Boss not mention coming over? Am I overestimating my importance to him? Or am I overthinking? At least he is okay with you being close to me, and that's something because you are the one person I can completely rely on at this point."

"Thanks for the vote of confidence. You are the only friend I have, but you know that," Oti said, sounding sad. "You really think he is okay with me being around you? I don't think he trusts me that much... I don't even think he knows me, judging by his earlier attitude."

"You are in good company, because the Boss doesn't trust anyone."

* * *

Naliaka smelled before she saw.

It was the smell of warm toothpaste laced breath, then the unmistakable scent of Boss's cologne. She fluttered her eyes and when they were fully open, Boss was bent just inches away. He pulled back a little and smiled, running his finger over her cheek. Without turning her head, she let her eyes roam the unfamiliar room. She looked at Boss in confusion.

"Hey beautiful," he whispered, kissing her gently on the lips.

"Where am I?" She tried to sit up but gave up when the pain in her head immobilised her. "Ouch...'

"Shhhh... stay still. I will call the doctor."

"I am in hospital? Why? What time is it?"

"If you are asking in relation to how long you have been here, you have been out for twenty-four hours." He was still rubbing her cheek gently with his thumb.

"Why?"

He nodded, pointing at her head. "You have quite a gash on your head from when you fell." Then he smiled. "Perhaps you should consider growing some hair for cushioning if you are going to make a habit of hitting your head on hard things."

She smiled.

"You will be fine, though... if you can recognise me, then you are fine. You do recognise me, don't you?"

"Of course I do... why wouldn't I?"

"Concussion can play around with your memory."

Then it all came back to her.

"Julia! I need to talk to her."

The nurse came in within seconds of Boss pressing the summon bell.

"Oh, good. You are up... let me inform the doctor."

Naliaka got a clean bill of health, but with a warning to rest as much as possible.

"You may feel sleepier than usual, and that's normal with a concussion."

When they were ready to leave, Boss led her not to the exit but next door to Queen's room.

Queen was sitting up in bed. The two women hugged as Naliaka cried, because it finally dawned on her, how gaunt and weak Queen looked, how she should have noticed it earlier.

When she calmed down, Naliaka sat on the bed and told them about the phone call.

All through the narration, Queen remained expressionless. Boss stood against the wall with a blank stare. She could understand Boss's expression, he had no personal relationship with the dead, and he was used to dead people. What she did not understand was Queen's attitude, even made worse when she said, "But why would you react so badly? Their death is good riddance to bad rubbish." Naliaka looked at Queen in confusion.

"Don't you care? They were your friends," she told Queen.

Queen sniggered, "Nope. I don't feel much for either of the brothers, though I feel bad for the kids." If Naliaka could read minds, she would have seen tears flowing in Queen, alongside her blood. She was hurting, but a mother's instinct, only active in her when it involved Naliaka, got her acting the opposite of what she was feeling. If she let Naliaka know how sad she felt, Naliaka would feel guilty.

"And Julia…"

Queen chuckled. "Ha! Julia will look at it as a blessing. Now she can enjoy her children without worrying about her husband. Probably end up with all the money. I am sure that idiot did not have a will."

"I still feel terrible."

"Those two buffoons have finally done something good for the world by dying. Do not beat yourself about it." Queen squeezed Naliaka's hand. Naliaka nodded, sniffling back tears. "You need to rest. So do I." She turned to Boss, who was still leaning on the wall. "Come on, you two lovebirds, go home and relax. I will be fine."

"Please be fine."

Naliaka assumed that Boss would drop her to Ndenderu, but when they got to the hospital reception, he tagged her. "I summoned Mambo for you."

"Who is Mambo?"

"Your usual cab…"

"Oh… Why, though? Are you going somewhere?"

He shook his head, a distant look in his eyes. "I still do not think it is safe for you to be seen with me."

"How long is this going on? When can I see you?"

He shrugged. "I don't know, but as long as I do not think it is safe, I will stay away from you."

Naliaka's eyes were misty. "I miss you."

"I miss you, too." And right there, in front of sick people and medical personnel, Boss pulled Naliaka to him, kissed her on the mouth hard and long. She let him, drinking safety from his very mouth. "Come on now, your cab is outside."

* * *

The night before, the OCS came this close to wetting his pants when the two burly men forced him to walk with them. The men, one following so closely behind with a gun stuck on his back, escorted him to another car at the far end of the parking lot.

He was nervous, not only because he had no idea what was about to happen to him, if he would survive, but he also felt vulnerable. He had always used the power of the crown to feel invincible, but in less than twenty-four hours, he had accepted there were people who did not respect the crown. It scared him.

"*Afande*, we need your help." That made him sigh so hard.

For an hour, at the back of a car, he listened in disbelief. What was being proposed to him would get rid of all his enemies within a day, it would make him a darling of his bosses, give him the power, and the money he constantly craved for. What was more unbelievable was it came with close to zero risk from him. All he had to do was sit and watch and appear at the right time, and read a statement to the press.

When they let him go, he did not enter the pub, but headed to his girlfriend's house.

When morning came, his adrenaline levels were so high, he moved faster and swifter than usual. He was not supposed to be anywhere near the epicentre of the action, but he was in Ngumo Estate by seven, and parked his unmarked car a few gates from Boss's house. Then waited.

He saw them arrive. He saw his new best friend, waved, but his new best friend ignored him.

* * *

At the dining table, Jonte and Oti had half-drank cups of tea on the table. Jonte was holding one gun, another one was on the table. They had spent part of their breakfast with Jonte teaching Oti the basics of shooting.

It was as Oti reached for the gun that they were interrupted by a hard knock on the door. They sat up straight, looking at each other in confusion.

"Who could that be?" Oti jumped from his seat and rushed to the window, slightly drawing the curtain and looking through the sheer. Outside the door were two burly men, and Boss. "Boss?" he asked, turning to look at Jonte who stood up slowly, picked the gun and joined Oti.

"Do you want me to open the door?"

Jonte paused, because he was trying to work out why he had a bad, sinking feeling. "You do that as I get into some decent clothes." He was still in the clothes he had slept in, a vest and a pair of shorts. So was Oti.

Oti waited for Jonte to disappear upstairs before opening the door, coming face to face with Boss.

435

"You… Do you live here too? You are everywhere!" Boss said, pushing Oti aside.

"Sir… you…" Oti was about to tell Boss that he was the one who gave permission for him to be there but he was roughly pushed aside.

"Where is Jonte?"

Oti pointed up the stairs. His throat was dry, his lips were stuck together. He wanted to shout at Jonte to jump over the balcony, but his throat suddenly lost the ability to remove any sound because even though he could not explain how, he had just worked out what was happening.

The three men were halfway upstairs when Oti decided to follow them. He had just reached the top of the stairs when he heard the first shot, then he heard another one that could have been from his own gun, because he felt like someone had pushed him, and he fell back. Many years later, he would wonder why there were no human sounds. No screaming, no groaning. Just gunshots that rendered him deaf for a few hours.

Then he heard another shot, and he ran out, still wearing his shorts and vest and a pair of socks. At the door he bumped into two security guards who had just managed to free themselves after they were tied at the gate.

"Get the hell out of here! Run, you idiots!" Oti screamed at them.

The dogs that lived in the compound but were locked in during the day were going crazy in the kennel. Oti, who did not stop to see if the security men followed, went through the gate, ran back and threw his gun, ran out of the gate again, and kept running. He stopped when he got to his own house, then realised he did not have the keys. He kicked it in with one hit, and for a moment wondered why nobody had ever tried to break into his house, like he just did.

* * *

The OCS heard the gunshots, all six of them. He tried to leave the car, went as far as to open the door. He sat back and took deep breaths to stabilise himself. When he saw Oti run out of the gate half-naked, his first instinct was to shoot at the fleeing man, and he tried, but his gun was still in safe mode. By the time he cocked it, Oti was too far gone, and there was a dog crossing the road. He did not want to shoot an innocent dog but truth be told, he did not trust his shot.

With more speed than he had moved with in years, he entered the compound, bumping into the two security men running out. The impact dropped him to the ground. He cursed, but quickly got up and rushed to the house.

Head in first, three seconds of pause. "Hello..." He called. It was quiet. Whole body inside. "Is anyone here?"

He heard the sound coming from upstairs, a bang, but unlike the ones he had heard earlier from the guns, it sounded like somebody banging the wall, repeatedly. With a gun on the ready, he walked up the stairs, his weight stopping him from walking silently or fast. Running from the gate had already exhausted him, and he was heaving. For the umpteenth time, he promised himself to lose some weight.

He stopped outside a slightly open door, and listened. The sound had stopped but he could hear loud human breathing. He pushed in the door, but something was stopping it from opening wide. He put his head through, and gasped. Or screamed. "What the..." right by the door was a body. Then another one. And another one, and a last one. There was only one man still alive.

* * *

When Mbogo saw Naliaka alight the taxi at the gate, he raised his hands to his head. "Madam why do you have a bandage on your head?"

"I fell, but it's nothing serious." Smiling was giving her a headache but the last thing she wanted was to spend a moment explaining her injury. Her legs were already shaky and she needed a seat.

It had rained the night before, and the grounds were wet. The paths in Queen's compound were paved, but her sandaled feet were wet by the time she got to the house. She shivered as she pushed the door, because the thought of facing Julia scared her.

Julia was waiting just inside the door, Malaika supporting her. They both had red eyes. "Are the eyes red from crying or lack of sleep?" Naliaka asked cautiously. She did not shut the door behind her, and she stood with enough space between her and the two women.

"What happened? You did not come back and your phone was off," Julia asked instead, cautiously. "You had us sick-worried."

"I am sorry. My phone fell and broke."

"But why did you not come back?" Malaika asked as she released Julia, then closed the distance to hug Naliaka. That was when she noticed the bandaged head. "What the hell? What happened to you?" She turned Naliaka around to study the bandage.

"I fell and hit my head. It's going to be okay though…"

"It's bleeding!" Julia gasped as she covered her mouth. "There is blood on the bandage. Why do you have a bandage on your head?"

"I said I fell. Look, I need to sit down, please… I need to shower, I need to eat and I need to organise my thoughts."

Julia and Malaika exchanged looks, then led Naliaka up the stairs.

"I have a lot to say, and none of it is good news. Can we meet at Queen's balcony in about half an hour, please?"

"Queen does not like the rest of us up there…"

"I want you up there, because we need privacy. Also, Queen is not coming back today…" or ever, she added in her mind.

Julia nodded. "I will come up with your breakfast. You have a shower."

"Come with wine glasses."

* * *

At the hospital, Boss gave Naliaka a five-minute head start before he walked to his car, his bodyguards in tow.

"Take me home," he instructed.

They drove in silence, with Boss staring outside the window throughout.

"Don't leave… just… just stay around. Get something to eat while at it." He told his bodyguards when they got to the house. Usually, they waited for Boss to enter the house, they would check if everything inside was okay, and then would go to their houses next door.

Boss was feeling paranoid, and not his usual one. This one was a dark, unsettling feeling. There was doom lurking around, and he was afraid, something he was unfamiliar with. The feeling that had started eating on his sixth sense days earlier seemed to reach a sort of a peak. The metallic taste was so strong, he was sure there was blood in his mouth. He spat on the sink to check. Nothing. Yet,

439

not only could he taste it, he could smell it as well. His tummy was queasy, but when he sat on the toilet, not even a fart came out.

He had spent the night at the hospital, sitting by Naliaka's side on a seat provided by the kind nurse. He didn't have to sleep there because they had sedated Naliaka enough to knock her out for hours, but the hospital had given him a sense of security he had not felt in days in his own house. On the plastic seat covered by a hospital blanket, he had slept more than he had slept over the week.

He brushed his teeth for the second time in hours, and only realised he had done it for too long, when his gum started aching. He had a shower and lost track of time. He was dressed in blue jeans trousers, a black tee-shirt, a hat and a blazer. He tried to eat, but he could not go beyond a bite of loaf. He drank coffee as he tried to work out what was bothering him.

Whatever was bothering him was at the tip of his brain, but whenever he was about to unveil it, it would disappear. He went to the bedroom and lay on the bed, shut his eyes, and willed himself to sleep.

But someone was knocking on the door.

"What is it?"

"Mike is at the door."

Boss shot up and sat on the bed. "Mike? What does he want?" Mike was his body-double, and he never turned up without an appointment. Boss thought he may have missed Mike's call, so he quickly checked his phone. It was off. Out of battery. "Oh. My phone battery died. Still, what could bring him here so early? Is he inside?"

"No, Boss. I wanted to ask you if it is okay to let him in."

"Let him in. I will join you in a bit."

Five minutes later, Boss walked into the sitting room. He expected to find Mike and his bodyguards, but he was alone, and pacing up and down the room.

"Where are your bodyguards?" he demanded, feeling alarmed.

Mike shook his head and studied his feet.

"What is it? You look like shit."

"You need to leave the house. Now…"

"Why?"

"Because if you do not, they will kill you. I have information that they are on the way. I could not even call, because they may be tracking your calls."

"Information? From whom?" Boss asked suspiciously. That feeling again. Then he mentally slapped himself because it would be ridiculous to suspect Mike.

"Boss, can we talk about this on the way out? We do not have time… please… but I can tell you that they almost killed me, thinking I was you. The bodyguards are dead. I was lucky to escape."

Boss studied Mike for a few seconds, so many questions running in his mind, questions he knew he should ask before doing what Mike was asking him to do, but the urgency on Mike's voice and body language discouraged him. Boss looked at his bodyguards.

"We got you," one of them said, "I will call downstairs for them to be on the ready. We got you." The bodyguard already had his phone out and barked orders on the phone.

Boss nodded, feeling slightly reassured. He turned to Mike. "Where do you have in mind?"

"You have enough safe houses. Pick one… come on, we need to go!"

They all started towards the door. Boss stopped and looked back at the house, one last time. He had lived in this house for years. This house was home for a lot of his favourite clothes. A week or so before the bad feeling took over his life, it had been home for a lot of his fortune. He had moved the safe elsewhere. He nodded at it, like it was a living being, and followed Mike and one bodyguard out of the door. One bodyguard was behind him.

* * *

Kirinyaga Road was a mess.

People who witnessed the pandemonium would narrate the story hundreds of times in their lives to hundreds of people, and each of those times, nobody would believe them. Each of those times, somebody would accuse them of having watched too many action movies.

They would tell how they witnessed a *Mama Mboga* transform into Lupita Nyong'o's character, Nakia, in *Black Panther;* how she threw off her *leso* and jacket and unleashed a gun from somewhere, nobody was sure whether it was from under her clothes or from the *kiondo*, how she had lain on her back and started shooting, rolled and shot again, like they did in the movies. How one of the bullets from her gun had landed on a man's groin, splitting his trousers and body parts, how she had then somersaulted towards two men, knocked both out and carried one of them on her shoulders into a building.

The people would tell about how Chizi Samuel, the resident mad man of Kirinyaga Road, had abandoned his sack, shed off in seconds the other sack he used as his jacket and revealed a clean white vest and arm muscles of someone who lived in a gym.

How, with a gun hanging from his right hand, he ran across the road, jumped on a moving car's bonnet, somersaulted and landed perfectly with both feet on the ground, rolled on the ground as he shouted at people to take cover by lying on the ground, and when he had stood up, he shot two men, one on the leg and the other one through the chest. Eye witnesses would tell how someone had shot Chizi Samuel on the shoulder, how the bullet had gone through him and hit a wall, and how he had continued shooting with the same arm, bringing down two more men. How he had disappeared into the same building that *Mama Mboga* had disappeared into.

There would be others who would tell how the tall beautiful girl, the one who owned a hardware shop and fed Chizi Samuel two meals a day, had run so fast, leaving formidable wind behind her, gun hanging on her left hand, cursing at people to make way, then she had started shooting as well. Some people would remember the cursing more than they would remember the action; they would tell how shocked and ashamed they had been at such a beautiful girl using such rude words.

They would tell about the pin-drop silence that had followed.

All those people would be telling the truth. In fact, the events happened too fast for them to take in all the nitty-gritty details.

* * *

Before the action.

Cecilia had been on her spot for exactly seven minutes, and already trying to ignore the stink of danger that threatened to choke her. She was tense, and the hairs at the back of her neck were as erect as a porcupine's spikes, probably as hard. On a typical day, Kirinyaga Road was a hustlers' street, and in her short stint there, she had grown familiar with the smell of concentrated sweat. Today's sweat was not just sweat, it was laced with adrenaline.

Trying to ignore the tension on her shoulders, she started scanning the crowds around her and across the road. It took her a few minutes to pick what was wrong. To a casual observer, there was nothing off, but Cecilia was anything but a casual observer. People on Kirinyaga Road walked fast. It did not matter if they were traders or customers. Even those who sat on pavements sat on the ready, like they were waiting to be launched—except Chizi Samuel.

Before making a hasty decision, she observed them walking up and down, pretending to be window-shopping, but making the classic mistake of looking at bare walls that had no windows, wearing dark glasses when the weather was grey. She caught the expressions on their faces, and they were most telling: set.

Her body jerked with the realisation that *it* was here, that thing they had all been waiting for, was here.

She looked across the street and everywhere else her eyes could reach, hoping to spot Chizi Samuel. He was not there. She called Kerubo. The phone rang four times and Cecilia decided she did not have time to wait. She turned around to look at the street boys. Today they were two, both eating *mandazi* and laughing at something one of them had said.

"Psst…" she called them. They did not hesitate. They had become borderline friends by virtue of familiarity, and that Cecilia kept giving them fruits. "I am about to tell you something that may shock you, but please, I do not have time to answer questions."

They opened their eyes wide in confusion then looked at each other.

444

"Do you promise not to act stupidly?" They nodded hesitantly. "There are strange men on the street... have you seen them?" The two early teenage boys looked around and shook their heads. "Do you see the man standing by the next shop?"

"*Huyo ni karao...*" One of them identified him as a cop.

"He is not alone. They are after Boss." They both gasped and covered their mouths and took a couple of steps back at the mention of Boss. "Don't worry, I work for him too," she lied. It worked because she saw them relax. "You need to run to the person you report to, right now, and tell him that there is trouble on the streets. Tell him I have counted five of them so far, there may be more. Do you understand me? Tell them to keep Boss inside... scoot!" The two boys disappeared.

Cecilia nearly screamed in joy when she turned and saw Chizi Samuel. He was his usual slow self, and she guessed he had not picked the atmosphere, a realisation that disappointed her a little because he was supposed to be the best among the field people, then she remembered he was probably tired, that the streets were not a five-star hotel.

She picked a random apple and a banana and crossed the street to where he was, offered the fruits to him, speaking under her breath.

"Shit about to hit the roof. Look around you." Chizi Samuel nodded and accepted the fruits. He put his sack between his legs as he felt for his gun. It had been cocked since the threat to Boss was upgraded to orange.

If Cecilia had walked to Samuel a few seconds later, she would have easily spotted Mike as he entered the building.

Now that Cecilia had told him, Samuel spotted them easily. In fact, he picked seven, two more than Cecilia. His heart started beating dangerously.

* * *

Kerubo was in the backroom laughing with Selina, when the phone rang. It was still in her handbag at the counter. Twenty minutes later she went to the counter to serve a customer. Five minutes later, when she was through with the customer, she checked her phone and found two missed calls from Cecilia. When she called back, Cecilia told her, "Get the hell down here and have your gun ready. You have five seconds."

* * *

Cecilia will never be able to pin-point what exactly made her make that first move that triggered a plethora of events that would see Kirinyaga Road turned into a live action movie set. It could have been pure instinct, and that would suffice because for years, her instinct had been responsible for many right trigger timings.

But it could also have been because from the corner of her eye, she did see two of the police-looking men tense, just for a second, before reaching for their guns, and taking quick steps towards Boss's entrance. From the other corner of her eye, she saw Boss and his bodyguards in the company of… the other Boss.

Just as she made that decision to act, she saw the bodyguard in the lead pick a call, tense for that one second, look around before pushing Boss down to the ground and covering him. The street boys had delivered the message.

She jumped up from her sitting position and by the time she was upright, her jacket was off and her gun was on the ready on her left hand.

One of the shooters picked her; saw his eyes grow wide with realisation that he was exposed, saw him pointing a gun at her. She could swear she saw the bullet from his gun head towards her, but it missed her because she was already on the ground and shooting back at him. His bullet made a hole on the wall behind Cecilia before deflecting and hitting a random person on the shoulder. The shot person screamed, setting pace for everyone to do the same and run.

Cecilia secretly mourned for her vegetables, now squashed and sprawled all over the street. People were running in all directions, bumping into one another, sliding on her tomatoes. Falling over one another. Crawling over one another. Cecilia was screaming at people to stay down, but her screams were swallowed by the other screams.

Her first shot was a good start. It landed right bang in the middle of the man's groin. She saw two of the man's partners who were walking behind him hesitate in confusion, trying to locate the person who shot their colleague, seemingly deciding there were bigger fish to fry and started shooting towards Boss. The bullets were indiscriminate. The body of the bodyguard who had covered one Boss a moment earlier went limp. The other Boss screamed and held his stomach as he went down as well, writhing in pain. The Boss who had been pushed down by the bodyguard was unmoving.

Cecilia rolled towards the entrance, towards possible death, because the bullets were still pinging on everything in and around the two Bosses. A couple of seconds before she got there, the shooting stopped.

By the time she picked herself and carried on, her adrenaline pumped, Samuel had shot at the original shooters, himself taking a shot on his shoulder for his trouble. He could see two more shooters, but they were having the same trouble as he was making clean shots with people running in every direction.

The stampede would cause more injuries than the bullets.

The centre of the storm cleared, giving Samuel a couple of clean shots at the people shooting towards the entrance.

The shooting stopped. Samuel quickly scanned the crowd around him and when he did not pick a shooter, he rushed towards the building.

Just as he disappeared within, he heard one more shot, hesitated for a moment then ran up the stairs, taking three at a time. He may not have been to Boss's hideout, but he knew the way.

The shot that Samuel heard had come from Kerubo's gun. It had taken her a little more than two minutes to run to get there. It would have taken her less time under normal circumstances, but everybody was everywhere on the streets, the vehicles were hooting nonstop and bumping into people and each other as they tried to drive from the chaos, the motorbikes were being ridden dangerously, there were people running to the opposite side of where she was running towards, the *mkokoteni* pushers had abandoned their carts on the road, and she stepped over a couple in high speed.

Kirinyaga Road was just as she imagined—an Armageddon.

It was nearly over by the time she got there, heaving from the running and adrenaline. From where she stopped to take in the scene, she saw nothing for a few seconds, then she picked him because he was so conspicuous in the midst of running people and others on the ground writhing and screaming. She saw the overweight man peeping from behind a parked car, looking towards Boss's building, and pointing his gun towards it. Kerubo stopped and closed her eyes for a moment. She had been on the street long enough and was familiar with the type of people who surrounded Boss. The fat man could never have been one of them, and in her books, if he was not for Boss, he was against him. She took her shot. A shot that dislodged the gun from the man when it hit his shoulder. His lone scream echoed to the end of the street.

For a moment, an eerie silence befell the street. The footsteps stopped. The screaming stopped. All movement stopped, the smell of gunpowder overwhelming. Kerubo coughed and pulled down her hood. She was the only one standing. Every shop door was shut. She felt like the one who had missed the apocalypse.

Something made her look up. She gasped. The shops and offices on the street level may have been quiet, but up on the buildings were heads hanging out of the windows, all of them with phone cameras focused below. She was part of the below.

She groaned, knowing that she would be starring in many of those videos and photos on social media. Somebody was probably streaming live. Instinctively, she pulled down her hood farther, tucked in her gun and jogged back towards the shop, on the way stepping over injured people, some of them not moving, others groaning in pain and cowering in fear.

She found Selina and all the shop staff standing outside the shop, listening to someone who claimed to have been a witness.

Selina broke from the group when she saw her.

"What the hell is going on there? We heard gunshots."

"I am not sure," Kerubo answered, entering the shop because the man recounting his story to her shop assistants was peering at her.

"It was over by the time I got there."

"Why did you go? That is so dangerous. I never thought you to be one of those Kenyans who run towards danger." Selina had followed her to the shop.

Kerubo laughed. She was struggling to keep her heart rate stable. Her adrenaline was going down very fast and she was starting to worry about Samuel, Cecilia and Boss.

"I… I just found myself going there… look, can you look after the shop for the rest of the day? I need to take care of something."

"What *something?*" Cecilia was looking at her. Kerubo avoided her eyes.

"I will tell you about it later." She picked her bag and started walking out.

"Kerubo, you…"

"Please. I will call you later, I promise…"

The man was still outside the shop, still giving his version of events to an unbelieving audience. He paused again when Kerubo emerged. She ignored him and quickly walked away in long and quick steps, only stopping when she got to her house.

Her first stop was the fridge to fetch a beer, then she removed her phone and with shaky hands dialled Cecilia's number. It rang, which was a good sign, but Cecilia did not pick up. She dialled Samuel's, it was off. She drank half the can of beer without pausing before dialling Onyango's line.

"What the hell is happening?"

"Goodness knows. We only have bits and pieces so far. Were you not there?"

She could hear him heaving, like he was walking fast, or even running.

"I got there when everything was over… nearly…"

"What do you mean, nearly?"

"I shot some fat dude whose movements I did not like."

"Ah… ha. That would be the OCS."

"Oh ooooh…"

"Don't worry. Not yet anyway. He is not one of the good guys."

"I cannot raise Cecilia or Samuel."

"I can't raise them either, but from the initial information, I believe they got away. I am about to enter the cop station now. I will call you as soon as I have more information."

Kerubo opened another can and turned on the television and as she expected, all the local television stations were on "Breaking News". She took her position on the sofa, covered herself with the blanket and with bated breath started watching and checking social media. There were reporters everywhere, interviewing eyewitnesses. In the background she could see blurred images of police activity.

There were tens of clips shared on social media. She saw herself on two of them, one of them captioned as, "Does anyone know the identity of this female shooter?" None of the clips she appeared on were clear enough, but anyone who knew her well would easily identify her, especially her staff at the shop who had seen how she was dressed.

Her phone was ringing. It was Selina. She ignored the call. Joe was next. She ignored his call too. They both called her repeatedly, she ignored them all. She could see WhatsApp messages coming in. She ignored them all.

* * *

One bodyguard was dead.

The surviving bodyguard sighed with relief when he saw the relatively small woman lift Boss up and enter the building. He knew her as the *Mama Mboga*, but he decided he would worry about her real identity when Boss was safely inside. He got behind her to cover her. When she stopped at the top of the first flight of stairs, looking like she was about to drop Boss, he took over.

"I will carry him. Cover my back."

With ease that made Cecilia feel slightly inadequate, he ran up the stairs, a slumped Boss on his shoulders. She followed, scaling the remaining staircases backwards.

"Get the keys from my pockets." Cecilia dug into his pockets with one hand, the other hand still holding the gun, eyes looking towards the stairs. It was silent, but that meant little. She was good at moving with zero sound and if she could, others would as well.

She had just retrieved the keys when a figure appeared at the end of the stairs. She pulled the trigger and cursed because her gun was empty. She then breathed in relief because it was Samuel.

"Samuel! I almost shot you…"

"Thank goodness for the limited number of bullets."

"You know him?" It was the bodyguard, looking both confused and relieved.

"Yes… we are on your side."

It was a single key. Cecilia opened the door, let in both men and then locked the door immediately, taking time to breathe in relief as she leaned on the door.

"He's bleeding a lot," the bodyguard said with concern. Boss was lying on the sofa, the bodyguard and Samuel standing over him, checking him everywhere.

452

"He got a shot on the stomach," Samuel declared as he untucked Boss.

"It looks bad."

"Is… is he alive?" the bodyguard asked, taking a step back.

"He is," Samuel said, checking his pulse. "Slow pulse rate though. We need to stop the bleeding first and hope no vital organs were touched."

"You are bleeding too!" Cecilia said in panic.

She had just seen blood trickling down Samuel's arm. His white vest was no longer white.

"It's just a graze. I will sort it out in a bit."

"Who are you people?" the bodyguard asked, standing up and looking at them menacingly.

"Sit down!" Samuel commanded as he started checking Boss's wound. "If we were bad people I wouldn't be trying to save your boss's life. Come on, bring some towels… we need to stop this bleeding or he will bleed to death in minutes."

The bodyguard ran towards one of the rooms.

"Do you know what you are doing?" Cecilia asked, still leaning on the door.

Samuel shrugged. "I am the closest to a doctor, any non-doctor will ever be. They make sure of that in the army."

"Will he survive?" she asked, approaching.

Samuel shrugged. He was staring at the wound at the side of Boss's stomach. It was pulsating *better* than the heart, regularly rising up and down, gushing some blood every time it gushed up.

"We will never be able to get out of here!" Cecilia said, looking around the house in search of escape routes. "This is a dungeon!"

she declared in frustration. "You would think that someone like Boss would have an exit…"

The bodyguard was back, carrying five towels.

Samuel covered the wound, pressing it down gently.

"Has it stopped bleeding?" Cecilia asked when Samuel lifted the towel to look. The bodyguard had taken a spot near the window, looking at them worriedly.

"It's certainly slowed, but we need to get help."

Cecilia turned to the bodyguard. "How the hell do you guys not have an escape route?

"There is an escape route."

"Where?" Samuel and Cecilia asked simultaneously.

"Up the roof."

"Huh?"

"There's a way out."

"Get us to the roof. It is not safe here."

The bodyguard carefully lifted Boss and headed towards the bedroom. He placed him on the bed that got red wet immediately, opened a wardrobe and pressed something that let in light from above.

"Wow," Cecilia said.

"I will be damned! I am impressed!" Samuel, for a minute seeming to forget about the dire situation, was peeping up at the ladder. "This… this is genius."

"I will carry him up. When we are all up on the roof, we press a button. That way, unless someone knows about it, they would never guess where we are. You go up first," he addressed Cecilia. "Then you can help me haul him up."

As the two disappeared up, Samuel was left rummaging through Boss's wardrobe. He picked a random tee-shirt and a zipper jacket but before he wore them, he tore a shirt and tied his own wound. Lastly, he undid the bloody bed, used the bed sheets to wipe off blood from the floor, and dumped the bed sheets into a wash basket at the corner of the room. He entered the wardrobe, started walking up the ladder, pressed a button that covered the open hole behind him, and hoped that by the time anyone else discovered the escape route, the bodyguard would have unleashed another genius.

* * *

No. He couldn't afford to lose his mind. Not before he was ready to and no way would he be ready before he sat in a bus on the way to anywhere out of the city. Anywhere but a hundred-kilometre radius of where he was. Several times, his mind and body colluded against him, threatened to give in, give up. Every one of those times, he managed to pick himself up in the nick of time.

It had been three hours since Oti came face-to-face with death. It was surreal then, it was surreal now. He knew he had run for several kilometres, half-naked, no shoes, over tarmac, rocks, out of Ngumo, across the roads into Kibera but somehow, he could not remember that run. There were always a lot of people in Kibera, whatever time of the day, yet he had no memory of seeing anyone's face.

As soon as he caught his breath in his house, it had been an easy decision; to get the hell out of his house, out of Kibera, out of Nairobi, and never, ever return. If they wanted to kill him, they would have to do so as he ran. Within minutes, his money was in a backpack and he covered it with a few clothes. Then he dressed.

In an A4 envelope, he stuffed as much money as he could.

Then he walked out of his house, not bothered about the broken door. He would never return to the house. That he was sure of. He was making an open invitation to anyone, seasoned thief or opportunistic thief, to raid his house. With as much calm as he could summon, he walked to his parents' house... And knocked...

There was no answer. He pushed the door and it gave in. He peered inside. The stove was on, and there was a half-drank cup of tea. His mother was probably in the toilet. He placed the envelope on a stool and quickly disappeared out of the house, walking all the way to Uhuru Park.

It was nearly six in the evening. He was shivering and wishing he had worn a jacket. He sat on a bench, his two bags trapped between his legs.

Jonte was dead. Oti whimpered at that thought and shivered some. He gasped, like he had just found out. No way could Jonte have survived the head gunshot. Oti had seen the blood spreading around the head.

Then he, Oti, had somehow shot the others through the door. He was not sure. It was either that, or they had shot each other. His recollection of the events was hazy. Him, the same person who did not know how to load a gun until Jonte demonstrated how, only a few moments earlier. He had used the same gun to shoot, then he had panicked and done the only thing that made sense at that point, running away.

"...it was a drama! So many people were shot..."

Two men interrupted Oti's train of thoughts. They were sitting on the grass behind the bench Oti occupied. Oti picked his bags, just in case he needed to leave in a hurry, and then like an antenna, he adjusted his ears to hear them better.

"See... they are all over. I hear they were all wanted criminals... even the policemen."

"You cannot trust anyone these days..."

"The police are the worst..."

It was after a minute of eavesdropping, a minute of Oti trying to work out if they were talking about the shooting he was involved in. He pulled down his hat and turned around.

"Excuse me... where were the shootings?"

"You must be the last person to know about it... Kirinyaga Road was like Hollywood."

Oti was both relieved and newly-stressed. What were the chances that it was Boss? He cursed that he did not have a phone, no way to get online. As he stood up to walk to the city to look for a cyber café, he silently, posthumously, thanked Jonte for showing him how the internet worked.

* * *

Kirinyaga Road was clear of chaos, but a cautious excited mood had taken over. Those who survived, those who watched from the windows, were competing to narrate what they had seen to the press and anyone else who cared to listen.

The numbers were in: ten people dead. Five of them from gunshots. There were no names given, but the inner circle knew that among the casualties was Boss's bodyguard, Mike, and three policemen. The other deaths were through the stampede and shrapnel from broken windows.

Kerubo watched everything from the discomfort of her couch. By two, she had finished six canned beers, and she was itching to open the bottle of vodka. She didn't think any of the dead or injured

457

were Samuel or Cecilia, neither did Onyango, but that did not lessen her worries, because they still had not returned her calls, yet Cecilia's phone was still ringing off the hook.

Boss was dead. She had seen his photos circulating on social media, along with those others of dead people. She never could understand how people felt alright sharing photos of dead people but just this once, she was happy they had been shared. That she was alone when she saw the photos had allowed her to mourn loudly and shamelessly. His death left her feeling empty. Hopeless. Widowed even. Seeing his body lying awkwardly on the ground had made her cry, wail.

His death, besides feeling like it was the death of a loved one, brought reality home, that it really was the end of an era. She and Samuel no longer had to be on Kirinyaga Road. They could not. It would take decades for their faces to be wiped off the memories of Kirinyaga Road dwellers.

She scrolled through photos that had her images countless times, and although none of them had a clear shot of her, she was too tall for the people familiar with her not to know it was her. The #KirinyagaRoad had been trending for hours, and included photos of Samuel and Cecilia.

Samuel had inspired people to tell stories of undercover agents they knew. There were many madmen who turned out to be intelligence officers: hawkers, newspaper vendors, *Mama Mboga* and shoe shiners. Kerubo imagined all the shoe shiners and vendors receiving very strange looks from people for a while.

Over the coming days, there would be a television report on Kerubo and Samuel. How she used to feed him on a daily basis. How people thought she just had a kind heart "while she was actually collecting intelligence". The feature would have interviews with one of her shop assistants, shop owners on Kirinyaga Road who would recount how they had been against her feeding Chizi Samuel, and how she had ignored them. The feature would have the mechanics on the streets, among others. The police would deny any knowledge of undercover agents on the streets.

Kerubo would be happy that Selina was nowhere to be interviewed.

She was about to go to the kitchen to open the bottle of vodka when they interrupted the Kirinyaga Road streaming. The police were giving a statement.

"Fellow Kenyans. This morning, something happened on Kirinyaga Road. In the unfortunate incident, several police officers and gangsters died in a fire exchange, and five civilians lost their lives, with many others injured. Two gangsters, one of them a most wanted criminal, were shot down. That would be something to celebrate, but we as a force are mourning our own who lost their lives in the line of duty. We have launched an investigation and a full report shall be published in the next few days. Please remain vigilant, and feel free to report to the police any suspicious activities. Thank you, and stay safe."

Kerubo walked to the kitchen and opened the bottle of vodka.

* * *

The bleeding stopped, but Samuel worried, because Boss was metal cold, and breathing like someone refusing to take their last breath. He kept force-feeding Boss with water, most of it ending on the clothes. The bodyguard had been back to the house a couple of times to get more blankets to keep Boss warm.

"At least the pulse is not getting lower." Cecilia was pacing the rooftop nervously. The bodyguard was stuck on Boss's side, fighting tears. Samuel was the one who finally walked to the edge of the

459

building and peered down, head first, inch by inch. He returned after a minute.

"What do you see?" Cecilia asked.

"Nothing much. Definitely less people but nobody seems to be running from anything anymore." It had been an hour since the shootings happened.

"Do you think it is safe to leave through the front door?"

"Definitely not. I bet there are several pairs of eyes keeping watch," Samuel said, turning to the bodyguard. "Did you say you can use a ladder to get down?" The bodyguard nodded. "Where is the ladder?"

He pointed at one corner. "The parking boys usually have the other bit of it."

"How do you communicate with them?"

The bodyguard looked thoughtful before suddenly appearing to snap himself out of the gloom they were all beginning to get used to.

"We call them… I can call them," he said excitedly, standing up to retrieve his phone. "Oh, but how do we get him without people noticing?"

"Leave that to us," Cecilia said as she fished out her phone from her back pockets. "Shit! I forgot the most basic thing!"

"What?"

"To check it. I have a million missed calls from Kerubo and Onyango… they must be worried sick!"

"Don't beat yourself too hard. We have been busy."

* * *

When Cecilia finished explaining to Samuel what Onyango had suggested, she took a deep breath before turning to the bodyguard.

"You are sure we have the right Boss, right?"

"I have spent the last ten years with him, seeing him every day. Of course I know it is him!"

He looked so hurt, Samuel coughed to suppress laughter. "Who was the other guy?"

"Mike... his..." He looked at both of them hesitantly.

"His double, I know," Samuel finished for him.

"Well, he is dead..."

"Good. Because he set up Boss."

"And you know that? How? "

"I just do. I... I have never trusted him, and when he came in alone this morning, I had a really bad feeling." He was clenching his fist.

Cecilia took a step back. "How long is your man going to take? I do not like how Boss looks... he looks... he looks dead!"

Samuel took Boss's pulse again. "He is barely alive and that is good news because it is better than dead."

The bodyguard stormed away to the end of the building.

"You do know you are not very funny," Cecilia said accusingly. "On a serious note, how is he?" She was folding her hands across her chest, looking down at Boss.

Samuel shook his head. "Dude is on hell's door... nothing I can do about it. I don't think the bullet got any vital organs, otherwise he would already be dead. It's the blood loss."

"Did the bullet go through?"

"Nope. He is the newest cyborg in town."

"I told you, you are not funny!" Cecilia said, but she was giggling.

"So why are you laughing?"

He started giggling, too, turning away so the bodyguard would not see him.

"Come on, call Kerubo."

"The hell!" Samuel clearly heard Kerubo screaming on Cecilia's phone. Cecilia held it away from her ear. "Where the hell have you been?"

"Gosh, stop screaming… we were busy."

"You and who?"

"Samuel."

There was a short silence on the other end. Cecilia heard a gasp and a sigh.

"You two are okay?"

"More or less… we will survive."

"Boss is dead. It is all over the news."

"No he is not. Just half-dead. He is here with us."

"But they are saying oh, wait. It's his double."

"Everyone but me knew about him! I am so hurt… oh, can I call you back? There is an incoming call."

As she waited for Kerubo to disconnect, Cecilia turned to Samuel and whispered. "She loves you…"

Samuel smiled and stood straighter.

* * *

If there had not been too much excitement on Kirinyaga Road earlier, someone would have noticed that it was odd how on the road behind Kirinyaga Road, four men, all wearing reflective workers' overalls and hard construction hats, went up a building using a ladder that was being supported by excited street boys. That the same men had stayed up there for twenty odd minutes, and when they came down, there were not four, but seven of them, and they were carrying a huge carton.

People saw them, some even stopped to look, but they did not want to waste time with events that did not include shootings.

"I hate it when things are easy," Samuel remarked. He was sitting at the back with Cecilia. Boss and the bodyguard were in a different vehicle, the one that had a doctor.

Cecilia scoffed. "You call that easy? You are mad. I have been doing this for a decent long time and what happened this morning made me feel like I am ready to retire... how is your arm?"

Samuel shrugged and ran a hand over the bandage he just got. "Too much ado about nothing."

"Alright, Mr Tough Guy. Do you know where we are going?" They were driving out of the city through Globe Roundabout.

"I hope we are driving to Timbuktu... I *kinda* need a holiday."

"And your idea of a holiday is a desert?"

"Isn't it a holiday destination? Anyway, what do you think we should do about Kerubo?"

Then the vehicle stopped.

"Oh, look, we are outside her gate. Driver, why are we here?"

"I am supposed to pick someone from here."

"The more the merrier... oh, there she is."

Kerubo, wearing a different set of clothes, was waiting outside the flats, hands folded, hood pulled down her face. She saw the vehicle and quickly walked towards it.

"Oh lord!" Kerubo gasped then started crying. "I am so relieved to see you two..."

"You speak for the three of us... this is going to be a big party, wherever we are going."

They pulled out, heading farther into Thika Road.

* * *

Safe house.

The first vehicle to come into view in the compound was an ambulance, Samuel recognised Onyango's car and the one that had ferried Boss.

Onyango, the bodyguard and three other people were gathered outside the ambulance, talking in low tones. They all turned when the last vehicle pulled in.

Samuel led the others out of the car, joining the group.

"What's going on?"

Onyango pointed at the ambulance with his mouth. "Doctor is operating on him."

"In an ambulance?" Samuel asked incredulously.

"Do you have a better idea? A place where they will not ask questions about gunshot wounds?"

"Oh... makes sense."

"Is... is he going to be okay?" Kerubo asked no one in particular, looking towards the ambulance.

"Join the queue to find out."

"I have a better idea," Cecilia cut in. "Let's go inside and sit down... those who pray can pray. As for me, I am going to get drunk... all safe houses have alcohol. Are you coming?"

Kerubo and Samuel nodded and followed her.

* * *

Oti twice attempted to board a bus to Kisumu. Twice he changed his mind, because he knew if he left before doing that one thing that was bothering him, he would not be able to rest. He believed in ghosts, his mother always invoked the spirits on them when they were younger to discourage them from mischief like lying and stealing. Not that it had worked on him, but he was still afraid of ghosts.

He had spent hours at the cyber café, checking each and every information and misinformation about Kirinyaga Road shootings. He checked about other shootings in the capital and its surroundings, it all came out nil. Was it possible that after all those hours nobody had discovered the bodies in Ngumo?

So he walked back to Ngumo, because he could not imagine Jonte's body lying there for days, undiscovered, rotting, being fed on maggots and flies.

The gate was still open. The dogs were whimpering, having barked themselves to exhaustion. As he put his foot inside and looked around, he hoped that this would not be the most stupid idea he had ever had, and he had had many of those. The compound was deserted. One step. Two steps. Stop, look around, and repeat.

The front door was open. Head in. Listen. Look around, and that was when he realised most of the furniture was gone. So were the electronics.

He made it upstairs. The smell of death choked him. Whoever had robbed the house had not gone up there, or perhaps they had seen the dead bodies and freaked out. When he saw Jonte's body, he fought down a wail. Jonte's phone was still on the dressing table and charged at a hundred per cent as it had been charging since morning.

There were thirty three missed calls, from Selina and someone saved as Bodyguard Boss. Nobody else had tried to call Jonte, and the only reason Oti could think of, was because everybody else had been wiped out. He paused and apologised one last time. On his way

465

out, Oti picked his own phone that had also been charging all day in the guest bedroom.

He went to the kitchen and tried not to be surprised when he found the refrigerator and the microwave missing. But he found what he was looking for. The night before, he and Jonte had eaten chicken. Both had been too lazy and high to clean up. The plan had been to clean up after breakfast.

Chicken bones and other leftovers. He put them on a plate and filled a bowl with water, carrying both to the kennels. He placed them by the door in front of the kennel, closed his eyes and opened the door. Oti sighed when the two German Shepherds ignored him and went for the food. His work was done. He left the gate open and wished anybody who would try to walk in good luck.

* * *

As the fields of Kirinyaga Road were figuratively burning, Naliaka pretty much remained ignorant about it all. In the morning, Julia and Malaika had joined her at the balcony, carrying breakfast for the three of them. For minutes, they all silently munched on their food. Naliaka searched for the right words to say everything that needed to be said. Julia and Malaika waited impatiently.

"Argh... just get it over with already!" Malaika finally snapped as she crashed her second cigarette in one of the flower pots.

"I agree. Whatever it is needs to be said. My blood pressure is stretched out!"

Naliaka studied both women for a while, then cleared her throat. Her hands were busy too, patting her bandage, scratching her nose and rubbing them together. "Queen is dying," she finally said, using the softest tone she could summon.

"What was that?"

"Queen has cancer. Stage four. Irreversible," she repeated more boldly, eyes averted from her subjects. She expected them to cry, scream... react somehow, so when ten seconds later there was no sound or movement from either, she looked at them. They were both staring at her, wide-eyed in disbelief, mouths open.

"It's true. She is at the hospital now... I don't think she is coming back..."

"Where is she going?" It would be the first time Naliaka would hear Malaika's voice squeak.

"Did you hear me say that she is very sick?"

"You want to say she is dying?" Julia's voice was more controlled, but she still looked shell-shocked. Naliaka nodded. "There is more... she is closing down the house."

"Oh... fu... what? I knew it! I knew something was off..."

"Yeah, me too, but... cancer? Dying and Queen in the same sentence?"

"So what happens to us when she..." Malaika's deep voice was back. She paced up and down, unlit cigarette in her hand. Julia stayed in her spot, studying Naliaka, like she was waiting for Naliaka to say it was a prank.

"She wants to leave the house to me."

"Huh?"

"Said I can do whatever I want to do with it."

There was silence. Malaika finally stopped pacing and stood next to Naliaka. Julia finally shifted on her seat.

"What do you want to do?" It was Julia who asked.

"Not sure, but I know I don't want the men anymore, but I will not kick out anyone."

"How do we earn a living?" Malaika started pacing again.

"We shall talk about that later," she took Julia's hands and squeezed them.

"There is something else... Kaggai is dead!" Julia pulled her hands from Naliaka's grip so fast that she, Naliaka, nearly fell off.

"What the hell are you talking about?"

That morning, in the taxi, she had called Jamie back to explain why she had gone off-line, and why Julia had not got in touch. Jamie, sounding calmer than Naliaka would have expected, explained how the two men died within minutes of each other.

"He was shot. At home."

"By who?"

"By your husband..."

"W... wait... wait... you are telling me my husband killed his brother?" Naliaka nodded. For a moment, Julia looked like one about to faint, or scream, or wail but what she ended up doing was laughing. A few seconds later, Malaika joined her. Naliaka would have joined, too, but her headache was denying her luxuries like laughing.

"It's not funny," Naliaka said.

"Oh, come on!" Malaika said between laughs. "You have to admit that it is funny... that oaf is no more. There is justice in the world, after all."

"There is no justice if my husband is still alive..."

"He is not!"

"What?"

"He died. Of a heart attack."

Julia lifted her arms to the ceiling.

"Oh joy! Long live poetic justice!" Julia said in between giggles.

For the next five minutes, Naliaka watched her two friends laugh. Stop. Look at each other. Laugh again. Eventually, her headache was too much and she stood up.

"I am going to bed. My head is killing me."

"Wait… you never did tell us how you got injured."

"When your son called me with the news, I was so shocked that I fainted and hit my head on a metal rod."

Julia and Malaika looked at each other and started laughing again. Naliaka shook her head and walked away, intending to sleep for not less than twenty-four hours.

She almost did.

* * *

The surgeon and the nurse had been in the makeshift theatre for a couple of hours, still stitching up Boss. Nobody else knew what was going on, because they asked not to be disturbed.

As the medics worked, the other ten or so people sat inside the house, watching television that was still intermittently streaming news from Kirinyaga Road, checking social media, trying to piece together the events of the day, all pretending they were not worried about what was going on in the ambulance. There was one black leather sofa that could not hold more than Onyango, Samuel and Judas, so everybody else was sprawled on the carpet, holding on to a beer.

"So, what do you think really happened?" Samuel asked Judas.

By this time, everybody knew who everybody else was. They had even bantered with one another about their roles for a few minutes.

Onyango answered after a swig of his beer.

"Mike, is what happened. He must have been upset about not being picked to take over from Boss." The bodyguard then told them what had happened that morning.

"So, he went to the very person who wanted to topple Boss. What a scumbag!" Samuel, following suit with the beer, added.

"I don't think he is more scumbag than the next guy," Onyango said, playing devil's advocate. "Imagine being with someone for so long, playing second fiddle, knowing nearly all the secrets of that person, living your life to take a bullet for that person, and then you are bypassed for a promotion? I say 'Boss is the scumbag.'"

"But if he did not pick him, he must have had his good reasons. Perhaps he did not think he was up to the task."

"He was not. He was weak. He should have just been happy playing Boss and getting paid a lot of money for it. He was going to get compensated very generously," the bodyguard, the only one not drinking, said.

"What did he do when he was not playing Boss?"

"He used to be a lawyer, but now runs some business." the bodyguard answered. "They met when Mike worked as Boss's lawyer. Everybody kept commenting how alike they looked. After the first murder attempt on Boss, he approached Mike to ask him to be his double. Mike didn't even think twice… he had a nose job, though. He had a very ugly nose."

Everyone laughed. Even the bodyguard who had been all tense, laughed.

"Who was going to take over?" Cecilia asked.

"Jonte," Judas answered. "He is a brilliant guy. I found him more user-friendly than Boss."

"Where has he been in all this?" Samuel asked.

470

Everybody shrugged.

"I think we need to know where he is," he turned to the bodyguard. "Do you have his phone number?"

The bodyguard nodded, and dialled Jonte's number. It rang but there was no answer.

"Do you know where he lives?" Onyango asked.

The bodyguard did.

Onyango turned to Judas. "You should send someone to check out the house."

"I agree."

Kerubo poked Samuel, signalling him to follow her outside. When they were safe in the compound she whispered, "I should check up on Selina. I have not been picking up her calls, or responding to her WhatsApp messages... Do you think Jonte is..."

"Dead? I don't know... but if I were Mike, I would have started with Jonte..."

"Cecilia and Jonte had lunch yesterday. She was still euphoric this morning... this would break her."

Selina picked the call. "What the hell is wrong with you? Why have you been ignoring our calls and messages?"

"You and who?"

"Joe, of course. We have been looking for you all day! Where are you?"

"Listen, a quick question. Have you spoken to your brother?" Silence from the other side. "Selina? This is important. Have you spoken to Jonte today?"

"Why?" Kerubo could hear the shakes in Selina's voice.

"Have you?"

"Who are you?"

Kerubo sighed. "I am Kerubo. I know you have questions and I promise I will answer them at the right time. One thing you should know, I am with the good guys," she punched Samuel when he chuckled. "Please, have you spoken to Jonte?"

"No, I have called him so many times but he is not answering."

"Okay… is Joe with you right now?"

"Yes, hold on a sec."

"Joe?" Kerubo lowered her tone. "Hi… please, no questions at the moment. I will tell everyone at the right time. There is a possibility that something terrible has happened to Jonte. Stay with her, please."

Joe swallowed so hard, Kerubo heard it over the phone. The swallow, and the shaky voice when he said okay, then disconnected the line.

"So, you with the good guys, ey?"

Kerubo grunted, pushing Samuel away.

"You stink by the way. I think you should have a shower."

As Kerubo walked by the ambulance, she had her fingers crossed. They would remain crossed for a few hours.

* * *

For minutes on end after the call with Kerubo, Selina was inconsolable. She did not want to be held. She kept hugging herself, rubbing her arms. Pacing up and down the room, throwing herself on the bed. She vomited a couple of times. She hit her head repeatedly against the wall. They were gentle hits, but they worried Joe all the same. He stood leaning against the wall, watching her helplessly repeat, "*I know he is dead. I know he is dead…*

Then her phone rang. It was Jonte's number. She squeaked and threw it on the bed. "Pick it!"

Joe picked the call. "Hello?"

"Hello... erm... hi. Is... who is this?"

"Is that Jonte?"

"Erm... no. My name is Oti... I am looking for Selina."

"Why?"

"Erm... well. It is Jonte... he... he was shot this morning. Thugs broke into his house and shot him."

Joe disconnected the line and turned to Selina, who was standing by the toilet door.

"I am sorry..."

She ran to the toilet to throw up again.

* * *

Oti breathed in some sort of relief. The bile in his mouth was tasting bitter with every minute, but he felt better after the call. Now it was up to Selina to follow up.

He walked to the city, feeling lighter, yet heavy hearted; feeling relieved but newly burdened. He was about to throw Jonte's phone into the nearest bin when it rang. Bodyguard Boss was calling again. He only hesitated for a second before picking it.

"Jonte?"

"No. Jonte is dead. It is Oti..."

"What happened?"

"Why are you asking me? Your Boss killed him."

"Where was he killed?"

"Ngumo," Oti said and clicked, then threw the phone in the nearest bin.

He walked on, towards the bus that would take him to Kisumu. His parents were originally from Kisumu, but he had never been there. He had never had the desire to go to Kisumu, until now.

* * *

A call came through Judas' phone. He listened, then disconnected without talking.

"Yep. Jonte is dead. They found his body, and those of three others. The dogs almost tore the team sent to retrieve the bodies into pieces."

"Don't tell me they shot them... the dogs I mean!" Cecilia shook in horror.

Judas looked at her with amusement and shrugged. "Of course they shot them. How else would they have gained access?"

Cecilia clicked her tongue.

"The other dead are the police officers who were working with the OCS. Good riddance."

Just then, the front door opened, and the doctor, still wearing his scrubs and looking worse for wear, walked in. They all stood up.

"He will live."

They all breathed in relief.

"Of course, I would rest easy if he were in a hospital."

"We all know that is not going to happen," Judas cut it. "Everyone out there thinks Boss is dead. That is the only narrative that will kill this whole story, and we can all move to different things."

"He will need to stay in the ambulance for at least twenty-four hours."

"It's your ambulance, I am sure you can make that possible."

"I guess."

"You will be compensated for it... especially if Boss comes out with his life."

"Right. In the meantime, my nurse will stay with him overnight. Another one will come to replace her in the morning..."

"Thank you, doctor."

"I will get out of these clothes and leave." He disappeared into the bedrooms.

"Well, that's a relief. As for the rest of you, you only have twenty-four hours to be in this house," said Judas.

"What do you mean?"

"This is government property. If they know we are housing you, and a supposedly dead criminal, my boss and I may become roomies with the OCS. Not a nice prospect especially when I am hoping for a promotion."

"Where are we supposed to take him? He is your problem, remember?' Onyango demanded. "You employed us to look after him. You cannot dump him on us."

"Watch me."

"You are kidding, right?"

"Nope. After tomorrow, we have never met. Boss no longer exists."

"Hilarious!" Samuel declared and laughed. Kerubo and the bodyguard were looking at Judas incredulously. Onyango was growling at him.

"Oh, come on, Onyango! You are a very resourceful man. If I didn't have my job and promotion to worry about, I would hide him in my house, knowing I would be well compensated when he recovers..."

"So it's all about money?"

"When is it ever about anything else?" He sneered. "By the way, somebody in this house stinks real bad…"

"Okay, okay! I am going to take a shower," Samuel said and walked away.

* * *

When Naliaka left Malaika and Julia at Queen's balcony, she fell asleep as soon as her head hit the pillow. Naliaka blacked out for eighteen hours, woken up by hunger pangs.

It was the middle of the night, and the house was eerily quiet. Her headache was less painful, but the hunger pangs were painful. She warmed some food in the microwave, ate in the dark, because she did not want to turn on the lights in the dining room, swallowed her medication, and went back to sleep.

She woke up hours later, feeling physically better, until she remembered everything that was happening. She was trying to not feel responsible for the deaths of the brothers, but from whatever angle, she ended up taking responsibility. But she felt no guilt.

If she had not told on Kaggai to his brother, he would still be alive but then again, if she had not, he would STILL be alive, and she hated to breathe the same air with him.

She checked her phone. There were several missed calls from Queen, Julia and Malaika, none from Boss. After a shower, she went downstairs and found all the women, except Julia and Malaika, chatting in low tones.

"Morning…where is Julia and Malaika?"

"They went out and didn't come… is it true what they told us? That Queen is dying and shutting down this house?"

Naliaka took a seat before answering. "Yeah… it's true."

"What happens to us?"

Naliaka smiled. "The only thing that will change for now is there will be no clients coming in. We can talk about everything else when I am better."

"So, you mean we can eat and sleep and..."

"... leave if you want to. Take your time to decide. You will not be getting any pressure from me."

"Can I get you breakfast?" one of them offered.

"Oh no... I will get it myself..."

"I insist."

Naliaka cringed and sat back.

She was in the middle of her breakfast, sitting alone at the table, smiling because there was happy laughter from the backyard, when her phone rang.

Boss was calling.

"Hey..."

"Kiki?" It was not Boss—he no longer called her Kiki. It was a woman.

Naliaka looked at her phone screen with confusion, sure that she had misread the name on the screen. Nope. It was definitely Boss. Then she decided it had to be a line mix up. It had happened to her before; calling one number and the system picking a different number. She disconnected it and dialled back.

A woman's voice, the same voice as before, answered. "Don't disconnect!" The woman barked.

Naliaka took a sharp breath, feeling dread taking over her body, like a poison serum. Why was a woman picking Boss's phone? The answer, whatever it was, could not have been good, and that was the answer she did not want to hear, yet the answer she needed to hear.

477

"Who is this?" she finally croaked, holding the phone against her ear with the right hand and her left hand holding the right wrist to stop it from shaking.

"It doesn't matter, not for now. Where are you?"

"Why?"

"Oh for Christ's sake!" the woman sounded exasperated. "Listen, Boss is seriously injured, and is asking for you."

Naliaka did not know how long she was silent for, but she was, for a considerable amount of time, considering that she was on the phone. There was a woman on the phone, telling her Boss was injured, badly. But she didn't say dead, and *injured* had to be better than dead.

"Hello! Are you there?"

That snapped her back. She shook her head slightly. The shivers were now all over her body.

"I am here. How is he?' she whispered.

"No way to know for now. I asked, where are you?"

She was about to answer truthfully, then she changed her mind.

"How do I know it is not a trap?"

The woman groaned. "Listen Kiki, it is up to you to come or not. Your boyfriend is injured and he is asking for you."

"I can come to you. Tell me where you are and I will come to you."

"We… hang on," the line went quiet, and for a second Naliaka panicked that it had been disconnected.

"Kiki?" It was a man this time. But it was not Boss. This voice was much deeper, and familiar.

"Who is this?"

"This is Samuel."

"Should I know you?"

"Yes. Remember the Mt Kilimanjaro view?"

"What about Mt... Oh. My. God! What the hell is going on? What are you doing with Boss? Who the hell are you?" Naliaka was now pacing up and down the room.

"It's a long story. One I can tell you when we have more time. For now, you need to come to where we are. For Boss."

She stopped in the middle of the room, shut her eyes and cringed her face.

"Where are you?"

"I would rather come and pick you up."

They met in Ruaka.

They did not talk when Naliaka got into the passenger seat. Samuel nodded at her. She stared back blankly. They drove to the safe house, and parked next to the ambulance. She followed Samuel silently to the ambulance. When she peered inside and recognised Boss, tubes running to his body, she gasped and took a step back.

"What's wrong with him?" she demanded. She was crying.

"He got shot."

"Why was he shot?" it was a whispered question.

Samuel, putting hands in his pockets, chortled. "So many reasons to shoot Boss. So many people who would want to shoot Boss, you of all people, should know that."

Naliaka took several steps back, and studied Samuel, wide-eyed.

"Who are you?"

"Come on inside. I will tell you everything."

Samuel walked away, towards the house. He knew she was not following but he also knew she would eventually follow. He left the door open as he joined Cecilia, Kerubo and the bodyguard.

"How is she?"

"Shocked, obviously."

"I bet. Does she know how you fit into all this?"

Samuel shook his head. "We haven't discussed that."

He was trying to control his feelings. He had not had enough sleep, he had pumped enough adrenaline in such a short time and he was blaming his state of mind for feeling jealous of Boss. The way Naliaka had reacted to Boss, how worried she was about him... how, how he had wanted to take her somewhere and make love to her, for long.

Naliaka walked in but hesitated at the door, taking in the people inside who, except for one woman, stood up when they saw her. "Hello..."

"Naliaka... so good to see you." It was the bodyguard.

He walked to her, hugged her and held her hand, walking her in. It was the first time the two had had any physical contact.

"Hi... my name is Cecilia..."

"Down, Cecilia!" Kerubo growled at a drooling Cecilia.

"Hi... erm..." Naliaka was trying to pick familiar faces from the people seated.

"Would you like a drink?" Samuel asked.

Naliaka wanted water.

"I will get the water, then we can fill you in. Please sit down."

An hour later, Naliaka knew as much as she could about what was going on. She gasped, she cried and gasped again, she growled and gasped some more, she sneered and gasped. She had been unable to ask questions because the shock had left her feeling insecure about her voice.

There was Samuel. He knew who she was all along.

There was the tall, and very beautiful woman, one emitting negative and uncomfortable vibes to Naliaka. Naliaka kept her eyes averted from Kerubo's. There was Cecilia who was nice and friendly, perhaps too friendly—but too friendly was better than the aloofness she was getting from Kerubo. There was Onyango and the other man who had bled his name.

"So, there you have it," Samuel finished. "Unfortunately, we need to leave the house tonight."

"Where are you going to take him?"

"Onyango is working on it. It has to be a place that would be the last place for anyone to look for him, for now."

"Your house?" Cecilia asked.

Naliaka shook her head, looked thoughtful for a moment then sat up straight.

"I may have the perfect place, but I need to call somebody first. Give me a minute." Five minutes outside speaking on the phone, she returned with a smile and gave a thumbs up, then turned to Samuel.

"Can I talk to you... alone?"

"We will give you some privacy..." Kerubo started getting up but Samuel stopped her.

"No... I will take her upstairs."

They all glared at him.

"To the balcony," he added defensively.

He led Naliaka upstairs, knowing all eyes were on them.

"Oh... they are so going for a shag... lucky! I could do it with such a woman..." Cecilia giggled.

The bodyguard frowned and shifted on his seat before crossing his legs. Kerubo's face fell as she walked out, heading straight to the ambulance.

* * *

Samuel opened the bedroom door and held the door for Naliaka to enter, then shut it behind him.

The first slap caught him off-guard. So did the second and the third. She was two inches from landing the fourth one but he managed to grab her by the wrist. He felt her knee head to his groin and jumped back a step, just in time. It was not by strength that he managed to turn her body around to face away from him, it was by technique. He would for a long time wonder how such a skinny woman had such strength.

Imprisoned in his embrace from behind her, it was easy to push her towards the bed, the same bed he had spent the night in, one he had not straightened. She was still fighting him, and cursing at him when they landed on the bed, he on top of her.

"Get off me, you bastard!" She screamed but her screams were muffled by the duvet. He tightened his grip. For a minute, she fought and struggled and cussed before her body relaxed in submission. Then she started crying. For another minute, she cried and he felt her every heave, lying on top of her. "Get off me." This time round, it was an appeal.

"Promise not to go feral on me."

"I won't. Just get off me. I can't breathe."

Slowly, he released her and lay next to her, breathing as heavily as she was.

"I am sorry."

"Piss off!"

"I am sorry."

"For what, exactly? For using me to get to Boss?"

He sniggered. "I did not need your help to get to Boss."

"Then why?" She sat up on the bed but did not turn to him.

"Naliaka, you are a prostitute."

"Was!" She snapped.

"Good for you! Remember the day you set me up? I was so excited when I saw you again… but I knew something was different right from the word go."

She turned her puffed face to him questioningly.

"What do you mean?"

"It's not like you and Jonte were doing a good job at pretending you did not know each other. Also, I was already familiar with Jonte. I put two and two together."

"And you let them rob you? What if they had killed you?"

He shrugged, still lying on the bed.

"It was not their thing… I wanted to know how it worked."

Naliaka looked away towards the window.

"So… at your house, was that part of finding out how it worked?"

He shook his head although she couldn't see him.

"No, it wasn't. That was pure fun."

"I agree," she whispered, bringing up her knees and hugging them.

"I want to do something, but I want you to promise you will not beat me up again."

Naliaka giggled and nodded. Samuel pulled her down to lie next to him; she let him. He ran a hand over her bandage.

"What happened?" he asked, bringing down his face to hers.

"It's nothing," she whispered and closed her eyes. "What happened to your arm?"

"It's nothing," he whispered.

And they kissed. Then they made love. Then they giggled when Samuel said he hoped they had not made too much noise for the people downstairs to hear them.

"Does it matter?" She asked, snuggling close to him, then felt a flash of guilt when she remembered Boss was outside, critically ill.

He thought about Kerubo, felt guilty for a moment and shook his head.

"No, it does not matter. How about… you know, Boss? What if his bodyguard tells him?"

Naliaka did not hesitate in shaking her head.

"Nah… we are not like that."

"What? What is he, impotent, because that would be the only explanation?"

Naliaka was glad he couldn't see her face.

"It's complicated. Who is the woman downstairs?"

"There are two?"

"The tall one…"

"Kerubo? She would be my best buddy, actually. Also a partner in the field… Why do you ask?"

"I don't think she likes me."

Samuel knew that already. What he could not work out was if she was doing it because of his history with Naliaka, or her history with Boss.

"Kerubo is awesome," he said truthfully. "She is just not very people friendly, but once she gets to know you…"

"The other one? Is she gay?"

Samuel laughed loudly.

"Is your *gaydar* that good?"

"It's very good."

"If it wasn't for her, Boss would certainly be dead." He was about to kiss her again when she pulled away.

"I found a place to hide Boss."

"Oh yeah. Nearly forgot about that. Where?"

"A priest's house."

"Come again?"

"A Catholic priest. He is a friend. Does not know exactly what Boss is, but he would do anything for me."

"Including abetting crime? Why would a priest hide a fugitive?"

"He... he was my client, but we became friends."

Samuel burst out laughing.

"A priest was your client? Is anyone really going to make it to heaven?"

* * *

Three days on.

Naliaka sat in what should have been absolute silence, but there was the near comforting meditation-like hum of the water pump.

During the three sleep-deprived days, her brain was beginning to protest and from inside her head, there were on and off sounds of an overheating computer. During those moments of near-brain explosions, she would slap her forehead lightly, and then look at the bed and the comatose figure in it.

She sat by the window and stared outside through the sheer curtains that had to remain drawn, because the last thing they all needed was to attract any sort of attention. Sometimes, she stood by the window when her buttocks threatened to go numb, but eighty per cent of her days and nights were spent in this room, sometimes staring at the sifted life beyond the curtains, sometimes at the figure

485

in bed. Once in a while, unable to keep her eyes open and body upright, she slipped in bed with him, but would soon wake up, afraid that he had died while she slept.

How did they all get here, with so many dead bodies on the trail?

The door opened slowly. She turned her head as slowly towards it to see Father Joshua, carrying a cup of coffee. She smiled at him. She and Boss had been in his house for three days; he had cooked for them, reminded her to go to the shower, sat with her as she ate, and stayed up with Boss as she took a few hours of sleep. He had not complained. And it was making her feel guilty.

"Mind some company?"

She stood up and stretched, accepting the hot cup of coffee. "Thank you. I feel so bad for making you do this."

Father Joshua took the sofa next to the bed.

"Don't be silly. I feel like this is my chance to reclaim my spot in heaven."

"You joke too much."

"It's not a joke. From what you have told me, this man has been a victim of circumstances. I do not think he is a bad man at all, just someone who has constantly been given a hit after another. You push a cat to a corner, you have to be ready for the scratch of your life. Now, if I can help him follow the right path."

"You mean religion?"

Father Joshua shrugged. "Not necessarily. You cannot force religion on people. But he sounds like somebody who has not been shown a lot of kindness by people. I am glad you have been good to him."

"Thank you."

"Besides, this house has been lively since you moved in… I like it when the nurse and the doctor come, and I make food and coffee for them. I even like it when Samuel comes, and he can be rather annoying."

"He is not!"

"Touché. But I understand. When you love someone, you do not see their faults."

"I don't love him."

"Tell that to the birds. I like the girl, too. She is uptight, but she looks like a lovely person."

"I think she loves Boss."

"Good. That makes a crowd of people who love the dude…"

He turned to look at Boss and nodded towards him. "He looks better though."

"Yeah. The doctor said he should be able to reduce his sleep medication starting tomorrow."

"Samuel called to say he is coming to pick you up."

"Take me where?"

"I did not ask."

"Who stays with Boss when you are away?"

"Kerubo is coming too."

"Oh…"

"Come on, Naliaka. You have a man who loves you, one you love back. Let the girl love Boss."

"Does he not have a say?"

"Has he said no?"

* * *

Kerubo nervously sat on the same seat Naliaka had been occupying a few hours earlier, talking to the unresponsive Boss like she had never spoken to anyone, because she read somewhere that unconscious people could actually hear and understand. She told him she loved him. She told him, in so many words, that she would understand if he did not love her back, but she would not regret her words, or her feelings.

She saw him flutter his eyes several times. She patted his head, caressed his overgrown beard, kissed him lightly on the lips, apologised for taking advantage of him, told him it was because she needed to have something to remember him by, just in case he did not want her when he woke up.

Like Naliaka did for three days, Kerubo sat with Boss. For hours. Sat or slept by his side, careful not to touch the tubes running into his body but making sure part of her skin was touching part of his skin.

It was at two in the morning when Boss stirred. Kerubo, a light sleeper but sleeping even lighter next to Boss, sat up and turned on the bed switch. Boss had his eyes opened and he was looking at her, brow furrowed, looking confused.

"You are up," Kerubo whispered, suddenly feeling naked. She had been sleeping in a see-through night dress. She pulled it up a little to cover her cleavage. Boss looked at her cleavage and blinked.

"Eem… water," he said, attempting to move.

"Careful… don't move too fast. You have tubes all over you!"

Boss looked at his left hand and cringed.

"Water."

Kerubo rolled her eyes; he smiled at that. In his deep sleep state, he had dreamed about a woman like her, and no wonder he felt like he knew her. He had listened to that voice for long enough to have it memorised, and he was wondering if the confessions of love he had heard were real, or dreams.

Kerubo returned with a glass of water.

"Here is the deal. You will drink a sip at a time. If you try to drink too much, I will take it away."

He smiled. "I just need water…"

She sat at the edge of the bed, supported his head and gave him a sip, then took it away. "That's enough… how are you feeling?"

"Like shit!" He tried to sit up and groaned in pain.

"Don't do that, yet."

"What's wrong with me?"

"You were shot, of course. You could pretend they removed your appendix…"

"Are you making jokes?"

"Would I? I don't know any shooting jokes. Anyway, I am glad you are up. A lot of people will be glad you are up, including Naliaka."

His face brightened. Hers darkened. He saw hers darken, and furrowed his brow.

"Where is she?"

"Away. She needed to rest. She refused to leave your side, so we had to force her to."

"Where am I?" he looked around. "This does not look like a hospital."

"You are in a Catholic priest's house."

Boss gasped. "Effing Father Joshua?"

"You know him?"

* * *

For the rest of the night, in between Boss's episodes of sleep, Kerubo stayed up, mostly studying him and updating him on what she knew. He lay on his back and listened, holding back emotions he could not identify. What was clear, however, was that by Mike dying, Boss had been given a second chance by his very traitor.

"You are the woman who was with *Mama Mboga*, right?"

Kerubo nodded. "That *Mama Mboga*, otherwise known as Cecilia, saved your life."

"I knew she did not fit in, but my people couldn't find anything on her."

At eight in the morning, when the doctor arrived to check on Boss, Kerubo called Samuel.

"Can you talk?" she whispered.

"She is in the bathroom. What's up?"

"He is up."

"That's good news. We can return later."

"You will do no such thing. You will stay where you are for two more days. If Boss does not show any interest by then, I will bow out."

"Kerubo, you are asking me to lie to Naliaka…"

"You owe me, dammit! You are happy with her. I want a chance to be happy too… please…"

He took a deep breath. "Kerubo, you know I love you?"

"I know. And I love you too. I also know you and I could never be what you and Naliaka are. I have a feeling Boss and I can be that… I just want a chance."

"I am rooting for you."

When Kerubo returned to the bedroom after a shower and breakfast, the doctor was gone, so were the tubes on Boss's body. He was sitting up, having a conversation with Father Joshua.

"You are okay?"

"Yep! I can start walking around the house today... if you help me, of course."

"Say no more. Come on."

Kerubo and Father Joshua helped Boss ease out of bed, helped him with his wobbly legs and supported him to the door and back to the bed.

"Well, that was a whole marathon," Boss declared with a laugh.

"It shall get better. I can massage your joints. That should help."

"You are a wonder woman."

Kerubo massaged Boss intermittently, exercised his joints, fed him, gave him his drugs, spoke to him, and snuggled next to him when he fell asleep. She had been giving him sponge baths when he was still unconscious, not since he woke up, two days earlier. Samuel had earlier told her Naliaka was insistent on returning and Kerubo was feeling the pressure.

Boss liked her, that one was clear. Enough times she had caught him looking at her with unmistakable lust. He often held her hand gently. He liked to brush her face gently as he looked deep into her eyes. Because she was now openly sleeping next to him, when she fell asleep, she would find herself in his arms, him holding her tight. She felt his desire on her thighs. She would pretend to be still asleep as she listened to his deep breathing.

Kerubo decided to take matters into her own hands.

She warmed water, took a face towel, sprinkled Father Joshua's scented shower gel, and then matched into the room, pausing at the door to study him.

Boss returned her gaze. He did not speak, but he nodded. She approached. Their eyes locked, Kerubo undressed him, slowly. He closed his eyes when her long fingers massaged him in the process. In silence, he let her clean him, head to toe. With relaxation he did not know he possessed, he felt his penis rise when she massaged it, and it stayed up. Boss had figured, if it went wrong, he could blame his health.

"Remove your clothes, please," Boss whispered. Kerubo did, slowly, revealing a body so toned, that Boss forgot, just for a second, what he wanted to do.

"Come here."

She lay next to him, careful to stay away from the wound.

"You are a very beautiful woman…" Kerubo felt herself go hot on the face, and everywhere else.

"So beautiful…"

Then they kissed.

"If I disappoint you, let us just blame the gunshot." He was not joking, but she thought he was.

"If it does not happen today, we have the rest of our lives to try."

"Rest of our lives?"

"Of course… you think I go sleeping around with every Tom, Dick and Harry?"

They both laughed, and they kissed again.

When he slid in her, he nearly screamed. When he hit an orgasm, he screamed. So did she.

MWISHO–END